LUCKY IN LOVE

"How in the hell did your brother let you come out wearing that dress?"

Bennie's mouth fell slightly open, but before she could speak Clay continued.

"If my sister even thought about wearing something like that I would lock her up. Donnie should be shot."

Bennie just laughed in his face.

"You don't like my outfit?" she asked innocently. "I think it's a sweet little thing," she continued, looking down at the front of the dress and striking a sultry pose.

She looked up to see if Clay was taking it as a joke. He wasn't exactly, but he wasn't being prudish or censuring, either. His eyes were warm with frank admiration, actually.

"Benita, you are absolutely breathtaking. I always knew you were pretty, but you are gorgeous, baby."

Clay had crossed the room and was caressing Bennie's shoulders as he spoke.

Bennie put her hands on Clay's hips and slid them up under his jacket, where she could feel his nicely muscled body.

"You know what? I think you're pretty gorgeous yourself."

She leaned into him for the lingering kiss that she wanted, and found herself kissing air. Clay stepped back.

"Okay, see, we need to talk."

He removed his big, warm hands and started pacing around the room. Bennie tilted her head and observed his growing agitation.

"Is this going to be a long talk? Because if that's the case, I'm going to sit down," she said, suiting action to words.

Bennie arrayed herself in what she hoped was a seductive manner in the corner of one of the two pillowy sofas that decorated the suite. Satisfied that she looked alluring, she tossed her hair back and prepared to listen to whatever Clay had to say.

"Okay, shoot. You look like a man with something on his mind," she said cheerfully.

BOOK YOUR PLACE ON OUR WEBSITE AND MAKE THE ARABESQUE ROMANCE CONNECTION!

We've created a customized website just for our very special Arabesque readers, where you can get the inside scoop on everything that's going on with Arabesque romance novels.

When you come online, you'll have the exciting opportunity to:

- View covers of upcoming books

- Learn about our future publishing schedule (listed by publication month and author)

- Find out when your favorite authors will be visiting a city near you

- Search for and order backlist books

- Check out author bios and background information

- Send e-mail to your favorite authors

- Join us in weekly chats with authors, readers and other guests

- Get writing guidelines

- AND MUCH MORE!

Visit our website at
http://www.arabesquebooks.com

LUCKY
IN
LOVE

Melanie Schuster

BET Publications LLC
http://www.bet.com
http://www.arabesquebooks.com

ARABESQUE BOOKS are published by

BET Publications, LLC
c/o BET BOOKS
One BET Plaza
1900 W Place NE
Washington, D.C. 20018-1211

All Kensington Titles, Imprints, and Distributed Lines are
available at special quantity discounts for bulk purchases
for sales promotion, premiums, fund-raising, and educa-
tional or institutional use. Special book excerpts or customized printings can also be created to fit specific needs. For
details, write or phone the office of the Kensington special
sales manager: Kensington Publishing Corp., 850 Third
Avenue, New York, NY 10022, attn: Special Sales Department, Phone: 1-800-221-2647.

First Printing: August 2002
10 9 8 7 6 5 4 3 2 1

Printed in the United States of America

ACKNOWLEDGMENTS

This has been a long time coming, so please bear with me. I have so many wonderful people to thank!

To my mother, again, for all her love and support during some very trying times and for being the living example of grace under pressure.

To an extraordinary and very patient group of friends who read my work from the very beginning and gave me so much encouragement and support that I know I couldn't have done it without them: my personal focus group—Denise Sherman; Deb Suffety; Ann Davis; Yvette Russell; Aneesah Shabazz; RaeAnn Jandrewski; Toni McGlasker; Virgie Wilson (DUDE! This rocks!); Jennifer Woods, my very patient and forbearing sister; Augusta Woods, my exemplary sister-in-law; Tammie Johnroe (yes, you are forgiven for losing that manuscript, but you'll be buying all your copies from here on out!); Felicia Watkins; Nicole Beasley; Melissa Pritchett (give a sister a shout-out, would you?); and Steven Johnson. To Rickey Staves for technical support and friendship. And a special thank you to Susan Colette Cooper Addision for always making me feel brilliant.

To my newest victims who willingly lent their time to the cause: Nekeia Star Hopkins, Donna Hopkins, Toni Colton, Denae Williams, Sue Mott, Aletha Williams, Debbie Sims, Stefeni Hardy, Lisa Atkinson, and Michelle Green. You ladies have no idea how much your comments helped me believe in myself and stay on track.

To my fellow writers who gave me encouragement and made me believe that I could do it, too: Francis Ray, Raynetta Manees, Beverly Jenkins, Bettye Griffin, Rochelle Alers, and Gwen Osborne. A special thank-you to Bette Ford and most especially Janice Sims for their friendship and advice. You really made me keep plugging away and I can't thank you enough for your generosity and wisdom.

To Chandra Taylor, for her patience, understanding, and encouragement, and for giving me a chance to fulfill a lifelong dream. Thanks just isn't enough.

To the Saginaw Public Libraries, especially the wonderful staff at the Claytor Branch and most especially Rhonda Farrell-Butler and Vi. Your encouragement and prayers meant everything to me.

To Jack and Judy Haveman, for so many things that I can't even begin to list, thank you a thousand times over. To Nelson Salgado, who to this day doesn't know how much I appreciated his friendship when I was getting shaky, thanks again. To Randy VanHook, just for being a friend—this is public notice that I will continue to nag you about your writing! Get with it!

A very special thank-you to a very special friend, Wayne Jordan, who extended a wonderful opportunity to me. I learned so much to quickly with Wayne and *Romance in Color.* Your talent, dedication, and hard work still amaze and inspire me. You're next, Wayne!

To Brenda Woodbury, for always being positive and supportive. You're an inspiration! To all of the Arabesque writers whose beautiful works made me set a goal and achieve it. Thank you from the bottom of my heat.

To my indomitable aunts, Pauline Ragland and Theresa Cole, who always knew I had it in me; to my brother, Dwight, for being proud of me; to my cousins, Lisa, Stacey, Stephanie, Jason, and Charles (and my little cousins, too); to my extraordinary nieces, Amariee, Jilleyin and Jasmine (I told you English was good for something!). This one is for all of you!

To the brave and bawdy men of the SCFM, thanks for all the laughter. And the lessons . . . I'm a much wiser woman now. And a special thank you to the Hanlons—they know why. And to the Rev.—you have to read it, you promised. It'll give you something to do besides chase scorpions in the desert. . . .

To the best gnome a sister ever had, Joyce Hankins. You kept me grounded, kept me laughing, and kept me focused and sane. Words are not enough to express my gratitude. But an answering machine wouldn't hurt you any, either. . . .

To Danny Watley, for his humor, compassion, common sense, and for keeping my hair fabulous. And to the stunning Thursday night ladies of the Hair Gallery, especially Ms. Neesha, for the always stimulating discussions.

And to Jamil, who knew it would happen before I did. You always believed in me. That's what best friends are for, but you exceed all standards. Thanks for the laughter, the love, and for sharing the babies with me. Love you the best and the most!

One

"All I'm saying is, I am sick and tired of those radio stations. *Tired* of 'em."

Benita Cochran raised her head from the shampoo bowl to emphasize the last three words, then dropped her head dramatically with a huge sigh. Renee, who was her best friend and roommate, as well as her hairstylist, looked at her with amusement.

"You say that at least once a week, but you aren't going to do a thing about it, are you?"

She wrapped a towel around Benita's head as she spoke. "You're going to be running Cochran Communications until you are ninety-five with support hose, blue hair, and using a walker. Now sit up and shut up."

Benita rose up majestically from the shampoo bowl in the private booth. Trying to look hurt, dignified, and proper while she was wrapped in a towel wasn't easy, but she managed.

"You see how you do me? I was going to have your wake at my house, too," Bennie said plaintively.

She glanced at Renee out of the corner of her eye and they both started laughing, the loud, hearty way that very old friends laugh at very old jokes. They were very old friends at that—they met as college students and had stayed close through good and bad times. They were as close as sisters and had a lot of similarities, including a wicked wit, high intelligence, and extremely good business sense. They even shared Bennie's three-story home in Indian Village. People often asked if they were sisters, although there was no physical resemblance between them.

Andrea Benita Cochran was six feet, one inch tall in her bare feet. The fact that she wore heels a lot made her more than elegant. She was the exact color of a caramel, although there was a lot of red to her skin tone, especially in the summer. Her abundant hair was jet black without tints, and was often the bane of her existence due to its wavy texture that would, as she put it, "swell up like a sponge every time the temperature gets over sixty degrees." She often tried to get Renee to cut it, but Renee politely explained to her, "Your head would look the size of an aspirin if I did. Trust me."

Benita also had strong, exotic features that gave her an air of mystery and sensuality that was often directly at odds with her no-nonsense approach to life. She had thick, shiny black eyebrows that were always groomed to perfection, plus long, silky eyelashes that were the envy of all who beheld them—those who realized they were real. She had a strong jawline, a characteristic of her father's side of the family. It would have looked almost masculine had it not been for the fact that she also had perfectly shaped full lips and a long, slender neck. She was proportioned like an athlete—lean and lissome, with long arms, legs and shoulders that were wider that most women's, and another reason to keep her hair below shoulder length, as Renee kept reminding her. But she was unmistakably feminine, with breasts that were surprisingly full for such a long drink of water.

Renee, on the other hand, was five-foot-ten, and her skin was the dark, satiny color of chocolate. She had a soft, round face and huge, almond-shaped golden eyes that could bore holes in a brick wall if she chose, or look sweet and demure. Her hair was also shiny black and currently relaxed in a short, feathery cut. As one of the leading stylists in Detroit, Renee felt it was her obligation to change hairdos often. "You can't sell it if you can't show it" was one of her mottoes. Renee was also built on very different lines from Benita. Where Benita was rangy and athletic, Renee was full, lush and voluptuous. They also knew each other well enough to know when one of them was serious about something. This morning, however, Renee had misread her best friend.

"Yeah, well, I'm serious this time. I've been involved in the radio business most of my thirty-two years. Do you realize that Cochran Communications is the only thing on my résumé? I know that Daddy started this thing, but how did I get to be the one who has to carry it to my grave?" she asked plaintively as she combed out her wet hair.

"There are five other members of this family, and it seems to me that one of the others needs to step up to bat now. I'm *tired*." Benita underscored this last remark with a snap of the wide-toothed comb on the counter.

Renee looked at her for a moment before speaking. She had been telling Benita for years that it was time to move on, but her advice had always fallen on deaf ears.

"Are you actually serious this time, or is this another venting session?" she asked pointedly. "Because if this is just your preperiod vent-of-the-month, I have better things to do."

In fact she did not, since the two women were alone in the salon, but she had a "been-there-heard-that" attitude toward this particular conversation. Today, however, Benita surprised her. Settling herself in the styling chair while Renee prepared to blow her hair dry, Benita answered her quite seriously.

"Ne-ne, I've given my entire life to the company. All the boys have careers and families of their own—well, at least careers, if not families. I eat, sleep, drink, and *dream* those stations. I know I have the other businesses, too, but you and I both know that Cochran takes up way too much of my life. I haven't yet found a way to turn back the hands of the clock, and time is slipping away from me with a quickness. If I don't do something right now to pry myself away from that station—and my family—I *am* going to end up a dried-up, bitter old woman with a walker *and* a nasty attitude. Only I don't want blue hair—can I have that purple color instead?" she finished with a wicked grin. Then she got serious again.

"You're the only person I have told or will tell, for that matter, but"—she paused and straightened her shoulders with a hint of defiance—"I'm going to start looking for a buyer this week."

Andrew Bernard Cochran, Benita's father, had founded WWCC, "The Voice of Black Detroit," in the 1950s. He was a lgend in broadcasting and his stations were outstanding. WWCC was the parent station of the many owned by the family. They were scattered throughout Michigan and Ohio, with formats from adult contemporary to all news/talk, with a smattering of jazz and religious programming thrown in. Big Benny, as he was known, had done some groundbreaking things in his day and of all of his six children, it had fallen to Benita to carry on the family legacy. Benny Cochran and his late wife, Lillian, had a beautiful family—first had come a set of twins, Andrea Benita and her brother, Andrew Bernard Jr. Then came another set of twins, Andre and Alan, followed by two single births, Adam and Adonis. Sadly, Lillian passed away when the children were quite young—Benita and Andrew were only ten.

And they felt their position as the eldest twins quite keenly, particularly Benita, who was the older of the two by thirty minutes. She was definitely the alpha dog of the family. Benny was so overcome with grief and so overwhelmed by the loss of his wife that he turned much of the burden for the younger ones over to Benita. He also had no idea how to raise a girl—that had been Lillian's arena. So Benita grew up a tall, assertive, athletic woman in a family of tall, aggressive men. They all went on to have careers outside the family business; Andrew was a surgeon, Andre and Alan were lawyers, Adam was an architect, and Adonis was a marketing consultant. Benita, however, became her father's right-hand man. She had trailed him around the stations from the time she was a tiny girl, so there was no aspect of the radio business with which she was not intimately acquainted.

She had started working there in earnest when she was in her teens, something that she had thought would end when she entered college. That was when Benny had his first heart attack, which compelled Benita to stay on at Cochran. She actually left after her graduation from college. She married her college sweetheart and moved to Boston, but her husband died tragically in the second year of their marriage, and the familiarity and security of the station helped her heal. And that, as she often reminded herself, was history. Although she had other business interests, it was the radio stations that kept most of her attention. They occupied time that she could have been devoting to a family, a husband, or pursuing her secret passion, writing.

But there was always some family member, usually Big Benny, to convince her that without her steady and creative handling the stations would flounder. And unfortunately, there was precedent to prove that theory. Every time she left the station in what she felt was capable hands, the ratings would drop. Not enough to make *her* panic, but enough to bring the Cochrans out of the woodwork to entreat her back into place. And every single time, she would capitulate and let herself be guilted back into the role of executive manager, as well as that of company president. Benny, as CEO, was mostly retired and spent much of his time playing golf. Benita was even called Bennie—and some people went so far as to call her Little Bennie, which she could not stand.

Lately, though, it was becoming more and more of a task to parcel out her time between the station and her other interests. These included a gym, a beauty salon/day spa that she co-owned with Renee, and a bookstore, which she had started largely because she was tired of having to go to the suburbs to find the books she wanted. She was ready to concentrate on the things that brought her pleasure, and that included having a man in her life. As she told Renee over and over, "I would like to meet a man over six-two who I am not related to and who has no connection whatsoever to broadcasting." In her capacity as president of a radio station she met all kinds of men who were interested in her, but that interest was seldom returned—all they wanted to do was talk shop.

For the moment, however, she was going back into the lion's den—another day of keeping the barbarians from the gate, as Benita called it. She stood and removed the comb-out cape that was around her shoulders. Once again, Renee had worked her magic; her hair was a glistening, smooth length of thick blackness.

Bennie peered at her reflection critically. "And you're sure I don't need a relaxer?"

Renee snorted in disgust and snapped a towel at her. "Please! If all my clients were like you, I'd go broke."

Benita was not in the least convinced, however. "Yeah, just wait until the weather turns really humid and I come in here looking like a thundercloud; you'll see. Thanks again for getting up at the crack of dawn."

She glanced at her antique tank watch. It was just seven-thirty A.M., but for Benita that was the middle of the morning. She slipped on the long black jacket in wool crepe that matched her side-slit skirt and adjusted the red silk sweater that she wore under it. As usual, Renee had to arrange her patterned Hermès scarf—Benita had no patience with doodads, and the scarf would likely find itself tossed on top of the file cabinet in her office before the day was done. But her heart was in the right place.

And Renee naturally had to get the last word in on Benita's dilemma. "I've been telling you for years you need to get up out of there—the way you let those men twist you around their little finger is a scandal and a shame. I hope you're serious this time, because you need more in your life besides business. You need to get *busy,* and you know what I mean."

Usually that was where the conversation would have ended, but Benita was truly on a roll that day. She paused dramatically as she was leaving the salon and raised her Franklin Planner purse high.

"As God is my witness, Renee, I am putting that life-sucking monstrosity on the market. I'll sell it to the first so-and-so who comes by, for a double order of rib tips and a forty-ounce, if necessary. And Daddy and the boys can take a flying leap."

Benita took her time getting out of the parking lot—it was on Jefferson near Indian Village, and the station was practically down the street in downtown Detroit, so she didn't have to kill herself to get to work. Benita loved her Jaguar—it was one of the few acts of sheer ostentation that she allowed herself. She and the car were made for each other—they were sleek, elegant, and classically beautiful, although no one would ever convince Benita of her beauty. She tooled along on Jefferson, enjoying what would be one of the few moments of solitude that she would have that day. As she drove, she mulled over her day.

She had a sales meeting first thing, then a few sales calls on her biggest advertisers, something she did periodically to keep herself on her toes. Then a committee meeting for the chamber of commerce, a speaking engagement at a business luncheon, a trip to the gynecologist, and a quick meeting with her twin brother to discuss Big Benny's upcoming fiftieth anniversary in the radio business. Finally there was the last item: a quick meeting with the manager of her gym and a workout before heading home. And it was just Wednesday. The rest of the week didn't look too much better.

To the uninitiated, this seemed to be the stuff of which dreams were made—an exciting career, a beautiful home in Indian Village, a loving family, and a custom-tailored wardrobe. But all that glittered was truly not gold, as the old folks said. There was a tremendous cost to be paid for the kind of life Benita was living. No family, for example. Benita had always expected to have three or four children by now. No social life, to speak of; industry dinners, conferences, and so forth counted as socializing, though they certainly didn't count with Bennie. And no man.

Bennie wasn't the type of woman who equated happiness and success with having a man. But it had been so long since she had had a date with someone who was not trying to work some kind of a deal and do some kind of business, she had forgotten what it felt like. Bennie had never been able to understand why she had so much trouble attracting and keeping a man, but it was ever thus. She could attract them by the droves, but the ones who were brave enough to approach her would usually turn tail and run after a couple of dates.

As a teenager it was because they were terrified of her brothers. The shortest man in Bennie's entourage was six-foot-five. Her dates always had the feeling that they would be crushed to death in some kind of primitive ritual if they had laid a hand on her—as indeed they would have been. Plus, Big Benny looked and acted like the type of man who would have no trouble putting out a contract on someone who caused his daughter any pain—as he certainly would have: Big Benny had known quite a few high rollers and racketeers back in the day.

Even when Bennie went off to college, away from the watchful eyes of her menfolk, she had problems. Benita was like some sort of superwoman in the eyes of many. She was smart, funny, and personable, and could beat the crap out of most men in basketball, pool, tennis, or any other activity, including golf and bid whist. Growing up in a house full of men had left her no choice—she had to sink or swim, and as she was the eldest, she had a responsibility to show her brothers the way. And her way was to excel at everything. In addition she was a superb cook, she could dance like Judith Jamison, and she had a great singing voice. Moreover, due to growing up in radio, she was a musical genius. There was no kind of music, from blues to zydeco to classical, that Bennie could not discourse upon at length. Altogether, Bennie was a little bit too much for most men to take, something she never understood.

To tell the truth, she didn't fare too well in the girlfriend department, either. Women tended to be reluctant to befriend her because she was so beautiful and accomplished, even though she was the sweetest soul on earth and a loyal friend. When she and Renee had met in college it was a godsend for both of them—Renee also had few friends, primarily because she had a problem suffering fools gladly. Her razor-sharp wit and impatience terrified most people, but Bennie found her hilarious, and a mutual friendship was born. Renee often tried to school her in the ways of men, to no avail.

"Men don't like women to whom they feel inferior. You've just got to tune it down a little so they will feel comfortable," Renee would tell her over and over.

Bennie would always counter with a timeworn argument about being herself: "Look, if I have to pretend to be someone I'm not, it's not going to work. Why can't I just be myself and be liked for who I am? I'm not a perfect person or some kind of superbeing—quiet as it's kept, kryptonite has no effect on me whatsoever. And I'd feel very condescended to if someone lowered his performance to a level that he felt was acceptable to me. Screw that noise."

Which was how she had found her true love, Gilbert Crittenden. Gilbert had lived in the dorm next to Bennie's and was in graduate school, although they were the same age. Gilbert was an undisputed, total, complete card-carrying genius, already sought after by all the major scientific consortiums in this country and several others. While other people were off playing during spring and summer breaks, Gilbert had fellowships to places like MIT and the Centers for Disease Control. Gilbert quite frankly terrified most people because of his laserlike intelligence. The fact that he possessed a devilish sense of humor was no help—he would crack arcane jokes that no one else would get, which put people off even more. He and Bennie met in the cafeteria and set off sparks immediately. She had seen him around campus but never talked to him.

She sat down at his table with a tray piled high with food. Gilbert immediately started in on her.

"That's a lot of food! You gonna eat all that?" he asked with amusement.

"Yep, I sure am," Bennie replied. She was so active that everything she ate seemed to metabolize instantly—she had a good, healthy appetite. Gilbert persisted in his quest to rattle her.

"You're seriously going to eat that meatloaf—do you know what red meat can do to you?"

Bennie shrugged. "Yep, red meat can fill me up and make me not hungry. *Green* meat might make me sick, but red meat is my friend." She grinned and speared a large chunk of meatloaf.

Gilbert pretended to be appalled. "Do you know that meat is probably full of parasites and bacteria? You have no idea what kinds of germs and filth you're ingesting right now." A couple of their tablemates started looking queasy, but Bennie ate on, unperturbed.

"Look, I grew up with five brothers. You can't gross me out, you can't scare me, and you can't beat my behind, so chill, okay?"

Gilbert was delighted. Helping himself to one of her desserts, he remarked, "You know, you'd be a pretty woman if your nose wasn't so long."

Bennie didn't miss a beat as she helped herself to his soda. "And you'd be an okay man if you weren't so short." Then they just smiled big, goofy grins at each other, knowing that something wonderful had started.

Gilbert wasn't really short, but he was only five-ten, which gave Bennie a good three inches on him. He was very dark, with baby-smooth skin and curly hair that was quite unruly unless Bennie cut it for him. They made a somewhat odd-looking couple, but they were so happy together that no one really gave it a second thought. He had a lean, muscular body and was virtually without physical grace of any kind, but he was the smartest, sweetest, sexiest man in the world as far as Bennie was concerned. He adored her for who she was and never asked her to hold back in any way. With Gilbert, Bennie blossomed—her successes were Gilbert's, and vice versa. There were no power plays, no petty games, no insecurities or jealousies. Sometimes Bennie thought she would miss him until the day she died.

Bennie slid into the parking structure of the building that housed the "Voice of Black Detroit" and sighed. Shouldering her Franklin Planner and picking up her expensive Mark Cross black attaché, she paused for a moment before entering the subbasement-level elevator. She knew that once she entered the building she would be "off and running in the jackass races," as she delicately phrased it. Then she straightened her shoulders and went in to meet her day head-on. She smiled in spite of herself. When all else failed she would remind herself that her career, hectic though it was, was better than a sharp stick in the eye.

By the time she got to her office, she wasn't all that sure that she would have minded a sharp stick or two. There were messages galore, her phone was ringing off the hook, her sales manager was running late, and there was a delivery problem with some promotional items that were going to be needed in two days. And none of that was going to be handled without coffee. Since she was the first one in the office, with the exception of the broadcast personnel, she took it upon herself to make a pot of fragrant brew. She began her usual walk through the station, dropping by the booths and chatting with various employees about matters both personal and professional. Bennie was held in very high esteem because she treated everyone as they wanted to be treated, to the best of her ability. She didn't take crap from anyone, but she didn't give out any attitude, either.

Bennie didn't believe in micromanaging, that habit of leaning over people's shoulders and making sure they had done everything they were expected to do. People, she felt, could not grow if you did that—they needed to have the freedom to make mistakes, if necessary, in order to have a sense empowerment. She was fair, generous, and supportive of the people she employed, which was why they would walk through fire for her. Unfortunately, it was another reason that she had always felt reluctant to leave. Bennie looked up from sharing jokes with Tawny Carleton, the morning deejay who interspersed news bulletins and weather during breaks in the Tom Joyner Morning Show, the syndicated program that got everybody's morning rocking, to see her receptionist, Lavinia Reed, heading her way.

Tawny was a small, curvaceous woman who often had Bennie in despair with her proclivity for hooking up with just the wrong man. Tawny's microbraids were flying around animatedly while she regaled Bennie with the story of her latest encounter.

"Girl, he's handsome and employed and single and he seems to be intelligent. I'm going to see him this weekend. He may be the BMW I have been looking for," she finished happily.

Even Lavinia, who was old enough to be their mother, knew that a BMW was a Black Man Working. Bennie raised her hand in caution, however, she had seen too many of Tawny's affairs blow up in her face.

"Tawn, honey, just make sure he's not another chew toy," she advised. Even Lavinia was taken aback by that one.

"Chile, what do you mean, a chew toy?" Lavinia asked, her brow furrowed in question. Bennie was happy to explain.

"A chew toy is something that pets play with to exercise their teeth and sharpen their reflexes. It's soft and pliant and provides hours of entertainment. Besides, it keeps the cat from scratching the couch, or the doggie from chewing the master's shoes. Keeps them from running wild in the streets and humping people's legs and things." Bennie smiled innocently as Lavinia sniffed and Tawny burst out laughing. She continued: "Just remember that a chew toy is not the real thing—that's where the trouble comes in, when you start thinking that rubber T-bone is real meat!"

Far from scandalized, Lavinia looked amused. In her late fifties, she was well versed in the ways of the world, even the world of workaholic young women.

She snorted and intoned, "Seems like to me there's somebody around here could use a chew toy of her own."

After Bennie returned to her office and started going through her messages in earnest, she found one that was of significant interest. It was a formally worded letter suggesting that there was a strong mutual benefit to be derived from a meeting between the heads of the Deveraux Group and Cochran Communications, doing business as WWCC. The missive read that due to their convergent interests, a follow-up call would be made to set up a meeting between the two concerns. It was signed by Clayton Deveraux and was on rich, heavy stationery with the logo deeply imprinted at the top of the page. To say that Bennie was intrigued was an understatement.

The Deveraux Group was a media conglomerate. It owned a string of magazines and newspapers and had been in cable television from its beginning. If Bennie wasn't mistaken, there might also be a radio station or two in the mix. She immediately turned to her computer and accessed the Internet to do a little research. At the same time, she pressed the intercom button to summon someone from the research department. As she scanned and printed every article she could find with information about the Deveraux Group, a member of the news research team came ambling into her office. Bennie barely glance up from her terminal.

"Hi, Alvin. Listen, do me a huge favor, would you? Find

out everything you can about the Deveraux Group, okay?" Bennie looked intently at the screen as she spoke.

"What kind of stuff do you want to know? And how much?" Alvin asked. Digging up arcane bits of knowledge was his specialty.

Bennie sat back and smiled widely, looking at Alvin directly for the first time. "Alvin, I want every newspaper article, magazine spread, gossip column, TV interview, radio tidbit, scandal sheet scoop, credit rating, and anything else that is floating out on the down-low." She smiled again and said, "I want to know Clayton Deveraux's shoe size."

"Kool and the Gang, boss lady, you ain't said nothin' but a word," Alvin said confidently as he took his leave. When he got through, the Deveraux Group would be an open book to Cochran Communications.

Bennie was more energized than she had been for a long time. The only reason that the Deveraux Group would come calling on a fairly small potato like WWCC was a possible buyout. If they were ready to deal, so was she . . . but Bennie liked to have all her ducks in a very straight row before getting down to business with anyone. Before she could mull over the potential any more, her sales manager, Austin Tinsley, finally arrived.

If Austin hadn't been very, very good at his job, he would have been in for a thorough dressing-down from Big Benny for his tardiness, and at the very least a "come to Jesus" talk from Bennie. "Come to Jesus" was how the staff referred to Bennie's periodic lectures to the recalcitrant or the slacker—either you got the spirit and repaired your behavior, or you prepared to meet your maker as the result of one of those talks. Bennie was happy that few had to actually meet their maker—most people shaped right up. And Austin had very good news indeed regarding a new account. Austin's dark, narrow face fairly radiated excitement, and was darned good-looking as well.

"Bennie, we got the package we wanted from Delphi Foods—they came on our terms with the exact deal we offered," Austin reported with pride. Bennie's face lit up.

This would mean big advertising revenues for the station, as well as a nice commission for Austin. She was about to congratulate him when her youngest brother, Adonis, entered the room.

"Well, what are you doing here, Donnie?" Bennie asked. No one ever called him by his given name. It was certainly fitting, but, in Donnie's eyes, terribly embarrassing. "Not that it isn't great to see you; it's just unexpected." She accompanied her words with a kiss on his cheek.

Donnie was Bennie's youngest brother and her baby. He had been only two when their mother died, making Bennie more of a mother figure for him. He was six-foot-seven and absolutely beautiful to look at, as were all of the Cochran men. They all had the same caramel coloring, striking black eyebrows, and strong jawbone, plus the thick, wavy hair that was a coarser version of Bennie's mane. Like his brothers, Donnie kept his hair cut neat and close. Like his brothers, too, Donnie had an exciting career outside of WWCC and Cochran. Unlike his brothers, though, he had some interest in the station, which was why he had dropped by.

"Well, Benita, this may cause you to faint, but I remembered that you had a sales meeting scheduled, and I am taking you up on your invitation to attend." Donnie looked anxiously at Bennie to make sure his welcome was still extended.

"Honey, you know you're welcome at any and all functions of this company. You don't ever have to wait for an invitation from me!" Bennie exclaimed. "In fact, Austin has some very good news to share."

The meeting got off to an auspicious start with the news of increased advertising sales and promotions. Advertising revenues were what kept radio and television stations running in the black—if someone was not buying time to sell their products on the air, the station would not survive long. Strong advertising revenues plus a good air product and good promotions were what had kept WWCC in the forefront for the more than fifty years that the station had been operating. The station had been family owned and operated for all that time, and had not once gone outside the family for financing of any kind. Which may have been what made the Deveraux Group want to pay them a little visit. Bennie confided in the two men about the letter that she had received so they would be up to speed on whatever new developments might take shape.

Austin frowned. "Aren't those the people who have that huge conglomerate in Atlanta? They are pretty much media sharks, from what I hear."

Bennie nodded thoughtfully. "They are indeed the big dog in the meat house. So why they would come sniffing after a little weenie like us is beyond me." She paused and looked out the window at downtown Detroit, then turned and smiled happily at Austin and Donnie. "But it sure is going to be big fun finding out what they want."

"What we at the Deveraux Group want is to develop a coast-to-coast network of small to midsize radio and television concerns. At the Deveraux Group we believe that there is strength in numbers. The power of communication in the New Millennium cannot be underestimated, and we intend to make that power accessible," said Marcus Deveraux emphatically. Leaning forward, he took a sip of coffee and cleared his throat before continuing.

The meeting was taking place in the large, well-appointed conference room of the radio station. In attendance were Bennie, Donnie, and Austin, representing WWCC. Also in attendance was Rich Lowenstein, the company accountant. The men of WWCC were chomping at the bit to get their turn to speak. Bennie, however, looked as though she did not have a care in the world. She had a lot of practice in looking benign and interested when drivel was being spouted, and it had come a-gusher that day. She was also looking quite fine in a red Chanel suit with huge mabe pearl earrings and her fabulous hair tamed into a chignon. She sat at the head of the table quietly, waiting for the ordeal to be over.

Marcus Deveraux, an extremely tall, extremely handsome man in his late twenties, represented the Deveraux Group. Darnell Washington, another looker about the same age as Marcus, assisted. They were both nattily attired in Armani suits and suitable Italian footwear—they fairly bristled with energy and importance. The problem was, they were spewing rhetoric—pretty, impressive phrases with not an ounce of meaning or substance, which Donnie was happy to point out in less-than-polite terms.

"Before you get wound up again," he said, "can we cut to the chase? You've been talking for twenty minutes now, and you have not said a thing. You keep mouthing phrases that came straight off your annual report, and none of them has any relevance to Cochran Communications that I can see." Donnie did not bother to hide the irritation in his voice.

Marcus nearly choked on his coffee, but was gamely trying to rally. In the meantime, Darnell spoke up. "Well, if you would let us finish our presentation, we would be able to show you the big picture." He glared as Austin smothered a snicker at the overused phrase, and blundered on.

"The Deveraux Group, which is based in Atlanta, Georgia, is the parent company of Media Deveraux, which is attempting to . . . in the middle of establishing a network of radio stations . . ." He stopped when he realized that Rich Lowenstein had made a slashing motion across his throat.

"Okay, this has been very illuminating, your little flip charts and all, they're quite lovely. And these four-color handouts are quite nice, too. But the bottom line here is that you are ham-handedly making an offer to buy this station, which leads me to two pertinent questions—why and how much?" Rich leaned back and crossed his arms behind his head to wait for the next volley.

Marcus had the fair complexion that was prevalent in his Creole heritage, so he visibly flushed with anger at Rich's tone, which was loaded with insolence, as Rich had intended. Darnell was visibly disturbed at the reference to the flip charts, since he was standing right in front of them to make a point. Then Austin felt compelled to make a couple of snarky remarks, and it was, well . . . *on*. Tempers and voices rose until it was virtually a shouting match. Bennie finally spoke.

"Okay, the pissing contest is officially over," she said authoritatively. Dead silence fell. "Boys, I'm taking charge here," she said calmly as she rose to her full six-one, even taller today since she was wearing a killer pair of Manolo Blahnik pumps. She surveyed the table with remarkably well controlled humor.

"I think we're all a little edgy today. This unpredictable spring weather probably has something to do with it. I know it always affects me in that way." Which was a lie, but it served as filler to give everyone a chance to calm down. She walked over to the credenza and poured a glass of ice water before continuing.

"Fellows, I'm sure that the Deveraux Group may have a proposition that may be of interest to Cochran Communications at some time in the future. But I feel that for today, at least, we have exhausted the possibilities of conference. I will meet with my staff"—she looked meaningfully at Austin, Donnie, and Rich—"in my office in fifteen minutes," she said, glancing at her Piaget watch. "In the meantime, you gentlemen enjoy your flight back to Atlanta."

Marcus wasn't finished, though—he still had one more volley to attempt. "Well, to be perfectly honest, I had prepared this presentation for the president of the firm, Benny Cochran. I'm sure that if he were here . . ." His voice trailed off as he looked into Bennie's long-lashed eyes that had suddenly turned into flames.

"Sweetie, I *am* Bennie Cochran, and that means as far as you are concerned, *I* am WWCC. Nothing goes through this company that doesn't go through me first. And you might want to tell your big brother that when you get home, *Chip*." She turned to leave the room, leaving a faint trail of Amarige perfume as she went, and stopped in the doorway to flash a brilliant smile with no hint of malice. "Have a nice trip."

Austin, Donnie, and Rich left the room quietly, like the guilty schoolboys they resembled. They knew a "come to Jesus" talk was inevitable. No such solace awaited Marcus and Darnell, however. With the conference room empty, they looked at each other in silence until Darnell finally blurted out what was uppermost in both their minds. "Man, Clayton is gonna be *pissed.*"

"Okay, gentlemen, what went wrong today?" Bennie asked rhetorically. She was sitting behind her big oak desk playing with her heavy silver pen. She did not look at the three men arrayed on the deep forest green leather sofa and club chairs that gave her office the appearance of a richly appointed private library. Bennie seemed to be in a kind of trance, actually. She was looking in the direction of her collection of prints and photographs by significant African-American artists, but anyone could tell that she wasn't paying any attention to them. She sat up abruptly and rephrased the question: "I don't mean what our guests did wrong, guys; I mean, what could *we* have done differently?"

Suddenly the toes of their shoes became topics of prime interest to all three men as none of them ventured to speak. Finally, Donnie, who knew Bennie the best, broke the silence. "Well, it was obvious that they were kind of new at what they were doing. And we could have heard them out before we started in on them," he said honestly.

Bennie nodded her agreement. "For one thing," she said, "it's just good manners. They came to visit, so it really doesn't matter if they eat with their feet; it's our duty to be gracious hosts." Austin and Rich both started to speak, but Bennie held up her hand and continued.

"Besides—and this is critical, guys—we don't know what possessed Clayton Deveraux to send in Frick and Frack. He had to know that they weren't ready for this, or he told them to come up here and act like buffoons, I'm not sure which. But there has to be some kind of method to their madness."

The men fell silent as they pondered the wisdom of what Bennie had just said. Then the ever-ebullient Austin had to get his two cents in.

"Yeah, but Bennie—you did spank them and send them home to mama. It was a beautiful thing to watch, I must say." The ice was broken, and general laughter ensued until Bennie had to shoo them out to take a phone call.

A few days later, the unpredictable spring weather took a turn that anyone in the Deveraux family could have predicted. In the sunny corner office that belonged to the CEO and president of the Deveraux Group, thunder crashed and lightning roared, in the person of Clayton Deveraux. He faced his younger brother with an expression of absolute fury.

"You did *what?*" he said with menace. "Please tell me again slowly, because I just know I did not hear what I thought I heard." The fact that he was not yelling was no help—his voice was so deep and gravelly that he sounded brusque when he was in a good mood, which he was definitely not in now. His thick, jet-black eyebrows were knit in a solid line of fury across his fine brow. Marcus took a deep breath and tried to explain.

"Okay. You know how you have been talking about getting some stations in Michigan, right? Well, we thought . . . that is, *I* thought, why not go after WWCC? I mean, it's in a great location, right in Detroit and all, and it's a top-performing station, and it's been around for a lot of years, and it's solvent and . . ." His voice trailed off because it was painfully obvious that Clayton was not being swayed in the least. He was slumped in his chair with his fingers steepled, looking at Darnell and Marcus as if they had each grown another head.

"Marcus, you just gave all the reasons why we should

not approach WWCC. It does not in any way fit the profile of the kind of station for which we are looking. We are looking for family-owned stations that have low ratings, that are in financial difficulty, and that are in pretty rough shape, generally. When you have a proven product like WWCC you keep your grubby hands off." He paused and looked at the two men, shaking his head before he went on.

"I specifically told you two not to try any grandstanding stunts until you knew the business better. Now you've put these people's backs up, and I don't need that. I need to have good relationships established with these people, and in this industry Benny Cochran is *the* man."

The Deveraux Group was a newcomer to radio, having built its reputation on print media. The walls of the reception area were full of awards and commendations that various publications had won over the years. The cable industry was also no stranger to the Deveraux touch. Clayton had seen the possibilities and promise of the industry in its infancy and was growing right along with it. To complete the family, he was just getting into radio, which was why he had exercised such caution in his dealings with the power players. In addition, Cochran Communications was private—no one outside the family knew very much about how they did and what they did—the Cochrans let outsiders see only the results.

And now, in his eagerness to prove himself, Marcus had gone up to Detroit and made a fool out of himself, and no doubt alienated Big Benny Cochran. Clayton could feel his temper rising when Marcus hastened to assure him that they had not met with Big Benny.

"See, that's what I'm trying to tell you, man—we met with this *woman* named Bennie Cochran, his daughter. We never met the old man at all," Marcus said emphatically. That got Clayton thinking for a moment, until Darnell interjected something.

"Yeah, but it's like she said. As far as we are concerned,

she *is* WWCC. She said it real nasty, too. And how did she know your nickname was Chip?" Darnell finished.

Marcus cringed—he was trying to forget that bit. Clayton, on the other hand, perked right up. This was the kind of information he could use, since there was so blessed little to be had on the Cochrans, particularly this Bennie, who seemed to be camera-shy. In all his research he had not found one blessed picture of the woman. But the fact that she had ferreted out his brother's nickname suggested someone who was methodical, if nothing else.

"Start from the beginning and tell me everything you said and everything she said. And before you do that, tell me this—what does she look like? How does she relate to people?" Clayton wanted to know.

Darnell was only too happy to enlarge on that theme: "Man, she's a big, manly moose," he said darkly. "She's like nine feet tall and as mean as a black snake," he said, shaking his head. "And she cuts people down like a schoolteacher, just like that woman on that show."

Clayton looked totally perplexed. "Boy, what are you talking about? What woman? What show?"

Darnell frantically scanned his internal hard drive and then snapped his fingers in triumph. "Julia Sugarbaker! On that show about those women who . . ." His voice trailed as Clayton looked at him with very little patience. "My mom watches it on Lifetime," he finished lamely.

Clayton sighed deeply and decided not to kill them. What was done was done, for now. He dismissed Darnell, and as the door closed he looked wearily at Marcus.

"You know, you two could screw up a two-car funeral." Marcus opened his mouth to speak but Clayton continued. "I thought I taught you better, but I see I still have my work cut out for me. Marcus, you could have done a lot of damage with your little trip to Detroit. You could have jeopardized the entire undertaking."

Marcus drew a deep breath and apologized. "I know I was out of line, and I am really sorry. We weren't as prepared as we should have been, and there are obviously a lot of things I need to learn. But Clay . . . I was trying to get my feet wet, man. I mean, I've been in school for years, and now it's like this MBA is burning a hole in my brain. I want to put all that education to use. I want to start some wheels turning, prove myself; you know how it is."

Clayton was still angry, but he was not unsympathetic.

"So you have a fire in your belly, do you?" he drawled. "Well, that's to be commended. And yes, I know that feeling well. That very feeling is what brought me to this point in my life. But you can't just jump in at the top, bro; you have to start at the bottom and *learn* your way up. Which is why I set up this training program the way I did, to expose you to the business in an orderly fashion. You have got to develop self-control. I am not asking you to have patience, but *control.* You have to always be the most prepared person in the room—you have to virtually know what the other person is thinking and what they are going to say before they speak. The only way you can do this is by research, attention to details, and observation. And, in your case, practice."

He stopped speaking abruptly and looked out the window at the panoramic view of Atlanta. He suddenly swung around and looked at his younger brother.

"And now I have to go to Detroit to make up to some angry Amazon in order to talk to her daddy. And she's mouthy, too?" He looked sternly at Marcus. "I should make you go, too, but she might aim for you and hit me." He waved Marcus out of his office, leaned back in his custom-built leather chair, and took a couple of deep breaths.

So Big Benny had a big, mean daughter who kept the gates, did he? Clayton smiled to himself and thought about how very uncomplicated life could be when you planned. The plan was to call Ms. Cochran and sling a little snake oil, then slide right past her to Big Benny. Then her feathers would be soothed and his path would be clear to get what he wanted, which was the stamp of approval from the *real* Benny Cochran.

Clayton started perusing the mail that had accumulated

in his absence. He came across an elegant, simple cream envelope that his efficient secretary had not opened, thinking it was personal correspondence. It was not hard to see how she would have made the mistake, as the envelope was written in a feminine hand that was both graceful and aristocratic. Inside was a note in the same handwriting expressing regret that the meeting had not gone as smoothly as anticipated, and the hope that the lines of communication would stay open for further dealings. It was signed *Benita Cochran.* For some reason, the note infuriated Clayton.

It was bad enough that Darnell and Marcus had gone up there acting like Beavis and Butthead, but now this woman had the gall to try to get him on the head and say "nice try"? It may have been that the note arrived on the heels of the disclosure of the bungling presentation or that he had just returned to town after a protracted series of meetings and presentations. It may have been that he was truly concerned about the outcome of the project, but Clayton was furious. He could feel his blood pressure rising to a dangerous level. Not even bothering with the intercom, he bellowed for his secretary. Annie Stidham, his assistant for fifteen years, poked her head in the door and looked at him warily.

"I'm sorry, but I'm not coming in here until you put your teeth away. If you bite my head off, how can I apply for another job?" she asked calmly.

"Sorry I yelled. Make me a reservation, would you? I need to go to Detroit tomorrow. Early." Clayton stood and shoved his hands into his pockets. "I have to see a man about a horse." He thought about it for a second and corrected himself. "Moose."

Annie looked at her boss, who was obviously in a very bad mood, and clicked her teeth as she closed the door. In the mood he was in, she would be glad to be rid of him for a couple of days.

* * *

Renee stared at Bennie in amazement. "You mean you actually found a buyer? That quickly?"

She and Bennie were in the sitting room of Bennie's bedroom in the arts-and-crafts-filled house in Indian Village that they shared. Bennie's sitting room also functioned as an office when she was home. It was furnished with an eclectic mixture of antiques and contemporary furnishings. Bennie's bedroom was all 30s and 40s decor, very art deco. The ivory, teal, and copper color scheme was soothing and gentle, intensely feminine without being girlish or froufrou. At the moment, Bennie had a sheaf of papers spread out on her desk and was studying them intently.

"No, no, no! I didn't find a buyer, because I haven't looked for one. *Yet,*" she finished hastily as she caught the look of disdain from Renee. "I haven't said one word to Daddy or to the boys, especially Andre and Alan, so there is no way I'm going to entertain any offers."

Andre and Alan, the other set of twins, were the family attorneys, as well as members of the firm that looked after all legal dealings of Cochran Communications.

"Besides," Bennie finished, "I have no idea what the Deveraux Group wants. You remember the meeting I told you about?"

"The one where the two young men from Atlanta made fools of themselves? Yes, of course."

"Well, after that debacle I sent Clayton Deveraux a nice note, and then I get this phone call today from his office. He wants to come up and make amends in person. So now I'm going over this information again with a fine-toothed comb. I want to be prepared."

Renee leaned over to inspect the neatly arranged pages, some with photographs and some with organizational charts and so forth. "So who is this Clayton Deveraux, anyway?"

Bennie shook her head. "I guess he's like the John Johnson of the South or something," she said, referencing the world-famous publisher of *Ebony* and *Jet* magazines.

"His family owned a couple of newspapers back in the day, and now they own around twenty-five different magazines and newspapers." Bennie rattled off a few names, which were quite impressive.

"Hmmm. That sounds prosperous," Renee offered.

"Oh, honey, there's more. There's also a few cable companies, and they own BlackVisions."

No further explanation was needed—anyone over the age of three was totally familiar with the black cable network that ran original movies and dramas, as well as topical news programs and talk shows. Bennie kept reading from the list of holdings until Renee begged her to stop. Bennie stopped reading aloud, but she was fascinated. To think that virtually one man had done all of this! It didn't seem possible, but Clayton Deveraux did not seem like an ordinary man. Bennie started reading again.

"I think he's only around thirty-eight or thirty-nine. Damn, he must be brilliant," she mused.

"Enough, please! Let's get to the critical part—what does this erstwhile media tycoon/giant look like? I ain't talkin' about his brain or his aura, either. What does this man *look* like?"

"Well, the only picture I could find was from years ago, when he was still a photojournalist. It was in Africa, when he was taking pictures of—" Bennie stopped talking when Renee gave her the look that said *Cut to the chase.* Bennie sighed. "Okay, try to picture a black Frank Zappa with dreadlocks."

Renee looked genuinely horrified, and her expression did not change when Bennie passed her a copy of a grainy photograph. It was a likeness of a very tall, very thin, fair-skinned man with a huge, hooked nose, a big, unkempt mustache, and some frantic-looking dreads.

Renee stared at the picture for a long time before murmuring, "Yikes. We won't be having *his* babies, now, will we?"

* * *

The next day, Bennie took particular care with her attire. Of course, she did this every day, but today was special. For some reason she wanted to send a message to Clayton Deveraux. Just what the gist of that message was, she had not a clue. It just seemed as though she should be making a statement of some kind. She settled on a cream silk blouse that buttoned up the back, and her favorite cream wool crepe pleated slacks with cuffs. She wore ivory hose and cream Chanel flats with a black patent toe and heel. She also wore an exquisitely tailored jacket in black cashmere. Bennie's clothes cost a small fortune because she had many of them custom-made. But she kept them for years, so she didn't beat herself up about the expense.

Her hair was in a soigné French twist with no softening twists or tendrils floating around her face for effect—today was not the day for that. She put on her mother's pearl necklace and a pair of pearl earrings that just missed being plain studs by the addition of a tiny diamond that nestled under the rather large pearl. Her makeup was understated as usual for the office, but instead of her usual neutral lip color, she applied rich, resounding red. She looked wonderful—powerful, in control, and approachable—but the slacks lent her an air of insouciance, as if the meeting was important but not crucial. She had no idea why she had reached for the red lipstick, but she certainly didn't have time to ponder. And she wore a light cloud of Chanel No. 5, her power fragrance. Lavinia buzzed her to let her know that Mr. Deveraux was there to see her.

As was her custom, Bennie went to personally escort each visitor to her office. When she rounded the corner and came face-to-face with Clay Deveraux for the first time, she began to realize that this was going to be a very interesting day. Clay Deveraux was quite possibly the handsomest man she had ever seen. He was at least six-foot-seven, and was thin no longer, if indeed he ever had been. He was lean and trim in his Italian suit, with broad, muscular shoulders that Bennie found devastatingly attractive. But it was his face that Bennie was drawn to—he was rather fair-skinned, a sort of light golden color. He had thick, shiny black hair that was almost straight, except for a slightly unruly wave over his brow. The rest of his hair was barbered to perfection—short on the sides but past his collar in back.

His eyes were almost black and his eyelashes were unfairly long for a man. He had thick, shiny brows that were almost too perfect, and an equally thick, lustrous, perfect mustache. He indeed had a killer nose, but it wasn't hooked; it just had a high, aquiline ridge. His lips were firm and sensual, and Bennie was filled with a sensation that was totally indescribable, other than to say she was finding it hard to breathe. She extended her hand in welcome and said in what she hoped was a normal tone of voice, "Welcome to Cochran Communications, Mr. Deveraux. I'm Benita Cochran."

"It's a pleasure to meet you, Miss Cochran, and thank you for seeing me on such short notice." The sound of his voice was what almost did Bennie in. As she was to tell Renee later, he made Barry White sound like a soprano. Clayton Arlington Deveraux was one of the finest specimens of man Bennie had seen, and that deep, rich, cultured voice was truly the cherry on her sundae. But Bennie had years of poise and business sense working for her, in addition to her sense of appreciation for masculine pulchritude.

"Why don't you come with me, Mr. Deveraux, and we can get started," Bennie said easily. "My father is in the office today, and I know he would like to meet you," she added.

Bennie luckily didn't see every female employee within earshot gather in their wake to watch this majestic man follow their boss. Nor did she hear what Lavinia had to say on the matter. Lavinia stood and watched the two tall, beautiful people walk away and said softly, "Now, that ain't *nobody's* chew toy. Ummm-*hmmm.*"

TWO

Bennie escorted Clayton into her office so that she could hang his vicuña overcoat in the closet. She offered him his choice of seats and then offered coffee. He refused rather abruptly. Bennie paid him no mind and turned to the credenza that held a heavy silver tray already set with a silver coffee service and Bennie's own art deco cups and saucers. She needed something to do with her hands, which might or might not have been trembling . . . she wasn't quite sure. At the same time, Clayton was not too happy with developments, either.

He had another nail for that idiot Darnell's coffin. *Big, manly moose, my foot.* Bennie Cochran was a very pretty woman. Not necessarily his type—he tended to small, sensuous-looking women—but still *very* attractive. She was very well dressed and she smelled wonderful. And she was being extremely gracious. This was not the scenario for which he had prepared. He did not like having to regroup like this; he liked being in total control. He looked over at the credenza, which was actually an antique dry sink that had been converted for use in the office, where Bennie was pouring coffee. She was graceful and unself-conscious and had long, slim hands. For some reason, the sight of her made Clayton rather anxious and unhappy. The fact that he had a roaring headache was no help, either.

Bennie turned to him with a dazzling smile.

"I took the liberty of pouring you a cup of coffee anyway, Mr. Deveraux. I know I can't start my day without it, and you just don't seem like a tea man to me." She placed a cup and saucer before him on the coffee table, along with a plate of tiny muffins and croissants. She then sat down across from him and smiled again.

"Mr. Deveraux, after I received your gracious letter, I took the opportunity to do a little research on the Deveraux Group. I wanted to be as well prepared as possible for our meeting. I must tell you, I am extremely impressed with how much you have accomplished. It must be very gratifying to have achieved so much at such a young age." Bennie paused to take a sip of coffee, while Clayton regarded her balefully.

He was the one who was supposed to be slinging the snake oil, not her. How dared she sit there looking like that and being professional and gracious? And what was the idea of telling him that she had done her homework? Nobody was that candid in business.

"Laying it on a little thick, aren't you?" he said in a snarl. No sooner were the words out than he regretted them.

Bennie did not react right away. She took another sip of coffee, regarding him over the rim of the cup as she did so. When she took the cup away, Clay could have sworn that there was a twinkle in her eye, but she did not smile. She looked at him with her big, bright eyes and spoke very slowly.

"I am almost positive that is not what you actually meant to say." She didn't wait for a response, but went on as if they were the oldest friends in the world: "Would you like some Tylenol for that headache?"

Clay had no choice but to say yes. How the hell had she known that his head was pounding? And why was she being so nice? Of course, she had effectively flung the ball into his court, so he had to apologize.

"I'm sorry; you were absolutely correct. I have no idea why I said that, other than this stupid headache. But even that doesn't excuse my behavior. Please accept my apology. And please call me Clay," he said.

Bennie thought, *Honey, with that voice, you could steal my Jag and I wouldn't care,* but all she did was smile.

"Certainly. If you call me Bennie." She gave him a glass of ice water with which to take the Tylenol she handed him. "Just make yourself comfortable, and as soon as you are ready, we can go meet with my father. That way you don't have to say everything twice. How's that?" she finished brightly.

Instead of being relieved, Clayton's heart was sinking. For some reason he felt as though he had just taken his first steps out onto quicksand and had no hope of going back. Or getting rescued, for that matter.

Andrew Bernard Cochran was a fine figure of a man. He had been one in his twenties when he started WWCC, and he was one now in his seventies in his current role of CEO of Cochran Communications. Any observer could tell where the Cochran children had gotten their looks after meeting Benny. Like his sons, he was well over six feet tall. He also had caramel skin and wavy hair, although his was quite white, which was a striking contrast to his skin. He had a beautifully kept mustache and goatee, and he still favored exquisitely tailored suits and expensive shoes. Big Benny Cochran personified the old-time glamour and pizzazz that African-American men had personified for decades, right down to the fedoras that he still affected.

Even though he was not as active with the station as he had been in years past, he still kept busy with board positions in various charitable organizations and so on. When Benny Cochran spoke, people still listened. He was still considered the dean of urban radio in Michigan and, indeed, throughout the Midwest, which was one of the reasons that Clay wanted to be someone whom Benny could trust and respect. And Benny was still as sharp as he had ever been—he could still spot BS coming around the corner, as he often liked to remind people.

After the introductions had been made, Benny saw no need for niceties.

"So what can I do for you today, young man?" Benny asked genially. He had stopped smiling, though, which made Clay all the more persuasive in his choice of words.

"Well, Mr. Cochran, the Deveraux Group is in the process of establishing a consortium of small to medium-size radio stations for the purpose of sheltering them until they gain enough strength to function effectively on their own. We view it as a sort of incubator in which they will receive the funding, the training, and the consulting to make them viable. What we are trying to do is to protect as many of these stations from going under as possible. There is no startup fee for them to join, and what they receive in return is a chance to establish themselves and flourish. Everyone benefits from this approach—the stations, naturally, but also the recording artists who will get the airtime that they are not necessarily going to receive anywhere else. The black businesspeople who will have opportunities to advertise their products at flexible rates will also benefit. The banks will be thrilled, because the Deveraux Group will underwrite the loans. This is as close as we could come to a win-win proposition for all concerned," he finished.

Bennie was extremely impressed, as well as a little relieved. If Clay Deveraux had really walked in there trying to buy WWCC, her father would have handed him his head. And Benny had good reason for wanting that beautiful head to stay right where it was. She roused herself from the reverie that Clay's voice had brought on, and made herself listen to the conversation. Benny was saying that he thought it was a wonderful idea, but that Clay would have his work cut out for him with some of the old-time stations that were held together with spit and glue but were unwilling to accept help from outsiders. Bennie spoke without thinking.

"Well, Daddy, you might want to make a few phone calls. And maybe you could somehow issue some kind of statement endorsing the program, or make an appearance or two on behalf of the Deveraux Group." Turning to Clay she added, "If there's anything that I could do to promote the program, I'd be more than happy to do it. It sounds like a wonderful opportunity for everyone involved."

By this time, Clay felt as if he had been somehow tipped into a parallel universe where everyone was beautiful and kind and floated around doing good deeds all day. *This is too easy; something bad is bound to come of it,* he thought, but when Benny agreed with everything his daughter said, Clay began to feel more at ease.

"As you are no doubt aware, I am mostly retired. I putter around here and there, but Bennie does the day-to-day running of Cochran Communications. Just get in touch with her for anything that you might require. Pleasure meeting you, but I have a couple of meetings."

And with that, Clay found himself following Bennie's graceful figure as she returned to her office.

"I think I should be taking you out to lunch to thank you," he said sincerely.

Bennie was more than happy to agree with that, and said she would drive, since Clay was cabbing it all around town. But first she offered him a tour of the station, stopping to introduce him to everyone she encountered and making him feel as at-home as possible. Finally they collected their coats and proceeded to the parking garage below the building. Clay stopped in midstride as they started walking to Bennie's pride and joy.

"That is the exact same make and model of car that I drive," Clay said.

Bennie was oddly pleased with that tidbit of information. It made them seem as though they were operating on the same wavelength. She liked that feeling, although she couldn't say exactly why. She glanced over at Clay, who looked even worse than when she had first detected the fact that he had a headache.

"You feel really rotten, don't you?" she asked sympathetically.

Clay felt too bad to lie.

"I usually don't get headaches, but this one is a killer," he agreed.

Bennie looked over at her defenseless passenger and made up her mind in about a nanosecond.

"Do you trust me?" she asked him. At his startled look, she pressed again: "Do you trust me?"

Clay looked at her for a long minute before he answered. "Sure."

"Well, hang on; lunch plans just changed."

In a very few minutes, Clay and Bennie drove down an alley and into a garage. Exiting the car, Bennie pressed the automatic door opener, which lowered the garage door, and then opened a door on the far side of the structure. When she saw Clay hesitating she beckoned him on.

"Come on; we're just going to my house to get some medicine for that headache." With that, she left the garage and started walking along a path that led across the lawn to her back deck.

Clay was amazed—not because of the majestic house, but because of her kindness. He thought of all the women he had dated who would have never just looked him over, decided he was harmless, and offered to nurse him out of a headache. Then again, maybe Bennie was just reckless. He caught up with her long strides just as she reached the back door.

"Hey, are you sure about this? I mean, your bringing me home with you—I might be an ax murderer, for all you know."

Bennie looked at him with great amusement. "I don't think so. You look trustworthy enough to me. Besides, I know who you are, where you work, where you live—the state, at least," she amended, "and I have at least twenty-five people who saw me leave the building with you. Trying to bump me off now would be extremely unwise."

By this time she had opened the door, disarmed the burglar alarm, and put her purse down on the huge butcher-block island in the middle of the kitchen.

She turned to Clay and said, "Come on in and make yourself at home. Let me run upstairs and get you something for that headache." She led him into the house and took off his coat.

By now the pain that had assailed Clay was unbearable—he didn't care that he was back in the parallel universe; he just wanted the pain to stop. He allowed Bennie to take his coat and lead him to a comfortable chair in what appeared to be a living room. Bennie went away for a few minutes and returned with a small glassine envelope and a glass of what appeared to be cola. She knelt next to his chair and handed him the packet. He felt utterly foolish by now.

"What am I supposed to do with this?" he asked.

"That's a headache powder," she said cheerfully. "Everybody's granny took these things—it just so happens that they work very fast and very well. You pour the contents on your tongue and wash it down quickly with this cola and you won't feel a thing. Your headache will be gone in about fifteen minutes, guaranteed."

Clay wasn't in any position to refuse. His head felt as though there were huge stones grinding around in it. He took the packet and tried to open it, but he was having trouble focusing on the task. Bennie took it from him and unfolded it quickly and neatly. She shook the contents so that they would be ready to pour out and tipped the little folded packet at Clay.

"Open your mouth," she said. Bennie smiled at Clay's hesitation. Men could be such babies! "Come on; open your mouth so you can feel better," she coaxed. This time he did open his mouth wide enough for her to pour the vile-tasting contents onto his tongue. She quickly handed him the glass of soda and said, "Drink this all down fast, so you won't taste it."

He did as he was bidden, but there was still a brief, acrid aftertaste.

"God, that's nasty!"

Bennie smiled sympathetically.

"I'm heating some soup for you, which will be ready in about five minutes. That will take all the taste away. In the meantime, you can wash your hands or whatever down the hall." She waved an arm to indicate the general vicinity of the downstairs lavatory. Then she picked up the glass and headed for the kitchen.

When Bennie reached the kitchen she had to collapse onto one of the tall stools that surrounded her work island. Now that she was alone, she could breathe normally, which meant that she was practically panting due to the rapid pounding of her heart. When she was giving Clay the headache powder, her finger had made the slightest contact with his tongue, nearly giving her a heart attack. She had been outwardly cavalier and collected all day, but inside she was a boiling mass of sensation.

Clayton Arlington Deveraux was not only *fine;* he was smart, powerful, and, as she knew only too well now, the sexiest man in the world. Even when his eyes were bleary with pain, he was incredibly beautiful to behold. And that *voice* . . . when he had been explaining his hopes for the Deveraux Group in her father's office she had about gone out of her tiny mind. He could have been reading the back of a box of Jim Dandy grits for all she cared, as long as she could hear that *voice.* Bennie looked at her reflection in the small mirror that hung near the back door. It had always come in handy for last-minute checkups, but now it served another purpose—to make sure her face did not reveal what she was feeling.

Satisfied that she didn't look like a love-addled twit, Bennie quickly stirred the soup. She ladled it into a big bowl and put it on a nice wooden tray on which she had already placed thick slices of homemade bread and a dish of fruit salad. She went back to the living room to ask Clay what he would like to drink and stopped dead in the doorway. Stretched out to his full length on her gigantic sofa was Clay, fast asleep. She had forgotten to warn him that those powders often had a soporific effect. Maybe she hadn't wanted him to know.

She went over to him and stood there for a minute, taking in his totally masculine beauty while he was completely at peace and unaware. She sighed deeply and unfolded the handmade throw on the back of the sofa to put over him. A loud thudding sound on the stairs alerted her to the fact that her cat, Aretha, had come looking for her. Aretha was the nosiest creature on earth, so naturally she had to come inspect Clay, standing on her hind legs to give him a good sniff.

"Doesn't he smell good?" said Bennie dreamily. She laid the throw over Clay's sleeping form and dared to touch that silken wave of hair. She picked up Aretha, who was making the little barking sound that meant she wanted to be fed.

"Okay, cat, I'll feed you. And Aretha, you'd better get used to him—I'm keeping him."

When Clay awakened, he was refreshed but disoriented. He did not recognize his surroundings, nor did he remember having a large, furry pillow attached to his body, yet there one was, and it seemed to be vibrating. Clay closed his eyes again. He was back in the parallel universe, but he was completely peaceful. Just then he heard Bennie's voice and remembered the events of the morning.

"Aretha, that is so impolite. We don't sleep on people until we know them better." *Lord, why did I say that? Did he hear me?* She made as if to take Aretha away, but Clay held her wrist to stop her.

"No problem. I like cats." He focused more carefully on Aretha's huge expanse of sleek black fur. "She's a big girl, isn't she?"

Aretha promptly became offended and departed, which left Bennie leaning over the sofa with Clay holding her slender wrist. She gently pulled away while Clay stood and stretched. He did it thoroughly and effortlessly, giving Bennie a chance to continue her inspection. He was absolutely perfect, as far as Bennie could tell. With his suit coat removed she could see not only how his broad chest tapered into his lean waist, but also that he had a perfect butt. And Bennie would know, having been a connoisseur of the male posterior for some time. She was so engrossed in her assessment of Clay's attributes that it almost startled her when he spoke.

"I should be thoroughly embarrassed by falling asleep in your house, but for some reason I'm not. I feel too good, for one thing, and you were too kind, for another," he said nicely.

Bennie sat there beaming like the proverbial Cheshire cat as he continued: "You know, I was so out of it when we came in, I didn't even notice your house. This is a big house for a single woman, isn't it?" Clay was looking around the massive living room of the huge old house as he spoke.

Bennie's house was large, but she had decorated it in such as way as to make it as comfortable and inviting as possible. In keeping with the arts-and-crafts sensibility of the house, Bennie had used simple mission- and Shaker-style furniture as much as possible, with rich colors like forest green, burgundy, and gleaming gold. Everything was simple and elegant, much like the owner. There were family pictures on many surfaces, and art by prominent African-American artists and photographers was everywhere.

Clay surveyed the room in which he stood, taking in the fresh flowers, the polished wood tables, and the intriguing items placed here and there that encouraged a visitor to sit and linger awhile. The late-afternoon sun washed over the room and gave everything a golden patina that for some reason made Clay feel very much at home. He repeated his earlier statement as a question.

"Don't you get lonely here all by yourself?" he asked.

"I have a housemate—my best girlfriend from college. Besides, this house is hardly ever empty. If you listen, you will hear the thundering hooves of my brothers." Just then

Clay became aware of the sounds of human invasion. "They come over every two weeks so that I can whip them in basketball and so they can eat all my food. Wanna play?"

Clay finally noticed that Bennie had changed clothes and was wearing sweats. She also had a well-used basketball under one arm. Clay smiled—it had been years since he had played some pickup basketball. Then he looked down at his clothes and sighed.

"If you're worried about attire, there are tons of my brothers' clothes around here, and shoes too. And if you need to change your flight, there's a phone," she said.

She wasn't going to push, but she wanted him to feel welcome. Which he apparently did, from his next words: "Let me make a couple of calls and I'll be right with you. But only as a referee."

Bennie smiled and said, "I love them all dearly, but I must tell you—they gloat when they win and they pout when they lose, so call plays at your own peril."

About an hour later, Clay conceded that Bennie was correct—there was no way he was about to wade into that churning mass of arms and legs that was Cochran family basketball. All of them played loudly and with much gusto, including Bennie. Or especially Bennie; he wasn't sure. Her hair was pulled up in a messy ponytail and she was wearing her brothers out on the court that was next to the garage. Clay was amazed and amused—gone was the sophisticated businesswoman of the morning and the solicitous nurse of the afternoon—the cutest tomboy that Clay had ever beheld had replaced her. He thought about his own sister for a moment and tried to imagine her dribbling and shooting with the same kind of precision that Bennie was showing. Not possible—his sister was too much the little princess for that.

He said as much to Bennie in the kitchen. Bennie had left the game early to shower and fix the men something to eat. She was rapidly slicing tomatoes for the giant sandwiches that would accompany the rest of the vegetable soup.

"Is your sister younger than you?" she asked. When he conceded that she was the youngest of five, Bennie nodded. "I'm the oldest. It would not have been possible for me to be a girly girl around here."

As if to prove her words true, her brothers filled up the kitchen and breakfast room with cries for food and lies about how well they had played.

"Damn, Bennie, I'm hungry as a bear," said Adam, leaning over her shoulder and trying to grab a piece of something—anything that would keep him from starving. Bennie shooed him away and told him to go wash his dirty hands.

"And please act like you have some house training; you know we have company," she scolded. Adam was repentant, but there was no restoration of decorum as each of her brothers in turn continued to meddle with her or try to ruffle her in some way.

Bennie was completely serene in the middle of chaos, however. She was glad of the noise and commotion because it was keeping her from concentrating on Clay. He was so sexy that the fine hairs on the back of her neck were tingling. It was a pleasant sensation, but frightening. She was glad that Clay seemed perfectly relaxed and was at the moment deep in conversation with Donnie. She was looking at Clay out of the corner of her eye while making herself a sandwich at last. Of course, Alan came and took half and Andrew took the other. She looked at her brother with exasperation.

"Not you, too! How can you treat your twin that way?" she said in mock reproach. Andrew looked completely innocent.

"You mean you didn't make this for me? I'm sorry; I'll put it back," he offered. Bennie pushed his hand away.

"Oh, no, you don't, Bunchy. Nobody wants it after you've had your hands all over it. I'll make another one. Better yet, you make it for me. Please," she added as she went to join Clay and the others in the breakfast room.

To Clay's surprise, the men, disheveled as they were, all stood when Bennie entered the room, and remained standing until she sat down. She was truly the queen of that outfit whether she acted like a "girly girl" or not. Alan had brought over his new laptop for Bennie to peruse, which she was eagerly doing when Donnie started in on her.

"Clay, isn't my sister beautiful?" he asked innocently. He reached over and twisted a lock of her hair. Bennie ignored him, but he kept on. "I mean, she is really pretty, don't you think?"

Bennie kept playing with the laptop, totally unaffected by what Donnie was saying. She never took her eyes from the screen, but she did respond.

"I'm not keeping your dogs," she said mildly.

Light dawned for Clay at that point. This was yet another way that Bennie's brothers had of teasing her. Adonis kept showering Bennie with extravagant compliments, which she ignored, engrossed as she was in some new program. Eventually she spoke with certain finality.

"I am not keeping your dogs, you may not borrow my car, I am cosigning *nothing,* and I am not upgrading your computer again. Go away."

As Donnie sighed with exaggerated pain and Clay laughed out loud, Bennie glanced at her watch.

"We had better get going if we are going to get you to the airport, Clay." Andrew emerged from the kitchen, which he and Adam had thoughtfully cleaned after eating the sandwich they had supposedly made for Bennie.

"Airport? I can take you to the . . . shortcut to the airport that I just discovered. Oh, never mind, it's blocked off. Road construction," he finished lamely.

His sister had shot him a look that meant *back off, butt out, or die,* and he took it seriously. Then he smiled.

On the way to the airport, the brief reprieve that Bennie had gained by surrounding herself with her brothers was over. She was completely alone with Clay, and his sheer masculinity was doing crazy things to her. Every time he spoke, for example, little flickers of electricity would envelop her. His smell was intoxicating—it was one she had never smelled on any of her brothers, thank goodness. Nothing was less arousing than being reminded of a family member in a romantic situation, and nothing about Clay Deveraux was remotely reminiscent of any man she had ever met.

Clay broke the quiet reverie into which she was slipping with his deep voice.

"You know, being with your family made me feel a little guilty. I don't get together with my brothers often enough. And when we do, it's mostly business," he said ruefully. "But I can tell that you really know how to enjoy yourself." He looked over at Bennie as he spoke.

"Guilty as charged," Bennie replied. "We're very close, and we tend to rely on one another a lot. And as you might have noticed, my brothers are all quite crazy and have to let off steam regularly."

Clay laughed quietly. "I think you let off a little as well as your brothers. This was quite a day, Ms. Cochran."

Bennie flushed a little at that comment—an understatement, if ever there was one. Here the man had come to Detroit to talk business and Bennie had virtually kidnapped him and subjected him to torture by Cochran. Everything had seemed normal enough while it was happening, but in retrospect, it was going to be hard to explain. She tried to voice this opinion and was immediately cut off by Clay.

"Oh, no, you don't! Don't go getting conventional on me! This is one of the most relaxing days I have had in about five years, maybe ten. The fact that you act from the heart and do things your own way makes you unique. Don't even think about apologizing or explaining. I should be thanking you right now. The pleasure was truly all mine."

Those words, spoken in that magnificent voice, were enough to put Bennie over the edge. For some reason, her underwear felt constricting and she was having trouble getting enough air. Luckily they had reached Detroit Metro by then. She pulled up to the terminal where Clay's flight was reserved and was headed for short-term parking when Clay insisted that she not wait but leave him to his own devices. Risking the wrath of airport security, Bennie parked in a no-parking zone and got out of the car. She opened the trunk so that Clay could retrieve his briefcase. Then she stood there in the chilly early-spring evening and waited.

Clay smiled down at her and she felt the warmth of his smile spreading over her like a cashmere blanket. He set the briefcase on the curb and put his arms around Bennie for a tight hug, which was followed by a kiss on the forehead. Saying something about being in touch, he waved and disappeared into the terminal. Bennie stood there blinking until the security guard suggested strongly that she move her car.

Bennie drove home in a fog. She didn't know whether to be happy or frustrated that Clay had not given her a real kiss. She was frustrated, because she had really, really wanted to kiss him. And she was happy because that kiss would have sent her completely off her rocker; she just knew it. Just experiencing his arms around her for that brief, rhapsodic—albeit brotherly—hug was making her ears ring and all kinds of little alarms go off in all parts of her body. What she was going to do about it, she did not know, but in her heart she knew that things were just beginning with Mr. Clay Deveraux.

Renee also knew that something was up the minute Bennie entered the back door with a goofy look on her face—and with Jordan and Pippen, Donnie's golden retrievers.

"What have you been up to?" she asked suspiciously. "And why did Donnie leave those monstrous dogs on the back porch?"

Bennie did not answer her directly. She let the dogs into the basement, then hung up her Burberry trench coat on a peg in the mudroom by the back door. She floated into the kitchen and sat down on one of the tall stools, extending her hands to Renee. Renee put her hands into Bennie's and they clasped fingers the way they used to in college when one had something of deep significance to impart to the other.

"Renee—I'm in love." Renee clicked her tongue in disgust and started to pull away, but Bennie would not let her. "I'm serious! I think he might be the one."

Genuinely mystified, Renee said, "Who?" impatiently.

Bennie sighed deeply and freed her hands. "Clayton Arlington Deveraux," she said dreamily.

Renee cocked an eyebrow to the ceiling. "Not that Rasta Frank Zappa wanna-be! Girl, have all my teachings gone astray? What is the matter with you? Ewww!"

Bennie came down out of the clouds for a minute and looked at Renee quite seriously. "Oh, honey, that was a *bad* picture. Or an old picture. It was an evil, not-true, horrible picture. This man is *gorgeous* . . . I mean he is sen*sa*tional."

Bennie described Clay from head to toe for Renee's edification and to simply enjoy talking about him.

"He has lovely manners, and that voice . . ." Her own voice trailed off for a moment. "Renee, his voice is like rolling naked on a chinchilla blanket in front of a roaring fire in the middle of a snowstorm in Vermont with chilled champagne and strawberries waiting and Kevin Mahogany playing in the background." Spent, she dropped her head into her hands and sighed.

Renee pressed for more details, which Bennie was happy to supply.

"Let me get this straight. You actually changed into grubby, manly gear and let that man watch you galumphing around with the brothers Cochran? In what way is that supposed to make you appealing? And please tell me that you did not take him to the airport in that *shmatte,*" she finished, using the Yiddish word for old clothes.

Bennie looked down—she had on a perfectly nice pair of chinos and a silk turtleneck.

"I look fine. And there wasn't much I could do about

this afternoon. It was too late to cancel, and if I had told them I was trying to get with some guy it would have made it worse—they would have all come over here and drooled and bayed at the moon or something, just to be cute. You *know* this. So I was just myself," she finished defensively. "And he liked it." Bennie smiled, remembering his warm words in the car.

"Yeah, as a novelty act, maybe. But be that as it may, what exactly are your plans for this person?"

Renee dated very wealthy, much older men exclusively, and there was not a lot of tearing around and hand-wringing in her dating life. She was not one for plotting and drama, but she saw no reason for Bennie not to indulge. Bennie, though, was clueless.

"Renee, all I know right now is that I want this man *bad.* I have a feeling that he has had women lined up around the block since he was two, and I'm equally sure that he has been exposed to every little trick in the book. Not that I would be any good at that kind of thing, anyway," she said truthfully.

"Right now I am going to play it by ear, unless I don't hear from him again, which seems unlikely." She rose and went to the refrigerator to get a bottle of Perrier. Turning to Renee, she raised the bottle in a mock toast. "In the meantime, there's always shopping."

Bennie was right: she did indeed hear from Clay again, and much sooner than she would have expected. The very next day she received an extremely beautiful bouquet of flowers that were the very essence of her—colorful, dramatic, and fragrant. The fact that they were delivered at the office made the speculation that had hummed along since the previous day burst into rampant gossip. It just wasn't like Bennie to disappear from the office with a handsome man—with any man, for that matter—and just turn up the next day as though nothing had happened. No one dared ask, however, and Bennie just drank in the flowers and minded her own business. Or she planned to, until she got home and found another floral tribute, this one in the form of Bennie's absolute most favorite flower, tulips. These were an amazing shade of baby pink that looked almost iridescent on the sleek, shiny petals. Bennie was wiped out.

She started to call Clay to express her thanks, then thought better of it—she would send him a handwritten note. She just had a feeling that Mr. Clay Deveraux had a standing order at many Atlanta florists for just this sort of thing, and she wasn't going down like that. *No, sir.* Win, lose or draw, Clay was going to have to realize that Bennie was one of a kind.

Which was critical at this juncture, because Bennie had been right about something other than the fact that she would hear from Clay—she was absolutely correct about the women falling at his feet. Clay, while not exactly a player, was a man who enjoyed the company of women. He socialized frequently, got bored quickly, and moved on, always leaving the women better off for having had a relationship with him. To his credit, he never misled anyone and he was not cruel or capricious. On the contrary, he was gentlemanly and generous to a fault. He knew in his heart that he would go spiraling off the deep end once he found the object of his soul's desire, and until that fateful day, he intended to enjoy every minute of his time.

Clay had a variety of ladies to choose from both in Atlanta and in most major cities. That they were all essentially the same woman had not once occurred to him—they were all pretty and pleasant and did not require too much of his intellect. The typical woman Clay dated was small—petite, dainty, and not terribly ambitious, which was why they got along so well. Clay could come and go as he pleased without having to account for himself, explain himself, or share himself. When he found his true soul mate, he had no doubt that she would be the best of this particular breed—well-groomed, housebroken, and acquiescent, if not obedient. In his defense, however, it was kindness and not ignorance that made him that way.

Like Bennie, Clay was the oldest of a large family—four boys and one girl. Twins also ran in his family—his second-oldest brothers were identical twins. Like Bennie, Clay had lost a parent—his father had died when Clay was twenty-one. He, too, took over the stewardship of the family, making him protective in the extreme, especially where women were concerned. His mother did not have to raise a hand if she chose not to. His sister did not know the meaning of the word *work,* and as long as Clay was in the world she did not have to unless she chose otherwise. That *work* was not a four-letter word as far as women were concerned did not occur to him—he genuinely thought, given his origins, that this was the best course of action for all concerned. Not for nothing was the road to hell paved with good intentions.

Nothing in his experience had actually prepared him for someone like Bennie. For some reason he could not stop thinking about her. She wasn't his type at all, but there was something about her that was so vital, so exciting, and so much fun that he couldn't put her out of his mind. He actually found himself calling her from time to time just to talk, a practice to which none of his previous companions had been exposed. At first he would use the consortium business as an excuse—now he just called or e-mailed whenever he felt like touching base with her. He always got a little charge every time she picked up her private line at the office.

"Bennie Cochran, how may I help you?"

Bennie had a clear, direct voice that Clay could listen to for hours.

"Well, you can tell me you're going to this media conference in Chicago. That would help me a lot," Clay drawled.

He could almost see Bennie's eyes light up on the other end of the phone. He could always tell when Bennie was smiling, and he tried to make her do it as often as possible.

"Hello, Clay, how are you doing? And yes, of course I'm going to the conference; I wouldn't miss it," she responded warmly. She flashed a smile at Renee who had stopped in to take Bennie out to lunch.

Across the room Renee's eyes got big and her mouth puckered into a *girl, you know you lyin'* O. She listened to Bennie continue to chat happily and shook her head slightly. Bennie had it bad. She wasn't gushing or drooling—yet—but from her animated conversation, giggles and batted eyes were soon to follow. She said as much when Bennie got off the phone.

"You know, you been chittin' and chattin' with this Clay person for several weeks now, and I see nothing happening. And I see you getting more interested by the minute. No, make that by the second—Midwestern Media Conference, indeed. You know how much you hate conferences. You normally wouldn't be caught dead at one of those things, so what gives?"

Bennie smiled lazily at Renee. She was feeling too good to defend herself at that point. The very sound of Clay's voice gave her fever. If he could do that talking over the telephone, there was no telling what he could do in person. Which was why she was going to make sure that she was at that stupid conference. That and the fact that she was taking Donnie. Donnie had at long last expressed his desire to become an active part of WWCC. This was what Bennie had prayed for and hoped for, and now it was going to happen. Someone other than Bennie was going to assume the leadership of the family business. In a few months she would be able to take a very happy back-burner role and pursue other interests. Which was what she tried to sell Renee, who wasn't buying.

"Okay, try again. You know and I know that this has something to do with that Frank Zappa boy. Don't try and kid a kidder; I know your moves," Renee said, narrowing her eyes slightly.

Bennie gave up.

"All right, I do have a little something planned for Mr.

Clay Deveraux. But please stop calling him that Zappa thing—when you see him, you'll understand. In fact," Bennie said with inspiration, "why don't you come too? You can shop on Michigan Avenue while the seminars are going on, and there's going to be a big dinner dance. It's usually as boring as hell, but this year it's going to be very, very different. Very."

Renee immediately looked more cheerful—shopping and subterfuge were her two favorite things, as long as she wasn't directly involved in the machinations. Shopping was truly one of their favorite things, and if a Chicago engagement was in the air, a new frock was a must-have item.

"Okay, let's hit it. I have the feeling there is something out there with my name on it," Renee said happily. "And if it doesn't answer to Renee, I just know it'll respond to American Express Gold."

Despite her normal misgivings, Bennie was enjoying the conference. It was a chance to meet with old friends and acquaintances and share resources and information. It was also a great opportunity to introduce Donnie to people who knew him vaguely as one of those good-looking Cochran boys and not as any integral part of the station. As far as Bennie was concerned, the sooner she could get Donnie up to speed on certain issues, the better. Big Benny normally came to these events, but he had decided at the last minute to stay at home, another move that was much appreciated by Bennie. The last thing she wanted was Big Benny dragging her around from person to person shouting the praises of his little girl as though she were a one-trick pony.

All in all, Bennie had nothing but great expectations for the conference. She had already seen Clay briefly—he gave her a quick, brotherly hug that set her insides reeling but seemed to have no effect whatsoever on him, the cad. But she was all right with that because the plans had already been laid. She was scanning her schedule of that day's seminars when two enormous hands accosted her from behind.

"Bennie, baby, ya look so good I could put ya on a plate and sop ya up with a biscuit!"

Bennie was whirled around to face one of her biggest fans, David Hawkins, a well-known radio personality and one of the organizers of the event. She gave David a big kiss on the cheek, unaware that Clay was observing the entire scene. After she and David exchanged greetings, one of the reasons for his effusive hello was revealed.

"You know, Bennie, everybody in broadcasting is not as dedicated as you and your family," David began humbly.

Bennie's eyes flashed and she immediately said, "No."

David looked hurt. "Aww, Bennie, now, you know . . ."

Bennie did indeed know. "One of the scheduled speakers dropped out and you want me to substitute at the last minute, don't you?"

David hung his head in mock shame. "Dang, Bennie, when you say it like that it sounds so cold . . . so harsh. Why you wanna playa-hate a brother like that?"

Bennie burst out laughing.

"David, this is the second year in a row you've tried this on me. It worked last time, but it's not working again. If you wanted me to speak, you should have asked me six months ago, like you did with the guy who didn't show up. When you give me my propers, you'll get yours."

Bennie was laughing at the same time she was giving him attitude. She started to walk away, only to have him follow her giving his best James Brown "Please-baby-please-baby-please-please-please-baby." Finally she stopped and put out a hand.

"Okay! But this is the last time, and you owe me big!"

David's big, handsome face took on a huge smile of relief, and he began to kiss her hands in gratitude. Bennie laughed helplessly at his antics, while Clay continued to observe from across the lobby. *What the hell was that all about?* he wondered. He continued to wonder the rest of the day, until it was time for dinner.

As at many conferences, lunch was served on both days, but participants were free for dinner on their own the first night, after a cocktail hour that served as a time to network. Clay and Bennie found each other at the cocktail hour after the long day of seminars.

"Well, how about dinner?" Clay asked. "Are you hungry?"

Bennie assured him that she was starving.

"But my housemate and my brother and I were going out to eat—would you like to join us?" she suggested.

Clay found that idea agreeable, and after changing from business attire they hit the town. The group finally settled on Chinese and found a restaurant that specialized in Pacific Rim cooking, offering an exciting and tantalizing array of food.

One of the high points of the evening for Bennie was the look on Renee's face when she at last met Clay. Renee's back was to the door when Clay knocked, so she did not see him when Bennie opened the door. When he said "Hello, Benita, are you ready to go?" Renee froze. Renee slowly wheeled around to see for herself the source of that heavenly voice and almost tipped over. She rallied, however, and managed to return Clay's greeting with her usual aplomb.

For Clay, the high point was that the whole evening was spent with Bennie. He hadn't been wrong about her—she was clever, classy, and more fun than anyone that good-looking had a right to be. She also had the healthiest appetite of any woman he had ever seen. He was so accustomed to women who would order a small salad and a glass of mineral water and act full that he was unprepared for Bennie. She eagerly ordered an appetizer, soup, and an entree. Anything that looked good, she wanted to try, which was how she ended up with two appetizers and two entrees that she happily shared. She also knocked back a couple of Chinese beers with abandon. Clay could not remember ever being with a woman who admitted to drinking beer. And despite her hearty appetite, Bennie ate daintily and neatly, wielding her chopsticks with precision. Her only regret was that no dessert was to be had.

"I'm sorry, but a fortune cookie is just not dessert to me. A dessert should ooze some sort of sauce or have cake or be frozen or something. Fortune cookies are cute, but they're not dessert," she said regretfully. Then she brightened.

"Okay, this is fun—someone told me that the fortunes make sense only if you add three words to the end of them. Are you game?" she asked of the table at large. They all agreed to go along with the game.

"All right, everyone read your fortune out loud and at the end you have to say, 'in the bedroom.' "

This elicited laughter from everyone. Renee insisted on going first.

"A long journey is best begun soon—*in the bedroom,*" she said with a raised eyebrow.

Donnie went next. "Things are not always as they seem—*in the bedroom.*" By this time, everyone was cracking up.

Bennie, ever dramatic, peeked at hers and howled. "The prize you seek shall soon be yours—*in the bedroom.*"

Clay was last: "The road to success is directly ahead—*in the bedroom.*"

By this time they were wiping their eyes and laughing. Bennie suggested walking back to the hotel to work off their meal. Renee immediately declined.

"Not in these heels, honey. I'm taking a cab. *To the bedroom.*"

Donnie yawned and agreed with Renee.

"Okay, you win," Bennie said, and was preparing to cab it with the rest of the group when Clay stopped her.

"Well, you didn't ask, but I'm game. I could use the exercise."

Bennie was thrilled, although she tried not to let it show. She and Clay saw Donnie and Renee off to a cabstand and then started walking the twelve or so blocks back to the hotel. The night air was cool and slightly windy, but not uncomfortable. It could have been the dead of winter instead of the middle of spring and it would not have mattered one iota to Bennie—Clay's company warmed her inside and out. They took their time walking back to the hotel, looking in the glittering shop windows and talking about anything and everything.

"Do you spend much time in Chicago?" Clay asked. "It seems like your kind of town."

Bennie hesitated before answering.

"I used to come here quite a bit. My husband was from Chicago," she answered quietly.

Clay was dumbfounded.

"I didn't know you had been married. When did you get married?"

Bennie sighed.

"Right after I got out of college. Gilbert was my college sweetheart. I graduated from University of Michigan, and he had just gotten his doctorate at MIT and was working there. So we got married and I moved to Boston."

Bennie spoke matter-of-factly, but she sounded so sad that Clay wanted to hold her. But he had to satisfy his curiosity.

"How long were you married?" he asked.

Bennie looked away before speaking.

"We were married twenty-two months, three weeks, four days, eighteen hours, and fifty-two minutes," she said.

Clay was astounded.

"You actually kept count?"

Bennie did not answer.

"So what happened in the fifty-third minute?" Clay asked. Immediately he wished he hadn't.

"He died," Bennie said quietly.

Clay stopped in his tracks.

Two little words, but their impact was like that of a freight train. Clay began stammering out an apology for his crudity when Bennie put her hand over his mouth.

"Clay, you don't have to apologize to me or feel sorry for me. I had absolutely the best years of my entire life

with Gilbert. He was my best friend and we loved each
other dearly. People spend their whole lives looking for
what we had."

She stopped speaking and wiped a tiny tear from the
corner of her eye. Then she smiled.

"Besides, Gilbert swore that if I got maudlin about him
he would come back to haunt me. So don't go there,
okay?"

She took his hand and they walked back to the hotel in
a comfortable silence, but Clay's head was reeling.

Bennie was truly an amazing woman. Just when he
thought he had her pegged, another dimension revealed itself. Clay insisted on escorting her back to her room instead
of parting in the lobby. Their hands were still entwined as
they left the elevator.

Once again Bennie found herself waiting to say good-
bye to Clay. This time there was no brotherly hug. This
time they stood facing each other without speaking for
what seemed like hours. Finally Clay leaned toward her
and touched his lips to hers in what should have been a
brief, chaste good-night kiss. He held both of her hands in
his and their lips touched softly and sweetly, then firmly
and insistently. Their lips parted at the same instant and
their tongues swirled around each other in a soft, pulsing
rhythm that was like the fusing of two souls. They finally
broke apart and stared at each other. Clay raised his hands
to cup Bennie's face and lowered his mouth to hers. They
had barely made contact when a loud thump came from
the other side of the door. It was just enough to break the
spell. Hands pulled away, deep sighs followed, and good-
byes were regretfully said. Then Bennie went into the suite
to kill her best friend.

Renee was soaking wet and contrite, wrapped in a big
bath sheet. Bennie pointed the first two fingers of her right
hand at Renee and hissed in a demonic voice, "You die!"

Renee was trying not to laugh as she apologized.

"I'm sorry, I'm sorry, I'm sorry! But I heard something
in the hall and I looked through the peephole, and— By

the way, he looked to be doing an *excellent* job," she volunteered. At the look on Bennie's face, Renee hurried on. "Anyway, when his hands went up to your face, I kind of lost my balance, and . . . well, you know the rest," she finished lamely. "So, you have a nice walk?"

Bennie found it too difficult to be aroused and enraged at the same time, so she let go of the anger. She tore off her leather jacket and dropped it on the floor, then staggered into her bedroom and fell face-forward across the bed. It was just as well that Renee had broken up that clinch. She rolled over to face Renee, who was standing in the doorway looking amused and concerned.

"Actually, I should be thanking you—God knows I would not have stopped on my own," Bennie admitted. She paused to taste her lips again and savor the slight essence of Clay that still remained. *Great day in the morning!* Their bodies had not even touched and she was on fire, from the soles of her feet to the very top of her head and every vital point in between. There was no part of her that was not quivering helplessly in the wake of that kiss. Abruptly, she turned to Renee.

"I've got to take a shower, a *cold* shower, right *now*. Then I'll tell you everything; I swear."

Leaving Renee in the middle of the bedroom, Bennie put action to words. She hurriedly stripped off her clothes and leaped into a tepid shower, which she promptly turned ice-cold. Even that wasn't enough to completely cool her off. Bennie leaned against the clammy tile wall of the shower enclosure and tried to breathe normally. What was she getting herself into?

On a different floor in the same hotel, Clay was asking himself the same question. What in the world was going on in his life? Everything was going along just the way he wanted it until along came a tall, beautiful, sweet, funny woman who could level him with one sweet little kiss. Clay took a swallow of the brandy that he was knocking back in the main bar of the hotel, but it still could not take away the taste of Bennie on his lips. He snorted. *Bennie.* What a ridiculous name for a beautiful woman. He refused to call her that, referring to her only as Benita. Benita, who tasted like peaches and kissed like an angel. She was amazing, and it wasn't just because she was smart and sexy.

There was something different about Benita. She had endured a terrible loss, yet she could talk about it with composure and a kind of quiet joy. He thought about what she had said about her husband threatening to come back and haunt her if she got maudlin. God, they must have known he was going to die. Clay stared out at nothing in particular. How could someone so young have lived through something like that? He tried to imagine any of the women he socialized with dealing with that kind of tragedy, and came up blank. He remembered his mother's absolute grief and despair and tried to imagine Bennie going through the same thing. It was just too much to bear.

Clay could feel his control slipping away from him. He wanted nothing more than to go back to Benita's room and kiss her some more. A lot more. But that would have meant exposing himself and losing even more control. This was not the way his relationships went. He started them, he ended them, and he decided what went on in between. He scowled, remembering that kiss. Benita's hands were long and slender and fit perfectly inside of his. For some reason, reliving the feel of her soft hands made him even more agitated. There was no way he was going out like this, not over a kiss that made him feel like an anxious schoolboy. No matter how spectacular the woman was, it wasn't going to happen like that. Glancing at the clock, Clay decided it wasn't too late to call an old friend. So, fortified by brandy and frustrated by emotion, he took out his cell phone and did something truly stupid.

Three

After a mostly sleepless night, Bennie decided that she was ready to take on the world. She had not expected Clay to kiss her, but on some deeper level she had known that his kiss would be just as potent as she remembered. And on that deeper level, she knew that being with Clay was inevitable. How she was going to get from point A to point B she wasn't sure, but she was ready to get started. She and Renee had talked a long time the night before. In Bennie's experience, there was nothing so murky that it could not be made clear by having a long talk with Renee, who was more than happy to serve as Bennie's sounding board. Plus, Renee was feeling so mellow afterward that she actually volunteered to curl Bennie's hair for the dinner dance, something that would fill Renee with dread because Bennie had so much hair, but not this time. So there was no reason that Bennie should feel anything but spectacular, and no reason that she should not look the part.

She was wearing black, which was a staple in her wardrobe, but this time it was in the form of an Azzedine Alaia suit that was a little bit shorter than she normally wore her work attire, and whose jacket was a bit more formfitting. She also had on her favorite Italian T-strapped shoes, which did wonderful things for her legs. And she was wearing real silk hose in a color so well matched to her skin that she appeared barelegged. Extravagant lingerie was another one of Bennie's indulgences, one that she allowed herself frequently. Her hair was in a French braid with a few wispy tendrils—she was saving the mane for the dance that evening, when she planned to throw the ball into Clay's court once and for all.

She was not at all surprised to not find him in the crowded lobby area, where a continental breakfast was being served—Clay did not seem like a man who would get up early to eat breakfast. Bennie, however, ate heartily, since she needed energy to get through her presentation, which was right before lunch. After dodging several would-be players and a couple of blowhards, Bennie found the ballroom where she would be speaking. She sat in the back of the room to collect her thoughts and make a few notes.

The room began to fill with the participants for the first seminar, which had something to do with human resource responsibilities in a changing society. It was extremely boring and seemed to go on forever. Finally it ended and the participants dispersed for a much-needed break before Bennie's session began. She went to the front of the large room and took a deep breath to compose herself. There were many more participants than she had anticipated. Since her talk came right before lunch and the first speaker had been so ungodly boring, Bennie figured that only a few people would return to the ballroom. She was wrong; not only was the place filling up, but when David began introducing her, she realized that he had not let people know that the expected speaker wasn't coming and that there would be a substitute.

She could only hope that there would not be a revolt when people realized that she was not the well-known motivational speaker they expected. Worse yet, she happened to look up and spot Clay sitting between two very attractive women, each of whom seemed thrilled to be where she was, clinging to the side of the best-looking man in the room. *This is what hell is like,* Bennie thought. She turned her attention to David, who was trying to explain that Ayala Taylor was not able to make it due to a serious family situation, and that Benita Cochran, president and owner of WWCC, would be substituting. Bennie leaned over to him and said sotto voce that she wanted to have a little talk with him afterward. She then went center stage and threw back her shoulders.

Clay realized that he was anxious for Bennie, more so when he saw that those assembled were really looking forward to the scheduled speaker. The woman on his left made that completely apparent as she leaned across him to speak to her friend.

"Girl, this is lame. We could go get our hair done for tonight instead of staying here for what's-her-name."

"Girlfriend" was about to nod in agreement when Clay drawled, "But that would be rude, wouldn't it?"

The woman sat back, flushed with embarrassment at having been overheard, and stimulated by Clay's sexy voice. She was about to start flirting when Bennie started speaking.

Refusing a microphone, Bennie gave the audience a wide smile.

"Good morning, and thank you for allowing me to substitute for Ms. Taylor. You notice I say 'substitute' and not 'replace,' because I am sure that you will agree that she has no equal in motivational speaking."

Moving to the edge of the stage, Bennie stopped for a moment and surveyed the group.

"I'm sure you are all dying to get to lunch, and I assure you that you will get there on time. I am going to take about twenty-seven minutes of your time to share some very basic management techniques that I learned firsthand from an expert in the field—my dad."

Bennie descended the stairs while still speaking. She was a rarity—a speaker who could move around easily and with grace and keep all the attention focused on her without resorting to staged trickery. Of course, the fact that she had legs like a Rockette didn't hurt either; every time she moved, Clay could sense every man in the room running his eyes up and down Bennie's legs. Bennie had her audience eating out of the palm of her hand. With a combination of common sense, shrewd insight, and anecdote, she charmed and educated every person in the room, even the clingers who were glommed next to Clay.

"In conclusion," Bennie said brightly, "remember to have fun. We're not machines. We were not put here to slave away mindlessly without ever taking the time to enjoy our lives and what we have accomplished and will accomplish. Enjoy your families, cultivate interests outside the workplace, and learn to relax. If your career choices are not bringing you satisfaction, you should seriously look at doing something else."

She looked around the room intently—Clay could have heard a pin drop.

"We spend too much time working to not enjoy what we are doing. We work too hard not to derive a sense of satisfaction from our lifestyle. Frankly, one of the reasons I enjoy radio so very much is because it is show business, at least as close as *I'm* going to come to show business. It is magic, it is entertainment, and it is *fun*. The secret to having a long and happy life is to figure out a way to make money by doing what you love to do most. The fact that I can make a great living and get free concert tickets, well, that just proves that life can be good."

Everyone burst into laughter and applause. Bennie glanced at her Piaget and smiled.

"Twenty-six minutes! Let's go have lunch."

Clay knew it was fruitless to try to get to Bennie through the crowd of people that surrounded her. He also knew that the decision he had made the previous night was the correct one. Bennie Cochran was a woman with whom he could not become involved without losing himself totally, which was why he had provided himself with a buffer. After watching yet another facet of Bennie emerge, polished and flashing fire, he knew he was doing the right thing. When the crowd had dissipated and Bennie was free, he went over to tell her how much he had enjoyed her speech.

Before he could approach her, though, David Hawkins

grabbed her in a huge hug. "Bennie, baby, you were great, as always. I just can't thank you enough!"

Bennie smiled sweetly and said, "Oh, but you can. How much were you paying Ayala Taylor for her appearance?"

David actually paled at the innocent question. Bennie did not wait for a direct response; she merely pressed on.

"Well, David, my time and services are equally valuable. So I will expect a check for that amount to be sent to Habitat for Humanity of Detroit in the name of WWCC. And next time you want me to speak, make sure I am your first choice and not a stand-in, okay?"

Clay was amazed. *Damn, she's smooth. She got exactly what she wanted without fronting or whining.* A small chill went down Clay's spine—this woman was truly formidable. And adorable. He finally went over to Bennie and told her how much he had enjoyed her talk. She thanked him with a huge smile.

"Are you hungry?" he asked solicitously.

"Yes, and thirsty, too. Running my big mouth makes my throat so dry!" she said. "But I really don't want to go into that huge room and wait in line forever. . . ."

Before she could finish her sentence, Clay had taken her arm and spirited her off to a small bistro off the main lobby. It was dark, secluded, quiet, and mostly empty. Sitting on a velvet banquette in a quiet corner across from Clay was just what the doctor ordered, as far as Bennie was concerned. She smiled happily while their server poured her iced tea with no sugar and lots of lime, the way she liked it.

Clay, on the other hand, was kicking himself. *This is exactly what I did not mean to happen. I do not need to be alone with this woman.* All she had to do was . . . nothing, and he was leaping to do her bidding like a sex-starved sixteen-year-old. Thank God she was unaware of his inner turmoil—if she knew she had this kind of effect on him she could walk all over him. *Now is not the time, and Benita Cochran is not the one,* Clay thought. Although when he looked across the table he couldn't quite remember why he was adamant that he avoid her.

Bennie was completely oblivious to Clay's angst and was chatting happily as she put away prodigious amounts of shrimp scampi, rice pilaf, and a green salad with Roquefort dressing on the side. She blissfully drained the last of her iced tea and turned the full power of her smile on Clay. Bennie was completely happy. She had done an excellent presentation, had an excellent lunch, and was with an excellent companion, albeit a quiet one. Bennie put her hand on top of Clay's and tried to get a two-way conversation started.

"You're awfully quiet. How was your lunch?" she asked.

Clay looked down at her long, slender fingers and started to drift back to the previous night. Then he caught himself.

"I'm just a little tired," he answered. *Tired of thinking about you all night long.*

Bennie made a comical face and teased him.

"Not too tired to dance tonight, I hope? I was planning on saving you at least one."

Her statement reminded Clay at last of the evening's mission.

"Oh, I'll be dancing all right. And so will you. I have a good friend who lives here in Chicago, and he is going to drop by tonight. He's a super-nice guy. I think you two will really hit it off," Clay said.

Bennie's slow smile did not betray what she was feeling, and that was a very good thing. Clay was trying to fix her up! It had gotten too hot for him and he had decided to bail. *Well, well, well! I am getting to Mr. Deveraux and he is running scared. Well, baby, you can run but you can't hide.*

The evening was well under way when Clay and his friend Bryant Porter entered the ballroom. The music was jazz and the atmosphere was charged with the energy of people out to relax and have a good time. The men were handsome and debonair in evening wear, and the women were arrayed in every type of finery. Glitzy frocks, glitter, sequins, and cleavage were the order of the evening. And there seemed to be a never-ending supply of lovely women from whom to select a partner.

Bryant's head swiveled from side to side as she surveyed the embarrassment of feminine riches. He was almost as tall as Clay and as broad of shoulder, but that was where the resemblance ended. He was as dark as Clay was fair, and his head was clean-shaven. A neatly barbered beard set off his white, even teeth. All in all, Bryant was quite a delectable man.

"Damn, Clay, if this woman you want me to meet looks better than that woman over there, I'm going to have a heart attack."

Clay smiled grimly. "This woman is very special. Believe me, you won't be disappointed."

Just then, a subtle flash of pale color in the midst of all the richly colored gowns caught his attention. Bryant must have caught the same glimpse, because his eyes went to the same place as Clay's. The men were staring at a long, lissome pair of legs that led up to lusciously curved hips in a dress that had no back whatsoever.

"Clay, forget that other woman, whoever she is. I want to meet that woman in the pink dress."

Clay was about to agree, but not because of the woman in pink. The more he thought about what he had done the more idiotic it seemed. The woman in pink, however, seemed to have heard Bryant, because she turned around slowly to look directly at Clay. All of Clay's breath left his body in an audible rush, and he felt as though he had been turned to stone. It was Bennie, looking as if she were wrapped in starlight.

Bennie smiled sweetly and started walking toward Clay, then stopped and walked directly into Bryant's arms. Bryant wrapped his arms around Bennie and held her as if he would never let her go.

"Baby, baby, it's been so long! Let me look at you!"

Bennie obligingly allowed Bryant to walk all the way around her, shaking his head as he did so.

"Woman, you are beautiful," he said reverently.

Bennie gave her most beguiling smile and held his hands as if she had just won the lottery.

Clay stood there hoping that he did not look like he felt, which was like the world's biggest fool.

"I take it you two know each other," he said dryly.

Bennie and Bryant stopped cooing over each other long enough to remember that Clay existed.

"Clay, what a wonderful coincidence! I knew Bryant when he was at Harvard—we were neighbors in Boston," Bennie said happily.

It evolved that Bryant also knew Renee, having dated her when she made trips to Boston to see Bennie and Gilbert. Bennie immediately dragged Bryant off to the table where Renee and Donnie were sitting, and the three of them started having old home week. Clay followed in their wake, outwardly composed but inwardly boiling with self-directed rage.

Bennie—*Benita*—looked absolutely amazing. He had never seen her with her hair down, and tonight it was a mass of deep waves and curls that cascaded around her shoulders. It was satiny and glossy, and he knew just what it would feel like in his hands. One side was pinned up with tiny, sparkling flowers, and the other side framed her beautiful face, which was turned adoringly to Bryant. And that dress—for some reason it was the most provocative garment he had ever seen, although Bennie was a lot more covered up than most of the women present. The dress had long sleeves and a straight neckline, so it wasn't as though her breasts were bared. But her long, lovely brown back was completely exposed to other men's eyes and other men's hands, and the thought was driving Clay mad. In addition, even though the dress was a soft, innocent pink, it was almost impossible to tell where Bennie ended and the dress began due to the sheer gossamer quality of the fabric, which had a soft iridescence. *That's worse than being naked,* Clay thought savagely.

Yet she looked so demure and innocent it was hard to fault her. Or so Clay thought, until Bennie and Renee rose to go to the ladies' room. The dress clung to every curve and outlined Bennie's body in such a way that she looked like a bronze Venus clad only in a spray of sparkling moisture. Clay naturally rose with the rest of the men at the table as the ladies left, but he did so with difficulty. All he had to do was look at her in that dress and all hell had broken out in his body. He set his jaw grimly. *This is going to be a long night.*

Actually, the dress was having exactly the effect that Bennie intended. She had gone to see her favorite dressmaker in Detroit, the woman who made almost all of her clothes, and explained the situation.

"Joyce, I need the frock of *death*. I need a dress that is going to bring a strong man to his knees and make him beg. I need to look totally sensuous, sexy, and provocative, but completely innocent at the same time. Okay?"

Joyce, bless her heart, didn't even blink.

"So we're going for a 'virgin whore' look, is that it?" Joyce asked, giving the street pronunciation—*ho.*

Bennie thought a few seconds and arched an eyebrow.

"Yes. That would definitely be it."

Bennie had expressed her reservations a couple of times during the fittings when it became apparent that it was not going to be possible to wear a bra or much else in the way of underwear with this confection. Bennie had eyed herself in the mirror at Joyce's atelier.

"I don't know about this, Joyce." Bennie narrowed her eyes and cupped her full breasts. "My girls need a house. I've never let them just run loose in the street, so to speak."

Joyce laughed.

"Don't worry about it, girl; this double Lycra underlining will hold you in place better than a Wonderbra. Never fear; Joyce is here!"

And she had indeed worked wonders. To be honest, Bennie did not really know how the dress was affecting the men she left quivering in her wake, because she had eyes only for Clay, a fact that was not lost on Bryant.

Upon her return to the table, Bryant leaned over to her and said so that only she could hear, "My friend has it bad, doesn't he?"

Bennie smiled up at Bryant.

"Yes, and I have it just as bad, but I'm not fighting it. *He's* the one going through changes."

Bryant put an arm around Bennie and pressed his lips to her temple.

"How about we turn up the heat for him? Raise the stakes a little? I know Clay very well, and he is not going down without a fight," he whispered.

Bennie widened her eyes slightly.

"I can't do that, Bryant. This dress is about as far as I was prepared to go. I can't resort to low tricks."

Bryant gave the smile that had left a string of broken hearts up and down the eastern seaboard.

"Don't worry," he said. "I can."

And with that he stood and pulled Bennie out onto the dance floor without so much as a word to Clay or anyone else. Bryant was a wonderful dancer, and the ice seemed to have been broken. Now that Bennie was not sitting at a table with someone whose laser glare would cut a man to ribbons, other men were asking her to dance. She was gone for the full set, dancing to jazz, R and B, and salsa with handsome men old and young. Clay's mood did not improve.

Finally she returned to the table, looking dewy and moist and energized. Dancing seemed to have improved her already good mood considerably. She sat right next to Clay, daring him to keep ignoring her.

"Well, Clay, I have to thank you for bringing Bryant here to meet me," she said cheerfully. "Although I'm not completely sure why you felt the need."

She looked directly into Clay's eyes and offered a sweet little smile.

"I told you—he's a nice guy, and I thought you would have a lot in common," Clay said shortly.

Bennie found this hilarious, but she kept it to herself. She couldn't resist looking around the room slowly, as if she were counting something.

"So," she said, "there aren't enough men here for me to pick from. You had to import me one, is that it? I'm just too big and homely to attract one on my own?"

Clay felt the back of his neck getting hot. *She's laughing at me.* At least she saw the humor in the situation, something to which Clay had been blinded. They both laughed out loud, at last.

"Okay, now that's the real Clay," Bennie said. "The evil twin is gone! Now, do I get my dance?"

Clay stood at once and held out his hand.

"I have been remiss. Let me remedy that right away."

He led her out to the dance floor and pulled her close. He looked into Bennie's eyes and gave her the kind of smile he had been holding back all evening.

"Is that better?"

Bennie smiled right back at him.

"Oh, my, yes. Yes."

The music was an oldie, Chaka Khan singing "Sweet Thing." Bennie melted against Clay. He was by far the best dance partner she had ever had, partially because they fit together so well. Clay's hands slid down Bennie's bare back to clasp her waist. The sensation that swept over her at his touch was shared by both of them. Bennie tried looking into Clay's eyes, but he looked so sexy and enigmatic that she gave up and laid her head on his shoulder with a little sigh. Clay pulled her even closer.

"You are the only woman I have ever danced with who didn't strain my neck," he said.

Bennie raised her head with a smile.

"Now, *that* was romantic. What a smooth talker you are!"

Clay took one hand away from her waist to bring it up to her face.

"So, you want romance, do you?"

Recklessly, Bennie said, "Yes. Oh, yes, I do."

Clay continued to hold her for a few moments after the song ended and a faster one began. Their eyes never left each other; they stood motionless, surrounded by people, lights, and music, but they saw only each other. Finally Clay lowered his head to her ear.

"Do you trust me?" he asked.

Bennie smiled and closed her eyes.

"Do you trust me?" he said again, with his lips touching the small, sweet hollow beneath her ear.

"Yes. Yes. *Yes*," she said breathlessly.

Clay finally pulled away from her long enough to take her hand in his.

"Come with me."

When they arrived in Clay's suite, Bennie wasn't sure what to expect. *Something along the lines of total abandon and ravishment, with clothes being thrown this way and that and the inevitable final shuddering clinch in a pile of bedclothes,* she thought, *with recriminations and doubts to follow.* What she had not expected was that Clay, after escorting her to his suite, would adjust the light, start some very nice jazz playing, and then turn around and look at her with his arms crossed and a deeply serious look. Nor was she prepared for the words that he spoke.

"How in the hell did your brother let you come out wearing that dress?"

Bennie's mouth fell slightly open, but before she could speak, Clay continued.

"If my sister even thought about wearing something like that I would lock her up. Donnie should be shot."

Bennie just laughed in his face.

"You don't like my outfit?" she asked innocently. "I think it's a sweet little thing," she continued, looking down at the front of the dress and striking a sultry pose.

She looked up to see if Clay was taking it as a joke.

He wasn't, exactly, but he wasn't being prudish or censuring, either. His eyes were warm with frank admiration, actually.

"Benita, you are absolutely breathtaking. I always knew you were pretty, but you are gorgeous, baby."

Clay had crossed the room and was caressing Bennie's shoulders as he spoke.

Bennie put her hands on Clay's hips and slid them up under his jacket, where she could feel his nicely muscled body.

"You know what? I think you're pretty gorgeous, yourself."

She leaned into him for the lingering kiss that she wanted and found herself kissing air. Clay stepped back.

"Okay, see, we need to talk."

He removed his big, warm hands and started pacing around the room. Bennie tilted her head and observed his growing agitation.

"Is this going to be a long talk? Because if that's the case, I'm going to sit down," she said, suiting action to words.

Bennie arrayed herself in what she hoped was a seductive manner in the corner of one of the two pillowy sofas that decorated the suite. Satisfied that she looked alluring, she tossed her hair back and prepared to listen to whatever Clay had to say.

"Okay, shoot. You look like a man with something on his mind," she said cheerfully.

Clay stopped roaming around and looked at Bennie.

"You just won't behave, will you? Benita, what am I going to do with you? You have no business being out in a dress like that. None whatsoever. I still can't believe Donnie let you out of his sight looking like that."

Bennie wanted to hear him say the words.

"Looking like what?" she urged.

Clay looked down at Bennie, who in fact looked like a delicious, decadent fruit full of intoxicating aroma and flavor, and gave up.

"Edible. Like I could devour you and come back for more," he said in a growl.

Bennie brightened considerably and started to get up from the sofa to join him.

"Don't you move. Stay right where you are," he warned. "I will not be responsible if you come over here," he admonished, but he did not sound as if he meant it.

The living room of the suite was dominated by a huge armoire that held the TV and stereo. Clay was leaning against it with an unreadable expression on his face. He had removed his suit coat and his tie, and in his dress shirt with the top buttons undone and his thick, wavy hair slightly mussed, he looked pretty delicious, too. Bennie decided to take matters into her own hands. She rose from the sofa, once again looking like a living work of art.

"Well, Clay, I think I need to share a few things with you," she said. "In the first place, this dress was not an accident. I had it made just for you."

Clay's expression became even more guarded. Bennie continued to walk toward him while she spoke in a soft, sultry voice.

"That's right, I had this dress specially made so that you would look at me just the way you are right now." By this time she had reached him and was sliding her hands up his strong, muscular arms.

Clay pulled her closer.

"And how am I looking at you, Benita?"

Bennie pulled his head down to hers and touched his lips with hers.

"Just . . . like . . . this . . ." she said under her breath.

She tasted Clay's sexy lips with her lips, at first softly and daintily; then she began delicately licking his lips with her tongue. Clay groaned with pleasure and tightened his arms around her. Bennie continued to tease Clay's lips with her tongue and started pulling gently on his lower lip with her teeth. Clay finally placed his hands in Bennie's hair to gain control of the kiss. The sweet, sexy teasing ended and the passion began in earnest as Clay and Bennie moved in each other's arms to try to satisfy the fiery sensations that had overtaken them.

Clay finally broke away from her lips. He put his forehead against Bennie's and tried to breathe normally. When that didn't work, he straightened his shoulders and led her over to the sofa, pulling her down into his lap.

"This is exactly what I am talking about, Benita. This should not be happening," Clay said.

He was momentarily silenced by Bennie's lips on his face, his throat, his eyes, and his mouth. Her hands stroked his face and neck, and Clay, for the first time in his life, started to lose all control with a woman.

"Benita . . . *stop*. Stop, baby . . . before . . ."

Bennie finally raised her head and stilled her hands.

"Stop before what? Before I take advantage of you?"

Bennie looked at Clay, who was trying to control his breathing. His eyes were glazed with passion and he looked incredibly sexy. Bennie sighed and slid her hands into his thick, glossy hair.

"I'll still respect you in the morning, I promise," she said.

Clay shook his head, removing her hands from his hair. He pulled them down to his lips and kissed each one.

"Benita, this is not going to work," he said slowly.

Bennie looked at him closely to see if he was kidding. He was completely serious, however, and his next words confirmed her fears.

"Benita, I like you a lot. A *lot*," he emphasized at the look in her eyes. "You are a person whom I respect, whom I admire, and with whom I enjoy working. You are talented, brilliant, beautiful, and a lot of fun."

"And these are somehow bad things, Clay?" Bennie inquired.

Clay sighed deeply. This was not going to be easy.

"No, those are good things, wonderful things. Hell, if I could put you in a bottle and sell you I'd have more money than Bill Gates. *Please*. But Benita, we can not have the kind of relationship I think you want."

Bennie got very still and looked down at her hands. This was not going the way that she wanted. Clay seemed to sense her withdrawal and lifted her chin to force her to look into his eyes.

"Benita, we are too much alike. Any relationship we have is bound to end in disaster. First of all, you are not the kind of woman I am attracted to. . . ."

Bennie drew back from Clay's chest and stared at him as if he had lost his mind. She moved her hips sensuously in his lap. At Clay's harsh groan, Bennie said brightly, "So that would be a pistol in your pocket, hmm? You're not really happy to see me, is that it?"

"Okay, you win; just . . . don't . . . move. Please."

Clay's eyes squeezed shut as if to aid him in his battle to resist the allure that Bennie presented.

"I didn't mean that I wasn't attracted to you; it's obvious that I'm attracted to you. It's just that there is a certain type of woman whom I usually . . . um, date."

Bennie surprised him totally by agreeing with him.

"That's understandable. You aren't the type I usually go for, either."

Clay's jaw tightened a little. "Oh, yeah? And what kind of men are you usually drawn to?" he asked, scowling.

Bennie was happy to explain, seeing that she had him slightly ruffled. "Well," she said slowly, "I am not a person who has a definite physical type in mind. I mean, as long as a man is intelligent and honest and respects and appreciates me, who cares what he looks like?"

Bennie took advantage of Clay's silence to rise from his lap. She stretched like a cat before she continued to speak. "But I must say that I've done my share of man watching from time to time, and I tend to like tall men, for obvious reasons. Tall, *dark* men," she added thoughtfully. She strolled over to look out of the French doors that opened out onto the suite's balcony. Looking over her shoulder at Clay she finished, "And I like men who are really big and muscular, and not as . . . um, *perfect*-looking as you."

Clay immediately started fuming. How dared she admit

to liking a physical type other than his? The fact that he
had just done the same thing notwithstanding, he did not
like the sound of that at all. He stood and turned around
to glare at Bennie, but he couldn't. She looked too sweet,
standing at the French doors looking out over the lights of
Chicago. Just then she opened the doors and went out on
the balcony. The night air was what she needed to cool the
turmoil inside, for despite her outward appearance, Bennie
was rather displeased with the evening so far. She didn't
really trust herself to speak, so she stood quietly and
thought about how she could gracefully exit the suite and
leave Clay to his sulk. Unfortunately, Clay walked up behind her and put his arms around her.

"Benita, I have to ask you something. When you came
up here with me, what were you planning?"

Well, that's a fair question, thought Bennie, and she answered him honestly.

"Clay, I have no idea. I do these things and I wonder
just what evil demons put the ideas in my head," she admitted ruefully. "I don't think that I came up here with
seduction in mind, but you're an awfully pretty package,
so who knows. I know that I wanted to be with you, and
to touch you and kiss you. I guess I figured that everything
would magically fall into place after that." Bennie sighed
deeply.

"I have no idea why I'm forever blurting things out
around you, or acting in a totally inappropriate manner, but
there you have it. I think I am socially retarded," she said
glumly.

Clay closed his eyes and inhaled her silky, fragrant hair.
"You are honest and direct and uncomplicated. So am I—at
least, I *think* I am," he amended. "You are the most exquisite, most brilliant, sexiest woman I have ever met, and
I do not want to lose your friendship and respect. I don't
want to take a chance on ruining everything we have now,"
Clay confessed.

As he spoke he drew Bennie closer to him within the
circle of his arms and committed her scent to memory.

"Damn, you smell good. What are you wearing?"

"Pine-Sol," Bennie said shortly, but she was laughing.

She turned around in Clay's embrace and looked him in the eye.

"I don't see why we can't have a nice, adult relationship and still be friends. If we know what the pitfalls are, we can avoid them, can't we?" she said reasonably. "I like you, too, Clay, and I admire you more than I can say. And I simply do not accept that once people start having an affair they go crazy. We will still be the same stable, mature, intelligent adults that we are now . . . we just . . ." Her voice trailed off as she moved closer to Clay, to feel all of him against her.

Clay's deep voice brought her back from the reverie she was about to go into.

"We just . . . what, Benita?"

"We'll just be a lot more . . . *satisfied*," she said dreamily, and laid her head on his shoulder.

Clay held her tightly for a minute or two and then put his hands on her hips to set her away from him.

"Let's go inside. I can't think like this," he said abruptly.

Bennie allowed him to lead her back into the suite, and watched while he carefully closed the French doors. Clay turned around to face Bennie, who was wandering around the living room, looking at the artwork as though she had not a care in the world. God, she was gorgeous. All he had to do was look at her and he was as horny and out of control as a college boy. His resolve grew. There was no way he was going to get involved in something he knew would lead directly to catastrophe.

"Benita, I'm still not convinced," he said emphatically. "I am not ready to get married, and you're the marrying kind of woman. This is not going to work."

Bennie gave him a huge smile and said, "Aren't we a little too sure of ourselves? What makes you think I'd want to marry you?"

Clay felt himself on safer ground.

"Well, you're what, twenty-seven, twenty-eight? I know

about that biological clock thing. You're at the age where marriage and babies are all you think about. And I am *not* the one, not now."

He actually felt pretty good about that statement until he looked at Bennie, whose arms were crossed and who was looking at him with a very odd expression.

"Oh, puh-*leease*, spare me! First of all, Mr. Man, I will be thirty-two on my next birthday. And I do not understand why men think that having babies is the most wonderful thing, in fact the *only* wonderful thing, that a woman can do with herself. And this biological clock thing—please! My own gynecologist was singing the 'If-you-want-to have-a-baby-you'd-better-have-it-now' blues to me the other day and for no reason other than my *age*. Scared me to death for nothing! People act like your uterus is going to shimmy down your leg and run out into traffic as soon as you turn thirty, or something. Honestly! Clayton Deveraux, I thought you had better sense!"

Clay had been trying with varying degrees of success to keep from laughing, but when she made the uterus crack, he let go with shouts of laughter.

"Benita Cochran, you are one of a kind. This was not, in my wildest dreams, how I ever imagined this evening ending," he said.

He walked over to Bennie and hugged her hard. Looking down into her eyes, which were still bright with indignation, he stroked the soft skin of her cheek and then kissed her again, a slow, lingering kiss that started the banked fires of desire roaring again in both of them.

"Oh, baby, what am I going to do with you?" he asked.

Bennie kissed him back, her lips hot with remembered anger and with unsatisfied passion.

"If you're not going to make love to me, you can take me back to my room, you ol' chicken."

Clay looked into her laughing eyes.

"Did you just call me a chicken?"

"Yes, you big baby. And you're also a chauvinist, but

I'm too tired to go into that now. If you're not going to put out, let's go," she said, laughing.

Clay was laughing, too, but inside he was terrified. Bennie was more complicated than quantum physics, more fun than an amusement park, and sexier than any woman he had ever imagined. He tried to ignore that dull thudding in his ears that signaled the end of life as he knew it, but all the signs were there—he was holding in his arms his fate and his future. He just wasn't ready to face it at that moment. So he took the coward's way out and returned her to the suite she was sharing with Renee.

Before they left, Bennie took the time to repair her hair, which actually hadn't been too badly mussed, and to apply more of the soft, glossy pink lipstick that Clay had enthusiastically kissed away. Clay noticed her tiny handbag for the first time. It was pink and shaped like a flower, covered in tiny Austrian crystals. He commented on how appropriate the bag was.

"It's a Judith Leiber," Bennie said. "I love her handbags—they're sweet and unusual. Like me," she said comically.

Taking a last look at herself, she added ruefully that she didn't look like a victim of ravishment.

"But not because I didn't try." She smiled radiantly at Clay, and to his chagrin, started making soft little chicken noises. "Bock-bock-bock-bock-bock-bock . . ."

Clay was amazed.

"I can't believe you are still making jokes. The women I know would be really torqued right about now. They'd be royally pissed off and their feelings crushed."

Bennie turned to him with her eyes wide open.

"Are you *that* good, Clay?" she said in a phony, breathy voice. Then she laughed again.

Clay watched her as they rode down in the elevator. *What in the hell is wrong with me?* he thought. *This woman is perfect; why am I not grabbing her and heading right back to my bedroom with her?* Bennie stopped laughing and gave him a real smile this time, one full of such warmth and sweetness that Clay's very heart turned over. This was why he wasn't acting out any of the intricate fantasies that her touch had inspired. Bennie was too precious and dear to him to risk losing her.

He was about to express that thought when Bennie interrupted him.

"Okay, Donnie might be in here, Clay," she said. "And I wasn't exactly candid about my little frock, earlier."

Clay raised an eyebrow and she hurried on.

"Oh, it's funny, really. Cochran men have a one-two-three test for my attire. If you can't see down it, up it, or through it, they think it's okay. So they basically look for cleavage, abbreviated length, and transparency, when they notice what I have on at all, which isn't often. Sooooo . . ." Her voice trailed off.

Clay prodded, "Go on, Benita."

Bennie smiled devilishly.

"So he had me stand in front of a light and that was about it. My boobies aren't hanging out and it comes down to my knees, so he never noticed the rest. So if Donnie's in here, can you kind of stand behind me?" she said in a rush.

By this time she was swiping the credit card–sized plastic key in the slot on the suite door. Clay was shaking his head.

"I was right! I told you that dress was too much," he gloated.

Bennie turned around to face him before opening the door. "But you like the way I look in it; don't try to deny it," she said.

Clay bent down to give her a hot, hard kiss and whispered, "Baby, I *love* the way you look in it. Just don't ever wear it for anyone but me."

Before Bennie could ponder the meaning of that statement, Renee flung the door open.

"Well, there you are!" she said brightly. "Come on in; we just ordered room service."

"We" was Donnie, Bryant, and Renee. Renee knew how

to play hostess and how to ward off the suspicions of protective brothers, although she herself came from a family of girls. Luckily, Donnie was mellow enough not to be bothered by Bennie's absence from the dance floor and sudden reappearance with Clay. Nothing seemed amiss, as Clay had replaced his tie and jacket while Bennie had freshened her makeup.

So they enjoyed a nice little after party in the suite, laughing and talking about old times. Clay did more thinking than talking, if the truth were told. Bryant was tall, dark, and pretty much fit the description of Bennie's ideal man. And there he sat, right across the room and just as happy as a skunk in a pea patch. The fact that Clay was responsible for Bryant's presence did not seem to register with him—all he was feeling were base, primitive urges that were starting to wear him down. He kept his promise to Bennie to shield her from Donnie's prying eyes, though.

Clay had no problem playing the gallant date. On the contrary, he was enjoying it immensely because it meant that he could sit as close to Bennie as he wanted and keep her attention from Bryant. Bryant, however, was not aware that he was not supposed to be enamored of Bennie and was being unnecessarily charming, as far as Clay could see. Finally, Renee had enough of small talk.

"Well, I'm going to turn in. We're flying out tomorrow and I am positively dreading that whole checking-out business," she said tactfully.

The men immediately sprang to their feet and exchanged good-byes. Bennie felt she was home safe until she turned to give Bryant a farewell kiss on the cheek. It was then that Donnie got a full view of her dress in all its glory.

"Benita, what in the Sam Hill happened to the rest of that dress?" he roared.

Bennie's face froze and she darted a quick look at her coconspirator, Clay. He leaned over and quickly kissed her cheek before leaving.

"Serves you right," he whispered, and left her to mollify

her flabbergasted brother. After the door closed behind them. Bryant turned to Clay with a huge smile on his face.

"Well, my brother, I think it's time for a talk, don't you?" he drawled. "I've been looking forward to this all night."

Rubbing his hands together in anticipation of getting into Clay's business with a vengeance, Bryant waited for the elevator with Clay. They went into the main bar and found themselves a table. Bryant took great pleasure in informing Clay that Clay was going to pick up the tab, and proceeded to order the most expensive cognac available. Then he sat back and looked at Clay with great amusement.

"And what was that all about, my brother?"

Clay dropped his head and groaned. His long, strange trip through hell was not yet over for the evening.

Meanwhile, Bennie and Renee managed to soothe Donnie's ruffled brotherly feathers and get him back to his own room by reminding him of their early departure the next day.

As soon as the door closed behind him, Renee turned to Bennie and said, "Well? You care to tell me just what was going on tonight? I turn my back for a minute and you're dancing with Clay. Then you've disappeared with Clay. Then you're back, in much less time than it takes to do anything really interesting, yet you are looking like the proverbial cat that swallowed the canary. Or like butter wouldn't melt in your mouth—I'm not quite sure which one. All I'm sure of is that some hanky-panky went on tonight, so dish."

Renee was following Bennie as she walked around the living room of the suite, and continued to follow her into the bedroom. Bennie used the lecture as undressing time, and by the time Renee was finished, Bennie was in her nightgown and was taking the little diamond flowers from her hair.

Picking up her facial cleanser, she went into the bathroom to remove her makeup. Sighing, she turned to Renee.

"Honey, I was there and *I'm* not sure what happened! First of all, I told you he had this demented notion to set me up with someone else, which idea I interpret as meaning he can't resist me without reinforcements. Then the blind date turned out to be Bryant, which did not seem to make Clay too happy—and it serves him right if he was miserable about it."

She paused long enough to wet her face, apply the cleanser, and give her face a needlessly brisk scrubbing. After splashing water on her face—twenty-one times—the proper number of times needed to rinse clean—she stood and patted at her face with an astringent-damp cotton pad.

She sighed as she and Renee went back into the bedroom, where they both flopped on the bed. Staring at the ceiling, Bennie continued to regale Renee with the events of the evening.

"So I think what he was saying is that he respects me too much to get involved. Or something. Anyway, I think it is just another way of saying he's not interested."

Bennie rolled over and looked at Renee. "Just what I need, another brother," she said glumly. "Although I must say, he kisses like a man who is very, *very* interested. I don't know, Renee; this is just too much *work*."

Renee looked at her dear friend with pity and love.

"Oh, you poor, besotted child! That man is not interested in being anybody's brother. Have you not seen the way he looks at you? If Clayton were any more interested in you, my dear, the top of his head would blow off. Honey, when we were sitting at the table in the ballroom and you stood, he looked like the wolf character in one of those Tex Avery cartoons. His jaw hit the table and his tongue rolled out like a red carpet while his eyes were doing the googly dance. He's smitten, all right; he's just putting up a big struggle."

Bennie raised her head to utter a plaintive "Why?"

Renee smiled and said, "Because men are stupid, that's why."

"Clay is brilliant," Bennie said in a dreamy tone of voice. "He is absolutely one of the smartest people I have ever met. And he is so handsome. God, he looked good tonight."

Renee had heard enough.

"Yeah, well, just you remember, he may be smart, but that does not render him any less idiotic when it comes to *les affairs de la coeur.* And you were absolutely gorgeous tonight, but then you always are. *You* are the prize, honey, and don't let him forget it. Just because he's cute and looks good in a suit and has a few bucks, that does not make him any more deserving of consideration than you. *You* are the prize," she repeated as she prepared to go into her adjoining bedroom.

Bennie lay there, trying to decide how she felt. On the one hand, she had dazzled Clay and she had gotten a few things off her chest. On the other hand, she hadn't been completely candid about her feelings. She wasn't trying to be deceitful, but she did not think anyone needed to know that she was feeling deep, dangerous feelings for Clay— feelings that went way beyond friendship or a casually sexual relationship. *This way lies madness,* she thought.

She lay there and pondered her fate for a while and then prepared to go to sleep. Just as she was drifting off, her phone rang.

"Hello?" she said with a sweet sleepiness.

Clay's deep voice responded, "Hello, yourself. Sorry to wake you up, but I have to ask you a question."

Bennie murmured something that signified agreement, and Clay continued.

"I know it's against some kind of statute for me to ask you this at such a late date and hour, but I wondered if you would consider taking a later flight tomorrow and spending the day with me? I want to start with brunch and then go on our first official date. How does that sound?"

Bennie thought it sounded just peachy, and told him so.

"I'll pick you up at about ten tomorrow, if that's okay. And Benita? Sleep well, baby."

Bennie lay there cradling the telephone handset for a long time after she disconnected. She sighed and closed her eyes. *Wow.* Without realizing it, she began humming one of her favorite old standards: about almost being in love.

Four

In the next few weeks, the lyrics of that classic song became reality for Bennie. By the time summer began to emerge, Bennie was past *almost* being in love; she was in that truly-madly-deeply stage. It started with the sunny spring morning in Chicago when she and Clayton had their first real date. Clay had come to collect her as arranged and proceeded to take her to a lovely restaurant for a brunch so delicious she could have wept. Clay enjoyed watching Bennie eat, and told her so while she was making short work of an asparagus-and-prosciutto frittata.

"You have the best appetite of any woman I have ever seen," he remarked.

Bennie took a swallow of very well prepared coffee and dabbed the corner of her mouth with her napkin.

"I don't know, Clay," she said dubiously. "That's one of those things that sounds like a compliment but really isn't. Like it's a nice way of saying I'm a glutton. Which I am," she admitted cheerfully.

Clay was not paying any attention to Bennie's commentary; he was too engrossed with the way she savored each bite, the delicacy with which she wielded her silverware, and the gusto she applied to the process of consuming a fine meal. *Damn,* he thought, *she's even sexy while she's eating.*

But he had resolved not to act on this or any other primal thought until the time was right. A long talk with Bryant had helped set him on the right path. That, plus the fact that Bryant had offered to leave his body in a shallow grave if any harm, real or imagined, came to Bennie through any act of Clay's. Of course, the conversation had not started out with thinly veiled threats and innuendoes; it had started as two old friends sharing a good cognac. Bryant had smiled his big, beautiful smile and asked an innocent question.

"Did you hit your head recently? Because you are acting like you have major brain damage," he said.

Clayton was too engrossed in brooding to answer Bryant. He looked at his drink with little liking and abruptly drained the snifter. Bryant was really amused now—he had never seen his friend so agitated, especially not over a woman. Although in his opinion, Benita Cochran was no ordinary woman. He continued to try to get a rise out of Clay.

"I mean, you must have some vision problems or depth perception or something if you were going to just hand over a beautiful woman like that. You knew what she looked like before you set up this so-called introduction, didn't you?" he goaded.

Clay was too done-in to go there with Bryant.

"Okay, I'm an idiot. I'm the king of stupid people, you win, whatever."

He continued to scowl and indicated his need for another drink to the passing waitress. Bryant wasn't about to let Clay off that easily, however. He wanted to hear Clay acknowledge what he could see with his own eyes to be true: that Clay was falling for Bennie like a ton of bricks and was too stubborn to admit it.

"So, Clay, since you're obviously not interested in Bennie, I'm sure you won't mind if I follow through on the idea that she and I should start seeing each other."

Pure fury lit Clay's dark eyes. Unaware, Bryant went on.

"After all, we already know each other. We've always been tight, so there's no reason why we couldn't—"

Bryant did meet Clay's eyes this time, and the barely contained rage in them made Bryant stop speaking. The two men looked at each other for a long moment before Bryant spoke again. Dropping the teasing, he addressed Clay calmly and sincerely.

"So if it's like that, what the hell are you doing? Why in the world would you try to bring someone else into the mix? And you'd better be damned glad it was not some real player who you picked instead of me. Without looking the way she was looking tonight, some dog would have tried something on her," Bryant pointed out.

Clay actually smiled, a thin and strained smile, but close enough.

"Benita would dislocate somebody's collarbone if they tried something," he said.

Bryant laughed. "You're right about that. Bennie don't put up with much. And she is *strong*. Only woman on this planet who can beat me playing one-on-one."

He took another sip of cognac and addressed the main issue again.

"So what is the problem, Clay? Why are you trying to dump Bennie?"

Clay sighed deeply and leaned forward with his arms on his knees.

"Bryant, I'm not completely deranged. Really stupid, maybe, but not crazy. I'm trying to save Benita and me a lot of grief."

At Bryant's incredulous expression, Clay went on: "Look, the two of us are just too much alike. There's no way that we belong together. Sooner or later one of us would have to make some kind of major compromise, and it would continue to escalate in one way or another until the relationship would disintegrate. Two people like Benita and me have no business getting together," he finished glumly.

Bryant looked at his old friend, who was obviously in misery. Clay's nose was open wide enough for a 747 to go into a holding pattern, and he was terrified. Bryant could not remember ever seeing the cool and collected Clay even mildly upset about anything, and here he was, agitated, brooding, and rash, sure signs of acute love. Bryant shook his head and was about to say something profound when Clay asked him a question.

"You knew Benita's husband when you lived in Boston. What was he like?" Clay inquired.

Bryant was caught off guard by the question.

"You mean what he looked like, how he acted, what?"

Clay took another sip of cognac before answering.

"How was he with Benita? How was she with him?"

Bryant thought for a moment before answering. Bennie and Gilbert had been joyously in love. They tried to pack every minute of their lives with every bit of the love they had for each other. With each other they could be silly, giddy, rhapsodic, hilarious, and exceptional. They relied on each other totally for everything. In some ways they were like one person, they were so closely joined. Bryant did not think that was what Clay wanted to hear, but he had asked, so Bryant told him the truth.

"They were crazy about each other, and it showed. There was nothing that they wouldn't have done for each other. They had a lot of fun, too. Even after Gilbert got sick, they laughed and made jokes and tried to be as normal as possible," Bryant said.

Clay narrowed his eyes when the illness was mentioned. Bryant immediately picked up on Clay's expression and jumped on his comment.

"Gilbert had what is known as non-Hodgkin's lymphoma, a kind of cancer. He fought it as hard as he could, and Bennie fought with him, but it was fast-acting and hopeless. Bennie took care of him all by herself, too. Her family wasn't too hip on the idea of her marrying Gilbert in the first place, so she got very little support from them. At least from her father—her brothers were pretty cool, especially her twin. And Gilbert's parents died in a car accident right after he got out of high school, so there wasn't anybody else," Bryant said reflectively.

"I used to wonder how she kept going. She was always smiling, always cheerful when she was with Gilbert. They made jokes right up until the end. But one day, I had taken her to the grocery store because their hoopty was on the skids, as usual. She was trying to find the right kind of gelatin or soup or something, the only kind Gilbert could tolerate." Bryant paused, the remembered pain evident in his eyes.

"All of a sudden she looked at me as if we had just met and said, "My husband is dying, Bryant. Gilbert is dying." She said it as if she were hearing about it for the first time. I took her out of that store and we sat in my car and she cried for about an hour. Then we had to get ice so she could bathe her face before she went back home because she didn't want to upset Gilbert by coming home with her face all puffed up. I didn't see her cry again until the day that he died, but I'm sure she did. She just hid it, like she hides a lot of things."

Clay felt like an idiot. No, that was too kind for what he was feeling. All he had been doing was thinking about himself—how *he* was feeling, what *he* wanted. The central issue was that he was used to being in control. He controlled all of his relationships because he deliberately chose women who he *could* control. And the minute he was lucky enough to meet a tigress like Bennie he went straight to Nutsville without passing Go or collecting two hundred dollars. He looked at Bryant, who gave him a condescending smile that meant, *I know what you're thinking and you're absolutely right.*

Bryant was kind enough not to go there, however. He could not resist giving Clay a piece of advice, however. "Clay, you're a good friend, and I like you. But I will not hesitate to give Bennie anything she wants anytime she wants it."

Bryant was not impressed with the look of fire and death that came from Clay's eyes.

"I have always had bad timing where Bennie was concerned. But I am not in a relationship right now. Neither is she, from what I can see. And if you want to keep it like that, I will be more than happy to—" Bryant stopped speaking because he could see that Clay was about to erupt.

Clay took a deep breath and excused himself to make a phone call. Within minutes, Bennie's cell phone was ringing. He came back to the table looking much more normal. He looked, in fact, like a man who had just been given the title to a brand-new Maserati with no strings attached.

Bryant smiled and said, "Well, my work here is done. And just because I'm crazy about Bennie, I have something for you."

He handed Clay tickets to the Cubs game the next day.

"Box seats. Bennie loves baseball. On one condition," he said, pulling the tickets away. "I get to be best man."

Inhaling Bennie's sweet smell, Clay decided that he had made the best decision of his life when he had asked her to remain in Chicago with him. They were on their way to O'Hare at last, after a day spent brunching and going to a Cubs game, much to Bennie's delight. Clay had arranged for a chauffeured limousine to drive them around the city, so they had the luxury of lots of legroom and privacy as they headed for the airport. Bennie was trying to be demure, but it was Clay who was the aggressor. He couldn't keep his hands off her, kissing her face, her neck, her hands, and whatever else he could reach.

"Clay, what has gotten into you?" Bennie demanded, trying to push him away. "One day you act like I have the plague, and the next day you're on me like a cheap suit. You need help. You need *Jesus,* that's what you need," she said, laughing.

She was momentarily able to push him away long enough to straighten her clothes and make sure that the soundproofed panel behind the driver was secure. Clay took a deep breath before moving closer to Bennie.

He turned her face so that she was looking directly at him.

"Benita, I have to apologize for yesterday. I was acting

like a fool, I know, and I'm sorry I said all those stupid things. The truth of the matter is that I want very much to see you as often as I can and be as much a part of your life as possible," he said sincerely.

Bennie's heart caught in her throat.

"Just like that?" she said shakily.

For an answer, Clay pulled her as close to his chest as the confines of the car would allow and kissed her with all the passion he was feeling. For once, Bennie was speechless. She just sighed and gave him a sweet smile. It was Clay's turn to speak.

"Just like that, Benita. You know, I love the way you smile. When you smile at me like that, it makes me want to give you the whole world," he confessed.

Bennie gave him another radiant smile. "I think you did. Didn't you just ask me to go steady or something? Are you not my boyfriend now?" she teased.

A brief look of surprise flickered across Clay's face as though he were trying to recall the definition of the word.

"Damn, I haven't had a girlfriend since I was . . . like, sixteen or something," he said slowly.

By way of answer, Bennie got into Clay's lap and started kissing him thoroughly.

"Well, you've got one now," she purred.

Having a girlfriend, as Bennie referred to herself, was fun, something that Clay had not foreseen. Bennie's presence in his life was a lot more satisfying than his progression of Barbie dolls had been. Even though they had not consummated their relationship, he felt happier, more relaxed, and more complete than he had with any other woman. For one thing, Bennie was the only woman who had ever written him letters. He had certainly received more than his share of sentimental mass-produced cards, but Bennie wrote him letters. In reading her amazing calligraphy, on an array of expensive writing papers that were sealed with wax, Clay felt as if he were gaining entry to her soul.

He also had come to love the sound of her voice. He called her every morning at the office and every evening at home, and if for some reason this routine was interrupted, his day was off, like a picture on a wall knocked slightly askew. Clay was addicted to Bennie's conversation. He loved the way she answered the telephone, and the little burst of warmth that would follow when she realized to whom she was speaking. The only downside was the fact that speaking to Bennie often left him frantic with desire. It was the only time in his life that Clay had gotten an erection from the mere sound of a woman's voice.

Clay would have been gratified to know that Bennie felt the same way about him. He was fairly sure of her feelings, since pretense was not her strong suit. But the fact that his voice sent hot thrills into parts of her body unused for years . . . well, that would have been news to him. She tried to explain to Renee how he made her feel.

"Let's see . . . have you ever been *really* hot, inside and out? Like after you've played a couple sets of tennis, or something?"

Renee nodded slowly—tennis was her game, after all. Bennie went on, sure that Renee would grasp this.

"Okay. Well, when you're really hot and you take a swallow of iced tea and it just radiates through your body and you feel it in your nipples—that's how the sound of Clay's voice makes me feel."

Bennie leaned back in her chair and sighed. Renee looked at her with great alarm.

The two women were sitting on the deck enjoying a Sunday afternoon with no activities planned. Sitting at the cedar table under the huge canvas umbrella, Bennie had been regaling Renee with stories of Clay's gallantry and delectability. Renee was impressed up to a point.

"Yeah, well, just remember that *you* are the prize. If he

is lucky enough, he might win you. Not the other way around," she said firmly.

Bennie sighed again. "Haven't you ever met someone who makes you feel . . . mmmmm, edgy, sexually charged, desirable?" she asked. "Someone who makes you feel more alive than you have ever felt before?"

Renee took another sip of iced tea before answering.

"No, I haven't," she replied crisply. "And I don't want to, thank you very much. It sounds a little bit too manic and disheveled for me. I prefer a more orderly romance," she went on, only to be interrupted by Andrew, who came around the corner of the house unannounced.

"That's why you only date cadavers, or soon-to-be cadavers," he said wickedly. "Old men tell no tales."

Renee gave him the kind of look usually reserved for piles of manure in a barnyard.

"And you ought to know about cadaver dating, since I never see you with a woman. Perhaps if you got hold of one you'd be a little less interested in my affairs," she threw at him as she rose to depart.

"Don't count on it," Andrew warned. "Anyone who runs as many old coots as you do has to expect a lot of speculation. It's like watching an accident on the freeway. You don't want to, but you can't help it," he called after her retreating figure.

Bennie shielded her eyes from the sun and glared up at Andrew.

"I wish you'd make a greater effort to get along with Renee. You two have been fighting since our freshman year of college," Bennie said testily.

Andrew didn't look ashamed in the least.

"She started it," he offered.

"No, Bunchy, she didn't," Bennie corrected, using his childhood nickname.

"Oh. Okay, then she owes me one," he answered, sitting down and drinking the rest of Renee's tea, something that would have had her screeching if she had remained.

Bennie looked at her handsome twin and shook her

head. He was, of all her brothers, the one closest to her heart. They had, after all, shared a womb, and knew each other better than anyone else ever would.

"So what brings you over here today, twin?"

Andrew raised his eyebrows comically and pointed at his sister.

"I came to get the dirt on this mystery man you're involved with. Who is this guy and where did he come from?" he asked.

Coming from anyone else the question would have gotten Bennie's back up, but this was her twin.

"He's not a mystery man. You remember Clay. You met here at the house a couple of months ago. The tall, handsome guy from Atlanta."

Bennie tried not to look smug as she said this, but her feeble efforts went unnoticed anyway. A light of recognition came over Andrew's face.

"Oh, yeah, I remember that guy. He seemed like a decent person. Does he treat you well? Is he good enough for you? Does he know how lucky he is? 'Cause I don't want to have to go after him with a scalpel or something," he said, seriously.

"Oh, Bunchy, he's wonderful. And I'm wonderful with him. Which isn't nearly often enough. But he is coming here this weekend for the cookout at Daddy's. So you'll get to interrogate him to your heart's content," Bennie offered.

Andrew looked impressed.

"You're going to expose him to the whole family? He's a brave man. A *very* brave man," he joked.

Bennie laughed too, trying to picture the interactions and responses of some of her relatives. Then she looked at her brother, who was handsome and brilliant and completely consumed by his work.

"So when are you going to start taking your own advice and get involved with a nice lady of your very own?" she asked. "I know how important your work is to you and to your patients, but it can't be the only thing in your life. Believe me, it can't."

"All things in time, Andie, all things in time. What you got to eat? I'm starving."

Bennie stood and headed to the kitchen.

"One day, Bunchy, you are not going to be able to change the subject. One day we are actually going to talk about this at length," she warned.

Andrew smiled and dropped a long arm over her shoulders as they went into the house.

"But not on an empty stomach. And not today."

Inviting Clay to the Cochrans' annual Memorial Day cookout was indeed an act of bravery or unbelievable folly. Bennie was not quite sure which as they drove over to the huge Palmer Park home in which she had spent most of her growing-up years. It had certainly seemed like the right thing to do while she was doing it. Clay had happily and warmly accepted her invitation. It had seemed right when she met him at Detroit Metro. They were so happy to see each other that any awkwardness had been washed away in their mutually warm embrace. And the fact that they stood right in the middle of the concourse kissing like there was no tomorrow had not embarrassed either of them in the least. Not even when a baggage handler added his editorial comments. *"Day-um.* I ain't mad atcha. If it was me, I'd get a room, but I ain't mad atcha, no *sir."*

Clay and Bennie collected his bag and more or less floated out of the terminal. Clay had wanted to stay in a hotel, but Bennie insisted on offering him the chauffeur's apartment over her garage. It was quaintly known as the Outhouse, and had served as living quarters for her younger brothers from time to time, as well as guest facilities. Clay was touched by her hospitality, especially when he saw how she had prepared the area for his visit.

It was furnished in the same style as the main house, but it had a more masculine feel, with sturdier upholstery and striped canvas roman shades at the windows. There were new magazines on the coffee table and fresh flowers in every room. The small kitchen was stocked with beer, wine, soft drinks, and an array of fruits and cheeses. It was small, but completely self-contained, with a bedroom, a living/dining room, and a tiny kitchen with a breakfast bar and a bathroom. There was even a small balcony accessed by French doors. And as a special touch, the regal Aretha lay in the middle of the bed like a harem girl awaiting her potentate.

"She likes to escape over here once in a while," said Bennie. "Feel free to kick her out. She'll be royally ticked off, but she'll come back to the house."

Clay scratched Aretha behind her ears, which caused the cat to go into a contortion of pure pleasure.

"Oh, she and I will get along fine. She obviously worships me," said Clay smugly. Aretha promptly bit his fingers and curled up into a fat ball of disdain.

Bennie laughed at his shock. "You do have a way with the ladies, don't you?"

After showing Clay around and making sure he knew where the towels and other necessities were located, Bennie started feeling needlessly self-conscious. As if he could read her thoughts, Clay took her by the hand and led her over to the comfortable couch, where they sat down. He indulged himself in one more mind-altering kiss, which he had difficulty ending. When he could speak, he said words that both relieved and frustrated Bennie.

"Look, beautiful, I'm not here to cop a quick lay and be gone. When you and I make love for the first time it is going to be extraordinary. And I can wait a little while longer for that. It is not going to be in some crappy hotel, or in your brothers' old rooms, or anywhere else on the sneak. It is going to be beautiful, private, and extremely special," he murmured as he continued to lick her neck and ear. "Do you have a problem with that?" he added.

Bennie moved onto Clay's lap and devoted herself to his lips for a few minutes before answering. "I was the kind of child who could not be trusted with presents," she said dreamily. "If you wanted to surprise me, you had to keep my gifts very well hidden. Like at somebody else's house." She breathed softly into Clay's ear, causing him to tremble. "So no, I don't have a problem with that plan. But I can't promise you that I won't try to shake the box every so often. . . ."

They offered beautiful smiles to each other and gave in to one last kiss. Before Bennie went back to the main house to finish preparing dinner, Clay had a surprise for her.

She opened the beautifully wrapped box, and under layers of exquisite tissue paper was a Judith Leiber bag in the shape of a chubby black cat with golden eyes.

"Oh! It's Aretha," Bennie cried. "Clay, how very sweet. I love it!"

Bennie threw her arms around Clay, who was startled by the genuine sweetness of her response. He had given many lovely parting gifts in his time; he couldn't remember ever giving one at the beginning of a relationship. And certainly not one that he had looked for and purchased himself. His assistant, Annie, had always been charged with picking up something nice for the brush-off. *I could get used to this,* he thought while observing Bennie's unaffected joy.

It wasn't until the day of the cookout that Bennie thought it might have been a bad idea to invite Clay. Her relatives were just too much for normal people. As usual, the cookout was the Saturday before Memorial Day, instead of Monday. They had no sooner entered the backyard of Big Benny's home than they were accosted.

"Smitty Smit, you, too, can have *fabulous* hair with Isoplus 'Cause we got to *mo-o-o-ove these kits!*"

Clay looked quite startled, but it was only Bennie's young nephews, Prescott and Brian. Using paper-towel cylinders for megaphones, they were loudly and happily imitating the popular commercial from the Tom Joyner Morning Show.

Bennie smiled and said, "Well, at least you're listening to the station. Come give me a kiss, you monsters."

They pressed their sticky lips to Bennie's cheeks, inspecting Clay closely at the same time.

"Bunnie, who is that?" demanded Prescott. It was obvious that he did not care for sharing his aunt with some strange man.

"This is Mr. Deveraux. Clay, meet my nephews, J. Anthony Brown and George Wallace."

Hearing their aunt refer to them by the comedians' names made the boys shriek with laughter. Bennie told Clay their real names and they shook hands solemnly before running off to move kits elsewhere. Clay looked at Bennie with amusement.

"Did they just call you Bunnie?" he asked.

"Yes," Bennie confessed. "I dressed up like the Easter Bunny one year when they were very little. For years they would tell anyone who would listen that their aunt was a rabbit."

Clay shook his head.

"No one seems to call anyone by their right name around here."

They had reached the patio where the tables were set up. Bennie stopped and thought. "You're right; we do have a lot of nicknames. Everyone calls me Bennie, except my brothers, who call me Benita. Except for Andrew, who calls me call Andie, for Andrea. I call him Benny, for Bernard, but everyone else calls him Andy. Except family, who calls him Bunchy. Adonis is Donnie, Adam is Bones, Andre is Bootsy and Alan is Skip."

At Clay's look of utter confusion, she teased, "But I have one name that no one calls me, and one name that only one person calls me."

Just then they were assaulted by more small bodies as her niece and other nephews joined them.

"Bunnie, Bunnie!" they cried, leaping all over her. Andre's wife emerged from the family room with a censuring look.

"Oh, please, give your aunt room to breathe!" Tina shook her head at the jolly offenders and came over to greet Clay.

"I'm Tina Cochran, Bennie's sister-in-law. We're so glad you could come," she said.

Tina was not as tall as Bennie, and to Clay's eyes not nearly as pretty, but she was attractive nonetheless. Alan's wife, Faye, another attractive, friendly woman, echoed her greeting. Both of them were assessing him without being too obvious. Before their scrutiny could become embarrassing, Clay was swept away in a round of introductions to various family members. Bennie, in the meantime, was busy helping greet what seemed to be an unending stream of guests.

The Memorial Day cookout had been a family tradition for years. It now encompassed family, friends, business associates, and employees of Cochran Communications. In fact, one never knew who was going to turn up. It was one of the social highlights of the spring in Detroit. Clay was pleasantly surprised to encounter Bill 'Bump' Williams, the jazz musician, apparently a friend of the Deveraux family for many years. Clay did not have time to wonder what the connection was between the Cochrans and Bump Williams; Bennie's arrival explained it all.

"Uncle Bump! When did you get here?" she cried in delight. After giving him a big hug and a kiss on the cheek, she turned to Clay.

"Clay, this is my godfather. Uncle Bump this is my . . . *boyfriend,* Clay," she finished with a wicked grin. Bump pretended to be appalled.

"You mean Big Benny is letting you court? I'ma have to have a talk with that man. You're too young to be going out with men!" he growled in mock indignation. "And especially with this fella. I been knowing this man a long time," he drawled. Then he smiled broadly. "I guess you're safe with him; he's a pretty good man."

Bennie smiled up at Clay adoringly.

"He's the best, Uncle Bump. Simply the best."

Clay went along with the older man's joke with a smile, but he did not miss the speculative look that Bump flashed him over Bennie's head. He could feel yet another lecture coming on. Since he and Bennie had first started the arduous path to dating, Bryant and Donnie had both warned him that to bring pain to Bennie was to imperil his health. When he had gone to pick Bennie up for their date in Chicago, Renee had let him into the suite with a big smile.

"Benita will be ready in a couple of minutes," she had said sweetly, offering him a seat. Renee had made small talk for about a minute, then went in for the kill.

"You know, you're a big man," she drawled, looking him up and down. "But if you hurt my friend in any way, there won't be enough left of you to bury. Okay?"

She said the last word brightly and happily, as if she had not just threatened his life. Clay was slightly amused and definitely bemused by this turn of events.

These people were so protective of Bennie, as if she were some kind of fragile flower. He assured Renee that his intentions were strictly honorable, and that he thought the world of Bennie.

"I know you don't know me," he had answered. "But I assure you that I'm a person worthy of trust."

Renee's expression did not change and her words held no warmth.

"Well, Benita certainly believes that of you. Let's just make sure you don't disappoint her."

Looking at Bennie now, he thought about the conversation with Renee. He could not conceive of a circumstance in which he would let Bennie down. He was seeing yet another aspect of Bennie that day. Her warmth and exuberance balanced her charm and beauty in a way that made her more desirable, if such a thing was possible. Clay was grimly amused by the primitive reaction he was having to Bennie; he was jealous for the first time in his life. People were continually touching Bennie—hugging her, touching her arm or her face, giving her kisses on the cheek or the lips—and it was driving Clay crazy. He had never been possessive of a woman in his life, and he was even jealous of her brothers.

All day long, one or more of them was in her face, eating off her plate, hanging on her, teasing her; it was perfectly normal behavior for a close family, but for reasons he was not willing to deal with, it was intensely irritating to Clay. Donnie went so far as to refuse to eat unless Bennie fixed his plate. The best soul-food restaurant in Detroit catered the huge buffet, but Donnie acted as though he would be poisoned if Bennie did not wait on him personally. Clay was snapped out of his brooding by Renee's arrival.

She was with one of her usual escorts, a retired military officer who now ran a bed-and-breakfast up north. His excellent posture and trim figure made him seem younger than his years, but the silver hair was a dead giveaway—he was at least thirty years older than Renee. This fact was not lost on Andrew; he immediately introduced himself and said something about how happy he was to meet Renee's father at last.

Renee smoothly corrected Andrew with a raised eyebrow and a tight jaw that promised later retribution. Then she smiled sweetly and asked where his date could be. To her surprise, Andrew actually had a date. A small, extremely busty woman suddenly appeared at his side. Andrew introduced her as LaKeisha.

LaKeisha lifted her meticulously woven hair out of her eyes with her thick acrylic fingernails and cooed, "Ooh, I love your contacts!" to Renee. "Where'd you get them? The color is so different!"

Renee paused for a nanosecond before saying, "They were a gift from God, dear."

Only Clay heard her mumble something in French under her breath. Bennie pulled Clay away from this amusing byplay. She sat down next to him with her three-year-old niece, Lillian, in her arms. Lillian's eyes grew huge at the sight of Clay. Bennie hastened to assure Clay it wasn't him that Lillian objected to.

"For some reason she has this thing about fair-skinned men," Bennie said. "She will not have anything to do with them."

Clay was not offended in the least. "So," he said in his deep voice, "you won't give the yellow brothers no play, is that it?"

Lillian gazed at Clay for a moment and then held out her arms to him. She settled herself in his lap and seemed perfectly content. Bennie was amazed. "Well, I always knew you were irresistible, but this is superhuman. I guess she knows a good thing when she sees it. Like her aunt."

Bennie leaned over and kissed Clay, right in front of God and everybody.

The rest of the day went well, even when Bennie's nieces and nephews all declared that they wanted to go home with Bunnie. Bennie was horrified—she hated to disappoint them, but she had other fish to fry. Surprisingly, Clay encouraged this arrangement. He knew better than anyone that six little chaperones were just what the doctor ordered. If he did not have some kind of buffer between himself and Bennie, there would be no stopping him that night. He wanted Bennie so badly that he was on fire in her presence, but he wanted her on his terms and no others.

So the day ended in an unexpectedly wholesome way, with Clay and Bennie supervising a pajama party. Renee had gone up north with her swain, so there was nothing but loud music and the sound of small children playing echoing in the house. Their parents would collect them by noon the next day, a rule that Bennie insisted on. Then she and Clay would spend the rest of the weekend enjoying each other's company and getting to know each other better. As Clay finally went to bed in the guesthouse with Aretha in attendance, he sighed. Nothing was ever ordinary when Bennie was involved, and nothing was ever boring. He closed his eyes, wondering what he had done for fun before he met her.

* * *

Clay was a wreck. It had been two weeks since his visit to Detroit, and now Bennie was coming to Atlanta—to see him, and only him. He had invited her while he was in Detroit, using an awards ceremony as an entree. True, there was a ceremony that the Deveraux group's publishing division put on annually, but that was hardly the reason for the invitation. He needed to get Bennie on his turf badly. He needed to have her in his comfort zone, because he wanted her desperately and because he was afraid of that desire. His longing for Bennie was primitive and basic, and it overwhelmed him at times.

The awards ceremony was on Saturday, but Bennie had agreed to come on Thursday so that she could visit with Clay and see Atlanta for a few days. He did not like admitting it, but he planned on showing Bennie the most amazing time she had ever had, similar to what had transpired in Detroit. The days after the cookout were some of the best that Clay could remember, and for his own purely male reasons, he wanted to top the experience.

After dispatching the nieces and nephews to their homes, Clay and Bennie had gone all over Detroit and its environs. Bennie had showed him her gym, and took him by Urban Oasis, the spa that she and Renee coowned. Then she had to show off a little and take him to the bookstore. Clay had stopped at a display of African-American romances and remarked that his company had just purchased the imprint that published most of the books. Bennie had looked quite impressed by that and told Clay that she read them all the time, which surprised him.

"Why is that a surprise? I love romance! It's exciting, mysterious, sexy, and fun—why would I not like to read about it?"

Another facet of the jewel that was Bennie was revealed.

They had gone to Greektown, to Eastern Market, and to the Somerset Collection, a very beautiful and expensive collection of shops. They ate out and ate in and went to a couple of jazz clubs. On Monday they had dinner with her father and his lady friend, Martha, before Bennie took Clay to the airport. By the time they arrived, Clay was wiped out by sensation. Bennie sensed his mood; in fact, she shared it. They were back at the airport where it had all begun so few months ago.

Clay again insisted that she not go to the trouble of parking and that he would find his way to his gate. But there was no brief brotherly hug this time. This time Clay took her in his arms and kissed her as though he could never let her go, a kiss that she was happy to return. She wrapped her arms around his waist and tried to control her breathing, but it was impossible. She stared at Clay, trying to memorize the way he looked at this exact moment so that she could hold on to the image. She loved the way his face looked when he was filled with passion, like now.

"Clay, I'm already missing you," she said. "I can't wait to see you again and you haven't even left."

Clay pulled her close and drew in his breath at the feel of her breasts against him.

"Baby," was all he said.

He couldn't trust himself to speak; he might have asked her to marry him on the spot. He kissed her one more time, just in time for their friend the baggage handler to stroll by.

"*Day-um.* Y'all back at it again? Woman that fine, I'd sho' hafta to get a room. But I sho' ain't mad atcha."

But all of that was two weeks ago, and now it was his turn. Bennie was coming to him, and he wanted to dazzle her. Unfortunately, he was not having a good day. In fact, it had been a day straight from the seventh level of hell. Everything that could possibly have gone wrong, went wrong, leaving him in a mood that could most charitably be described as foul. Plus, even though he had left the office an hour earlier, he was nowhere near the airport, thanks to a jackknifed semitruck that had backed up traffic for miles. And the fact that it was raining the proverbial cats and dogs did not make the situation any better.

When it became manifestly apparent that he was not going to be able to meet Bennie's flight, he picked up his cell phone to leave a message on her cell phone. Quite naturally, the battery had done what batteries do when they aren't recharged—it had died. When he was finally able to make it to the airport his heart was pounding and so was his head, for that matter. Bennie would be furious and justifiably so. When he reached the baggage claim area for Bennie's flight, he looked around anxiously for her forlorn figure. When he finally saw her, she was absorbed in a paperback novel, looking completely relaxed and happy. He walked over to her and was rewarded by a smile of pure happiness on her beautiful face.

"I'm sorry I was so late," he began.

Bennie put her book down and rose gracefully to embrace him.

"It's okay. I knew you'd be here." She placed one cool, slim hand alongside his face as she spoke.

"I don't get a kiss?" she asked. "Surely there's a few airport employees we can scandalize."

Clay smiled for the first time, remembering their admirer at Detroit Metro.

"Well," he replied, "if it's scandal you're after . . ."

He lowered his lips to Bennie's and gave her the kind of kiss he had been burning for since they had parted. The softness of her lips and the eagerness of her tongue were all he needed to release some of the tension that had been building all day. He felt anxiety flow away from him in a great wave, only to be replaced by a different kind of tension. As Bennie pushed closer to the growing source of heat between them, Clay had to pull away or risk total abandon right there in the airport.

"Let's get the hell out of here," he said in a growl.

Bennie licked her lips hungrily and immediately agreed.

In very short order they were nearing Clay's house. Bennie craned her neck to better acquaint herself with the rolling, lush green foliage along the way. Even in the slanting rain it was beautiful, and she said as much to Clay. The

Jaguar pulled into a gateway that was almost invisible unless one expected it, and proceeded up a long driveway. It looked as though they were entering a private forest until they reached the huge house at the end of the drive. Bennie was absolutely floored.

The house was three stories tall in its center, with two-story wings on either side. The style defied a typical description; it was made of a natural stone with timbers that made it blend into its setting. A huge Palladian window was the centerpiece, with multipaned windows on either side. Clay whisked Bennie into the massive double-entry doors and told her to make herself comfortable while he got her luggage. Bennie stood in the huge entryway, enchanted by what she was seeing. A double cantilevered stairway led to the upper level, and there the back wall contained another huge Palladian window.

To one side there was a living room with one wall given over to a massive natural-stone fireplace. The other side seemed to be a formal dining room. Although the rooms were graciously sized and inviting, it was sparsely furnished and gave no real indication of being a home. With the exception of a huge arrangement of flowers in the living room and its twin in the dining room, there was very little of Clay in the rooms. Clay answered Bennie's questioning look as he arrived in the entryway with her bags.

"I've lived here for a few years, but I really haven't taken the time to furnish it completely. I'm on the road so much and so busy working that I haven't given it the time that I should," he admitted.

Bennie nodded absently as she admired the workmanship of the fireplace.

"I can see that," she agreed. "But Clay, this is absolutely gorgeous." She sighed. "Show me the rest, please."

She removed her trench coat and handed it to Clay. Anticipation was all over her pretty face. Clay just stood and admired her for a moment. Her hair was loosed from its normal work updo, and she was casually attired in black raw silk trousers and a matching jacket. The ivory cream silk T-shirt she was wearing complemented her caramel skin and made it glow. He took her hand and proceeded to show her every room. By the time it was done, Bennie had a huge crush on Clay's house.

The kitchen was big enough for a small restaurant, and had the added bonus of French doors that led out onto a deck. The deck, in fact, spanned the entire rear of the house and was also accessible from the family room, which lay beyond the living room. There were four bedrooms and a study on the second floor, in addition to the master suite on the third floor. The master suite took Bennie's breath away. The green-tiled bathroom was huge, encompassing a gigantic Jacuzzi as well as a glass-enclosed shower. The shower was in fact glass on all sides; windows formed one wall. Bennie immediately turned to Clay upon observing this.

In answer to her unasked question he replied, "No one can see up here. There's too many trees, and it's quite isolated."

The master bedroom was also decorated in shades of green, from the raw silk wall covering to the watered-silk coverlet. It had a vaguely Oriental feeling, but the furnishings defied categorization. They were obviously custommade, especially the bed, which was enormous. It was on a raised platform and was simply the most magnificent bed Bennie had ever seen. The headboard and footboard were a carved teak that sloped away from the center and gave it the look of a throne of some unknown dynasty. There were also fresh flowers in this room, as well as a bedside array of scented candles, the kind Bennie adored.

Bennie could not resist sitting on the bed.

"Clay, this is the most wonderful thing I've ever seen in my life," she said softly.

Realizing what she was doing, she started to get up. Clay sensed her embarrassment and sat down with her.

"Don't you even blush. This is your room for as long as you are here."

He kissed her briefly, not trusting himself at the moment.

He was trying hard not to fling her across the bed right then and there, but just being near her was making it quite difficult.

"Why don't I bring your bags up, and you can get comfortable. I'm going to take a shower and get us something to eat. I was going to take you to a nice restaurant, but the rain doesn't look like it's going to let up."

Bennie smiled radiantly. A nice dinner at home sounded just the thing to her.

"On one condition," she said. "You let me help you with dinner."

Clay demurred, saying that she was his guest. Bennie stuck her lower lip out a little.

"I'll pout," she threatened.

Clay leaned over and gently pulled her lip into his warm, wanting mouth.

"Oh, please do. We may not get to eat, but it'll be enjoyable," he promised.

After he left to get her bags, Bennie fell back across the bed. *Hot damn,* she thought. *We should have done this months ago.*

Clay was thinking the exact same thing as he showered and dressed. Having Bennie in his home seemed so right it was frightening. Bennie was in fact the only woman who had ever been in his home for more than thirty minutes, and the only one other than his immediate family who had ever been above the first floor. It was a deliberate decision on Clay's part, one that he did not take lightly. Clay had always gone to the homes of his female acquaintances, and had never spent the night. The massive bed in the master suite had never held a body other than his own; the fact that Bennie would be the first and only woman to share it with him was incredibly exciting to him.

Clay had planned to take Bennie out for a night of dancing and dining at one of the many establishments in Atlanta designed for that purpose. His delay at the airport and the horrendous day he had had seemed to bode ill for the evening ahead, but the sight of Bennie looking radiant and relaxed pushed all those thoughts away. She was truly one of a kind. Anyone else would have been frantic with rage, but Bennie had the utmost confidence in him. "I knew you'd be here" was all she had said. Something about Bennie calmed his very soul. He knew that he was falling more deeply in love with her every day, but for right now he didn't want to question it; he just wanted to savor it.

He went upstairs to check on Bennie before beginning the preparations for dinner. She was asleep in the middle of the bed, still wearing her traveling clothes. She looked unbearably sweet lying there, and he didn't have the heart to disturb her. Actually, he was happy that she had fallen asleep. Despite her protestations, he wanted every bit of this evening to be for her alone, and that included making her meal. He turned on the lights in the bathroom so she would not be too disoriented when she awoke, and silently went down to the kitchen.

Bennie slept for about an hour and awakened curiously refreshed and without any embarrassment. She rose slowly and stretched sensuously. The night she had been waiting for was finally here, and she wasn't about to miss a minute more. She entered the bathroom, marveling once again at the spacious green room. She eschewed her normal shower, running a luxurious bath instead. She was touched beyond measure to find a big bottle of bath gel awaiting her. Clay had somehow ascertained the name of the fragrance she had worn for him in Chicago, and there it was, in its unopened peach-colored box. She poured a generous amount into the running water and stripped off her clothes.

After pinning up her hair, she unpacked her bags, taking special care with the garments she planned to wear that night. Then she got into the deep tub and sighed with enjoyment as the bubbling jets almost lulled her back to sleep. She couldn't stop thinking about how beautiful Clay was and how handsome he looked when he came to the airport. *It should be illegal for anyone to be that gorgeous,* she thought with a smile. But it wasn't just his sheer physical perfection that drew her to Clay. He was smart; he was funny, kind, and thoughtful; and he had a way with children. Bennie sat up straight in the tub when she realized that she was thinking of the possibility of having Clay's babies. Then she relaxed again. *Why shouldn't I be thinking that? I'm in love with the man, and I know it as well as I know my own name.* Acknowledging this indisputable fact gave Bennie a quiet happiness; she serenely accepted her fate.

Bennie finally got out of the sumptuous tub and patted herself dry lightly. She then applied generous amounts of the body lotion that matched the bath gel. She followed this with the body cream on her knees and elbows, although it wasn't strictly necessary; Bennie's skin was as soft as baby Lillian's. Bennie considered going without underwear but decided that there was such a thing as being *too* ready. She slipped on the sheer bronze-colored lingerie that gave her the appearance of being nude.

The only makeup she applied was a bit of shimmering gold powder to her cheekbones and collarbones, plus a curling-formula black mascara, which she did not really need. She then sprayed herself generously with perfume and donned sheer silk georgette harem pants in an opalescent copper. They hung low on her hips and were loosely gathered around the ankle. The pants gave the distinct impression of nudity, since their color was so close to her skin tone. The voluminous tunic trimmed in tiny copper beads was of the same fabric and did not do much more in terms of camouflage. *Another triumph for Joyce,* Bennie thought wickedly. Joyce definitely had a knack for creating outfits that meant business.

Bennie took down her hair and brushed it into a mass of waves on her shoulders. A little glimmer of lip gloss was all she needed to complete her makeup. After putting on delicately strapped gold sandals, she made her way to the second floor. The lower floor was darkened, which made her pause.

"Clay?" she called softly.

Getting no response other than the soft music that was playing, she continued down the stairs as her eyes got used to the dim lighting. She went into the living room, which seemed to contain most of the muted light, and discovered that it was completely lit with dozens of candles.

And not just any candles—these were expensive, beautifully scented candle in a variety of shapes and sizes that gave the room a look of complete enchantment.

"Oh," she said softly.

She stood in the center of the room like a child entering a fairyland. Clay entered the room in time to see her standing there looking more beautiful than even he could have imagined.

He crossed the room and took her hands, kissing each one on the back, and then flicked his tongue across the inside of her wrists.

"This is so unfair. How am I supposed to concentrate on serving you a meal when you look like this?"

Bennie smiled seductively.

"You look pretty delicious yourself, you know. How am *I* supposed to concentrate on eating?"

Clay did look magnificent. He had on a loose-fitting black silk shirt with no collar and drawstring pants. His long, aristocratic feet were bare. Bennie had always found men's feet to be quite sexy, and told him so.

"Okay, that's it. We're eating right now before you have your way with me and I'm too weak to chew," he told her.

Bennie's delight showed all over her face; Clay the perfect gentleman had retired for the evening, leaving Clay the impetuous lover. As if he could read her thoughts, Clay pulled her into his arms for a slow, fierce, erotic kiss that answered all of her questions. They were both wearing so little in the way of clothing that their mutual desire was obvious. Bennie's hands slid up and down the soft silk fabric on Clay's tight, muscled body; she moved boldly under his shirt to caress his back and hips and realized that he wasn't wearing any underwear. *So much for being too ready,* she thought vaguely.

She really wasn't thinking about anything but the feel of Clay's big, warm hands all over her body and the hot, sweet fire of that kiss. She raised her arms up around his neck and accepted his hips as he ground his hardness against her. Rising up to her toes did little to assuage the burning that she felt; she wanted more. The soft purring noise she was making escaped as a moan as Clay reached under her top to put his hands directly on her skin. Bennie cried out as Clay pulled her even closer. Lifting her into his arms, Clay carried Bennie over to the fireplace, where a huge pile of silk-covered cushions had been placed.

He laid her there in front of the fire and started to move away, but Bennie pulled him down on top of her body, which was shaking with desire.

"Don't you even think of leaving me here," she whispered breathlessly.

Her fingers found their way into the long, silky hair at the nape of his neck, and she pulled him into a kiss that expressed all of her desire. Her soft moans, coupled with the movements of her hips, were too much for Clay. He pulled away briefly to remove her gossamer top and the scrap of shimmering Lycra that passed for a bra. Bennie's feet slid out of the delicate sandals, and her toes curled in anticipation.

Her soft, full breasts felt like heaven in his hands; he lowered his mouth to them and added his lips to his hands. Bennie stilled him just long enough to get him out of his shirt, and gasped when his hard chest pressed against hers with no barrier between them. He lifted her hips up to free her from her remaining garments and looked at her beautiful body bronzed by the light of the flickering candles and the firelight. She was incredible and she belonged only to him. Clay covered her body with kisses that drove her mad with desire and branded her forever. He traced a line of fire from the base of her throat to her stomach, caressing every inch of her body from her face to the soft curls at the apex of her thighs.

The feel of his thick, silky mustache drove her into a frenzy. Bennie arched her back and trembled, calling out his name as he ran his tongue down the inside of her thigh to the core of her desire, gasping as he kissed her there as thoroughly as he had kissed her mouth. She was completely given over to the sensation that was Clay; he was claiming her, and in so doing he was giving her a pleasure that she had never dreamed existed. After the final shuddering climax she felt herself slipping into nothingness, only to be claimed again by Clay's lips on hers. They clung together, breathing as one person as the sweet aftermath overtook them.

As Bennie's breathing gradually began to return to normal, she realized that she was now wrapped tightly in Clay's arms. She was quite naked, and he was still wearing his drawstring pants. She had no idea what he was thinking; he was perfectly still, except for his hands, which were stroking her hair as she lay on his chest. She pulled away from him just enough to kiss him one more time and to look into his beautiful face.

"Let's go upstairs," she whispered.

She moved away from him so they could both stand. She slipped on his black shirt and they quickly extinguished the candles and went up to the big master bedroom.

Bennie had turned down the bed before coming downstairs, so all they had to do was slip into its inviting expanse. Before Clay joined her, he removed his last article of clothing, exposing his male beauty to Bennie's adoring eyes. It was Bennie's turn to claim the man she loved. He lay on top of Bennie, and for long moments they were wrapped in each other's arms, not speaking; they simply absorbed each other. Clay finally raised his head and brought his hand to Bennie's face, stroking her cheek with one finger.

Bennie in turn captured Clay's hand and brought it to

her lips. She parted her lips slightly and drew Clay's finger into her mouth, caressing it with her tongue and gently sucking on it until Clay's breathing became ragged with passion. Bennie seized her advantage and reversed their positions so that she was on top of Clay. Now she was in control, and she loved it. Sliding down until she was positioned on top of his arousal, Bennie braced herself on Clay's chest and moved her hips languidly until Clay was almost inside her.

Clay moaned with pleasure and said, "Not yet, baby . . . Not *yet.*"

Bennie sighed and moved so that she was close to his side.

She propped herself up with one arm and began stroking Clay's chest with the other. Clay was surprisingly hirsute; his broad chest was covered with soft, silky hair that felt indescribably sensual against her breasts. While the soft palm of one hand caressed the most sensitive part of his chest, Bennie brought her moist lips to the other side and traced the nipple with her hot, seeking tongue. Clay's hand, which was tangled in her hair, tightened for a moment before he gave in to the pleasure that Bennie was giving him. She continued to kiss her way down his hard, golden body, moving her hand as well as her lips. When she reached his arousal, he gasped; Bennie's tender hand slipped around his manhood with ease, and she boldly caressed every part of him, causing him to cry out with pleasure.

"Benita, baby, what are you doing to me?" he asked in a groan.

Bennie smiled and slid her hand up the length of his body. She gracefully arranged herself so that she was kneeling next to Clay, and she leaned over and kissed him thoroughly before answering.

"I'm loving you. What do you think I'm doing?"

Clay grasped her upper arms and pulled himself up so that their bodies were pressed against one another. Pulling her close, he answered gruffly, "I think you're trying to drive me out of my mind."

He levered her down so that he was once again covering her with his body.

"You feel so damn good, baby," he whispered.

Before he went any further, he leaned away to get the inevitable foil packet from the bedside table.

Bennie was happy to assist him in putting it on, demonstrating the erotic potential of the prosaic act. Clay sought her mouth once more as he entered her warm, wet femininity.

Raising his head slightly, he looked into her love-glazed eyes and whispered, "Tonight was supposed to be just for you, Benita. Just for you."

At that point Bennie was too far gone to answer. Clay filled her like nothing she had ever experienced. She raised her hips to meet the force of his desire and wrapped her long legs around his waist. The deep thrusts and sensual movements brought her to a spiraling peak of ecstasy that made her want to cry out, but she simply did not have enough breath.

She looked into Clay's eyes and thought she would die from happiness at the naked passion she saw reflected in their depths. Suddenly Clay pulled her to his heart and the world tipped over. Clay cried out her name over and over as their mutual climax made their moist bodies shudder in a frenzy of passion.

As they gradually returned to earth, Bennie found enough of her voice to breathe his name once: "Clayton . . ."

For Clay, it was more than enough.

Clay finally was able to release Benita, only to adjust their position. Propped up on the huge pillows, he cradled her to his heart. He was so profoundly moved by what he and Bennie had shared that it was impossible to speak. He turned her face to his, only to feel his heart stop at the sight of crystal tears on her lashes. Was she frightened? Unhappy? Unsatisfied? Then she smiled rapturously and laid her head on his shoulder, as trusting as a baby. *My baby*. Despite the amazing passion Bennie had just shared with him, that was what she felt like in his arms. He had known that she would be an assertive, formidable lover, but he was not prepared in any way for the sweetness and innocence she brought to his bed.

Benita was the ideal lover for Clay; their bodies matched perfectly. He could not stop stroking her, inhaling her scent, and marveling at the sheer length of her, entwined with him in the middle of his enormous bed. If he never touched her again as long as he lived, he would remember the way they had made love for the rest of his life. And it was apparently not over, as Bennie began stroking him again. Finally he was able to speak.

"You are trying to drive me crazy, aren't you?"

Bennie raised her head and smiled seductively.

"If that's what it takes," she purred.

Clay squeezed her tighter.

"Aren't you supposed to collapse in immediate slumber or something?" he asked.

Bennie's hands continued their quest.

"Sorry to disappoint you, but I am not sleepy in the least. I thought men were supposed to fall asleep directly after," she pointed out.

"Baby, with you in my arms I could walk to the moon right now," he answered.

Bennie's stomach picked that moment to indicate the fact that it was empty. It was a fairly delicate rumble, but unmistakable, since she and Clay were so close together.

"You're hungry," he said, making a statement rather than asking a question.

Bennie tried to lie her way out of it, to no avail.

"I'm hungry for *you,* sweetness. That wasn't my stomach, it was my—"

Clay laughed out loud. "Don't even try it! Come on and let me feed you so we can get back to bed. Quickly, before we starve for other things."

Bennie sighed and agreed. She really was starving, after all.

After a brief shower that consisted mostly of the two of

them kissing madly while locked in each other's soapy arms, they made their way to the kitchen. Clay retrieved the dinner he had so painstakingly prepared from the refrigerator. And in a very short time they were once again in front of the fireplace, this time feeding each other grilled shrimp on skewers, a salad of mesclun with balsamic vinaigrette, and sourdough bread with sweet butter. He even had dessert, huge strawberries with a chocolate ganache for a dipping sauce.

Clay had never known such contentment was possible. How had this beautiful, beguiling woman found her way into his life and his heart in such a short time? Bennie mentioned taking the dishes back to the kitchen, but Clay insisted on doing it.

"I keep trying to tell you that this night is all about you," he reminded her.

Bennie leaned over and caressed his face.

"Every time I do something for you, I'm doing it for me, too, Clayton. I want you to be as happy as you make me," she said simply.

It felt as though his heart were expanding throughout his chest. Not trusting himself to speak, he kissed her briefly and took all evidence of their fireside meal away. Returning to the living room, he held out his hand.

"Let's go make each other happy right now, baby."

As they walked up the stairs Clay posed a question that had been haunting him: "Baby, do you eat a lot of peaches?"

Bennie raised her eyebrows. "I love peaches, but I don't eat them to excess. Why?"

"Because," he said, smiling, "you taste exactly like a ripe peach—all over. And I seem to have an insatiable craving for peaches, . . ."

Five

The next morning, everything in Clay's life had changed. He knew the change was coming; on some level he had accepted it weeks ago. But to awake with Bennie wrapped in his arms put the cap on whatever he had been feeling. The thunderous passion of the night had given way to a quiet joy that permeated every inch of him. *So this is what love is like,* he thought. He had never, in his entire life, awakened with a woman in his arms. His rich and varied sex life prior to meeting Bennie had precluded that kind of intimacy.

In a way, it was always another job, his being with a woman. If you had a biological need to take care of, you did it in the most expedient manner, with the most willing and comeliest partner possible. Then you went on your merry way. Clay looked down at Bennie, sleeping so sweetly in his arms. Leaving her was an impossible idea; it would be like leaving his heart. Keeping her . . . that too, might prove impossible, but he would surely die if he did not try.

The realization of what he was thinking hit Clay like a fist. In a few months Bennie had sauntered into his life and made off with his heart, his soul, and apparently his common sense. The tension rippled through his body like a shock wave. Where was his much-vaunted control now? How could he have fallen so far, so fast? *What the hell have I gotten myself into?* he thought angrily. Just then Bennie stirred in his arms. Uttering a soft sigh of complete contentment, she stretched against him and purred. Finally she opened her eyes and smiled.

"Good morning, lover," she said softly.

Whatever lame defense Clay had been trying to marshal dissipated in the warmth of Bennie's eyes, her smile, and her touch. *I am the luckiest man in the known universe,* he thought. He was about to articulate that thought in some less pungent manner when Bennie's movements in the bed distracted him.

"What are you doing, baby?" he asked, sighing.

Bennie gave him a lazy smile. "What does it feel like?"

Clay moaned and stopped when he detected the scent of her toothpaste.

"You cheated. Either we both have morning mouth or we both brush," he said.

Bennie rolled away from him and stretched herself into an upright position. With her arms still over her head she said, "Well, you'd better get to brushing, honey. Unless you have something else in mind."

Bennie's hair was tousled, but her face was dewy and moist from the quick toilette she had made while Clay was still deeply asleep. She was blissfully unself-conscious of her state of nakedness; she seemed to enjoy showing Clay her body. Clay was out of the bed and in the bathroom in seconds.

When he came back, after brushing his teeth thoroughly (as well as a few other things), he was disappointed to see that Bennie was wearing a robe. It was a silk kimono covered in butterflies, but it was hiding her body from his view. Bennie had gone out onto the balcony that spanned the length of the master suite and faced the backyard.

"Clay, are you absolutely positive that no one can see up here?"

Clay assured her that no one could—there were no houses within view. Bennie immediately took off the robe, dropping it to her feet so quickly that Clay did not have time to react.

The rain of the night before had given way to a sweet,

hazy morning that was typical of Georgia in early summer. It was cool and moist, and the sun had not quite decided what it was going to do that day. The air was rich with the scents of honeysuckle and pine from the verdant growth that surrounded the house. And in the middle of this was Bennie, with her eyes closed and her head back to breathe in the essence of everything that surrounded her. She held her arms away from her sides and took in deep, intoxicating breaths. The sight of her gave Clay a rush of fever like nothing he had ever experienced.

When he could finally speak, his voice almost betrayed the emotions he was experiencing.

"Baby, what are you doing? It's cold out there."

Bennie remembered Clay was watching and turned to face him. She observed how he was drinking in every inch of her body and gave a slight shrug.

"This is me," she said simply.

She leaned her head back and closed her eyes, stretching her body as far as she could. She seemed to be in her own little world, but one she wanted to share with Clay. She crossed the balcony and took his hands, drawing him out to stand with her.

"I have always wanted to do this. I have never, in my entire life, been outside without a stitch on. I always wondered what it would be like to feel the air all over my body without any barriers. This is wonderful, Clay. Don't you feel it?"

She pressed the full length of her body to his and they held on to each other for long minutes. She pulled him to her, swiftly, effortlessly, and forever. Clay looked into Bennie's eyes before giving her the kiss that would bind him to her forever. Whatever happened from that point on was his choice; he accepted his fate and became the willing captive of her heart.

Much later, after a lot more lovemaking, Bennie remembered that she had brought Clay a present. It was an original photograph by James Van Der Zee, the famous black photographer who made artistic history by capturing Harlem in the early part of the century. Clay was absolutely stunned. He had never received anything from a woman other than his mother and sister in his entire life. In Clay's world, it was men who kept women supplied with their hearts' desire, not the other way around. The fact that Bennie had taken the time and trouble to unearth this very expensive photograph for him was touching in the extreme.

Clay examined his gift reverently. Bennie had had it custom-framed in an expensive manner. It was magnificent.

"Benita, this is so thoughtful of you, but—"

Bennie was kneeling beside him on the bed, loving the look of happiness on his face. She kissed him thoroughly to cut off whatever he was about to say.

"Don't say another word. If I can't spoil my boyfriend, who can?" she teased.

Just then, her stomach gave its now-familiar two-minute warning.

"Clay, you might want to reconsider this whole thing; it's impossible to keep me fed," she said in mock sadness. "But I *can* cook, so why don't I make us breakfast? Brunch," she amended after glancing at the clock on the dresser.

Kissing him again, she hurried off to the kitchen before he tried to stop her.

Bennie really was a great cook. Years of living with the bottomless pits that passed for stomachs with the Cochran men had taught her to cook well and to cook fast. Plus, she had always enjoyed it. One of the happiest memories she had of her mother was of learning to cook at her knee. She could recall following her mother around the big, sunny kitchen in the Palmer Park house, learning the right way to make pie crust, among other things. She shared her mother's love for old jazz, too; they had spent many an afternoon listening to old records and singing together, the timeless songs of the great ladies of jazz.

Bennie started to sing "A Sunday Kind of Love." Bennie

sang as she cut up the fresh fruit she found in Clay's refrigerator.

Clay stopped in the dining room, puzzled. He did not remember owning any CD with that song on it. Maybe Bennie had turned on the radio.

To his amazement, it was Bennie, singing in a beautiful contralto. *Damn.* The voice that was coming out of her was like everything else about her—amazing. He crossed his arms and listened to her while she finished her task. She looked up to see him standing there and stopped mid-word.

"Don't stop! Your voice is . . . stupendous. You could be doing that for a living, you know."

Bennie smiled and wrinkled her nose.

"No way. I grew up in radio, remember? I know just how hard it is to be a performer. And how nonlucrative it can be. For every Aretha Franklin or Diane Schuur or Cassandra Wilson, there are about a thousand broken, disillusioned women chasing after a dream. Do you like French toast?"

After he assured her that he did, she went about assembling the ingredients. Watching her swift, assured movements was relaxing and enticing at the same time. Clay could not resist coming up behind her and giving her a tight squeeze and a few kisses down her neck.

"I can't believe that there is so much talent in one person. Is there anything you can't do, Benita?"

Bennie snorted. "There are tons of things I can't do! I can't sew, I iron like a five-year-old and . . ." Her voice faded away.

"And what, baby?" Clay turned her around to face him.

She looked both serious and shamefaced as she admitted, "My biscuits are like hockey pucks. I can't make a decent scratch biscuit to save my life."

Clay laughed out loud at that, which earned him a punch in the stomach.

"Just for that, I'll make a batch tonight and make you eat them," she threatened.

She did no such thing, however. The rest of the day was a pleasant blur. Clay took her all over Atlanta, happy to show off the magnificent city. They went sightseeing like tourists and shopping like newlyweds. Bennie was particularly impressed with Clay's willingness to wander around the stores with her. He was sweet, patient, and attentive, as though pleasing her were the reason he was born. They decided to have dinner in again, since they would be going out black-tie the next night. They found a nice greengrocer and a great gourmet market where Bennie found everything she needed to make a superlative meal.

Clay had a minimum of outdoor furniture, despite the fact that he had a beautifully landscaped yard with a wonderful swimming pool. There was a table and chairs, though, where they opted to have their meal. The pool was designed in such a way that it blended into the grass and looked like a reflecting pond instead of the usual manmade pool. There was room for any kind of garden that anyone cared to have, although Clay had not gotten around to hiring a gardener. Still, it was a lovely, romantic setting for the two of them.

Clay had insisted on helping to prepare the meal, which consisted of pesto-stuffed mushrooms, salmon grilled with rosemary, oven-roasted asparagus, and potatoes Anna. Working in the kitchen together was almost as intimate as what they had shared in the bedroom, but with a sweet domesticity that filled Bennie's heart. *I could do this every day for the rest of my life,* she thought, hoping her face did not betray her utter contentment. She tried vainly to remember Renee's precepts for remaining aloof and desirable, but her mind was absolutely blank on that count.

Bennie led with her heart—whatever came up, came out, which was why her brothers loved to play poker with her. She couldn't bluff worth a damn in cards or in love, and she did not want to scare Clay away. But Bennie knew herself better than anyone, and she knew that she was perfectly capable of blurting out exactly how she felt about Clay, which was probably not the wisest course of action right then. She was therefore thrilled when Clay proved to be extremely talkative that night.

They each talked about their childhood, and how closely they paralleled. They both were the eldest children of a large family; both had taken over the family business as an act of necessity, and both had worked from a very young age. And both families ran to twins. Bennie was still amazed at everything that Clay had accomplished.

"Well, I can't take all the credit. All of my brothers work in the family business along with me, so it's not like I have done it alone," Clay said modestly.

Clay's brother Malcolm was in charge of finances for the Deveraux Group. His brother Martin was the chief counsel and ran the legal department.

Martin was the survivor of a tragedy—he had been gravely injured in a car accident, which left him with severe scarring. Sadly, he was Malcolm's identical twin brother and had as a constant reminder of what he should have still looked like.

"He's become somewhat reclusive as a result—he comes to Atlanta as infrequently as possible. He basically lives on his houseboat in the Florida keys and does everything from there. But he comes to the house on St. Simons Island sometimes. You'll probably meet him there," Clay said offhandedly.

Bennie tried to ignore the little frisson of pleasure that came when Clay made that statement. It sounded as though she was a permanent fixture in his life, and not a passing fancy. *Cut it out!* she told herself fiercely. *Enjoy the moment, live in the now, chill!* She had to drag herself back to what Clay was saying.

"And of course, you've already met Marcus. I don't know where he will end up in the organization when he gets through training," said Clay.

That reminded Bennie of something.

"I hope you weren't too hard on him after his little visit to Detroit," she said, giving the city its French pronunciation, *Deh-twah.* "We were pretty smug, after all."

Clay laughed. "Are you kidding? After I met you, I bought him a Porsche and gave him my office."

Bennie threw her linen napkin at him for his foolishness. Clay rose and came around to her side of the table, pulling her out of her chair.

"Okay, maybe I didn't get him a Porsche, but he is definitely my favorite brother right now. He brought you into my life," he said quietly.

Bennie could not have spoken if her life depended on it; luckily, she did not have to. Clay bent his head to hers and gave her a soft, sweet kiss. He cleared his throat and tried to inject some levity into the emotionally charged moment.

"So what's for dessert?"

Bennie gave him a sultry smile.

"Something I think you will really like," she said.

They cleared the table and Bennie insisted that Clay sit down so that she could bring it out to him. It was something she was inspired to create just for him; a parfait of crumbled amaretti soaked in Grand Marnier, layered with white peaches and Ben & Jerry's White Russian ice cream. Clay took one taste and groaned with pleasure. They shared the parfait, feeding it to each other, licking each other's lips, and laughing. Finally it was too cool to stay outside any longer, at least for Bennie, who was wearing peach-colored silk lounging pajamas.

They went in and made short work of the kitchen, working together like an old married couple. Then they went to the family room and listened to music while they talked some more. Clay learned about Bennie's mother, Lillian, and how she had taught her to cook, how to sing, and how to nurture.

"It's so odd, the little things I remember," Bennie mused. "How to set a table, how to accessorize properly, how to write a thank-you note, just basically how to be a lady, I guess. Not that it did a lot of good," she said ruefully.

Clay looked at her sternly. "You are a most proper lady, my dear. You are certainly a chameleon, but that's because you are so intuitive and adaptable. There is no situation in which you are not a perfect fit."

Bennie actually blushed. No one had ever said anything so sweet to her. Clay looked at Bennie, who was resting against his heart as they lay on the big plush sofa in the family room. She was as close to perfection as he had ever encountered, and she seemed to have no idea of her value. He'd have to work on that. How could Benita not know how special she was, how unique, how loved? *Loved.*

Once again Clay felt like a drowning man about to go down for the last time. The fact that he was drowning in a river of bliss was, at the moment, no consolation. Clay did not know how much longer he could continue to hold out against the inevitable. Sooner or later he was going to have to follow the actions dictated by his heart; he loved Benita passionately, and a commuter affair was not going to cut it. Unlike Bennie, though, Clay was a great poker player. No one ever knew what he was thinking unless he allowed it. So he would be safe for a while longer, at least. Thus love made fools of strong men.

Clay knew that he was in even more trouble when Bennie glided downstairs the next afternoon. The Image Awards show, an annual event sponsored by *Image* magazine, one of the Deveraux Group's premier publications, was televised. This meant that the program started rather early in the evening, so Bennie and Clay were beautifully attired in evening wear in the late afternoon. Clay was waiting for her downstairs; actually, he was admiring his new haircut in the powder room off the main hallway.

When Clay had mentioned needing a haircut before the gala, Bennie had offered to cut it for him.

"I barbered all of my brothers when we were growing up. Besides, I have had professional training. When Renee and I decided to open a salon, we both went to beauty school."

Clay shook his head.

"No way in hell could I do that," he said.

Bennie pointed out to him that she and Renee viewed it as a sensible investment.

"We looked at how much money is spent on hair care in this country alone, and we knew that, handled correctly, it could be a big moneymaker for us. We wanted to do it right, so we learned all we could from the ground up. And even though I don't work in the salon the way Renee does, I loved learning about hair and skin care. It's challenging, creative, and fun."

The word *fun* was one Clay have never thought of in connection with getting a haircut, but he had never had a haircut like the one Bennie gave him. She had him sit out on the patio, shirtless and swathed in a bath sheet. He looked at the tiny scissors in her hand doubtfully—these did not look like barber shears to him.

"I am a stylist, not a barber. These are the finest ice-forged German scissors made, and they cost about three hundred and fifty dollars, so relax," she informed him.

Clay found the feeling of Bennie's hands in his hair more than pleasurable—it was downright erotic. She was merely cutting his hair, efficiently and professionally, but the touch of her hands was driving him crazy. The fact that she seemed unaware of the effect she was having on him increased his libidinous urges. After trimming and shaping his hair to the desired effect, Bennie put down the scissors and comb and laced her fingers through his glossy hair. She then gave him a finger massage that made him want to moan from pleasure. She quickly ran the styling comb through his hair and held up a mirror for him to view the results.

"Okay, you're all pretty again. What do you think?"

Clay ran his hand through the finished creation.

"Damn, Bennie. It's perfect. It looks like I haven't had a haircut, I just look groomed."

Bennie smiled. Clay truly did not seem to realize that he was almost beautiful. Those sharp, strong features, especially his piercing eyes with those ridiculous lashes,

made her heart skip a few beats every time she looked at
him. And that mustache—every time she thought about the
way it felt on her skin she just melted. She sighed without
realizing it. Clay's eyes met hers, and without saying a word
they went into the house to act on their unbidden passion.

After a short shower and a long, sensual, shared bath,
they parted long enough to get dressed for the evening.
And the end result had Clay's heart in his throat. Bennie
did not descend the steps so much as float down them. She
was wearing a black silk jersey dress that was completely
without adornment. It was strapless, but offered no cleavage at all. It was not provocatively low in the back, either.
It would have looked shapeless and boring on most women,
but not on Bennie. It clung to her body in such a way that
it almost looked like body paint, yet it was not vulgar in
the least. On the contrary, she looked elegant and graceful,
like a sepia Audrey Hepburn. Her hair was up in a severe
twist, and she wore only a pair of stunning earrings that
she had purchased the previous day at Skippy Musket in
Phipps Plaza. The green and gold stones were the perfect
foils for what she considered the centerpiece of her ensem-
ble, the black cat purse that Clay had given her.

The only thing that kept the dress from being too severe
was the thigh-high slit on one side, which let a flash of
her beautiful leg show. Bennie presented herself for Clay's
perusal.

Slowly turning around she asked, "Will I do? Your family won't think I'm a skank, will they?"

Clay's eyes were hooded with passion as he looked at
her from her ridiculously fragile-looking shoes to the top
of her shining hair. Her lips were a dark, juicy red that
made him want to forget everything except devouring her
on the spot.

"My family is going to think the same thing that I do—
that I'm the luckiest man on earth."

Before Bennie could form an answer, he reached into
his pocket and fastened the choker that matched the earrings around her neck. He had purchased it while she was

occupied in another store, to Bennie's complete surprise.
Before she could thank him properly, he escorted her
through the front doors, where a limousine was waiting.
Clay hated driving to big events; he had the patience of a
boiling teakettle when it came to the logistics of parking,
valet or otherwise. Besides, he wanted to be able to concentrate completely on his evening with Benita. He had no
idea that his celebrated poker face had deserted him. From
the moment they emerged from the limousine, it was more
than apparent to everyone who knew him that Clayton
Deveraux was a marked man.

For one thing, precious few people had ever seen Clay
with a woman on his arm. And on the few occasions that
he brought a date to a social function, he certainly wasn't
as attentive as he was being to Bennie. Throughout the
evening, when they were not seated in the huge auditorium,
Clay's big hands encircled her small waist. As statuesque
as Bennie was, the gesture made her seem fragile and delicate. It was certainly obvious to anyone who knew Clay
that this was the real deal. Because even when he wasn't
touching her, he was looking at her in a way that all the
men understood and all the women envied.

He was right about his family; for the most part they
did indeed find her enchanting. When Bennie was presented to his mother, it was all the older woman could do
not to throw her arms around Bennie and thank God for
answering her prayers. But all she did was to smile warmly
and said," Please call me Lillian, dear."

Tears glittered briefly in Bennie's eyes.

"My mother's name was Lillian," she said softly.

His brother Malcolm kissed her on the cheek, almost
welcoming her to the family before he caught himself. Malcolm's wife, Selena, gave her a big hug after a smiling
assessment that took in every inch of Bennie from head to
toe. The Deveraux could not have been more welcoming
and appreciative of the obvious connection between Clay
and Bennie.

The only exception was the only Deveraux daughter, Angelique. Angelique was lovely, having inherited the dashing Creole looks of her father and brothers. Her mother's warm brown skin and petite frame were nowhere to be seen in Angelique's tall, creamy beauty; neither was her mother's graciousness and charm. She might as well have carried a warning label marked *Spoiled brat,* she was so toxic. When she spotted her oldest brother with an Amazon on his arm, she wasted no time in sauntering up to get a closer look.

The congenial group was gathered in the lobby of the Fox Theater, about to return to their seats after a brief intermission, when Angelique presented herself at Clay's side. She looked Bennie up and down with little liking and barely acknowledged her after their introduction. She tried to pull Clay away from the group unsuccessfully, and the flash of her eyes indicated that she was girding up for a fight of some kind. Bennie noticed a tightening of several jaws and heard Selena say sotto voce, "Lord today. Miss Thing is gonna go there, isn't she?" The group merged back into the theater, which forestalled any antics on the part of little sister, but Bennie doubted that she had heard the last of Miss Thing.

The evening's events and the after party that took place in a mansion refurbished as a restaurant were lovely. The awards show had brought out the famous, the infamous, and the nearly famous in droves. Bennie was thrilled to see many people she had known for years; as a direct result of the station, there many famous entertainers who knew the Cochrans well. She was particularly pleased to see Uncle Bump again. He was his usual irrepressible self, Clay's presence notwithstanding.

"Bennie, girl, you're nekked! Where's the rest of that dress?" he demanded.

"Uncle Bump, I am all covered up, practically. You can't see a thing," she defended herself, hoping that Clay did not hear this exchange.

Bump rolled his eyes comically.

"I didn't say you were n-a-k-e-d; I said you were *nekkid!* That's when you got on just enough clothes to fool somebody. But you ain't foolin' me, girl. You are nekkid!" After reducing Bennie to helpless laughter, he relented.

Then he turned directly to Clay and said, "Why don't you and I go have a cigar right quick?" As neither of them smoked, it was obvious that Bump was about to deliver the lecture that Clay had somehow escaped in Detroit.

They stepped outside onto the veranda that encircled the side of the mansion, thus assuring privacy. Bump wasted no time in getting to the point.

"Clay, I love that woman like she was my own daughter. She is truly my godchild, you understand?" Clay nodded without speaking as Bump continued: "I have known her family for a whole lot of years, since before Bennie or any of her brothers were born. I've known your family a long time, too. Your father and I went back a long way." At Clay's look of surprise, Bump repeated his last words for emphasis. "A *long* way, okay? I knew your father, and I think I know you. And you are not your father."

Clay's eyes closed briefly in pain. How much did Bump Williams know? In answer to the unspoken question Bump said quietly, "I know everything. I was not in the country when it happened, but I know everything." He paused to let his words sink in.

"You're a good man, Clayton. Benita is a good woman—no, she's an exceptional woman, as you are no doubt aware. You take care of her. You need each other; you make each other happy and you'll make some pretty babies. You got a great gift in there, son; you both do. Love is the greatest gift two people can share, and when you get it, you need to take it and run." At the look on Clayton's face, Bump burst out laughing. "You thought I was coming out here to threaten your life, didn't you?"

Clay finally spoke. "Something like that, yes."

Bump laughed again as the two men reentered the ballroom.

"I'm not the one, son. But I can't speak for Big Benny," he said with a wicked chuckle.

While Clay and Bump were outside, Bennie had a

chance to chat with Lillian Deveraux, who invited her to attend church services the next day. She also got to have a brief conversation with Vera Jackson, editor of *Image* magazine and a longtime Deveraux Group employee. She liked Vera right away; the two women were about the same age, and apparently shared similar tastes. Vera was strikingly beautiful in a unique way—she reminded Bennie of Dorothy Dandridge or some other vintage black star.

"I love your earrings and necklace, Bennie. Are they Hobé, by chance?"

Bennie smiled and said that they were indeed. Vera collected vintage jewelry, and the women were chatting happily about accessories and such when Vera noticed the cat evening bag.

"Girl, a Judith Leiber! I've always wanted one of these," she exclaimed.

Bennie smiled modestly. "It was a gift," she said.

Angelique drifted over just in time to hear this exchange. "They have knockoff bags like that at the flea market every week," she said snidely.

A collective gasp went up from the table from everyone except Bennie, who looked amused. No one saw Clay approach until it was too late. Looking down at his impetuous sister, he spoke carefully.

"I assure you that I did not purchase it at a flea market, Angelique."

Caressing Bennie's shoulder, he silently dared his sister to open her mouth. Luckily, someone asked Angelique to dance, and that was the end of that episode. Clay kissed Bennie on the temple and sat down. The irrepressible Vera could not help but give Bennie the slightly cocked head signal that all sisters recognize as the universal *you go, girl* nod.

The biggest surprise of the evening for Clay was not the scene in which Bump had offered his blessing to a union between Clay and Bennie, but the ease with which Bennie and Marcus were chatting. Marcus was thanking Bennie again for her offer, and said that he would have a lull in his training program soon that would allow him to take advantage of it. Clay looked completely mystified until Marcus explained.

Bennie had written him a letter even before Clay came to Detroit the first time. In it, she related an incident in which she had completely blown a presentation while in training to be sales manager of WWCC. She said that she had apparently forgotten what it was like to be ambitious and anxious, and she apologized for dismissing him and Darnell so cavalierly. She also offered him the use of the stations for an internship in order for him to learn more about the business of radio.

Clay was almost undone by his feeling of love and admiration for Bennie. It wasn't that she was trying to coddle Marcus because he was Clay's younger brother—she had done a genuinely nice thing because she was a caring, sweet, generous person. She did not owe anyone an apology, yet she managed to do the right thing quickly and graciously. Clay looked at Benita without realizing that his heart was in his eyes. Deveraux around the room were nudging each other and pinching each other at the sight.

By the time Clay and Bennie were able to take their leave of the festivities, the evening air was quite cool—cool enough so that Bennie shivered in the back of the limousine. Clay immediately took off his tuxedo jacket and wrapped it around her shoulder, then pulled her into his arms. Bennie sighed with contentment and cuddled close to his side.

"That was quite an evening," she said sleepily.

Clay did not answer for a moment; he was too awash with emotion to speak. It had been one of the best times he had ever had, and the reason for his enjoyment was right in his arms.

Benita was everything he had ever dreamed of in a woman: smart, sexy, independent, and beautiful. When he was with her, all things seemed possible—it was when he thought about her having a life separate from his that things got complicated. Watching her tonight, he realized more than ever that this was going to be a complex relationship. Benita had business concerns of her own, a corporation and a family and responsibilities hundreds of miles away in Detroit. In her own sphere she was as influential and powerful as he—she was not about to walk away from all that on a whim.

Clay tightened his hold on Bennie for a moment, then relaxed as she stirred in his arms. She seemed completely content right now, but this was a weekend, not a lifetime. *A lifetime. A lifelong commitment.* Was that what he wanted? He knew the answer on the most primal level: Andrea Benita Cochran was *his* woman, the only woman who could complete him. But at what cost? He certainly couldn't walk away from his responsibilities in Atlanta any more than she could leave Detroit. Long-distance marriages might work for some people, but Clay could not see how that would be an option. *This is why I should have never gotten started with this in the first place,* he thought angrily. In his mind, at this moment, it was a no-win situation.

The limousine purred to a stop, derailing Clay's train of unproductive thought. He stroked Bennie's face to waken her; her lashes fluttered but her eyes did not open.

"Oh, please tell me I wasn't drooling," she said comically.

"No, Peaches, you weren't," he answered. "Let's get you inside before you freeze." He helped her from the limo and they went inside the big house. "Do you want to go right upstairs to bed, or sit and talk?" he asked.

Bennie assured him that she wasn't tired enough for bed.

"What I want to do is dance with you," she said. "I want to put on some nice mushy music and light some candles and slow dance with you for a while. How does that sound?"

It sounded just fine to Clay, and it felt even better. Bennie had removed her shoes, and Clay loosened the banded collar of his tuxedo shirt, and they danced to Luther, Barry, and Will Downing. They weren't speaking, just holding each other. Neither one would acknowledge that what they were doing was memorizing the other—the touch, the feel, and the scent of each other. Finally Bennie had had all she could take. All she said was his name, and that was all she had to say. He kissed her once, softly, and led her upstairs.

In a very few minutes it didn't matter to Clay whether the relationship was right or wrong. He would never regret making love to Bennie, ever. Every time they came together the love was amazing, perfect, and life altering. And this night was no exception. When they reached the master suite, Bennie became the complete siren, luring Clay into her aura with her seductive eyes. She stood in front of him and loosened her hair from its French twist, tossing it with her hands until it fell loose and wild around her shoulders. She started unbuttoning Clay's shirt, kissing down his chest as each button exposed more of him. When the shirt was undone, she removed it and made him sit on the side of the bed.

She continued to undress him with agonizing precision. Clay was shaking with need by then and tried to help her, but she stilled his hands.

"Tonight is for you, Clayton. Just for you," she promised.

When he was completely undressed she pushed him down onto the pillows and kissed him thoroughly. Only her soft, panting breaths betrayed the fact that she was as eager as Clay for what was to come. She stood and slowly removed her jewelry, placing it on the dresser. Never taking her eyes from his, she unzipped the invisible side zipper of her dress and let it fall to the floor.

Clay drew in his breath sharply. Bennie had on an incredibly sexy strapless bra and a matching G-string panty in a sheer fabric that in no way hid her shapely frame. She stood there for a moment, loving the way Clay was looking at her. She slowly removed each item so that she stood before him as naked as he was. She went into the bathroom to take a bottle from her cosmetic bag, and slowly walked to the bed. She stepped onto the raised platform that held the bed and started to get in. Leaning over his body, she

captured Clay's lips in a fevered kiss, then whispered to
him, "Turn over. I am going to give you the best massage
you ever had."

Clay rolled onto his stomach and braced himself for the
sensual onslaught that he knew would come as soon as
Bennie touched him. She straddled his body, positioning
herself on his buttocks. The feel of her moist femininity
did wild things to Clay. He turned his head to the side to
say something, but his voice faded as Bennie's strong, soft
hands began rubbing his shoulders and neck. Bennie had
applied some kind of oil that had a light, barely detectable
odor. What it lacked in scent, however, it more than made
up for in sensation. The combination of the oil and the
warmth of Bennie's hands was astounding. He felt as if he
were floating, only in an atmosphere like nothing he had
ever experienced.

Bennie's strokes were strong, measured, and penetrating.
Her hands moved across his shoulders, down his arms, and
across his shoulder blades. When she reached the lower
part of his back, Clay thought he had died and gone to
heaven. Bennie was completely absorbed in her task,
kneading and caressing every part of Clay's body until he
was almost unconscious with pleasure. She went down each
leg in turn, and when she got to his feet, it was just about
his undoing. Clay had no idea that his feet were erogenous
zones until he felt Bennie's hands on the soles. She ma-
nipulated each toe and pressed on his feet in such a way
that he was sure that he was levitating off the bed.

"Oh, damn, Benita, that is absolute torture, baby," he
said with a groan.

Finally Bennie relented, to a degree. She eased her way
up the bed and made Clay turn over, so that she could
repeat the process. But she was sweetly merciful this time;
she rubbed and kissed her way down his chest, stroking
his firm golden flesh as she went. She didn't subject him
to the erotic torture of the back massage—she slid her
hands down his body and trailed her hot lips to his by
now-throbbing arousal. When Clay felt her soft lips sur-

rounding him, he was lost. Bennie had her way with him for as long as he could stand it; after a tremor of pleasure so intense that it felt like pain he pulled Bennie away from her task and reversed her positions so that he was on top of her.

This was not the gentle, sensual coupling of days past— Clay was as on fire for Bennie as she was for him. They came together swiftly; Clay thrust into her with one powerful stroke that had her gasping with desire. They were so intent on bringing each other to the ultimate level of fulfillment that everything else ceased to exist. He gave himself to Bennie in a way that no other woman would ever experience, and she met him stroke for stroke. At that moment there was nothing in the world except them, sealing their love in the most profound way that two people could share. When it was finally over, in a thunderous climax that rocked them both, it was impossible to say whether the tears that ran down Bennie's face were hers alone.

This time there was no laughter or intimate talk after their lovemaking—neither one wanted to break the spell. Clay enfolded Bennie in his arms and they clung to each other as the final tremors gave way to a powerful, dreamless sleep.

Six

It was the best of times and the worst of times, as far as Bennie was concerned. Coming back to Detroit and picking up her life where she had left it before her idyllic days with Clay was pure torture. She was back physically and even mentally, but her heart was in Atlanta with Clay. She was restless and edgy, and found her attention wandering when she was supposed to be working. Like right now, when she was reviewing the monthly sales figures for the stations.

Of course, being Bennie, she was the consummate professional at work. She was too busy with the day-to-day details of her various positions to spend inordinate amounts of time daydreaming. And now that her relationship with Clay was common knowledge to all of WWCC since the Memorial Day festivities, she did not have to pretend there was nothing on her social calendar. With Donnie fully on board at the station, she could, in fact, start grooming Austin Tinsley and Rich Lowenstein for greater management tasks. This, too, was part of her plan to secure more freedom for herself in the day-to-day operation of the family business. So Bennie's plate was as full as always with business matters. But every so often, sweet memories would creep in to fill her with longing.

She tried valiantly to keep her attention focused on the reports in front of her, but her mind would float back to the days that she had spent in utter bliss with Clay. Finally she leaned back in her chair and gave in to the impulse to remember every single thing that they had said to each other, everything they had done together, and all the nights of passion. Those memories stirred her so deeply that she often had to go into her private powder room and rinse her face and hands with icy water to cool the heat that resulted from reliving the delicious passion they had shared.

At those moments she would quickly try to jump to something more neutral, like the memory of going to church with Clay's mother. That Sunday morning had dawned bright and sunny, and Bennie had left Clay sleeping while she showered and began the process of getting dressed in suitable church attire. She was wrapped in a towel, combing her hair, when Clay's sulky face appeared in the bathroom mirror behind her reflection.

"What are you doing? And why are you not in bed with me where you belong?" he asked grumpily.

Bennie had smiled and said, "I'm going to church with your mother. And if you weren't such a heathen, you'd be going too."

Clay had looked at her as if he wanted to argue the point, but he merely shrugged and left the room. Bennie finished applying a touch of makeup and her French lingerie. She decided to wear her ivory linen Dana Buchman suit. She had just put on her mabe pearl earrings and her Prada pumps when Clay came back into the bedroom, his hair slightly damp from the shower. He was dressed in a beautifully tailored suit and looked sleepy but more than presentable. Bennie opened her mouth to speak, and Clay had held up a hand.

"Not a word. Let's go."

Bennie was so enthused at seeing Clay's family again that she had not noticed the general stir caused by their appearance. It wasn't until Clay was seated with Bennie in the family pew and the minister had looked directly at him and said, "Let the church say amen" that Bennie realized that this was quite an event. Clay was apparently not the most churchgoing of the Deveraux.

The church service had been followed by brunch at

Clay's mother's house, where Bennie got to meet his three adorable nieces. They were perfect little ladies and were obviously in awe of Uncle Clay's girlfriend. It was as though they did not know such a creature could have possibly existed. The food was wonderful, the company exquisite, and the atmosphere warm and welcoming, with the exception of a brief encounter with the lovely Angelique. She made no secret of the fact that she was not among Bennie's new horde of admirers, simply by ignoring her. She flounced into the living room, observed the assemblage, and left with a loud snort. Lillian was beside herself with embarrassment.

Bennie tactfully changed the subject by asking about Clay as a child, which led to a pleasant afternoon of anecdotes and baby pictures, much to Bennie's delight and Clay's chagrin. They finally took their leave and drove the long way home to enjoy the beautiful afternoon and each other's company. It was altogether a perfect day. Bennie sighed, remembering how much she had enjoyed being with Clay's family. It was that, in fact, that had sparked a serious conversation between Clay and Bennie.

Bennie gave up all pretense of working and went over to sit on the big leather sofa by the window of her office. That conversation could have been tricky and awkward, but as with every conversation with Clay, it had gone well. They had been in the family room, listening to music. Clay's head was in Bennie's lap, and she was stroking his beloved face and playing with his hair.

"Clay, why haven't you ever gotten married?" she wanted to know.

Clay had not jumped or recoiled or done any of the things that men do when cornered. He hadn't moved a muscle, in fact.

"I haven't been in a relationship serious enough to warrant thinking about it," he replied easily.

Bennie continued to stroke his hair.

"I find that hard to believe," she mused. "A big, smart, good-looking man like you? Mamas all over Georgia have been targeting you for their little debutantes for years, I'll betcha." She laughed as he swatted at her hands.

Clay laughed with her and said smugly, "Their eyes may shine and their teeth may grit, but Lillian Deveraux's boy they ain't gonna get."

Bennie made a comment about his giant ego, but she was still laughing while she did it. Then Clay turned the tables on her.

"So why have you never gotten married again?"

Bennie sighed softly. "Same reason, I guess. I truly mourned Gilbert after he died. I did not look at or think about another man for a long, long time. Like four or five years, I think it was."

She did not see Clay's look of shock, because she was focused on her own thoughts.

"Then I did start to date a little, but I never met anyone with whom I wanted to develop a close, lasting relationship. We'd go to a lot of free concerts courtesy of WWCC," she joked. Then she got serious again. "I have dated, *do* date, but I just never met that special person," she finished.

Clay was quiet for a long moment.

"Benita, I want to ask you something that is none of my business and that you certainly do not have to answer, okay?"

"All right, Clay, what is it?"

"How many really serious relationships have you had in your life?" he asked quietly.

Bennie got the least bit self-conscious for a moment. "Counting my husband and you?" she murmured.

"Yes, Benita, counting your husband and me," he said patiently.

Bennie appeared to be deep in thought. Finally she answered.

"Two," she said with a touch of the kind of defiance that a small child offered in the face of certain chastisement.

Clay rolled off Bennie's lap so fast that he fell onto the floor. He didn't seem to notice as he brought himself up to sit next to her. Bennie had waited for some kind of censuring comment, but none had come. Clay took her hand in his and kissed her on both cheeks, sweetly and reverently.

"Thank you," he said quietly, then pulled her to his chest and lay back with her. Then had come the really tricky part of the conversation.

Closing her eyes against the view of Detroit from her office window, Bennie slid down so that her head was resting on the fat arm of the sofa. She rubbed her flat stomach in circles, remembering every word of what she and Clay had said.

"Clay. Last night, we did not use any protection," she began.

Clay had tightened his arms protectively around her, and kissed her temple before speaking.

"Benita, I would never knowingly put you in jeopardy. To tell you the truth, that was the first and only time in my life that I have never used a condom. I guess I assumed that you were on some sort of birth control." He kissed her again, and turned her head so that he was looking into her eyes. "Are you saying there might be a little Deveraux in there?" he said, rubbing her stomach.

Bennie immediately answered in the negative.

"Wrong time of the month. All the little eggies are elsewhere right now. But I am not on the pill—I'm too old, according to Dr. Doom. And I don't have a diaphragm, although I can be fitted for one when I get home."

Clay shook his head. "No, I'll take care of you. It is my privilege as well as my responsibility," he said.

Bennie drew back and looked at him carefully.

"Okay, I can understand your not being married. But I can't understand why there are not hordes of women lined up outside this house ready to shoot me. You are not going to convince me that you lead the life of a monk. You are just too . . . well, I can't see that."

Clay chuckled wickedly and said, "They are probably in an ambush formation right now."

She had taken a playful swipe at him, which he ducked. Then he had addressed her sincerely and seriously.

"Baby, I'm not going to tell you that I have not had other women. But not since I met you. I am a simple man with a one-track mind, and I haven't thought of anyone but you since the day we met. And I won't."

Bennie had just melted against Clay at those words. Basking in bliss, they stretched out on the sofa and began kissing feverishly, only to burst out laughing when both their stomachs had sung a hungry song in chorus. Brunch had been, after all, hours ago. So they went out to eat and hurried home to make love again.

Stretching luxuriously, Bennie was just about to go into a serious fit of longing for Clay when she was interrupted by her intercom. It was Big Benny, summoning her to his office. Bennie made a face as she straightened her clothes. It looked like a "come to Jesus" talk for sure, one that she had been expecting. *This should be interesting,* she thought as she entered the reception area on the way to Big Benny's corner office.

Surprisingly, though, this was not a meeting in the real sense of the word. Benny was at his expansive, jovial best that day. He gave Bennie a bear hug and looked her over carefully.

"Well, daughter, you're looking well," he said, "considering that I haven't seen hide nor hair of you in a week or more. Where have you been keeping yourself?" Before Bennie could answer, he went on: "I was hoping you could join me for dinner this evening. Nothing fancy—I thought we could just get together and talk."

Bennie's eyes widened. *Okay, who are you and what have you done with my father?* she thought. Big Benny never asked anyone in just to inquire about their health. Nor was it his custom to have a quick bite on a weeknight. Weeknights were usually given over to his lady friend, Martha, a woman of whom Bennie heartily approved. Dinners were usually on Sunday, and business was usually upfront and to the point. Bennie agreed to meet her father for dinner with some curiosity. *What are you up to, Daddy? Inquiring minds want to know. Now.*

Bennie could not shake the feeling that her father was up to something. She had tried to no avail to get Renee to accompany her to this so-called casual dinner, but Renee had refused. Big Benny had not requested her presence, Renee pointed out.

"He did not say anything about bringing his surrogate daughter, did he? Or anyone else, for that matter. So no, honey, I am not going to run interference for you tonight." But then Renee relented, seeing as how Bennie was genuinely not looking forward to the evening for reasons she could not explain.

"Have you ever sat down with him and had a talk about Clay?" Renee probed gently.

Bennie looked at Renee with an odd expression on her face.

"No, I haven't. I think I'm a little bit old to be having a father-daughter talk about my latest beau, if you get my drift. And Daddy and I have never really related to each other like that," she admitted.

Bennie had always been like an assistant to her father. He relied on her as he would any trusted business associate. Before Lillian Cochran had passed away, all the minutiae of being a female in a house full of men had been mother's work. Afterward, it had been nonexistent. Bennie had not dated enough in high school for Bennie to get really rattled about it, and her one romance in college had been Gilbert. Benny had indeed disapproved of Bennie's getting married and moving away, to the extent that they had had a colossal row.

When he realized that nothing he could do or say was going to make Bennie change her mind, a rift had arisen between them that had not fully healed until she was back at home in Detroit after Gilbert's untimely death. They had never really talked through their separation; Big Benny merely acted as if she had been away for a few weeks, and Bennie was too stricken with grief to challenge this fallacy. Thus they picked up their lives and went on as though nothing had ever come between them.

"Bennie, come back, hon; you're drifting on me," Renee said, waving her hand in front of Bennie's face.

Bennie jumped guiltily.

"I'm sorry; I was lost in thought for a minute. What were we talking about? Oh, yes, that father-daughter thing. I'm too old for that, and there is nothing that Daddy is going to do or say that is going to change my relationship with Clay. So he need not go there," she finished with a flinty look in her eye.

Two hours later, Bennie still wasn't sure what her father was up to. Martha was not at the Palmer Park house; it was just Bennie and her father. Big Benny was still in the jovial mode of the office; he grilled steaks for them and they ate them out on the patio. Over the steaks, roasted corn on the cob, and a tossed green salad, they chatted amiably about first one thing and then another. Everything was safe and serene, and Bennie finally let her guard down and enjoyed the evening. After they cleared away the dishes, though, the other shoe dropped.

"Bennie, I'm concerned about what is going on at the station," he began. Bennie raised an eyebrow, but let him finish. "I don't think that the additional responsibilities you are giving Adonis are going to work out."

Bennie took a deep breath before answering.

"I don't know what you're talking about, Daddy. We all discussed the fact that Donnie wants to take on a leadership role with Cochran Communications. I don't *think* he can handle these new responsibilities; I *know* he can. Donnie has an MBA, after all, and he knows more about Cochran communications than you think he does. It's not like he's coming here fresh from a paper route, you know. Donnie was in business for several years and has a well-earned reputation as a brilliant marketing consultant. And what he doesn't know about radio, he is learning very rapidly. I certainly did, and it's his turn now. He wants it that way and so do I. And up until tonight, I thought you did, too. What's going on here, Daddy?" Bennie was tired of skirting whatever the main issue was.

"Benita, when I step down as CEO of Cochran Communications, I want to make sure that things continue to run smoothly. I don't want to see what it has taken me fifty years to build crumble because you are too involved with some man to give the company your full attention. This is more than a business; it's the legacy that I leave you and your brothers. I am concerned about the future of the company; that's all."

Having dropped this little bomb, Big Benny sat back to receive the reassurance he knew he would get from his daughter. He was so assured of victory that he did not recognize the fury that rippled across her face before she spoke.

"Not this time, Daddy," she said quietly, but with real heat. "You built Cochran Communications fifty years ago, but I have been working there since I was twelve, or don't you remember that? I have been carrying the weight of WWCC for the past fifteen years! There has not been a time since I assumed my position after Gilbert died that you have had cause to question my loyalty to the business, to the family, or to you." Bennie's face was flushed and her eyes were snapping as she paced around the kitchen.

"In all that time, did you ever ask yourself what it was that *I* wanted? Did it occur to you once that I might have wanted a life outside the station? Andrew has one; all the boys have one except me. And now Donnie wants to assume a role that he is just as entitled to as I am, and you don't *like* the idea? Well, you'd better get used to it, Daddy, because if you don't want Donnie running WWCC, you're going to have to hire someone from the outside. I am through being shackled to that place," she spat.

She could feel tears boiling to the surface, but she fought

them down. She could not afford to give an inch or her father would have her right where he wanted her. As it was, he seemed to read her thoughts. Benny raised his hands in a gesture of conciliation.

"Bennie, Bennie, I am not trying to upset you. Come on; let's go sit down and talk this out."

Against her better judgment, Bennie allowed herself to be led into the cozy family room that adjoined the kitchen. She sat on one end of the sofa, while her father sat down heavily in the wing chair next to it. He looked at her for a moment before speaking.

"Bennie, I know that I have perhaps expected too much of you in the past. I know that I treated you more like a partner than a daughter. But I didn't know what else to do. It seemed to work for us, and it was never my intention to make you unhappy," he said sincerely. "I agree that if Adonis wants to be more active at the station, it is a good idea, and I am certainly not going to object. But someone has to be CEO, and I always assumed that person would be you." Bennie started to speak, but Benny held up his hand to continue. "I am not saying it has to be permanent, but for the next two or three years, at least, while Adonis is getting his feet wet—"

"Two or three years? Do you realize what you are asking of me?" Bennie looked at her father as though birds were flying out of his ears. "Daddy, you are missing the entire point here. There is no reason why you can't provide some guidance for Donnie while he assumes the title. I am not the end-all and be-all of WWCC. Between the two of us, and with Austin and Rich moving into managerial positions, Donnie will be fine. The station will be fine. And I will be free," she said with finality.

Big Benny did not raise his voice—he had learned much more effective means of controlling his only daughter over the years. Instead, he looked almost satisfied with her outburst.

"Free to do what, Benita? Marry this Clay Deveraux

person? Has it gotten that far? Has he even asked you to marry him?" Benny asked softly.

Complete understanding dawned at that point. *So this is what he's up to,* Bennie thought. *Well, fire away, Daddy.*

"Daddy, this has nothing to do with Clay. And please don't refer to him as 'this' Clay Deveraux. Believe it or not, I wanted to pursue other interests long before I met Clay. And no, Clay and I have not discussed marriage. But when we do, it will be a matter strictly between the two of us; do I make myself clear?"

For long moments the two Cochrans stared at each other, taking the measure of each other and wondering what the next move would be. Both of them banked heavily on the old sales adage that the first one to speak after closing the sale was the loser. Bennie crossed her arms firmly and refused to look away. These were things that she should have gotten off her chest months—no, *years*—ago. Her father looked surprisingly calm—too calm, in fact. That he had another ace in the hole would not have surprised Bennie in the least. Sure enough, he had saved the best for last.

"Well, I can see that I am not going to change your mind about this," he said meekly. "I had planned to tell you this under more festive circumstances, but Martha and I plan to get married as soon as I retire. We had planned to do a lot of traveling, but that may not be possible now." He looked over at Bennie with a face of innocence and hope. "I'm sure that this will all work itself out, daughter. We've always taken great care of the family, and we always will."

The blood was pounding in Bennie's ears so hard that she barely heard her father's saccharine words. He wanted to get married and go play, so he was trying to entrench her even more firmly at Cochran Communications. *Not today, Daddy. I am not the one.* But she would let him think that he was going to get his way, at least for now. She knew what his game was, so it was just a matter of developing a new strategy. For the moment she gave him a hug and congratulations that she hoped sounded sincere. She really did love Martha and thought it would be a good thing for the two of them. *But not at my expense. This is not over, Daddy.*

Clay had developed a sixth sense where Bennie was concerned. He knew when she was tired, when she was overdoing it at work, and when she was just plain lonely for him. He knew these things because he was so attuned to her that if she broke a fingernail, he would feel it. Hearing her voice on the telephone, he knew that something was bothering Bennie.

"Baby, what's the matter?" he asked after exchanging greetings. "I can tell you've had a rough day. Tell me about it."

Bennie sighed softly. She couldn't get used to how perceptive Clay was. She hastened to assure him that it was a minor dispute involving her father.

"Nothing to worry about," she assured him. "Tell me how your day went," she said to change the subject.

Clay allowed her to have her way for the moment, and they talked easily about a variety of topics. Then Clay went right back to his original thought; something was on Bennie's mind that she was not sharing.

"Peaches, if you don't want to talk about it right now, I'll understand. But you have to know that I am here for you, whatever the situation. I don't want you to feel like you have to handle everything all by yourself. That's what boyfriends are for, isn't it?"

He hoped his lame joke would make her smile. Instead, he thought he detected a sniffle, which caused his stomach to twist.

Bennie fought back the urge to cry it all out to Clay. He was being so sweet and caring, yet she did not want to burden him with family business. So she told a half truth.

"I just miss you terribly, that's all," she murmured.

Clay knew she wasn't being completely candid, but he let it go for the moment.

"That's a coincidence—I miss you, too. More than you'll ever know. In fact, I was hoping that you would come down this weekend. By rights I should come up there, but I have something special planned. And it has been two very long weeks since I saw you. I think we both need some TLC this weekend," he said.

Bennie agreed wholeheartedly. They agreed to fix a specific time to meet when Bennie had made reservations. Bennie told him that he didn't have to pick her up at the airport, that she would rent a car or something.

Clay snorted. "Woman, are you crazy? I wouldn't miss seeing your face when you get off the plane for anything. Besides, I get some of your best kisses in major airports. Just let me know what time and what flight, baby."

This time the weather and the traffic cooperated, allowing Clay to get to the airport in plenty of time to greet Bennie as soon as she got off the plane. The only small snag in his impeccable timing was the presence of a former liaison, Lisa Williams. As bad luck would have it, he ran right into Lisa as he was headed for Bennie's gate. Lisa's eyes lit up at the sight of her former lover, and she took the opportunity to trail along with him and pepper him with questions about how he was doing and what he'd been up to.

"Clay, I don't think you're listening to a word I'm saying," she said in exasperation.

Clay finally glanced down at her small, pouty face. Lisa was a perfect example of the kind of woman he used to date: small in stature, with flawless brown skin and a short, perfectly cut bob with auburn highlights, Lisa was very pretty. And in truth, she was a very sweet woman. There was just nothing there to challenge him, to get his senses reeling the way they did with Bennie. *Benita. She's not going to understand this at all.* He was here to meet the woman he loved, and some other woman was clinging to his arm like a barnacle. It was not the prettiest picture in the world.

Clay made some desperate small talk and tried to extricate himself from the woman's grasp. He was so engrossed that he did not realize that deplaning passengers had started flowing out of the jetway leading to the plane until it was too late. He looked up and saw Bennie emerge with the other passengers, looking incredibly beautiful. She was wearing something in a hot shade of pink that he had never seen her in before, and the color did wonderful things to her complexion. She smiled her most radiant smile and walked right into his arms for a kiss.

"Hi, baby. I missed you." She sighed softly.

She was about to kiss him again when she became aware of Lisa at his elbow. Bennie's eyes widened slightly and she covered her mouth.

"I'm so sorry; you must think I'm terribly rude! I'm Bennie Cochran, and you must be a friend of Clay's. I was so . . . happy to see Clay, I didn't see you there."

Lisa was too bemused to do anything but shake the hand that Bennie offered, and say, "I'm Lisa Williams; nice to meet you."

Clay was, once again, done-in by the phenomenal life force that was Bennie. If he had gotten off a plane in Detroit and Bennie had been standing there with a handsome man, Clay knew very well that his reaction would not have been the same. He would have been on guard, at the very least, until he knew what the situation was. Not Bennie. She required no explanation of any kind; she was immediately sweet and gracious and polite. Clay did not know whether to admire her good manners or be a little piqued that she wasn't having a snit.

After collecting her luggage and getting on the expressway, Clay had time to think about the scene at the airport. Bennie had floated into his arms as though she belonged there—which she did. She was polite and kind to a woman whose only crime was being in a public place at an inconvenient time. And judging from the look of shock on Lisa's face, he was not the only one who was surprised by Bennie's gracious behavior. *So why am I thinking about it at all?* The answer was not reassuring—it was because he actually felt intimidated by Bennie for a moment. She had this way of always doing the right thing in just the right way. How in the world was he supposed to live up to a standard like that?

Bennie was completely unaware of his momentary crisis of conscience—she was chatting away happily and holding his hand as if she would never let it go.

"So what is this big surprise you have planned? You know how I am with surprises—I can't stand being kept in suspense!" she confessed.

Clay immediately relaxed. Bennie might be practically perfect, but she was as guileless as a child sometimes.

"I'm not telling," he said as they entered the driveway. "You can torture me, you can bully me, you can threaten me, but you won't get it out of me tonight," he answered.

Bennie scrunched her face up in frustration, then leaned over and whispered something to him. Clay's eyes lit up with comic lust.

"Oh, well, if you do *that,* I'll have to tell, no question."

Clay meant what he said, though: no amount of effort on Bennie's part could get him to tell her what he had in store for her. She certainly tried her best that night to prize the information out of him, but the only result was some truly innovative lovemaking on both their parts. When they finally lay sweaty and exhausted, trembling in each other's arms, Clay had whispered that she would find out first thing in the morning. Bennie sighed and closed her eyes to sleep.

"First thing in the morning," she threatened. "Or I'll have to torture you again."

Clay smiled to himself. *That's not the way to get a man to confess anything,* he thought before drifting off to sleep.

* * *

By noon the next day they were on their way to Savannah, where they would leave for the house on St. Simons Island. Clay had at last told Bennie that he wanted to take her to his family's weekend home.

"It's really pretty there. It's quiet and restful, and the islands are gorgeous. No distractions, just you and me." Bennie's eyes had lit up like stars. "I have to warn you: we'll either have to take a quick flight or a long drive," he cautioned.

Bennie immediately voted for the drive.

"No more planes, please! Let's drive and we can talk," she said.

After assembling the casual clothes suitable for an island weekend, and gathering the supplies Clay had provisioned, they were in his Jaguar, eating up the expressway between Atlanta and Savannah. Bennie grew uncharacteristically quiet after a while. Clay glanced at her and touched her hand.

"What are you thinking about, Peaches?"

Bennie turned to him with an incredible smile on her face. She actually blushed.

"I'm thinking about this morning," she confessed.

Clay winked at her and smiled. "Good," was all he said, but there was a wealth of meaning in the word.

Bennie had been brushing her hair in the bedroom that morning after her bubble bath.

"Clay, I'm definitely getting addicted to that bathtub," she had said. "I usually prefer showers, but that tub is wonderful." Realizing that Clay had not answered her, she called him. "Clay?"

Just then she heard his voice floating up through the open French doors of the bedroom. Going out onto the balcony, she looked down to find him standing in the backyard.

"Come on down here, Benita."

"Okay, let me get dressed and I'll be right down," she answered.

Clay assured her that her butterfly kimono would be just

fine. Shrugging, she slipped it on over her naked body and went downstairs to join Clay. He was waiting for her with a big smile—and a camera.

"Whoa. What's up with that?" Bennie asked suspiciously.

Clay looked perfectly innocent.

"I don't have any pictures of you. You don't have any pictures of yourself to give me. I have a camera"—he gestured to the beautiful yard—"and the perfect setting. So . . ." He let his voice trail off for Bennie to take in the whole idea.

Bennie's mouth opened and her eyes got huge.

"You want to take pictures of me au naturel in your yard? Right now?"

The look of surprise was replaced by one that Clay had never seen on a woman's face before: a look of innocence, seduction, feminine pride, and total freedom. Bennie undid the belt of her robe.

"Okay, let's do it," was all she said.

Clay took pictures of Bennie posing with her robe sliding off her shoulders, partially hidden by a tree, lying in the grass, and dancing like a nymph by the reflecting pool. For almost an hour he shot exposure after exposure, trying to capture the essence of Bennie. His mind was completely on the task at hand, but that did not stop the impromptu photo shoot from being one of the most erotic experiences he had ever had. His single-lens reflex camera was able to take incredible close-ups, so that without being near her he could practically taste her through the lens. Bennie was so natural, so graceful and unconscious of her nudity, that it was like being a voyeur, spying on some vestal virgin from an ancient civilization. But he wasn't spying—he was participating. Those innocently provocative moves were for him and him only.

As for Bennie, she was absolutely on fire. Her desire for Clay had heated her to the point where she felt that steam was rising off her body from the cool morning air. She knelt in the dewy grass and pulled her hair up on both sides while turning to look at Clay one more time. Her mouth was slightly open, and everything that was raging inside her showed plainly on her face. Clay abruptly put the camera down and walked across the lawn, ripping off his shirt as he did so.

"That's about enough of that." He groaned as he fell down beside her.

They managed to spread her robe out on the soft grass before removing the last articles of Clay's clothing and giving in to the fire.

Unbelievably, the best part, at least for Bennie, came later. When they finally made it back to the bedroom and were preparing to shower, Bennie pointed out to Clay that they had gone without protection.

"If I didn't know better, I'd think we were trying to get pregnant," she remarked.

Clay was relieved that she had said *we* were trying to get pregnant, and didn't think he was trying to force her into it. He tried to make light of her statement by repeating what everyone who had seen them had said: "Well, we would certainly have some beautiful babies," he said, trying not to sound too hopeful. *Where in the world did that come from?* Before he could get really frantic, though, Bennie started laughing.

"Clay, get real! Our children would look like flamingos. Any child we had would be nine feet tall, with a neck like a giraffe and legs like a stork! And I don't even want to think about the nose—baby, with our honkers, that child would look like a cross between Jimmy Durante and Cyrano de Bergerac!"

Bennie laughed heartily at this, but Clay didn't laugh with her. He pulled her into his arms almost angrily and took her into the bathroom to stand in front of a wall that was a mirror from floor to ceiling.

"When are you going to get it through your head that you are the most beautiful, most gorgeous woman I have ever seen? Not just on the outside—on the inside, too." Clay put Bennie in front of him and placed one hand on her hip. Bringing the other up to her face, he held her chin and made her look at herself in the mirror.

"Benita, if you could see yourself the way I see you, the way other people see you, you would know what I mean." His eyes reflected the passion and desire he felt whenever he looked at Bennie. "You have the most wonderful skin I have ever touched; you have the most incredible mouth, and when you smile, it makes my heart stop. When I look into your eyes, it's like looking straight into Paradise. Your body"—he stopped long enough to run his hands down her hips before finishing—"is perfect in every way." Clay brought his head down to kiss Bennie's neck briefly and whispered in her ear, "And if I am blessed to have a child with you, it's going to be as gorgeous as you are." He cupped her breasts and then brought his hands down to caress the soft, curling hair at the base of her stomach. "Coming from us, out of here, how could it not be?"

Tears were running down Bennie's face by this time, and she tried to cover her face with her hands. Clay would not permit that; he continued to stand with his arms wrapped around her, talking in a soft voice until she believed every word. There was nothing left to do but become one, and they had, with great tenderness and love.

Bennie sighed deeply and then realized where she was. They were still on the road to Savannah. She shook her head to clear it of the images that were so clear in her mind. She turned to look at Clay, placing her hand on his thigh.

"Clay, when I'm a very, very old lady, I'm going to still remember every single minute of this day and everything you said to me. I am an incredibly lucky woman; do you know that?"

Clay felt a little jolt at her words. Covering her hand with his, he said gruffly, "No, Peaches, I'm the lucky one."

Bennie just smiled. "Okay, then *we're* lucky, both of us. Want me to drive for a while?"

* * *

The St. Simons house was everything Clay said it was. The Sea Islands of Georgia were clustered off the coast of Georgia around Savannah. St. Simons was the largest of these islands and the biggest draw for tourism. Clay and his family had had a home there for years. It had started life as a rustic cabin that was not much more than a fishing shack, but over the years it had been enlarged and developed into a large, rambling home. It was covered with weathered cedar shingles and had a deep veranda that ran the length of the house in front, and screened-in porches on either end of the house that served as sleeping rooms as well as places for entertainment.

It still maintained an air of rustic charm and simplicity, although Lillian had charmingly decorated everything. The floors were of pickled pine, and the deep sofas and chairs bore washable duck slipcovers. There was a big fireplace in the great room, and a casual, friendly dining room with Lillian's plate collection displayed on the walls. Bennie fell in love with the big kitchen. It had sliding doors that led out to a huge patio that was surrounded by an herb border as well as wildflowers. Bennie was happily exclaiming over the bedrooms while Clay was bringing in the bags.

"I'm going to think you love me only for my real estate," he grumbled as he brought in the last box of groceries.

Bennie came up behind him and hugged him hard.

"Don't be stupid. I love you just for you," she said sweetly before releasing him and going to explore the backyard.

Clay was relieved that she left the room so that she could not see the look of shock, the total happiness that came over his face. Of course, she was just playing around, but to hear her say those words so naturally, without hoping for a jeweled trinket or marriage proposal or anything else—it was awesome and humbling to Clay at the same time. *I wonder what it would sound like if she really meant it?*

As with every event with Bennie, the weekend had its

surprise. Bennie and Clay were relaxing in one of the cool, shady rooms that were formed by the screened-in porches. They were talking lazily, and by some unspoken mutual consent had been about to merge into more passionate love-making, when a sound caused Bennie's head to turn. A large dog was sitting in the doorway that led into the great room, his head cocked to one side with canine curiosity. Bennie cocked her head in turn and nudged Clay, whose eyes were closed in anticipation.

"Baby? I think we have company," she said.

Sure enough, as soon as she finished speaking the doorway was filled with a tall, imposing stranger. He was obviously related to Clay—he had the same hawklike features, the same fair coloring, and the same glossy hair. But he wore a patch on his left eye and had a jagged seam of a scar down that side of his face. His hair was also much longer than Clay's—he wore it in a ponytail, which gave him the look of a pirate.

Clay looked surprised for a second and then smiled.

"Martin! Good to see you." He rose, pulling Bennie to her feet. "Martin, this is Benita Cochran. Benita, meet my brother Martin."

Bennie crossed the floor to shake Martin's hand.

"It's so nice to meet you," she said. Indicating the dog, she asked, "And who is your friend?"

Martin finally spoke, in a voice as cold and measured as Clay's was warm, despite the similarity in depth and tone.

"Satchel," he said grudgingly. Bennie held out her hand for Satchel to smell, and was rewarded by a lick across the palm. Encouraged, she wasted no time in scratching the beautiful dog's ears. Martin looked shocked.

"Normally he doesn't let anyone but me touch him," he remarked.

Clay thought it was time to intervene.

"Benita has a way with animals," he said. "So, are you hungry? We were thinking about getting something to eat."

Martin shook his head. "Look, I didn't know anyone was here. I'll just go back to the boat."

Bennie protested. "Oh, no, you don't! There's plenty of room here! You have to stay and get acquainted. I want to know all about Clay in his feckless youth, and your mother certainly wouldn't tell me," she wheedled.

Martin looked at the total love on his older brother's face and decided abruptly that he would stay. Clay looked as though he needed someone to keep an eye on this situation. Martin knew only too well what a beautiful woman could do to an unsuspecting man. *If Clay doesn't watch himself, this woman could destroy him.*

They ended up going to a restaurant on St. Simons that specialized in Low Country cooking, utilizing all the regional specialties. While Bennie freshened up in the ladies room, Martin ordered them bowls of Brunswick stew as an appetizer. Returning to the table, Bennie sniffed appreciatively at the steaming bowl in front of her. It contained tomatoes, potatoes, onions, corn, and some kind of meat in a red sauce with an appetizing aroma. Taking a big spoonful, Bennie moaned her delight.

"Oh, my, this is good!" she said happily.

Martin continued to give her his stony stare. "You know what it's made out of?" he asked. "Squirrel," he said unkindly, without waiting for her to respond.

Bennie's eyes lit up with glee. She took another big bite before answering. "Well, if they want some squirrels, I know where they can get some big, fat ones. Yeah, some big black ones that would probably have a lot of meat on 'em," she said emphatically.

She went on to regale Martin and Clay with the story of how the fat black squirrels that proliferated Indian Village in Detroit had made a hole under the eaves of her house and gotten into her attic.

"You can't shoot 'em, because it's against the law. You can't poison 'em, because they'll die up there and stink all to be-damn. You have to get someone to trap them, and then you have to patch up the means of ingress immediately or they'll get right back in."

Clay was cracking up by now, and even Martin was trying not to smile. When she related how she had finally gotten a reliable contractor to fix the holes, she was really animated.

"Okay, so that evening, after all the work was finished, Renee and I are in the kitchen drinking tea. Then we hear this racket and Aretha, starts going crazy. I look up, and there's this fat, shameless squirrel, beating on my kitchen window with his little hand or foot or paw or whatever it is. He had the nerve to look hurt! He was like, 'So why ya wanna playa-hate a squirrel? Whassa matter, baby? I been livin' here and it was all right. I mean, you ain't said nuthin' to a squirrel. So now you just gonna kick me to the curb, is that it?' All he needed was a Kangol cap and a gold chain to be the total player-squirrel."

By this time, tears were rolling down Clay's face, and Martin was laughing out loud, real belly laughs. Bennie picked up her spoon and daintily finished the last of her stew.

"Yeah, I used to think squirrels were fuzzy and cute— they're nothing but tree rats to me now. So you could give me squirrel pie and I'd eat it."

Their waitress overheard this last remark and assured her that their Brunswick stew was made with chicken.

"Squirrel and rabbit are more traditional, but the tourists don't like the idea," she confided.

Bennie was tickled that Martin had tried to test her with the squirrel business. She gave him one of her best *gotcha* smiles and held up her hand.

"Martin, please. I grew up with five brothers. There is very little left to gross me out with," she assured him.

Martin smiled back. "I was just having some fun with you," he said.

Clay was amazed. He was surprised and relieved when Martin agreed to stay, and even more so when he accompanied them to dinner. Martin, after his accident and subsequent desertion by his faithless wife, had become hard and hermitlike in the past few years. To see him as relaxed as he was now, especially in the company of a person he did not know, like Bennie, was nothing short of miraculous. He looked at Bennie and Martin, who were having a conversation about baseball. If he had been subconsciously subjecting Bennie to a series of tests—which he had not— this would have been the final exam. Martin had become, as the result of his past, the most distrustful man on earth. And in less than an hour Bennie had led him out of the thicket and had him eating out of her hand. At that moment Clay did not know whether he was afoot or horseback. He knew one thing for sure, and that was that his life was better than it had ever been, solely due to the laughing woman at his side.

Seven

Now it was Bennie's turn to be frantic, although her state of nerves had nothing to do with her and Clay. The past couple of months had gone by quickly, but not so quickly that she did not have a rich store of beautiful memories from which to draw. After the weekend on St. Simons she and Clay had gotten closer and closer; it seemed as though she had always had the big, golden man in her life. Martin had stayed only one night at the family house. He could see that Bennie and Clay wanted him there, but they needed to be alone even more. So they had had the rest of the weekend to spend totally enraptured with one another.

Bennie had not planned to be back in Detroit until Tuesday, but Clay had some business that could not be put off that Monday. Bennie surprised him by suggesting that she go into the office with him and even rent a car so that she could call on a few of her national accounts that were based in Atlanta. Clay thought this was a wonderful idea, although he would not hear of her renting a car.

"Just drop me at the office; I'll give you a tour and you can use my car. Are you going to be able to find your way around? Atlanta can be pretty frustrating for some," he said.

Bennie was touched by his concern but reminded him that she came from a place where a driver couldn't go anywhere without knowing where to get on and where to get off the expressway.

"Plus, we name our expressways. And we call them by

the name and the number interchangeably. Newcomers don't know what the heck the Chrysler or the Lodge is, but they find out fast or they stay lost forever. I can find my way around with no problem," she assured him.

Clay had been more than happy to show Bennie around his office building. It was a huge glass-and-wood building in a forestlike setting. The building was a hexagon from the outside, which yielded to a circular design once inside. The offices on each floor were windowed from floor to ceiling, while the hallways were like a continual balcony that encircled the interior. The center of the circle was the reception area, which soared up in an atrium full of exotic greenery. Each floor housed a different component of the Deveraux Group. There was the publishing division, sub-divided by newspapers and magazines. Then there was the cable division, the television studio, and the newest enter-prise, the book division. The administrative offices were housed on a separate floor entirely. Bennie was impressed, to say the least.

Clay's office was much like he was, masculine and authoritative without being macho. Clay, like Bennie, had leather furnishings, but his were a deep cordovan. There were art prints on the walls, but like Bennie, all his awards and honors were not in view—there was a wall in one of the conference rooms that held all manner of those things for everyone in the Deveraux Group. Looking at the pic-tures made Bennie blush mightily, remembering their inti-mate photo session. Clay had immediately read her thoughts and laughed gently.

"Like I would let anyone else see those pictures! I'm also developing them myself. No, Peaches, I'm afraid you still owe me a picture for the office," he said. "Not that I would get much done while I was staring at it."

Bennie scoffed, throwing her arm out to indicate all of the Deveraux Group. "Honey, you don't have time to day-dream! This is an immense operation. It's amazing that you get as much done as you do!"

Clay was pleased by her remark, and he was not a man

giving to boasting. He could not resist, though, telling her about some of the things that the Deveraux Group was about to undertake. The book division's acquisition of a romance imprint was the perfect tie-in for television movies with scripts based on the books.

"So this time next year, we hope to have several screen-plays optioned and ready for production," he explained. Bennie wanted to know what authors had been approached, if any.

"Well, everything is still in the negotiating stage," Clay said slowly. "There is this one author in particular who is kind of reclusive or something. She doesn't do publicity or signings or anything, and she writes under a pseudonym, so I don't know how cooperative she will be. She's written only a few books, but they have all gone into reprints. If I could get Elise Crittenden on board, I know I would have a winner."

Bennie didn't say anything, just put out her hand for Clay's car keys.

"You don't have to escort me down; I can find my way out of the building. And Clay, honey? You're going to sign Elise Crittenden; don't even worry about it."

Clay was touched by her confidence in him. "That's sweet of you to say, Benita, but even I'm not sure about this one."

Bennie kissed him sweetly and started backing toward the door of his office.

"Oh, you'll sign her, all right. I happen to know her quite well, and she is a sucker for a good-looking man like you."

Clay's jaw dropped. "You know her? How well do you know her?"

Bennie flashed him a feline smile as she slipped out the door. "Intimately. I *am* Elise Crittenden," she said gaily before departing.

Springing that little surprise on Clay was great fun, but he did not let her get away with it. He caught up with her before she got out of the building and demanded an explanation.

"It's quite simple. I always wanted to be a writer. I minored in creative writing with a major in journalism. And a few years ago, I got tired of hearing myself whine about it and sat down and started to write. I've written short stories and articles for magazines under different names, but I like romance writing the best. I can't devote as much time to it as I would like, but writing truly is my passion. And now you have all my guilty secrets, Clay. You, Renee, and my brothers are the only ones who know. Well, my publisher knows. But hey, you're my publisher now, so . . . there!"

Bennie still loved remembering the look of total surprise on Clay's face. She had seen many expressions of ardor and affection on his handsome visage, but that was the first time she had ever seen him dumbfounded. And she had seen him quite a bit over these past couple of months. He had come to Detroit three times; once was the week after the St. Simons trip. The second time was for her birthday on July 1, and he had stayed through the Fourth of July holiday. And once was just because he could not stand to be away from her for another minute. That particular trip was the best, by far. Bennie had no cause for complaint about Clay's level of attentiveness.

The cause of Bennie's panic was the fact that this was the weekend of the gala to celebrate the fiftieth anniversary of WWCC. In addition to the dinner dance at the legendary Roostertail on the Detroit River, there were breakfasts and lunches and golf outings and all manners of activities for the guests. The guests naturally included family and what seemed to be six thousand of her father's most intimate acquaintances. The banquet manager at the Roostertail was a model of efficiency and calm, which helped. Faye and Tina, Bennie's sisters-in-law, pitched in wherever they could, doing things like making reservations and hosting various cocktail parties and such.

Andrew had done as much as he was able, given his

job. Andrew was not just a surgeon—he specialized in reconstructive facial surgery, most often on terribly disfigured children. His career was demanding and consuming, but he was always there for Bennie whenever she called, which was not often. He had arranged for a video to be made of Cochran family movies to use in a special tribute to Big Benny. Adam had designed the programs and coordinated the decorations, and Donnie had planned the entertainment.

Bennie was truly grateful for every bit of help she had received, but the lion's share of the work had fallen on her shoulders. This was the first time that she had undertaken anything so massive, and she was quite sure it would be the last. *InStyle* magazine, as well as *Ebony, Jet,* and a few others would be there to cover the event. Even one of Clay's publications, *Image* magazine, would be there. Not to mention Clay and most of his family. That was the part where Bennie was shaky. What in the devil had made her invite the entire Deveraux family to what could very well turn out to be a debacle? *This could be the worst disaster since the Chicago fire, and I had little enough sense to invite Clay and his family.*

Bennie moaned more loudly than she realized, which caused Renee to look over at her. The two women were at the Roostertail going over the seating chart one more time.

Renee glanced at her friend and said, "Honey, you need to take a massive break from all of this. I booked you for an entire afternoon at the spa for Saturday. You've done all you can do, so relax, can't you?"

Bennie appreciated Renee's concern, but she shook her head all the same.

"I know logically that I have done everything. And the boys have really been wonderful, truly they have. And they're all going to be at the morning celebration thing with Tom Joyner on Friday, which I truly appreciate." Bennie pointed at her temple. "Up here, I know that everything is together." Dramatically, she patted her stomach. "It's down here that hasn't gotten the message."

Renee looked somewhat relieved. "Well, honey, you tell that stomach to get with the program. Now is not the time for queasiness. Okay, after we leave here, what do we do next?"

Bennie consulted her list. "Well, I sent limos to pick up Clay and his family—I thought that was a nice touch. I told Joyce we would be in to pick up our dresses at noon. The cocktail party is set for tonight at Daddy's house. We need to stop by the caterers for tomorrow's brunch at our house and . . . Oh, Lord—I need to be shot in the head. Aunt Ruth will be here in two hours."

Renee joined Bennie in a heartfelt moan. Bennie's aunt Ruth was her late mother's younger sister. *Piece of work* did not even begin to describe her. Aunt Ruth was what was euphemistically referred to as a pistol—like a handgun, she was liable to go off anytime, anyplace, and usually half-cocked, to boot. Everyone loved and feared Aunt Ruth. After her sister's death she resigned her army commission as a nurse and moved in to help bring up her sister's children. She was cranky, lovable, impatient, bossy, and charming, and could drive anyone up the wall in about thirty seconds flat if she chose. She could also charm the birds out of the trees if she took a notion. You just never knew with Aunt Ruth.

"So, Renee. You wanna go pick up Aunt Ruth?"

Renee held up her right hand with the palm and fingers slightly cupped. "Bennie, I'm too tired to slap you, so you just fling your face against my hand, won't you? I love you dearly, and sometimes I love Aunt Ruth, but so help me, God, I am not going to pick her up. Alone in a car with Miss Ruthie May in airport traffic. Unh-unh."

Renee shuddered delicately. Then she brightened.

"Call Donnie and get him to dispatch an underling. Or better yet, get him to go. She always liked him best—make him earn it!"

Bennie laughed out loud and said "Girl, that's why you're my best friend! You got some good ideas! Girl, you got *skills!"* Whipping out her cell phone, she did indeed euchre Donnie into collecting Aunt Ruth.

"Okay, Renee, let's go by the caterer and go get those frocks. It's time for us to pamper *us* for a change."

And with the exception of a very few minor snafus, it was indeed time to take care of Bennie. Bennie had made reservations for Clay's family at the Townsend Hotel, a very plush hotel in downtown Birmingham. With the exception of Clay, of course, who was to stay in the Outhouse. Problems arose when Aunt Ruth assumed that she was staying there. *Jesus. In a house with four guest bedrooms, she makes a beeline for the one place she can't have. In a city where she has relatives with at least twenty guest rooms to go around.* Bennie took it in stride, the way she was taking everything to do with the event. She looked directly into her aunt's eyes and took a deep breath.

"Aunt Ruth, someone else is going to be staying there. You are more than welcome to any of the other rooms, or you can stay with Alan and Faye. Or I can get you a hotel."

Aunt Ruth leaned back on one leg and crossed her arms to survey her niece. There was a vague resemblance between them, although Bennie was quite a bit taller. Ruth Bishop still had a slim figure and her hair had very little gray. It was cut short and stylishly and showed her attractive face to its best advantage. Aunt Ruth was deeply tanned, the result of her incessant globe-trotting. She was just back from an extended stay in Africa. She knew Bennie was being evasive about the Outhouse, but since she felt compelled to do so, there must be a good reason.

One thing about Aunt Ruth: she knew how to pick her fights. Surprisingly docile, she agreed to stay with Alan. But the look she gave Bennie said that it wasn't over yet.

"Oh, that's fine, dear," Aunt Ruth said sweetly. "I'm sure whatever arrangements you made will be just fine. By the way, you look a little peaked. Are you getting enough fiber in your diet?"

Thus Bennie had to endure a lecture on what constipation could do to the complexion as part of her punishment for nearly barring the woman from her home. *God does not love ugly,* Bennie chanted to herself.

Seeing Clay the next day was worth any pain she might suffer from the sharp tongue of Aunt Ruth. When he rang her doorbell on Friday afternoon, Bennie was so relieved she almost cried.

"What are you doing here? How did you get over here?" she asked stupidly. "I was going to come to the hotel and pick you up," she added.

Clay could see that she was frazzled; he put his arms around her and held her tightly for a moment or two before he answered.

"I rented a car. I got Mom settled at the hotel—she loves her suite, by the way—and came over to see if you needed anything. And you do."

Bennie looked up, puzzled. Clay bent his head and gave her a soft, sweet kiss.

"Oh, I did need that." She sighed. She immediately felt better. "Well, let's get your things in the—"

Clay stopped her before she started rattling on. He took her hands and led her over to the sofa in the living room, then pulled her down into his lap.

"Baby, I can get my things later. Right now we're going to sit here for a while so you can wind down."

Bennie did not offer any protest; she laid her head on Clay's shoulder and closed her eyes.

"Okay, that's fine. I'll just sit here for a minute and relax. Then I have to get dressed for the cocktail party"— she yawned—"and . . . and . . ." Her voice trailed off as she fell into a much-needed sleep.

Bennie slept for only about an hour, but it was golden time as far as she was concerned. When she awoke, she was lying on the sofa with a throw over her and Aretha breathing down her neck. The big black cat butted Bennie's forehead affectionately and then strolled off in search of sustenance. Bennie took that as her cue to get up and get dressed for the cocktail party that was being held at her father's house. She was surprisingly well rested after such a brief nap. She ran up the stairs to her suite and began to get ready for the party.

She had just stepped out of the shower when the telephone rang. It was Clay.

"I see you're up already. I was going to be your wake-up call," he said in his deep, wonderful voice.

"Thank you for being thoughtful. And for helping me relax. But I'm good to go now, or I will be as soon as I am dressed," she replied. "Is your mother about ready for us to pick her up?"

Clay hesitated a moment before answering.

Finally he said, "Mom isn't going to come tonight. Angelique arrived unexpectedly and she doesn't feel well, so Mom is going to stay in with her. I hope you don't mind," he added.

Bennie hastened to assure him that it was not a problem at all. She told him that she would be ready in about thirty minutes, and hung up the phone. Still in her robe, Bennie ran upstairs to the third-floor suite that was Renee's domain. She threw open the door without ceremony and said dramatically, "Take me now, Lord. The lovely Angelique is in town." Moaning, she fell across Renee's chaise longue.

Renee was amused.

"Not that spoiled sister of Clay's?" Bennie moaned louder. "Oh, girl, don't even worry about her. Clay's family knows how she is, and they'll keep her away from you. Plus, I haven't personally excoriated anyone in at least two months. Let me worry about the lovely Angelique," she purred.

Bennie brightened considerably. Renee could indeed quell an insurrection with her sharp tongue. So could Bennie, for that matter.

"Renee, I have no idea why I am so antsy over this whole thing. You would think I had never given an affair in my life. I don't know what my problem is—I keep thinking something weird or bizarre is going to happen, and I don't know why."

Renee looked at her friend and shrugged. "Opening-night jitters, honey. How about a glass of wine to relax?"

Bennie agreed wholeheartedly.

"How about two glasses?" She grinned.

Renee was right, Bennie mused. It was just the jitters. Everything was going perfectly. Her father was in seventh heaven, and there had not been the least bit of a snag in any of her well-made plans. Angelique's presence was a surprise, but it wasn't as though Bennie had not invited her. *I just didn't think that she would show up.* The biggest surprise was the fact that Renee and Andrew had decided not to kill each other and were actually going to the celebration together. That one took some getting used to, but as Renee patiently explained, it was a mere formality.

"Marshall is out of town," Renee said, referring to one of her steady escorts. "And neither one of us wants to mess up the seating arrangement by not having an escort. So we're being mature adults, that's all," she finished loftily.

Her sharply raised eyebrow dared Bennie to think anything else. Bennie threw up her hands in a conciliatory gesture.

"Hey, I have nothing to say, other than I'm glad you won't be drawing blood for a change."

They were in the dining room of the big Indian Village house, making a last-minute check of the brunch preparations. Aunt Ruth was happily settled into her room, and the other guests who were staying with Bennie and Renee had also arrived. Both women were wearing white. Renee was in a crisp sundress that made her chocolatey skin glow. Bennie was wearing a linen shirt and slacks with a pair of Italian flats. She looked collected and in control, although someone who knew her well would sense something the least bit off about her. Naturally that person was Clay.

After his morning shower he dressed and joined Bennie and Renee as they awaited the arrival of the guests for brunch. Bennie had seemed to relax at the happy and crowded party the night before, but something wasn't quite right today. Clay pulled her to his side and kissed her on the cheek.

"Everything okay, Peaches?" Bennie nodded with a smile, but Clay wasn't convinced. "Have you eaten?" he asked.

Bennie gave him a look of pure horror. "Ick. No, not yet. I'm not hungry, for some reason," she admitted.

Renee and Clay looked at each other. Bennie, not hungry? Before either of them could insist that she eat, the first guests arrived. From then on, there was not a point at which personal conversation was possible; in no time at all the house and yard were filled with people.

Clay kept his eye on Bennie the rest of the morning to make sure she was all right, and truly she seemed to be fine. She greeted guests and made sure everyone was welcome and served from the sumptuous buffet. She seemed perfectly fine as she introduced his family to her father and his companion, Martha Davis. He lost sight of her as she took his mother, his sister-in-law, Selena, and Vera Jackson on a tour of the house. Someone else, though, had her eye on Clay.

"Well, I think it's time we got to know each other a little better, don't you?"

Clay turned to the source of the voice to find the legendary Aunt Ruth at his elbow. Without waiting for him to speak, Aunt Ruth charged ahead in her forthright manner.

"From the way you have been eating up my niece with your eyes, I would say you are a permanent part of her life. And from the way she has been devouring you, the same goes for her. So we need to get to know each other fairly quickly."

With that remarkable statement, Ruth guided Clay into the sun parlor off the living room, which was deserted at the moment. She sat down on a love seat and indicated that he should do the same. Clay seemed helpless to do otherwise; this woman meant business. She was smiling, however, which boded well for whatever was on her mind. Ruth did not waste any time in getting to the point.

"Clayton, I don't believe in beating around the bush. I can see that there is a very strong connection between you and my niece. I know Benita well enough to know that you would not even be here if this were not a serious relationship. Benita has been wise enough not to squander herself on flirtations and foolishness. Benita is also a fairly good judge of character. If you were a jackass she would have tossed you long before this."

Ruth paused to take a sip of the glass of iced tea in her hand. Clay was more relaxed now—it was clear that Ruth did not intend to issue him some dire warning. He had, in fact, the distinct impression that Ruth might prove to be an ally. Her next words bore that out.

"Clayton, my niece is very special to me. She's very special to this whole family. I don't think she knows just how much she means to all of us. Benita has always put herself last and everyone else first. I thought she was safe when she married Gilbert, but then . . ." Ruth shrugged, a world of eloquence in the gesture. "You never know what life has in store for you. Does Benita ever speak of the time after her mother passed away?"

The abrupt change of topic surprised Clay.

"No. I know her mother died when Benita and Andrew were ten, but that's all, really."

Ruth pursed her lips briefly, and then a look of great sadness came over her face. "My sister, Lillian, was killed in a car accident. No death is pleasant, but there is something so cruel about having a life just snatched away like that. I was on a tour of duty in Southeast Asia, and even with allowances for a family tragedy, it was almost a month before I could get back to the States.

"When I got here, Big Benny was a zombie. When he wasn't drinking, he was at the station, although I don't think he was doing much good there. He kept telling friends and family that everything was fine, he had everything under control, when nothing could have been farther from the truth. Between the two of them, Andrew and Benita were running this house. Benita cooked and cleaned and took care of the younger boys like they were her children. Andrew washed and ironed and did all the outdoor chores."

Ruth leaned back against the love seat and closed her eyes. "I wanted to be terribly angry with Big Benny, but I couldn't be—I knew what he was going through. My sister was a very special woman. In many ways, Benita is just like her." Ruth sighed for a moment, and then continued.

"Even after I moved in, Bennie was still in charge. Donnie was so young when his mother died that he transferred all his affection to Bennie. She bathed him, changed his diapers, and even potty-trained him. Night after night, when she was supposed to be sleeping, she would go to the other children's rooms to check on them and make sure they were covered and sleeping well before she would go back to bed." Ruth shook her head sadly.

"Any childhood Benita had stopped the day my sister died. She and Andrew had always been hell-raisers and mischief-makers; they turned into model children, especially Benita. Everyone in this family became her personal responsibility, and she never shirked what she felt was her duty, not once." Ruth looked directly at Clay for the first time in this recitation. "I suppose you are wondering what this has to do with you," she asked wryly.

But no further explanation was necessary. Clay understood what Ruth was trying to say about Bennie, but she said it anyway.

"Clay, if you care about Benita the way I think you do, take care of her. It's her turn for happiness, and I think she'll have it with you. And regardless of what that selfish old man says or does, don't let this chance slip away for the two of you." Before she could elaborate on the "selfish old man," Bennie appeared with his mother and sister-in-law in tow. That they were having a wonderful time was apparent by the glow on her face.

After the ladies went to admire the garden, Bennie confessed to Clay that she was actually a little hungry. Clay put his arms around her and held her close.

"Baby, if you say you're a *little* hungry, you must be starving. Let's go get you some food before you faint." Kissing him sweetly, Bennie agreed, noticing the odd way he was looking at her.

"What's the matter—do I have something on me?" she questioned, brushing her cheeks with her fingertips. Clay assured her that she did not.

"You look beautiful as always."

Bennie smiled widely.

"Oh, honey, this is nothing. Wait until you see me tonight," she promised. "I'm going to knock your socks off." Clay did not doubt it for a minute.

Clay spent the rest of the afternoon processing the conversation he had had with Ruth. It answered some questions about Bennie and created more. The more he learned about her, the more he admired her. And the more he loved her. Loving Bennie was the most dangerous thing he had ever done, and the most rewarding. He didn't know if he was the right man for her; he probably wasn't the man she deserved, but he knew he would give up his life for her. The only remaining question was how he could convince her to give up everything that she had here in Detroit to be with him in Atlanta.

He glanced around her gracious living room while he waited for her to descend the stairs. Benita's family was here, her career and her home were here. There was not a single thing that he could offer her that she did not already have in abundance, and that she could not provide herself if she desired. *Benita does not need me.* She desired him, she craved him, and she seemed happy with him. But was that going to be enough?

Clay was so deep in thought that he did not hear Bennie until she was almost at the bottom of the stairs. He looked up and the entire world stopped. She was glorious, incandescent. Every time Clay had memorized every feature of her face, every expression, she threw him a curve. He had never seen her looking so incredible.

Bennie was wearing a shimmering gold gown that needed no ornament, other than her beautiful face and form. It clung to her curves and molded her body so that she resembled a golden statue. Her rounded bosom was barely visible in the modestly dipped bodice, but there was no mistaking the lushness of her breasts. The thin straps joined behind her neck and fanned out to form an intricate crisscrossed pattern; other than that, the back of the dress was bare. Perhaps because she was undeniably his, Clay did not resent this provocative dress—he reveled in it. Bennie turned around slowly so that Clay could take in the full effect. The back dipped slightly below her waistline and the slim skirt fanned gently into a demitrain. Her hair was in a style he had never seen; it was arranged in an elaborate updo with a deep wave at her brow. She was positively celestial.

Bennie gave Clay a saucy smile over one shoulder while she drank in his admiration.

"I clean up pretty good, huh?"

Before Clay could answer, Andrew joined them. "You'll do, in a rush," he said dryly. Bennie immediately punched him in the arm.

Faking great pain, Andrew moaned loudly and stopped when Renee floated down the stairs. She was wearing an incredible oyster-white dress with a halter-necked bodice. The top of the dress was handworked with pearl, crystal, and gold beading. The skirt was made of silk chiffon and swirled out above her knees—Renee hated wearing long dresses. Andrew seemed to have trouble breathing—he certainly had lost his ability to speak.

Clay, however, recovered quickly enough to assure both women that they were fabulous. They smiled little feline smiles at each other and sighed together. "Aren't we though?" Renee noticed that Andrew's bow tie was dangling from his fingers and she took it from him. Standing on the stairs so that she was eye level with him, she started putting on the tie. Andrew still had not spoken. Clay took the opportunity to take Bennie into the living room so that he could tell her how lovely she was.

Before he could get started, though, they were interrupted by the appearance of Ceylon Simmons, Bennie's dear friend and a popular singer/comedienne who was not only staying with Bennie; she was part of tonight's entertainment.

"Oh, dear, I'm breaking up a clinch, aren't I?" Ceylon's low, sultry voice was her trademark. She looked genuinely distressed for about a second, then smiled. "Too bad. If I'm alone and lonely tonight, everybody else has to be, too!" Laughing, she introduced herself to Clay.

Then Bennie's cousins from Philadelphia came downstairs, followed by Aunt Ruth, and it was just easier to leave than to try to hack out a moment alone in that mass of people. It was time to depart for the Roostertail, anyway. Everyone else got into limousines, but Clay and Bennie elected to drive her Jaguar. The ride over was mercifully brief, as Clay was about to burst into flame from desire.

"Benita, you are . . . spectacular, baby," he said as he glanced over to the passenger seat. Bennie looked at Clay, so handsome in his custom-made tuxedo, and sighed.

"Clay, you are without a doubt the best-looking man I have ever seen in my life."

Clay snorted, but he was pleased, nonetheless. Although he wished that for once, Bennie would just accept his admiration with a smile and not feel she had to return it. He was about to articulate that thought when they reached their destination.

Further conversation became impossible as Bennie was swept into the maelstrom of activity. In addition to greeting guests and circulating, she was the go-to person for the myriad details of conducting the evening. And what an evening it was. Everyone who was anyone was present: recording stars, politicians, athletes, and tycoons. Even the haughty Angelique, who was making her first appearance of the weekend, was impressed, although she tried to hide it. Of course, when one encountered the mayors of Detroit, Denver, and Atlanta at the same soiree, it was hard to pretend to be jaded. And when she spotted Samuel L. Jackson in conversation with Big Benny, she was definitely impressed.

Clay overheard the little noise that Angelique made, the one that signified her grudging approval. Glancing at his impetuous little sister, he couldn't resist a tease.

"So it's not quite the barn dance you were anticipating, Angel?"

Angelique gave him a sheepish look. Of all people, Clay was the one she never tried to buffalo; he could always see right through her.

"I must admit, this is very nice. For a hick town like Detroit." She couldn't resist getting in one little dig. "And there are some very interesting people here," she added as Jesse Jackson walked past with Martin Sheen. "And some fine men. I wonder who in the world they are," she said, nodding at two tall figures standing nearby.

Clay followed her gaze and chuckled as he realized that Angelique was staring at Adam and Adonis Cochran.

"Those are two of Benita's brothers. Would you like an introduction now or later?"

Angelique's shock was written plainly across her face, but she recovered quickly. Assuring Clay that she could wait for the privilege of meeting Bennie's family, she took herself off, ostensibly to mingle.

As the cocktail hour progressed, Bennie felt some of the tension leaving her body, although her stomach was still too wound up to accept food. Which was a shame, because the catering staff had exceeded her wildest expectations. The hors d'oeuvres included fried zucchini blossoms filled with chevre, grilled shrimp stuffed with crabmeat, and delicate crepes rolled with caviar. Bennie's mouth watered when she looked at the caviar, but she didn't eat a bite of it. Everyone else seemed to be enjoying the wide range of delicacies, though.

The room was bathed in candlelight from the tapers on each table, as well as cleverly designed muted lighting around the room. The decorations were gold and cream and crystal, in keeping with the fiftieth-anniversary theme. In fact, the decorations and ambiance were geared toward the era in which Big Benny had launched WWCC—the 1950s, the larger-than-life, big band, jumpin' and jivin' era.

Uncle Bump was in his element as he got back to his big-band roots to conduct a full jazz orchestra in the mellow music of the era. Later on there would be deejays mixing contemporary music for dancing, as well as musical tributes, but for right now it was fine and mellow. Gold lamé tablecloths with ivory damask overlays looked rich and inviting, as did the beautifully arranged tables with gold charger plates. Each table had a fragrant, heady array of flowers that evoked the ambiance of a posh 1950s supper club, which was of course, the intent. Each chair held a gold gift bag with mementos of the evening—Swiss chocolates in a small Baccarat box, imported cigars for the men, and crystal bottles of fragrance for the ladies, as well as a specially recorded CD, pressed just for this occasion.

The only fly in Bennie's personal ointment was the fact that her father would not let her more than a foot away from him all evening. Every time she would start circulating and conversing with someone it seemed that Big Benny would find her and she would be redirected into his wake as he chatted his way around the ballroom. It was a total relief when it was time for dinner to be served. At least he stayed where he was supposed to for the delightful meal, none of which Bennie could consume. She pushed the food around on her plate for a while, and then gave up all pretense of eating, although the grilled salmon, fresh asparagus, and wild mushroom ragout looked and smelled fabulous. Clay had no problem disposing of his tournedos of beef in béarnaise sauce, although he felt slightly guilty when he saw that Bennie was only sipping water.

"Baby, please calm down. Everything is perfect. The room is beautiful, you're incredible, and everyone is having a wonderful time. Relax, Peaches; you did a wonderful job."

Bennie squeezed his hand tightly under the table. Clay was right; this was a perfect evening. Dennis Archer, the former mayor of Detroit, rose to say a few words about Benny Cochran and his many contributions to Detroit, and to introduce Bennie and Andrew to begin the brief testimonial program. Clay felt his heart swell with pride as he looked at his beloved Benita, so poised and striking as she addressed the congenial group.

Bennie and Andrew resumed their seats as a popular comedian took over as emcee. Warm tributes and anecdotes followed from various celebrities, family friends, and recording artists who attributed much of their success to Big Benny. The most moving moment was when Bennie and Andrew resumed the podium to talk about their father as a man, and not a business icon. The lights were dimmed and the videotape Andrew had made was shown to laughter and applause as it depicted Big Benny's life from the very early days of WWCC to the present. To see him with people like Duke Ellington, Billy Eckstine, and Sarah Vaughan was evidence that he had truly been and still was a true mover and shaker in the industry. To see him with his family proved he was a man.

Clay was touched in ways he could not explain as he looked at clips from Bennie's childhood. He especially loved the ones of Bennie as a tiny girl—it made him long for their children to come. He had to drag himself back to the present when Andrew started talking again.

"Anyone who knows my sister and I well knows that we have a love for fine automobiles. We have a passion for a flashy ride, no question," he said frankly. Which was true—Bennie drove a Jaguar and Andrew's only nod to luxury was his Bentley. Andrew continued: "Well, this is the reason why—our dad never spoiled us. If we wanted something, we had to work for it. And this is the first car that Benita and I ever owned—the Pushme-Pullyu."

The room broke into laughter as the screen showed Bennie and Andrew at sixteen, standing next to the ugliest car in the entire world—a huge, poop-brown Monte Carlo of uncertain age. Andrew further explained that it had a string attached to the windshield wipers because they did not have the money to get them repaired.

"So whenever it rained, you had to roll down the window enough to pull that string and work those wipers. And it was big fun in the wintertime, too."

Bennie started speaking then, expressing the gratitude and love of the family for all their father had done for them.

"Daddy, we appreciated the fact that we didn't have everything handed to us, because we all know the value of hard work and the satisfaction of accomplishment that you experience when you earn your own way. We're all responsible adults because you cared enough about us to raise us responsibly." Her eyes twinkled merrily as she teased, "But Daddy, you didn't have to make us park the Pushme-Pullyu two blocks away from the house. That was kinda cold."

After the laughter died down, Bennie smiled her special smile at her father. "Daddy, the boys have a little surprise for you. They decided that this would be much more eloquent than a speech."

Bennie stepped away from the podium and her big, handsome brothers rose. Standing together at the podium, they surprised everyone with a beautiful a cappella rendition of Boyz II Men's "The End of the Road." The movies of their life continued to roll by on the big screen as they sang, and there were tears in more than a few eyes when they were finished, including Big Benny's.

Finally Andrew introduced their father, to a thunderous standing ovation. Big Benny stood and accepted the outpouring of affection from the crowd. Wiping his eyes, he smiled with joy and pride. When the applause had died down, he began to express his thanks.

"My heart is very full tonight. But before I can fully express that joy, I have to say there was only one thing missing. I didn't get to hear my baby girl sing for me."

Bennie had resumed her seat next to Clay at the head table, so he alone could correctly read the look that flashed across her face, and he alone could feel her turn as rigid as stone. As soon as it had started, though, it was over. As Big Bennie finished his request for a song, Bennie rose graciously and walked over to the orchestra. She turned to Bump and mouthed something, to which he nodded. Smiling, she faced her father and the many guests.

"This one's for you, Daddy," was all she said. The simple, lovely lyrics of "Unforgettable" took on an added beauty when Bennie's magnificent voice caressed each word.

The room was in awe as Bennie finished the song. People who had known Bennie for years had no idea that she could sing like that, and people in the music industry were shocked that she wasn't making a living with her voice. And to top it all off, she simply glowed in the soft spotlight. Clay was totally undone, although he tried hard to hide it. By the time Bennie finished, gracefully blowing a kiss to her father, there wasn't a dry eye in the house, including his. The evening had been in all ways a total triumph, although from Bennie's carefully inexpressive face, you might have thought she was attending a lecture on the history of lint instead of listening to her father's retirement speech.

Big Benny was in his glory now, recounting the humble beginnings of WWCC, and his trials and triumphs along the way. He made special note of friends and allies on his road to success, and took the time to thank many by name and anecdote. He publicly thanked Ruth for helping to raise his children after the death of his wife. He also introduced his lovely fiancée, Martha, thanking her for her love and patience.

"And in conclusion, I have to thank one other person without whom I would not be here today. For the past ten years, she has been WWCC. Without her strength, her wisdom, and her expertise, Cochran Communications would not be what it is today. Every man needs to know that the seeds he planted will yield a crop that will continue to grow in the generations to come. That's all any man really wants—continuity. To know that his work will go on after he passes on," Benny intoned.

He looked out over the audience, then looked at his family arranged on either side of the podium before concluding. "It gives me immense pride and pleasure to know that my legacy will continue into the next millennium. And even greater pleasure to know that the person who has contributed the most will be solely responsible for making that happen. I could not retire today if I did not know this." He raised a glass of champagne and called for a toast. "To the new chief executive officer of Cochran Communications, my daughter, Andrea Benita Cochran."

The rest of the evening was a blur of sensation for Clay. He felt as though he had been smacked in the head with a grappling hook. He knew abstractly that Bennie was the logical successor to her father, but hearing it announced like that had been an unpleasant jolt to his system. It was as though all his worst suspicions had been confirmed. There was no way that Bennie was just going to waltz away from Detroit and all of her responsibilities—no matter how much he wanted it to be otherwise, they were doomed to the relationship that they had now.

Clay was so immersed in his muddled thinking that he did not immediately notice that Bennie had withdrawn from everything that was going on around her. She had a placid, fixed smile on her face and seemed totally disconnected from the events at hand. When yet another cheery person started pumping her hand and offering her congratulations, it finally dawned on Clay that Bennie had retreated into herself and was not really reacting to anything. Waiting until her admirer had left, he put his arm around her and spoke into her ear. "Benita, what is it? Are you not feeling well? Do you want to leave?"

Bennie reacted at last.

"Yes! Clay, get me out of here, please!"

Clay heard the underlying panic and got Bennie out of the building and into the car as fast as humanly possible. They drove directly back to her house, and she leaped out of the car like a scalded cat, not even waiting for Clay to open the door. Instead of going into the house, Bennie paced back and forth in the backyard. She was obviously upset and agitated, although Clay had no clue as to why.

"Benita, baby, what is the matter? Why are you so upset?" he asked, mystified.

Bennie did not answer him directly for a moment.

"Clay, you don't even know what was going on tonight, do you?" she asked. "You have no idea how manipulative and conniving my father can be." She stopped pacing then and turned to face Clay. "This evening was not supposed to be about me, nor was it supposed to be my damned musical debut. That's just my father's way of keeping me under his thumb. Like a damned performing monkey or something."

Clay said nothing. He thought that everything tonight was perfectly appropriate, but he wasn't about to say so— Bennie was too angry and distraught.

"My father has known for some time that I have no intention of being CEO of Cochran Communications. I've had enough of Cochran Communications, of the Cochran Foundation, and especially of WWCC. He expects me to give up my life to his damned legacy just because he wants it that way. He wants everything in my life to be put on hold just because it's convenient for him," she spat. "Well, it's not convenient for *me!* Or for Donnie. I'm entitled to have a life of my own, a life away from here. He doesn't care about that. He's never known what I wanted and he's never cared either! Why can't I have what *I* want for a change?" It was a cry of anguish straight from her heart.

Bennie was truly worked up now. She had resume pacing with a vengeance and was also tearing loose her elaborate hairstyle. Tears were running freely down her face as she tossed hairpins aside and shook out the curls and waves so that her hair hung free and wild over her shoulders. Clay could not stand it anymore. He grasped her shoulders to make her stop pacing and pulled her close to him. Kissing her damp cheeks, he stroked her hair and murmured softly to ease her agitation.

"It's okay, Peaches. Everything will be fine, baby. What do you want? Tell me what would make you happy," he said.

Bennie looked up at him with tears starring her lashes.

"Do you really want to know?" she said softly. "I'll tell you what I want. I want to make love to you without having to get on a plane to do it. I want Donnie to take over the business. I want to write." She stroked his face and kissed him softly before continuing. "I don't want to be away from you anymore. I'm tired of being here when you're in Atlanta. I want to be with you every day, every morning and every night. Clay, I want to have your babies, lots of them." She paused for a minute. "You know, I thought I was pregnant for a few days. I found out last week that I wasn't and I cried. I actually cried, Clay, because I would have been so happy to be making a baby with you."

Before Clay could accept what he was hearing, Bennie wound her arms around his neck.

"Clay, I love you so much that when I'm not with you it feels like I'm dead inside. And when I see you I feel like someone just handed me the world. Clay, don't make me stay here alone anymore. I want to be with you forever," she said on a sob.

Clay was too overcome with love to speak. All he could do was hold on to Bennie as tightly as she was holding him. Gradually, the enormity of what Bennie had confessed was sinking in. *She loves me. She wants to marry me.* Clay had no idea what he had done to deserve this, but he was not about to question the Lord's bounty now that he had it.

First he kissed her, a long, slow, drugging kiss that quieted both of them on the surface and set a raging fire underneath.

"Baby, let's get out of the backyard. This is not the place to celebrate," he said, smiling down at her. Bennie let him take her hand and lead her up to the Outhouse. He sat her down on the sofa, then fetched something out of his suitcase. Sitting down beside her, he took both of her hands in his.

"Benita, I know this has been an emotional night for you, and I guess a gentleman would wait for a time when you were more composed to do this. But I am a man who loves you passionately and with all my heart, and I am not letting this moment get away from me . . . from us." Clay opened a small box and took out a ring. Slipping it on her finger, he said quietly, "Benita, I didn't know how I was going to convince you to marry me, I just knew that my life was incomplete before I met you, and since I found you I have been the happiest I have ever been. When I am away from you everything in here stops," he said, touching his heart. "When you're with me, I'm alive again."

Bennie's tears of joy were running unchecked down her face, but she looked radiant. Clay kissed the tears away and looked into her eyes.

"Marry me, Benita."

Bennie touched his face and looked at him with eyes of love.

"Yes, Clay," she said softly.

She was kissing him with great fervor when it occurred to her that she hadn't actually looked at her ring. She broke off the kiss and settled into his arms to look at what he had slipped on her finger. "Wow," was all she could muster.

It was a flawless five-carat oval canary diamond surrounded by perfect white diamonds in a Tiffany setting of yellow gold. Clay assured her that if she didn't like it, they could get whatever she wanted. Bennie looked at him as if he were mad.

"Oh, sweetheart, I love it! And I love you," she added. "You have no idea how much I have been wanting to tell you that," she said. "I thought I was going to explode, I wanted to tell you so badly."

Clay was forestalled from comment by the appearance of Aretha. She had the uncanny ability to insinuate herself into the most private of situations at the oddest times. This time, though, Bennie had news for her.

"Look, Aretha!" she said, waving the ring in front of the nosy feline. "We're getting married! And we're moving to Atlanta," she finished happily.

Clay looked at Bennie's flushed, radiant face, with her mussed hair and tearstained cheeks. He knew that he would move heaven and earth to keep her happy, but he could not help feeling a slight twinge of conscience. Bennie had laid her soul bare tonight, but had he really been fair to her? Had he unconsciously been as manipulative as Big Benny in getting her to expose her heart to him? Just then Bennie leaned over and kissed him on both cheeks.

"Clay, you have no idea how happy we're going to be. We're going to have a wonderful life. And we're going to have a houseful of beautiful babies. And I am going to love you with all I have from now until the day I die. I love you with all my heart, Clayton Arlington Deveraux." She kissed him softly on the lips and was about to kiss him some more, when her face got a familiar look. "Clay, I'm hungry. I haven't eaten in, like, two days!" she exclaimed.

Clay laughed and his heart felt light once more. If Bennie was hungry, everything was all right again. He stood up and pulled Bennie into his arms. Everything was going to be fine.

Eight

And even with such a tumultuous start, things did go amazingly well. The cap on the evening of the celebration was when Bennie and Clay were finally walking across the lawn to the main house. They encountered Andrew, who was leaving by the back door with an ice pack on his eye and a large quantity of Renee's lipstick on his mouth.

"Don't ask," were his only words.

Bennie held up her left hand by way of greeting—it seemed fitting that her twin brother be the first to know her momentous news.

Andrew wasted no time in congratulating Clay and offering Benita his best wishes. He looked the two of them over and smiled.

"You two are going to have a good life. I'm very, very happy for you, Benita. Clay, you take care of my sister, and let her take care of you." After a moment's reflection he ventured, "When are you telling Pop?"

Bennie confirmed that she and Clay would make an announcement the next day, before his family went back to Atlanta.

"If you want me for moral support, just let me know, Benita. And don't worry about tonight—after the talk we all had, Donnie is fine with what Pop said. You just be happy."

Realizing that the makeshift ice pack was starting to drip down his neck, Andrew stated that he had to go home before he froze his head. He kissed Bennie on the temple, and gave Clay a tight hug.

"That little pal of yours has a mean left hook," he added as he ambled away.

Clay turned to Bennie and asked, "What talk?"

Bennie explained that she had had a sit-down meeting with her brothers when it became apparent that Big Benny was not willing to let Bennie go from the family business without a struggle.

"We all know how determined Daddy can be when he wants his own way, and that no trick is too low for him to try. So I laid my cards on the table. I am more than willing to continue to train Donnie, and to handle the foundation business, but the day-to-day operation of Cochran Communications is not going to be my bailiwick—it's going to be Donnie's. And Alan and Andre are going to take a more active part in the business, too.

"Basically, we wanted to be able to present a united front when and if it came down to it, and it has. Daddy likes having the first word, the last word, and all the words in between, but that simply cannot be this time. I am going to be Mrs. Clayton Arlington Deveraux, for one thing, and I have a whole new life ahead of me, for another."

By this time they were in the kitchen, scrounging for something to eat, since Bennie's appetite had come roaring back like a rampaging wildebeest. Renee came into the kitchen wearing lounging pajamas and an extremely complicated expression. She didn't say anything; she reached into the refrigerator and withdrew a large bottle of mineral water.

She took a large, defiant swallow straight from the bottle and said testily, "I suppose you'd like to know why I engaged into hand-to-hand combat with Andrew."

"No," Bennie said mildly. "I would like to know if you're interested in being my maid of honor."

Renee's eyes, which had been dark and flinty, immediately got golden and watery from emotion. She looked from Clay's smiling face to Bennie's and burst into tears.

"Oh, honey, I'm so happy! Oh, of course I'll be your maid of honor! Hell, I'll be your flower girl!" When she saw the huge ring on Bennie's finger she almost swooned.

"My Lord, Clay! How long have you been casually hauling this thing around, waiting for the right moment?" she demanded.

Bennie turned quizzical eyes to Clay also—how long *had* he had the ring in his possession?

"A while," was all he would say.

It didn't matter—this was a time for celebrating, not interrogation. Like Andrew, Renee wondered about telling Big Benny on the morrow. Clay and Bennie were not the least concerned.

"Renee, you know how he is. At best he'll be civil and courtly while he's trying to think up a way to get over on me. At worst he'll blow a gasket. But nothing is going to change the fact that Clay and I are getting married," she said firmly. Renee demanded particulars, like when and where.

Bennie's vote was for Las Vegas the next day, but Clay would not hear of it. He actually wanted a wedding. Bennie had tried protesting when they were still in the Outhouse. She had pointed out to him that they weren't exactly kids and that she had been married before. Clay had listened to all her arguments patiently without saying a word.

"But Benita, I've never been married. I'd really like a real wedding ceremony," he said simply. Bennie looked bemused at the quiet longing in Clay's voice. Pressing his advantage, he asked, "What kind of wedding did you have with Gilbert?" Bennie admitted that they had gotten married at the courthouse in front of a judge friend of Gilbert's.

"It was strictly no-frills because we had no money and we simply weren't interested in a big wedding, anyway."

What she did not say was that Big Benny had made his disapproval so obvious that it would not have been a traditional ceremony in any case. At least not when it came to the father of the bride escorting his daughter down the aisle.

Clay, seeing that Bennie was lost in thought, drove home his final argument.

"So you really haven't had a wedding, either. At least say you'll think about it, Peaches. I would love to see you walking toward me in a beautiful dress. . . ."

Bennie had stopped listening to Clay then. *A beautiful dress? He means a real, honest-to-goodness wedding with flowers and stuff.*

"Clay, let's not decide right this minute, okay? Because you know you can talk me into anything. Let's get something to eat before we make any more life-altering decisions."

And she proceeded to drag him out of the apartment to the main house, where they had encountered Andrew and Renee.

Bennie mulled over their earlier conversation while she was making a roast beef sandwich. As she was laying lettuce leaves on rye bread, she looked up at her handsome Clay, who was chatting with Renee. Bennie was so overcome with love for him that she couldn't stand it.

"Okay, if you want a wedding, we'll have one. But as soon as possible. Definitely before your birthday," she said with finality.

Clay smiled with pure happiness. It was the second week of August, and his birthday was in November. In a very few weeks, he and Bennie would be man and wife.

"I can't say that I am completely surprised by this. But I have to say that I think this decision is a little precipitous, if not downright hasty."

Benny put down his cup of coffee and looked at his daughter and the man she had just told him she was going to marry. They were seated in the family room of his son Alan's Grosse Pointe home, away from the commotion of the barbecue that was taking place in the backyard. Clay and Bennie were seated on the sofa with Martha, Benny's fiancée. Big Benny was seated in a huge wing chair across from them.

He spoke in a carefully neutral, measured voice designed to give away nothing. He could have been a commentator on *Meet the Press* analyzing an international incident, he was so calm. Luckily, Martha Davis was more ebullient.

"Oh, for goodness' sake, Ben, they're in love! Why on earth should they wait? They aren't children and they know what they want. Not everyone has to be together for ten years before deciding to marry, you know."

The last remark was a pointed one, since that was how long Martha had been keeping company with Big Bennie. She shot him a look of pure exasperation.

Martha Davis was a vivacious, charming woman who ran a travel service that specialized in European and African tour packages for mature groups. She was often out of the country for weeks at a time, so it wasn't as though she sat around twiddling her thumbs waiting for Ben to grace her with his presence. In truth, she had kept Ben waiting quite a while before making a commitment of any kind to him. She had actually given Big Benny quite a few bad moments before accepting him as her main beau—Martha's dance card was always full.

Martha knew exactly what she was getting with Andrew Bernard Cochran—she did not kid herself in the least. She knew that he was stubborn, paternalistic, demanding, and bossy, but she could handle all of that. Big Benny was also generous, caring, and sweet, and he genuinely meant no harm. He really did think that he knew what was best for everyone, especially his only daughter.

Now Martha looked at him with a warning in her eyes. She knew how possessive Benny was with his only daughter, and she knew that if he did not tread lightly, he would be the loser. Directing her attention to Bennie and Clay, she reinforced her earlier words of joy. "Well, I couldn't be happier for the two of you. When is the wedding going to take place?"

Bennie smiled at her stepmother-to-be and squeezed her hand.

"October. I'll have a definite date when I contact the church tomorrow. I should be able to get a Saturday—October weddings aren't that popular. But that doesn't leave a lot of time to get ready."

Martha assured her that she would be more than happy to help Bennie plan the wedding. Throughout this exchange, Big Benny remained silent, sitting like a potentate surveying his subjects.

"Martha, could you excuse us for a moment? I'd like to speak with Benita and Clay alone for a moment," he said quietly.

Martha couldn't quite disguise her trepidation—what was Benny going to say to the couple that he did not want her to hear?

Bennie's words echoed her thoughts: "Daddy, Martha is going to be your wife, just like Clay is going to be my husband. I don't see why she can't be privy to anything you have to say to us."

It was like a tennis match. Game, set, and match to Bennie, who had returned every volley lobbed by her wily father. But Big Benny was not through.

In the same silky, civilized voice, he said, "Well, I am sure you won't mind if I speak to my future son-in-law alone. We need to have that traditional little talk," he added jovially.

Clay had not spoken much since Bennie had told her father that they were getting married. He could see from the older man's gestures and expressions that despite the little show he was putting on, he was extremely displeased with this turn of events. *Fine, if he wants a showdown, he can have it. And then Benita and I can get on with our lives.* He harbored no ill will toward Big Benny; he had a lot of respect and even affection for him. But the idea that anything her father could say or do would keep him from Benita was ludicrous, and it was best to get it over with as soon as possible.

Clay took Bennie's hand and said, "Why don't you and Martha join the others? We'll be out in a minute," he assured her.

He rose, pulling her up and kissing her on the cheek. Repeating the action with Martha, he waited until the women had left before resuming his place on the sofa.

As the two women joined the various family and friends gathered in Alan's spacious backyard, Martha couldn't help but look over her shoulder with a look of fear in her eyes.

"I hope that Ben doesn't jump salty with your Clay, dear. You know how your father can be," she fretted.

Bennie draped an arm around Martha's shoulders.

"It will be fine, Martha. Clay is not intimidated by anyone. And Daddy hates to lose, so he's only going to go so far. He thinks he's won only when he draws blood, and that will *not* happen with Clay. So he'll back off rather than lose face. The worse that will happen is that Faye'll have to replace the carpet after the pissing match, and that's about it," she said confidently.

The two women looked at each other for a moment and burst out laughing. Their laughter blended into the sounds of festivity that emanated from the various groups around the lawn. Marcus and Vera were deep in conversation with Bennie's other sister-in-law, Faye, and her husband, Alan. Clay's brother Malcolm and his wife, Selena, were chatting with Tina and Andre, comparing stories of their respective children. And most interestingly, Bump Williams was sitting in a quiet corner with Clay's mother, Lillian. They were sharing an old-fashioned glider with an awning, and talking about old times.

They had known each other for years and years, having grown up in the same Louisiana parish. They had in fact been childhood sweethearts until the dashing Clay Deveraux Sr. had stolen her away. Last night at the celebration had been the first time they had seen each other or spoken at length in years. And Bump was not about to let this opportunity slip away.

"Lillian, I'm getting old. And so are you, dear," he added kindly.

Lillian took umbrage at that remark. "Bill Williams, I am only fifty-five years old, and you know it. And you're only a few years older than I am. I don't know about *you* feeling old, but *I* am in my prime!" she snapped, but she was laughing as she spoke.

Bump brightened up at her words.

"Sweetheart, I'm glad to hear you say that. What I was going to say before you went off on your little tangent is that I am getting too old to be pining away after you. Lillian, I have been in love with you since you were twelve years old. You married Deveraux, and I got married after I realized I couldn't have you. Your husband has been gone for a long time, and my Anna has been gone for three years now." He reached over to take her hand. Leaning toward her with a look of utter sincerity and love, he asked, "Now what are we going to do about this?"

Lillian looked at his hand clasping hers for a long moment before she looked him in the eyes.

Raising her other hand to his cheek, she said softly, "Well, I guess you'll have to come to Atlanta for a visit."

Bump kissed her on the cheek and smiled a satisfied smile before saying, "Well, all right then."

Everything was idyllic in the sunny yard, with friends and family getting to know one another and enjoying good food, good conversation, and the fabulous weather. Of course, to look at Angelique was to dispute one's eyes. If the look on her face was to be believed, the happy gathering was a witch's coven. Donnie did not look much better. He had just returned from taking Angelique for a ride around the city, showing her some of the beautiful neighborhoods in Detroit.

He pulled Bennie to the side and said, "Good God, that girl is a piece of work! How one person can be so pretty on the outside and so ugly on the inside is beyond me, but from now on I am staying the hell away from Evilene." Donnie finished with a theatrical shudder.

Bennie smiled sympathetically and squeezed his arm. "That may not be possible sweetie—she's going to be my sister-in-law."

Donnie's eyes got big as he processed that bit of information. "Damn, Benita. I like Clay a lot, I do. I think you two are meant for each other. I'm very happy," he said, hugging her tightly. "But can't he put Evilene up for adoption or something? Or have her put to sleep?"

Bennie hugged Donnie for a long moment.

His eyes scanned the yard and he asked, "Well, where is Clay? Have you told everyone yet?"

Bennie made a face.

"He's having some kind of 'man talk' with Daddy even as we speak. And no, we have not made an announcement yet because, well, you know Daddy. So as soon as the little chat is over—"

"Assuming there will be enough left of Clay to marry," Donnie interrupted.

Bennie just smiled.

"Oh, honey, do not underestimate my man. Daddy has met his match at last," she said confidently.

Bennie was both right and wrong about what was transpiring in the house between Clay and her father. As soon as the two women left the room, all pretense of civility left Big Benny. The first words out of his mouth made it plain that this was not going to be a pleasant chat.

"Is my daughter knocked up?" he said in a growl.

Clay leaped to his feet with the speed of a jungle cat.

"I don't care who you are," he said in a low, lethal tone of voice, "do not ever presume that you can disrespect Benita in that fashion. She is not at this moment carrying my child, but when she does it will be a private matter that will concern you the least of all of us. Do I make myself clear?"

Had Benny been in a better frame of mind, Clay's protective instincts would have roused his admiration. As it was, his wrath only fueled Benny's fire.

"A private matter?" he spat. "Boy, that's my only daughter you're talking about. There's nothing too private for a father and his daughter. I'll be damned if you're going to drag my daughter off somewhere and have her having babies and me not be involved with my grandchildren. Private matter, my ass, boy, this is my blood you're talking about."

Clay was too well schooled in matter of multimillion-dollar deals to let Benny distract him with misplaced emotions. Adopting his most respectful face, the one he reserved for most of his Pacific Rim dealings, Clay let Benny fume for a minute or two, then turned on his voice of reason.

Resuming his seat he said smoothly, "Mr. Cochran, your concern for Benita is certainly admirable and natural. Let me assure you that you will never have cause to trouble yourself over the well-being of your daughter after we are married. I intend to spend the rest of my life making sure that Benita and our children have everything they could possibly need, want, or desire, and I have the means to do so. There will not ever be a time when Benita will have cause to regret this marriage. I would hope that after you have had time to think about the situation we will have your full support."

For just a moment, Clay's carefully polished veneer slipped and the ruthlessness that was a part of his business life surfaced.

"I would hate to think that any of Benita's family was not going to be an integral part of our future, but you see," he said calmly, lowering his already deep voice, "I cannot allow Benita a moment of unhappiness over anything or anyone."

Benny's power of speech left him for a moment. Clay had actually threatened, in so many words, to keep Benny out of his own daughter's life if he did not toe the line, but he didn't care.

"Boy, I don't think you know who you're fooling with here. If you don't know, you'd better ask somebody."

It was Benny's turn to stand up and look down at Clay with all the fury he could muster.

Clay let him have his moment, then rose to his full height, which exceeded Big Benny's by a few inches.

Still playing "good cop," Clay said softly, "Mr. Cochran, it's really not necessary—your reputation as a devoted father and family man is richly deserved. So is your legendary business acumen. I know you to be a man of good judgment and love for his family—a man who above everything else wants his daughter's happiness as much as I do."

Benny continued to glare at Clay for almost a full minute before seeming to retreat. Then, as though the last few tension-filled minutes had not happened, he asked calmly when they planned to make an announcement. Clay knew how to win graciously.

"Well, since we're all here, how about now? Let me go get Benita and we'll meet you outside."

Benny nodded as Clay left the room. Benny immediately went to the telephone on the credenza near the entryway and punched in a number he had long committed to memory.

"It's me. I have a job for you," he barked. In a few minutes, he laid the phone in its cradle. *Just who does that arrogant Creole bastard think he's dealing with?*

Bennie had several occasions to rethink her decision to have a wedding over the next few weeks. The dress was certainly not a problem—the ever-intrepid Joyce was willing to drop everything and design the perfect dress for Bennie.

"Joyce, I don't know what to tell you. I want to look stunning, of course. But you know I hate froufrou stuff, because it's just not me. So no lace, no sequins, no beads, and no ruffles. And no satin or taffeta, please! Something simple, like Vera Wang, but sexier. I definitely want to look sexy," she added. "And certainly not snow white—I know that everything goes these days, but honey, lightning would strike the church if I put on a white gown."

Joyce took in these directives without any protest—she had an unerring eye for design, and she had been making Bennie's clothes for so long that she knew instinctively what would suit her. As for the number of bridesmaids and their dresses, that was another question. Renee was, of course, the maid of honor. Faye and Tina were the bridesmaids, along with Selena. The wild card was Angelique. Bennie had hesitated about asking Angelique, since their few encounters had not been the sort that led to lasting friendship. But since Clay had all four of his brothers standing up for him, plus Bryant Porter as the best man, she needed five women. And she did not want Angelique to feel left out, despite her behavior at the announcement of the engagement.

Every time Bennie thought of that day she was amazed that she had gotten through it without knocking the young woman silly. Clay had joined her in the yard of Alan's house, and nothing in his attitude had indicated that he and Big Benny had just had an unpleasant incident.

"Come on, Peaches, it's time to let everyone in on our surprise," was all he had said.

Benny was at his most charming as he told friends and family that Clay and Benita had decided to tie the knot. There were tears of joy and happiness all around, especially from Lillian and Aunt Ruth. No one had anything but the sweetest of words for the happy, joyous couple, except dear Angelique.

To say she was caught off guard was like saying that World War II had been war games. Her mouth flew open, and the sultry posture she had been affecting on a lounge chair went south as she struggled to get up and the entire chair rolled over on top of her. Covered with the iced tea that she had spilled all over her linen outfit, she stammered something unintelligible and certainly uncomplimentary.

Bennie's nephews found the spectacle quite amusing and basically laughed their little butts off right in front of her. Angelique then scrambled to her feet and stalked into the house, muttering something about "country-ass hicks trying to put on a show."

Bennie's sympathetic heart made her race after her young future in-law to offer her comfort and aid. Not surprisingly, Angelique rounded on her and showed Bennie the very ugliest side of her personality.

"I don't know who the hell you think you are, but if you think you have a prayer of keeping a man like my brother, you can think again, Miss High-and-mighty. He has never been with a big, overgrown heifer like you, and what he sees in you other than the novelty is beyond me," she hissed.

Although she had been put sorely to the test, Bennie's sympathy did not dissipate—it relocated itself. This was clearly a very unhappy young woman, but her problems were way beyond what Bennie could handle. *Prozac, followed by a long course of psychotherapy,* was Bennie's first thought, but one she did not voice. Voices behind her alerted Bennie to the fact that they were about to be joined by Clay's mother, and Bennie did not want Lillian embarrassed in any way. So she quietly withdrew from the scene, making a mental note to avoid Angelique as much as possible.

Bennie sighed as she shuffled dutifully through catering menus. She still felt that asking Angelique was the right thing to do, yet she wasn't completely happy with her decision. She had too many other things on her mind. Color schemes, flowers, food, music, moving, business—everything swirled together in a mad mass. Thank God for Ruth, Martha, and Lillian—she would have been a nervous wreck had it not been for those stalwart women.

Ruth, that military genius, was taking charge of the moving issue. The things that Bennie had decided to take with her were being weighed, measured, packed, and whatever else was necessary. Martha was taking charge of the wedding itself, once Bennie decided on bronze as a suitable color for attendants in a fall wedding. Matters of music were left to Uncle Bump and Ceylon, who was taking time off from a tour to sing at her old friend's wedding. And Lillian, bless her, was in charge of the reception and the engagement party.

Lillian was beyond thrilled to be assisting. Malcolm and Selena had eloped with not a word to anyone, and it did not look like Angelique would ever marry, she was so headstrong. And as for her second-oldest son, Malcolm's twin, Martin, there was no possible way that he would ever remarry after the fiasco of his first marriage. So Lillian got to indulge all her wedding fantasies with this affair. Plus, Bennie was just what she had always wanted in a daughter—someone who was sweet, kind, accomplished, and clearly devoted to her son.

Bennie gave up looking at the menus and beseeched Lillian to put anything she wanted on the menu.

"As long as it's sit-down, I don't care what it is. I just hate the looks of desperation people get in serving lines," she said.

Bennie was willing to be cooperative about almost anything now, because she had bucked so many other rules. She refused to register for gifts anywhere.

"Oh, Lord, no! We have too much stuff as it is. Can't we just suggest that people make a donation to charity or something?"

She wasn't too thrilled about showers for the same reason.

"With the money we make, it's obscene for people to have to buy us gifts," she insisted.

And as for certain wedding traditions, she wasn't having any of it.

"Jump a broom? Not on the longest day I live will I jump a broom in public in high heels. I'd look like an idiot and fall flat on my face!"

Despite all her protestations and lamentations, Bennie was a happy bride-to-be. The only tradition she upheld was the one that was driving Clay mad—absolutely no intimacy before the wedding. Clay's reaction, when she made this announcement, was priceless.

"Oh, damn, Peaches, you've got to be joking! We barely see each other as it is, and you're going to put me on lockdown for, like, *three months?* That is cruel and unusual punishment, baby. That is so wrong."

Bennie laughed a seductive laugh designed to torture Clay to the limit. Luckily, they were on the telephone and not face-to-face when she told him; she had no doubt that he would have her naked and happy within minutes.

"Clay, look at it this way—when we have our wedding night it will be a real celebration in every sense of the word. It'll be fresh, new, and exciting because we will have been apart for so long," she purred.

Clay did not try to hide his frustration.

"This is payback, right? You're paying me back for wanting this wedding. Okay, let's call it off. Let's go to Vegas tonight and get married and get on with our lives. You were right; I was wrong."

Bennie laughed again.

"No, baby, I'm thanking you, not punishing you. This is going to be the most beautiful day of our lives. And our wedding night is going to be the most passionate, the most sensual night either one of us has ever experienced."

Clay was slightly mollified, but he had to get in the last word: "Peaches, every time I'm with you I feel like that. The fact that we will be man and wife will make it sweeter, but nothing could make it better."

The simple statement brought tears to Bennie's eyes. She reminded Clay that they would see each other over the weekend in Atlanta. Lillian was hosting an engagement party for them, and Bennie was anticipating and dreading it at the same time.

She was sure that Lillian would host a lovely party, but she was not sure about her father's behavior. Or even if he would appear. She and Benny had had their own little Gulf War–like set-to a few days ago, and like Desert Storm before it, the total sum of the destruction had not yet been measured. Big Benny had been so solicitous, so much the endearing father over the past few weeks that Bennie was about to be driven out of her mind. She confided in Renee about the situation.

"Ne-ne, it's downright bizarre. It's like Don King playing *Father Knows Best*," she said with a shudder. "It's creepy." Renee started to brush away her concerns when Bennie grabbed her arm to emphasize her point. "Renee— he's been calling me Princess and Kitten'. I'm telling you, he's turned into this . . . this Stepford dad. He's up to something," Bennie said darkly.

Renee had to agree. Benny called his daughter things like Slim, Red, and Sporty—syrupy endearments were not in his vocabulary.

"I'm afraid you're right, honey. Big Daddy is up to something, so just be on your guard. He'll either ambush you, kidnap you, or fake a heart attack," counseled Renee. "Just be ready for him."

But nothing could truly prepare Bennie for her father's course of action. He had summoned her to the house in Palmer Park, ostensibly for dinner. This was something he had done quite often as of late, so her radar was not up. When Benny pulled out a huge dossier on the Deveraux family, Bennie was devastated—not because of whatever was in the folders, but because of her father's chicanery.

"Daddy, how could you? How could you do this?" she demanded. "Don't you want me to be happy?"

Benny did not even cringe at the pain in his daughter's voice—he was too determined to convince her to leave Clay.

"Baby, you need to know what is in those folders. You need to know more about the man that you claim to love."

With the help of the private investigator that he kept on retainer, Big Benny had discovered some interesting things about Clay's father—namely that the man had been a womanizer who had died of a heart attack in the arms of his mistress in California. The woman was a lover of long standing, and was rumored to have a child by Clay Deveraux Sr.

She was the wife of a prominent businessman in Los Angeles, and the fact that he did not want publicity had made it relatively easy for the Clay, who was then twenty-one, to make it look as though his father had succumbed in his hotel. No one, it seemed, other than the cuckolded husband, the woman, and Clay, knew anything about the whole sordid mess. Benny might not have found out, except the woman was herself a prominent socialite and was about to write a tell-all book to celebrate her newly acquired sobriety.

Benny told all of this to his daughter in rapid, clipped sentences, rushing so that he could get to the punch line: "You see, Bennie, he's not good enough for you. Why would you want to tie yourself to a man who could keep that kind of smut under wraps? It's all going to come out sooner or later, and everyone will know him for the liar he is. You can't possibly want to marry him now," he finished triumphantly.

Her eyes filled with tears as she looked at her father. Bennie could not believe what she had just heard. How could she know so little of the man whom she loved so dearly?

"Daddy . . ." Her voice faltered, then grew strong. "Daddy, that was a lousy, stinking thing to do. I can't believe that you would stoop so low as to dig around in Clay's family history to come up with something so inconsequential and then throw it in my face. So his father was a player—well, so was mine, from what I hear." Bennie paused at the stricken look on her father's face. "Oh, Daddy, please—did you think I was deaf, dumb, *and* stupid? I have no illusions about you—especially now. Now I know what you are capable of to get what you want. I just don't know why you want it.

"Why am I not entitled to have a normal life? For twenty years I have been in bondage to this family and to the damned company. If this family was General Motors I could retire with a pension by now! Well, pension or no pension, I am retiring. Daddy, you cannot—*cannot*—keep me from spending the rest of my life with Clay. I have paid enough. I can not give you any more of me—I have to belong to myself now. And to my husband."

During all this time, Bennie had not raised her voice and her father had not moved a muscle. She took the sheaf of papers that he had shoved at her and threw them across the room, where they scattered silently. Bennie faced him for a long, long moment.

"Daddy, I sincerely hope that was your trump card. Because if you try anything else on me, if you even think about something ugly in connection with Clay, you will never lay eyes on me again, and I mean that. And factor this into the loop while you're at it: I have several brothers and a godfather, all of whom will be more than happy to walk me down the aisle. So I'd watch my salt and cholesterol intake, if I were you. Stay healthy, because this wedding is taking place on schedule with or without you. And no, I am not going to tell Clay about this little charade, because I don't want him to know what he's marrying into."

Bennie rose to leave, but before she did she looked her father full in the face. "I'm really disappointed in you, Daddy," was all she said before going.

If Bennie had not been so sure of the love she and Clay shared, she might have caved in when her father had produced his little catalog of filth. Not to the point of calling off the wedding, but she would surely have collapsed in tears and taken to her bed to deal with the pain. What her father's actions did was let her know that she was doing what was best for her—she was marrying a man who loved her and whom she loved desperately.

The revelation her father had intended to break them apart had only increased her love for Clay. It certainly answered some questions for Bennie—she believed now that she understood Clay's iron will when it came to matters of business. To her mind, it also explained why Clay was so precise in matters of the heart. No wonder he was reluctant to give in to his passion—having to clean up a mess like that at such a young age would make any man wary. Bennie wondered how much, if anything, Lillian knew about her late husband's carrying on. In Bennie's experience, women always knew much more than men thought they knew, and handled it much better.

She had no intention of discussing it with Clay—when he was ready, he would talk to her about it, she was sure. In the meantime, she and her father had managed once again to evolve some sort of cordiality out of the mess. It was the way they always did things—once something was over, it was over, and the less said about it, the better. Manipulative, demanding, and meddlesome he might be, but he was her only parent, and Bennie understood that she had to figure out a way of coping with him or she would have to cut him out of her life, which would be unbearable. So they would walk on eggshells for a while and then get back to their usual relationship. *If I looked up* dysfunctional *in the dictionary there we'd be, grinning like jackasses eating briers,* Bennie thought ruefully. But Big Benny was the only father she would ever have, and despite it all she loved him.

Unbeknownst to his daughter, Big Benny was not likely to miss the engagement party, not with his own grand-daughter's defection to the Deveraux camp. Lillian had attached herself to Clay's mother almost from the moment she met the lady. She had immediately started calling her Grandma, to Faye's chagrin. Faye vainly tried to get the toddler to call her Mrs. Deveraux, but little Lillian stubbornly refused, and Clay's mother certainly did not mind. She was enchanted with the little girl who so closely resembled her aunt Bennie and obviously had a strong personality.

Bennie was the one who figured out the connection between her niece and Lillian Deveraux. She had been sitting next to Clay's mother on the infamous glider, while Lillian was playing with Clay on the grass.

Bennie had referred to the older woman as Lillian, and her precocious niece said in triumph, "See? I tol' you she was my grandma!" Bennie gasped when she realized what was going on.

"She's always known she was named after her grandmother—my mother—Lillian. So when she heard people call you by your name, she just assumed—"

Little Lillian put an end to this speculation by clambering onto Lillian's lap. Patting the woman's surprised face, she smiled happily.

"You *are* my new grandma, I tol' them."

And that was that, as far as she was concerned. She even went so far as to announce that she was staying with her grandma on this trip to Atlanta. Which was fine with Lillian—she adored the three granddaughters that her son Malcolm had produced, and loved nothing better than their company.

This easy acceptance by his family of the Deveraux clan was just one reason that Benny was going to Atlanta on his best behavior. The other reason was that, regardless of how strained the relationship between him and his daughter, nothing was going to damage it permanently, at least nothing of his doing. Besides, Martha had threatened him with decapitation in a public place if he did not clean up his act. And she didn't even know about his little dossier— God help him if she ever found out.

So there was no reason to anticipate anything but a lovely weekend in Atlanta for the Cochrans and Deverauxes. The engagement party was on Saturday night, and as a special show of sisterly welcome, Angelique was giving Bennie a surprise shower on Saturday afternoon. After a morning of shopping with Renee, Lillian, Selena, and Vera, Bennie was really ready for a cold drink and a hot shower, but she managed to put on her sweetest expression when the doors to Lillian's patio opened and there was an assortment of women in residence. It took only a few seconds for Bennie to realize that something was amiss.

The patio was gaily decorated, and a catering staff was nearby with a lovely buffet table, but something was off. The guests, all of whom were naturally strangers to Bennie, looked quite uncomfortable. Lillian was clueless, but Vera gasped and then froze as light began to dawn for her. Bennie scanned the assembled guests and thought for a moment that they were all somehow related, they seemed so similar. All were petite and pretty and well dressed. Then two things suddenly made everything clear for Bennie.

Point one, she recognized Lisa Williams in the group of women. *That's the woman I met at the airport with Clay.* Point two, Miss Angelique was looking awfully satisfied with the proceedings. *I see—these are apparently all of Clay's old girlfriends.* Renee had also recognized that something was terribly amiss, and she was about to go off on her friend's behalf when Bennie rose to the occasion.

"Well. I think that this was intended to make us all uncomfortable, ladies," Bennie said with a wry smile. "In fact, if this was a poorly written romance novel, this would be the point at which I run out of here in tears. But I'm a little too old for that, and you ladies look like you have too much class. So I hope you all stay and tell me all about Atlanta. I'll be moving here in just a few weeks, and outside of a very few people, I don't know a soul." Bennie stopped and admitted, "Of course, if you'd like to leave, I can certainly understand why. This is a heck of a way to meet a lot of new people who look to be very nice!"

Lillian was suffused with embarrassment as the full import of what her daughter had done sank in. Angelique was attempting to sidle away from the patio, and everyone was glaring at her—except Bennie, who was sticking to the high road and introducing herself and Renee to the guests who were too fascinated to leave. Once the party was in full swing, with laughter and happy chatter floating over soft jazz, Bennie found Angelique in the bedroom, where she had taken refuge. Bennie did not mince words.

"Angelique, get a job," she said firmly. Angelique looked at her incredulously. Bennie repeated her words for emphasis. "That's right, get a job, get a hobby, get a life, and get you some business, girl. You are way too interested in your brother's love life—and that is not healthy for you. You're a beautiful woman, and you can't possibly be as stupid as you are acting now. Do something with your life, girl, something that makes you happy." Bennie looked carefully at the unhappy young woman who was trying to cling to her nonexistent dignity.

"This is the last time you are going to interfere in my life. I have no idea what has caused you to be so miserable or to view me as such a threat to your world, but you are going to find another way of handling those emotions as of right now. Please remember that—don't make me hurt you, hear?" With that Bennie left the room, shaking her head. At least she wasn't the only one with crazy relatives.

Near chaos was all around her, but Bennie was completely serene. Her wedding day had finally arrived, the day she and Clay would become man and wife. Despite the attempted interference from Big Benny and the sabotage by Angelique, all the planning had progressed unchecked to this very moment. With only a few alterations, the wedding was about to proceed. Vera Jackson had taken Angelique's place in the wedding party, for one thing.

After her wedding-shower caper in Atlanta, Angelique wisely decided to make herself scarce and took off to California to visit friends. Lillian had been absolutely mortified by the stunt. She had not known her only daughter could behave so badly. She kept apologizing to Bennie, who assured her that it was something that she and Angelique would work out over time. To say Clay was furious was a gross understatement. He was livid with Angelique and a bit put out that Bennie was not the one who told him what had happened—he got about five other versions from the women who had attended the so-called party. The fact that they were all singing Bennie's praises was small comfort to Clay. They almost had an argument over it, but Bennie managed to make him see that it was a relatively minor incident that served only to reflect how unhappy Angelique was. Clay had mumbled something about Bennie's being too forgiving, but he agreed to put it to rest.

Bennie was sitting quietly in the church dressing room, watching the commotion around her as if she were watching a movie. She was so serenely, supremely happy that she even wished that Angelique were there to share in the ceremony. It was enough that Martin was going to be there. Up until the very last minute Clay was not sure that Martin would attend. He was still reclusive, but showed some signs of mellowing. Martin genuinely liked Bennie and thought she was good for his brother.

Clay knew that Bennie had Martin wrapped around her little finger when he saw her give him a hug. Clay had, in fact, been shocked by the gesture, because since the accident Martin did not permit himself to be touched by anyone. Yet Bennie routinely hugged him or squeezed his arm or his hand as if he were just another of her brothers, and Martin did not mind at all. And he had come to the wedding rehearsal the day before and to the rehearsal dinner without any undue persuasion on anyone's part, so that meant he truly wanted to be there.

Everyone was dressed except for Bennie. Renee and Joyce shooed everyone out into a large anteroom so they could help Bennie into her dress. No one had seen the dress except those three—Bennie wanted everyone to be surprised when she walked down the aisle. Her hair was beautifully arranged in a style that would enhance the dress, since she was not wearing a veil. It was parted in the middle, and the sides waved away from her face into a mass of curls low on the nape of her neck. Soft tendrils escaped over her ears and along her nape, which gave her an ethereal quality. After getting Bennie into her dress, Renee and Joyce just stared in amazement.

Finally Renee said, "Bennie, you are just gorgeous. I

hope Clay has a strong heart, 'cause it's gonna give out when you come down the aisle." Bennie did not really hear Renee; nor did she clearly see her reflection in the mirror. All her thoughts were with her beloved Clay. The wedding director rapped sharply on the door to let Renee know it was time to join the wedding party lineup. It was also Bennie's cue to wait for her father to collect her.

At last, the wedding procession started down the aisle. The church was decorated with topiary trees that ranged down the aisle instead of the traditional pew decorations. The flowers that decorated the front of the church were, like the topiaries, in lush tapestry colors of purple and crimson and rose. The groomsmen, tall and elegant in their tuxedos, were each joined by a bridesmaid in a shimmering confection of bronze silk chiffon, skillfully cut on the bias to enhance the body. They each carried a cascade of flowers in shades of russet, mauve, and crimson that dramatically set off the gowns.

They looked elegant and sophisticated, but Clay honestly did not see them. Nor did he completely register his three nieces and little Lillian flinging flower petals with abandon as they trailed behind the bridesmaids in their deep rose frocks. Clay was waiting, with his heart in his throat, for the first sight of his bride. When the music signaled her entrance, Clay felt his chest constrict, and his breathing almost ceased.

The one traditional element of the wedding for Bennie was Mendelssohn's Wedding March. She had confessed to Clay that she would not really feel married unless she heard that music playing. The church was absolutely still as the doors at the rear of the sanctuary opened and Benny entered with his daughter on his arm. Bennie's radiant beauty was all that Clay registered at first. She was breathtaking in a gown that defied all traditions, yet managed to capture the essence of the woman wearing it.

It was a strapless sheath in a champagne hue that was suffused with gold. The deep décolletage and backless nature of the dress were minimized by the sheer overlay that gave it some modesty. The overlay was itself almost transparent—it would have blended almost totally into Bennie's skin tone except for the delicate and colorful embroidery that accented it. There were crimson and teal flowers, deep green leaves, and tiny violet and rose birds scattered about the dress. Only a few graced the bodice and sleeves, with more on the back and even more down the train that trailed behind her. The sheath skirt flared out at the knee, flowing into the train. With tiny flowers that echoed the shades of the embroidery tucked here and there in her hair, Bennie looked like the embodiment of a fairy tale.

But not to Clay—to him she looked like the beautiful wild creature that he had so lovingly photographed. It was as though Bennie had taken that magical morning and re-created their secret fantasy just for him. Which, of course, she had. Walking toward Clay carrying a sensuous cascade of ruby, crimson, and violet flowers, she smiled, remembering that morning. No one else saw the looks that they were giving each other, because everyone else was too taken with the sight of the tears coursing down Benny's face as he prepared to give his only daughter over to the man who would love her forever.

As they slowly approached the altar, Clay walked forward to take Bennie's arm and lead her the rest of the way. Bennie handed her bouquet to Renee and turned to face Clay. Clay looked into Bennie's face and could not resist touching her cheek and leaning over to kiss her temple, which brought a collective sigh from the women in attendance. As the minister said the vows that would make them man and wife, Clay could feel tears welling up in his eyes, tears of pure joy that he was damned if he was going to try to hide. Of course, Bennie's eyes were also moist from emotion. When the minister asked, "Who giveth this woman to be wed?" all five of her brothers rose with their father and said, "We do." Bennie almost wept then, but Clay touched her face again and she was fine. Finally, it was done—the minister pronounced them man and wife, and before he could admonish Clay to kiss the bride, they were in each other's arms.

Clay tried desperately not to make a spectacle of his lovely bride right there at the altar, but it took a Herculean effort not to drown her in passion right there. He reluctantly pulled away from Bennie's soft, luscious lips and looked down at her loving expression.

"I love you, Andrea Benita Cochran-Deveraux," he said solemnly.

"I love *you,* Clayton Arlington Deveraux," she answered.

Taking her bouquet from Renee, she joined her hand to Clay's and took the first step into their married life together.

Nine

The enchantment of the wedding did not end after the ceremony; the reception was just as beautiful. Even the lapse between the ceremony and the reception for picture taking was bearable, due to the entertainment provided by Uncle Bump's band and the lovely buffet of hors d'oeuvres to occupy the guests while they waited for the arrival of the wedding party. Bennie and Clay tolerated the endless flashbulbs because now that they were man and wife, they could contain their urgent desire for a while. They could not suppress the looks of passion they gave each other, however. Even in the most proper poses, it was not possible to disguise their feelings.

That was also the consensus of the guests when the formal dinner was over and the dancing began. The first selection was of course, the bride and groom's special song. Bennie and Clay had chosen, most appropriately, "I Only Have Eyes for You." As a special surprise, Vera and Marcus sang a sexy, jazzy duet of the song. Truer words were never sung than those lyrics; Bennie and Clay never took their eyes off each other as they danced their first dance as man and wife. The room was literally charged with emotion as everyone saw the genuine adoration that poured out of their eyes for each other.

The other traditional dances took place in succession— Bennie danced with her father while Ceylon sang "Unforgettable," and Clay danced with his mother to "Skylark," her favorite song. The biggest surprise was Lillian Deveraux taking the microphone and singing a sultry version of "At Last." And she was not singing totally for the benefit of the newlyweds, either. Her eyes locked with Bump Williams and did not waver for the entire song. The sexiest surprise was Andrew and Renee dancing to that song, locked in each other's arms as though they belonged there. Even Bennie, drowning as she was in love, noticed the two of them holding each other with every appearance of bliss. *Now, where did that come from?* she thought, but could not come up with a good answer.

For Clay, though, the sweetest surprise of the reception was when his beautiful wife sang to him. Bennie sang "For Sentimental Reasons" in a voice of such love that Clay thought his heart would burst. He knew how difficult the weeks before the wedding had been for Bennie; he had felt guilty about wanting a wedding when she was so reluctant. But looking at her in that incredible dress, and watching her as she sang to him, he knew he would do it again if he had the chance. He would never forget how beautiful she looked on this day, or how loved he felt. And Benita would never forget the honeymoon he was taking her on; he would make sure of that.

After the dinner and the dancing and the toasts, Clay was getting restless. It was time to start his married life. "Peaches, let's get out of here. Please," he begged. "I can't take this anymore. Let's go."

Bennie gave him one of her best smiles. She had thrown the bouquet—she was aiming for Martha but somehow it had ended up in Renee's arms. Renee had been as excited to see the bouquet as someone who had been handed a fresh road kill. Clay had tossed the garter over his shoulder without looking once he realized that Bennie was wearing some really provocative lingerie under the phenomenal dress. After he slid his hand up to retrieve the garter and found the top of her silk hose, he lost all interest in receptions. Andrew had just pulled out his cell phone to answer a page from the hospital when the garter landed on the phone's tiny antenna. Andrew looked as though a leech had attached itself to his phone and hastily flung it away from him. So much for tradition.

They had also gotten through the cake cutting without mishap. The cake was a five-tiered fantasy with champagne-colored frosting and embellished with the same flowers and birds that covered Bennie's dress. There was even a wedding couple on top of the cake—in a surprising twist they resembled Clay and Bennie, right down to Clay's mustache and longish hair to Bennie's fanciful dress. One of Bennie's dear friends was a master baker and could create any fantasy one could contrive. She had outdone herself with the magnificent cake.

Instead of smearing the cake on each other's faces, as at some weddings, Clay and Bennie fed each other small bites to signify that they would always take care of each other and nourish the other's soul. It was so sweet and deliberate, in fact, that it was almost too private to watch, especially when Clay licked the frosting from Bennie's fingertips and kissed her palm. It was then that Clay had begged Bennie to leave. And leave they did—not in a shower of rice and confetti or well wishes; they simply left.

As much as Clay wanted to whisk her off to their honeymoon that night, the logistics were too nightmarish to contemplate. So he did the next best thing—he booked the bridal suite at the best hotel in Detroit and arranged for the most perfect wedding night that he could conceive. And given his long separation from Bennie and their long period of deprivation, his fantasies knew no limits.

Everything was in readiness when they entered the suite—Clay had discreetly phoned the concierge to alert him of their imminent arrival. Clay insisted on carrying Bennie across the threshold of the suite to signify the start of married bliss. "But Clay, you don't have to do that until we get home!" Bennie said, laughing. "I could break your back, and then what kind of honeymoon would we have?"

Clay set her down on the bed before answering. "Peaches, anywhere we are is where home is from now on. And I am a big man—I could carry you around all day and not feel it. And"—he paused to kiss her thoroughly before continuing—"that is the most incredible dress I have ever seen, but I'm really tired of looking at it," he said suggestively. Bennie laughed the deep, throaty way that she did only when Clay was arousing her. Clay had learned to recognize that sound and tried to get her to do it as often as possible, because he knew that she was unaware of it and that he was the only one who could elicit that sound from her.

There were other sounds that he had become attuned to in their time together, like the soft sound of surprise that Bennie made every time she was on the brink of ecstasy. That was the sound he wanted to hear, and soon, before he lost all semblance of control. Bennie knew exactly how he felt, because she was as anxious as he was to celebrate their love. She stood up and confessed to Clay that she wasn't sure how to get out of her dress. "Renee and Joyce got me into it, but of course I wasn't paying attention," she admitted.

Clay immediately sprang into action, searching for a way out of the gown. Bennie knew there was a hidden side zipper, of course, but was at a loss as to how to get it over her head. Clay found some tiny hooks at the neckline, which, when undone, would allow Bennie to remove the dress. She smiled her relief and went into one of the suite's two bathrooms to get ready. Clay did the same, trying not to reveal his eagerness but failing miserably. Which was perfectly fine with Bennie; she did not want to be the only one looking like a passion-crazed newlywed.

Bennie had a small bag with her that contained everything she would need for the night. Clay had insisted on not only purchasing everything she would need for their honeymoon; he also packed it. He had kept the details of their getaway completely secret, and no amount of wheedling could get the information from him. After removing the dress, Bennie hung it on the padded hanger that was in the garment bag hanging on the bathroom door. She raced through her toilette, loosening her hair from its mass at her nape to curl wildly about her shoulders. She reapplied her fragrance in the form of a silky body cream to her shoulders, stomach, and the backs of her knees. Then she put on the most exquisite nightgown she had ever seen, a special gift to her from Renee.

Renee had been to Paris a few months before with one of her beaus and had purchased the virtually transparent negligee and gown for Bennie's wedding night. It was a sheer ivory silk with lavish amounts of ecru lace that turned it from something wanton into something feminine and delectable. Bennie stared at her reflection in the mirror and started to remove her earrings and necklace, then decided not to. They were her wedding gift from Clay, and she wanted to enjoy them a little longer. The earrings were brilliant-cut canary diamonds with teardrop-shaped peridots dangling from them. The necklace was the same, although there were also white diamonds alongside the canary brilliant. Fingering the pendant, Bennie sighed. She did not know what she had done to deserve such happiness, but she wasn't about to question it. Hearing soft music from the living room, Bennie went to join her husband.

Clay turned around to see his beautiful Benita walking toward him. He wondered if his heart would ever stop beating like a wild thing every time he saw her, then decided he didn't want it to. He crossed the room and took her hands in his so that he could stare at her beauty for a moment. "Peaches. Baby, you are . . . everything," he said reverently.

Bennie thought the same thing, looking at Clay. He was wearing silk pajama bottoms in a deep, creamy ivory color, and a beautiful silk robe in a deeper shade, open to expose his beautiful chest with its silky covering of hair. The memory of what that felt like next to her skin made Bennie blush. He looked like a model out of a ritzy men's underwear ad, but far, far sexier. He looked dangerous, in fact, and Bennie told him so.

Clay pulled her down into his lap on the overstuffed sofa and laughed. "How can I look dangerous to you, baby? You're the one who tamed me. If anything, I should be afraid of you," he confessed. Bennie was tired of talking. She slid her fingers into his hair and kissed him thoroughly, the kind of kiss she had been wanting for weeks. "I love you, Clayton," she whispered. Clay kissed her back with even more passion, and then he pulled away. "Baby, I can't wait anymore." He groaned. He had wanted to make this an evening of seduction and mutual pleasure, but Bennie felt too good in his arms, and he was too hungry for her.

It was obvious that Bennie felt the same, because she immediately got off his lap and led him to the bedroom, which was scented with the heady fragrance of the candles that were arranged everywhere. Pushing the robe off his shoulders, Bennie showed Clay that she was as eager for him as he was for her. She pressed a line of kisses down his chest and sighed her pleasure as he removed her robe. Before she realized what was happening, they were lying in each other's arms without any barriers of clothing. They held each other tightly for long minutes, savoring their reunion. It had been so long since they had been this close. Nothing had changed, yet everything was different. They had always belonged to one another, from their very first kiss. But now they were truly one, man and wife.

Clay ran his big hands down the length of Bennie's body as she stroked his chest. They stared at each other, almost overwhelmed by the love in each other's eyes. Clay repositioned himself so that he was covering Bennie's body with his own as they merged in fiery passion. "I love you, Benita," was all he said before they were lost to everything around them except their love. Bennie might have been right when she said that abstinence would make their lovemaking more exciting—it was better than it had ever been before. Whether it was due to the fact that he hadn't touched her silken skin and felt her warmth for so long, Clay did not know. The undeniable fact was that he had never experienced such profound passion in his life, not even when he and Bennie had made love before.

One minute it was soft and sweet and innocent, like two virgins coming together for the first time. Then it was wild and hot and erotic, like a pagan ritual—Clay could not get enough of her as he plundered her body over and over. Only the fact that she was giving him as much as and more than he got stopped him from pulling away from her.

Bennie was not one of those women who sank into the legendary sleep of the sated woman. At least not tonight— she was energized and wide awake, and more than happy to accommodate every mutual fantasy she and Clay had ever had. Clay finally prevailed upon her to pity him. "Peaches, baby, I'm older than you are. I think I'm broken, too. If you want a honeymoon, you'd better let me get some sleep." Bennie laughed her little laugh and purred, "Well, if I broke it, I'm pretty sure I can fix it." She started to demonstrate what she meant when Clay distracted her.

"I have something for you—I almost forgot about it," he said, rising from the bed and going into the sitting room. Bennie sat up in bed. "Clay, you have to stop buying me things. After this beautiful jewelry and the honeymoon, on which I am sure you spared no expense, I do not need anything else. Do you hear me?" By that time Clay was back in the room bearing a beautiful leather portfolio that was about twelve by sixteen inches. He sat down on the bed and scoffed at Bennie openly.

"In the first place, I will get you anything I want, anytime I want, just because I love you. And because I can," he said frankly. "And you are not one to talk about getting people presents," he reminded her. Before their engagement party in Atlanta, Bennie had given him his gift, a small box that contained a set of keys. Clay looked puzzled until she took him outside to show him what the keys went to—a white classic Aston-Martin with red morocco leather interior. And it was not a reproduction, either. Bennie had been tracking one down for years, and when her car sleuth had found this one, it seemed like the perfect wedding gift. Clay had been, and continued to be, totally knocked out by that gift.

Bennie decided to change the subject and look at what Clay had in the portfolio. She gasped when Clay took out the contents—it was the pictures that he made of her that misty morning in Atlanta. He had used a sepia-toned film and developed them on a heavy matte paper, which gave them a timeless elegance. The pictures were, even to Bennie's critical eye, incredible. There were a few that showed her in total nudity, but most were done with a sensual sleight of hand that suggested rather than displayed everything. Some were quite close up, so that all one saw was her face and shoulders. Some were rather distant, so that she looked ethereal and misty rather than blatantly naked. One thing was obvious in all the pictures, and that was that Bennie was deeply in love with the man behind the camera. The last shot she looked at was the one that had made Clay put down the camera and join her on the moist grass. Her face was so suffused with love and fever that it was a wonder the camera had not burst into flame. Bennie gasped and covered her mouth with her hand.

Clay looked distressed for a moment. "Don't you like them, baby? I think they're astounding, if I do say so myself," he added. Bennie shook her head and admitted they were lovely. "I was just thinking about what our grandchildren will say when they get a look at these," she mused. "You know that our children and our children's children are going to get a look at these someday," she said realistically. "Whatever will they think?" she said with amusement.

Clay said in a growl, "They are going to think their mother was hot and that their father was a lucky man, that's what." Clay put the pictures back in the portfolio and proceeded to show Bennie just how lucky he was feeling at that precise moment.

"Ooh, Clay, I thought you were broken, baby," Bennie cooed as he kissed and sucked his way down her body.

"You fixed me, Peaches, just like you always do," he moaned as he continued his trail of pleasure.

* * *

Bennie was never happier in her life than she was now as Mrs. Clayton Arlington Deveraux. Even now, as she surveyed the drop cloths and assorted paint rubble that would transform the room she was redecorating, she was blissful. She and Clay had settled into domestic life with a vengeance. Once they returned from their honeymoon, they had established a routine that was, to Bennie's mind, perfect. Clay had looked at her on the Monday morning after they returned to Atlanta and asked her what she was going to do with herself now that she wasn't a busy executive. Bennie had laughed and said she was going to be a busy wife.

And she was—and loved every minute of it. The honeymoon had exceeded all her wildest expectations. She knew that Clay was a generous and adoring man, but she had not anticipated the lengths to which he would go to ensure her happiness. The morning after the wedding they had checked out of the suite and proceeded to Bennie's house so that she could leave her wedding gown in Renee's care until she was back in Atlanta. And with a weird sense of déjà vu, they greeted Andrew leaving by the back door as he had the night of Big Benny's party. But this time, instead of an ice pack, he had a dreamy, happy smile on his face, caused no doubt by the sizzling kiss Renee had just planted on him. "Don't ask," was all he said. He kissed Clay on the cheek and shook Bennie's hand, then looked puzzled. "I think I did that backward," he said to himself as he continued to walk to the garage.

Clay and Bennie had stared at each other, Andrew's retreating back, and Renee, standing in the doorway with the unmistakable glow of a satisfied woman on her face. The newlyweds had proceeded with caution into the house, expecting any moment that the pod person who had obviously taken over Renee would burst out spewing slime. But it really was her old friend and roommate beaming and offering coffee and such. Bennie opened her mouth several times to ask some deep and probing questions, but she knew that the information would be forthcoming soon, as Renee and Donnie were going to drive her Jaguar down to Atlanta the next weekend with the lovely Aretha in a carrier.

Bennie and Clay could not linger, as they had to head right out to the airport. So after hugs and kisses and admonishments to call, they took off. They flew to Miami, where they got a flight to Providenciales, at the southern tip of the Bahamas archipelago. It was beyond anything that Bennie could have imagined. Clay had found an elegant resort called the Grace Bay Club for their honeymoon and had naturally secured the most exclusive suite, one that had no neighbors on either side. Each suite had a private walled garden, but this one was angled in such a way as to be isolated from the other rooms. It was absolutely enchanting, furnished in an elegant, tropical style that was cool and inviting at the same time.

The bedroom opened onto a very large veranda with a view of the beach that was a few feet away. The water was as blue as a Maxfield Parrish sky and as inviting. The cool, neutral tones of the cushioned rattan furniture seemed made for late-morning dalliances and late-night trysts, and that was exactly what Clay and Bennie used it for. There was no nightlife to speak of on the island, not that they cared. The week they spent there was for one thing only: to revel in each other and start their married life off in sheer bliss. They swam, ate wonderful meals, and made love for days on end.

Bennie particularly loved to sunbathe nude in their private garden. She put on a lotion with an SPF of 15, but as she told Clay, "I don't care if I burn to a crisp or end up as wrinkled as an old prune. This is the only time in my life that I am going to get to do this, so I am going to enjoy it." It was a moot point, since she never got to spend too much time actually sunbathing. Clay could not stand the thought of her naked in the sun; the sight of her gleaming, beautiful body made him crazy with love. He would inevitably pounce on her and lure her back to bed, to which she had no objection whatsoever.

And as much as Bennie had loved the passion-filled days

and nights, she also had no objection to going home to Atlanta after their fun in the sun was over. It was time for them to get to the business of real life. Bennie's routine now was to wake up before her husband, make a quick toilette, and fix his breakfast as he showered and dressed for the office. The first few weeks consisted of rearranging furniture, purchasing items here and there, and writing thank-you notes for the myriad of gifts that had, against her wishes, sneaked in anyway.

After that, Bennie's day consisted of making Clay's breakfast and doing a minimal amount of tidying, since they had a wonderful housekeeper who came twice a week. She would then shower, dress, and go to work in her home office. At least twice a week she devoted herself to the business of the Cochran Foundation, and the rest of the time she spent writing. As far as Bennie was concerned, it was the perfect schedule. She would have lunch a couple of times a week with Clay, and always had something wonderful in the way of a meal prepared when he got home. The weekends were devoted to long, leisurely brunches and dinners taken in a nice restaurant, or prepared by Clay. He was a very good cook, and delighted in preparing Bennie's meals.

Everything about married life delighted Clay, in point of fact. He was always a pleasant person to work with, but his employees and business associates noted a definite change in him. He had gone from being positive to being absolutely effervescent on most days. He loved nothing more than waking up with Bennie in his arms on the weekends; the weekdays when he could entice her back into bed for some quick, hot sex before work were equally memorable. But somewhere in the back of his mind he could not help thinking that Bennie would get bored. She was so accustomed to being her own person that he was not convinced that she would not get restless and unhappy with married life in Atlanta. Even when she dropped Cochran from her name, he wasn't convinced. They had returned

home from a dinner dance for one of his mother's charities
when Bennie brought it up.

"Clay, I am Andrea Benita Deveraux, not Cochran-
Deveraux. If I weren't willing to share your name I would
not have married you. I am liberated enough, thank you
very much. I have lived and worked in a male-dominated
business for years, so please, give me a break! Benita
Deveraux from now on, okay?" She had poked him in the
chest to emphasize the point, and although her eyes were
full of merriment, he knew her to be completely serious.
He was just chauvinistic enough to be pleased by the idea
that she did not view taking his name as losing her identity,
but he was not completely convinced.

It wasn't until his birthday that he realized how badly
he wanted to believe that Benita would be happy with her
new lifestyle. His birthday fell right before Thanksgiving,
and Bennie had made a lovely dinner for him, which included his family. Even Angelique had shown up, looking
and acting rather subdued, for Angelique. Bennie had gone
out of her way since the wedding to show Angelique kindness and consideration, never once reminding her of how
she had behaved. For some reason, Clay sensed it served
to make Angelique feel even guiltier about her behavior.
As Bennie said, she would have to figure a way out of her
distress on her own.

After everyone left and the two of them were alone in
the big house, Bennie took Clay into the living room and
sat him down on the sofa. She took a small box from behind a picture on the mantel and handed it to him after
sitting down in his lap. "Happy birthday, sweetheart. I hope
you like it," was all she said. Clay raised an eyebrow. Bennie had already given him wonderful gifts—a beautiful
cashmere sweater and a CD of Bennie singing just for him.
"It helps to have a godfather with his own recording studio," she had teased Clay when she presented it to him.
Now she was giving him something else. "Open it!" Bennie demanded. She never took her eyes from his face as
he slowly unwrapped the box and took off the lid. Inside

was a jeweler's box with a heavy gold link bracelet. In the middle of the bracelet were three block letters: DAD.

Clay stared at the bracelet for a moment; then his face lit up with joy. "Peaches, does this mean we're having a baby?"

Bennie nodded her head with a big smile. "In July, if the doctor's calculations are correct. It seems we brought back a little souvenir from our honeymoon," she added sheepishly. "Please tell me you're happy about this. We didn't talk about having one so soon or—" Her words were cut off by Clay's mouth on hers. After kissing her feverishly, he held her so tightly she couldn't breathe.

"Oh, Benita, baby, you have no idea how happy I am," he whispered. And it was true—Clay didn't realize how much he wanted to be a father until he realized that he was going to be one. He was ridiculously proud of the fact that she was carrying his child, as though they were the only people in the world clever enough to have pulled off such a miracle. He couldn't stop kissing her or holding her or thanking her. It was the thanking that got to Bennie.

With tears of happiness streaming down her cheeks, she laughed at her big, handsome husband. "Why are you thanking me? I enjoyed making this baby as much as you did," she reminded him. "And let's see how much you thank me when he wakes up for his two A.M. feeding." She laughed.

"I'll do it," Clay said immediately. "I'll feed him or her, change diapers, everything," he said seriously.

Bennie smiled and stroked his face. "Honey, unless you change equipment, you won't be feeding him for a while," she said sweetly. Clay's face softened into a look of pure happiness as he realized what Bennie meant. Bennie recognized the look as one of primal joy that she would be breast-feeding his child. She smiled again and promised to let him change as many diapers as he wanted, though. "It's not nearly as much fun as you might think," she warned.

* * *

Clay was the most devoted father-to-be in the known world. He was curious about every step of the process, even Bennie's morning sickness, which she had every afternoon like clockwork. Every morning she was dewy, radiant, and hungry, and every afternoon at one-fifteen she was, as she put it, "spewing like Mt. Vesuvius." Luckily, Clay was at work for most of these attacks, which made Bennie extremely happy. Clay was so solicitous that he would have tried to have the nausea for her. She tried to explain to Renee that she was feeling claustrophobic around Clay, but she didn't want to sound ungrateful.

Renee had come down for Thanksgiving with Big Benny, Martha, Donnie, and Adam. Big Benny was admirably restrained in his behavior, no doubt due to Martha's influence. At any rate, he was the very picture of a happy grandfather-to-be. Renee and Andrew had apparently gotten over their bliss and were back on barely speaking terms, which was partially the reason for his absence. Andrew seemed to have another liaison in the offing, which was the other reason for his absence—he stayed in Detroit with his lady friend. Bennie had searched Renee's face for some sign of unhappiness over this turn of events, but as usual, Renee seemed unmoved. She never let herself get so involved that she could not extricate herself painlessly.

Renee naturally proved to be the perfect sounding board for Bennie. "Ne-ne, I don't mean to be a cow, but every time I turn around he's *there*. Do I need anything, am I comfortable, can he do something for me—I feel like jumping out of my skin!" She looked at her friend with huge eyes made unhappy by guilt and confusion. "Now am I the most hateful, ungrateful witch you have ever seen in your life or what?"

Renee said one word, clearly and succinctly: "Hormones." At Bennie's puzzled expression she continued. "Honey, you forget that I have four sisters, all of whom are married and the mothers of my lovely nieces and nephews. And all of them, to a woman, were the most ornery heifers you ever saw when they were pregnant. It's just your body adjusting to the fact that you have a new life in there. This will pass in a few weeks; trust me. And you can't have been but so mean to Clay—the man is still drooling every time you enter a room."

True enough, Clay came into the kitchen, where the two women were sitting, and his eyes lit up upon seeing Bennie. She sprang up and went over to put her arms around his waist. "Clay, I found out why I've been such a shrew," she confessed.

Clay hugged her and kissed her lightly before taking the words out of her mouth. "Oh, I know, Peaches; it's your hormones. You'll be back to normal in a couple of weeks," he said knowingly. Kissing her again, he ambled away, whistling.

Bennie looked at Renee with her eyes narrowed. "See, I don't even get to be magnanimous and apologize. He's a *saint*," she hissed.

Renee wanted to laugh but was kind enough not to. All she could do was promise her best friend that it would all be over in a few weeks. And it was.

Christmas was a beautiful, festive affair for Bennie and Clay. The Christmas-morning festivities were at Malcolm and Selena's house, since they had small children. Lillian was happy to give over the Christmas Eve celebration to Bennie, who was thrilled to be able to have her first Christmas with her new family in her new home. She and Clay had devoted an entire afternoon to searching out just the right tree for the house, as well as ornaments that would begin their family traditions. Even though the afternoon sickness was still plaguing her, Bennie was as happy as a little lark throughout the holidays.

A memory that Clay would never forget was walking in on Bennie, who was supposed to be getting dressed for a holiday party. She had a small pillow stuffed under her crimson velvet tunic. She was unaware that he was watching her, and was turning this way and that to see how she would look in a few months. Clay's eyes got moist as he saw his happy wife stroking the pillow tummy in prepara-

tion for the real thing. Benita was going to be a perfect
mother; of that he had no doubt. His nieces adored her, as
did her own nieces and nephews. Children just seemed to
gravitate to her—though she always laughed it off. "They
know I have a childlike mind," she always said. "They
recognize their own."

Clay knew better, though. Bennie had a genuine sweetness and patience about her. She was tender, loving, smart,
and capable—his children would have the best of everything with Bennie as a mother. Sometimes the force of his
love for Bennie would come over him so strongly that he
would actually feel a tremor race through his body. It both
exhilarated him and frightened him. He had never experienced anything like the feelings he had for Bennie—sometimes he felt so humbled by her love that he could not
speak. At other times he felt like the monarch of the universe, powerful, privileged, and omnipotent. That day,
watching Bennie preparing to give birth to his child, he
just felt blessed.

After the holidays were over, Bennie's daily nausea
abated and she was full of energy. "It's that nesting instinct," she assured Clay. "Pregnant women always get it
so that they can finish up all their projects before the
baby comes." Which was why she was surveying the half-
finished room. They were converting the sitting room of
the master suite into a nursery for the time being. It only
made sense, as the master suite occupied the third floor
of the house and the other bedrooms were on the second
floor. Either the baby would come upstairs for its first
few months, or Bennie and Clay would have to move
downstairs. And Bennie had no intention of giving up
their beautiful suite.

By now, Clay was pretty much convinced that Bennie
could indeed do anything. She continued to handle business
for the Cochran Foundation—in fact, she was in the process
of helping Malcolm set one up for the Deveraux Group.
The Cochran Foundation was simply a means of conducting
the philanthropic business of Cochran Communications

without the burden of taxes. The Cochran Foundation raised money for and donated money to things like Habitat for Humanity, AIDS programs, historically black colleges and universities, sickle-cell anemia, and cystic fibrosis research, and similar programs. They also funded grants and scholarships for talented youth and provided internships and summer jobs.

Clay was impressed no end with Bennie's expertise in these matters. The Deveraux Group had long been involved with multiple charities, but he could see right away that something like this would benefit the company as well as allow them to be more efficient in matters of philanthropy. Malcolm, the financial chief, and Martin, the chief counsel, were happy to have Bennie to assist them in getting a similar program in place for the Deveraux Group. Bennie was more than invaluable to Clay in a lot of ways. Her presence in his life helped with many of the business decisions that he was making at that point.

Clay wanted to continue to diversify the Deveraux Group, and at the same time he wanted to consolidate some of the holdings of the company in such a way that they would not require his direct supervision. That required a lot of recruitment of new executives and rearranging corporate positions. Before long, Clay found himself relying more and more on Bennie's business acumen. He didn't have to, certainly—he knew what he was doing and he knew how to hire qualified headhunters. But Bennie's shrewd insights and assistance were invaluable. Besides, he liked the idea of working with her. He liked being able to discuss business matters with her, and the fact that she could do much more than pretend to be interested in what he was saying.

She was a superb hostess and could be relied upon to host a small dinner party for a viable candidate with virtually no notice. His wife was an absolute dynamo. Looking at her, it was impossible to believe that she was four months pregnant. She wasn't showing at all, and she had the energy of five women. Clay could not get over how lucky he was. Neither could anyone else. His business associates were constantly singing Bennie's praises, as was his family. Clay's heart was full whenever he thought about his life with Bennie—he really was married to a queen.

At that particular moment, the queen was feeling a little out of sorts. No, a lot out of sorts. She was sitting in the room she had designated as her office and was looking anxiously at a huge pile of paper. None of it pertained to the book she was trying to finish; it was all Deveraux Group stuff. How, in a short month, had she gotten so caught up in helping Clay that she had gone from full-time wife and part-time novelist to unpaid corporate drudge? Again? As much as she loved Clay and, yes, Martin, she was not thrilled about doing all the paperwork. It was enough that she was still doing Cochran Foundation work; she did not want this extra duty.

She put her elbows on her desk and rubbed her face with her palms. She did not want to review any more résumés or meet any more dewy-eyed hopefuls, either. But Clay genuinely liked having her input; he told her so many times. And there was no mistaking the fact that he liked working with her—he made absolutely no secret of that. Lately, she had even gone to some business functions in his place. Sighing, she sat back and surveyed her nails. They were thicker and whiter than they used to be, no doubt a result of her pregnancy and her prenatal vitamins.

There were other changes, too, even though she wasn't really showing yet. Her breasts were bigger, heavier, and exquisitely tender. It might have been her imagination, but she swore that her nipples were getting darker, too. And she might not have been showing in the front, but her butt was certainly doing its part to carry this baby. She smiled ruefully and patted the offending member fondly. She would be happy to be sticking out like a whale, and as soon as possible. Maybe that would remind Clay that she was his wife, not one of his underlings. Maybe it would give her the gumption to tell him herself. She could not bring herself to even tactfully broach it to Clay, so maybe the sight of her huge tummy would. A familiar sensation ripped through her and she glanced at the clock. Every so often, the baby still liked to get its one-fifteen spew in, and today was one of those days. Groaning, she ran for the bathroom.

"Peaches, please think about it. If you don't want to do it, I will completely understand, but if you choose to, I will be forever grateful," Clay said sincerely.

Bennie looked at him helplessly. "You rat. You know I can't possibly turn you down," she said. "This is so unfair. Okay, I'll do it, but on one condition: when I get back we are going on a romantic weekend just for us. No phones, no cable, no communication with the outside world at all," she insisted.

Clay's eyes lit up. "That's fine for me. What do you get out of the deal?" he said in a growl next to her ear.

Bennie squirmed with pleasure as his mustache tickled her neck. They were still in bed late on a Saturday morning, just enjoying being with each other. Or they would have been had Clay not asked her to fly to L.A. to accept some stupid award in the name of the Deveraux Group. Bennie had demurred at first. "Why can't Malcolm or Marcus go? These people don't know me from a can of paint," she pointed out. Clay had patiently explained that both he and Martin would be returning from Japan on the day of the banquet, so it would be impossible for them to attend. Malcolm had a series of important meetings regarding acquisitions and divestitures of the group. And Marcus was, as he reminded her, in Detroit doing the internship that she herself had arranged. Bennie did not even want to think about schlepping out to L.A. for some stupid award. It was bad enough that Clay was going to be out of town for a few days; it was ridiculous that she would have to disrupt her routine and miss her exercise class just for this. But she couldn't say no. Clay meant too much to her, and *no* was a word she simply did not know how to employ when it came to her loved ones.

Which was how she found herself on a plane going to the Bonaventure Hotel in L.A. to attend a stupid awards banquet to accept a stupid award for continued excellence in journalism from the NAACP. Yes, it was a very big deal, and yes, she was happy that the Deveraux Group was being recognized, but that was as far as it went. *No. No. No.* She practiced the word over and over again. *No. No. NO.* "No!" she said forcefully to the flight attendant, who looked alarmed.

"I'm sorry, ma'am. Most people like pillows on these long flights, " the woman said apologetically.

Blushing, Bennie accepted the pillow and a blanket. "I'm sorry," she said winsomely. "My mind was elsewhere."

It was indeed elsewhere—it was back in Atlanta, replaying the scene in which she had once again acquiesced. Bennie was disgusted with herself—she was an adult, about to have a baby. She had to be able to express her likes and dislikes to the people she loved. She could do it in business—nobody messed with Bennie Cochran in the boardroom. She knew how to express herself fully and forcefully when she had to, and no one thought less of her. She wasn't so neurotic that she thought that Clay would stop loving her if she did not leap to fulfill his every wish. Moreover, it was critical that she have her priorities straight for the remainder of her pregnancy.

She was going to be a mother, and that had to come before any business—Cochran, Deveraux, or otherwise. A little ashamed of herself for having let it go this far, Bennie closed her eyes to sleep. When she got back to Atlanta, she and Clay were going to come to a new understanding of what her priorities were. Clay was more than reasonable; he would understand and probably applaud her stance. Her lips curved in a sleepy smile when she thought about Clay and how lucky she was.

* * *

While Bennie was beating herself up for not communicating with Clay, he was doing the same thing half a world away. He was thinking about Bennie and how anxious she was to get the whole trip to L.A. over with. He grimaced, thinking that it had really not been necessary for her to go in the first place. Any number of people could have adequately represented the Deveraux Group, up to and including Marcus, who was not by any means glued to Detroit. There was really nothing that would have prevented him from leaving his internship for a couple of days to go out there and stand in for Clay.

Clay winced when he thought about how selfish he had been over the issue. Why was it so important that Bennie go? Because she was beautiful and gracious and everything she did, she did with style. And love, he admitted. Bennie had told him over and over that she was tired of business and wanted to be creative and domestic. She wanted a life with him and she wanted his babies. She had left her high-stress, high-profile life in Detroit with no hesitation whatsoever and proceeded to create a loving, warm home for him, and was carrying his child. And he showed his appreciation by working her like a Mississippi field hand. He swallowed hard, trying to remember the last time she had come to him to talk about plot changes in her newest book. She probably hadn't worked on it in weeks.

Clay looked across the living room of the suite he was sharing with his brother. Martin was sitting on the sofa, engrossed in a report. Clay stared at him before speaking. "Martin, I'm a real jackass," he said.

Martin did not look up from his report. "I never doubted it for a minute, bro. What brought you to that conclusion?" he drawled.

Clay was not going to be put off by Martin's jibes. "I'm serious, Martin. I have been screwing up, big-time," he said seriously. That got Martin's attention.

Clay explained what he had been doing as far as Bennie was concerned. "You know, I could see how much of her time she devoted to taking care of her brothers and her father. She was always doing something for somebody and hardly ever took time for herself." Clay was pacing around the suite with his hands in his pockets. "I used to be kind of annoyed by her brothers, or irritated or something. It was like I didn't want anyone but me getting any of her attention. And now look at me—I hang on her worse than they did," he admitted shamefacedly.

"Look at it this way, Clay," Martin said reasonably. "You'll both be back at home in a couple of days and you can sit down and talk everything out. And you can make sure that this does not happen again. I know you love Benita to death, but you have to talk to her, man. And you have to stop acting like she's superwoman. She may be smart and talented and all of those things, but she is a regular person like everyone else," he reminded Clay.

Clay knew that Martin was right, but it galled him to hear his brother tell him things that he already knew. It cut him deeply to realize that he had not been taking care of Bennie the way she deserved. But that was all going to end in a couple of days. Clay was tempted to try to call her, but with the time difference and her potential jet lag, he decided not to. *Just wait until you're back in my arms, Benita Deveraux.* Clay was going to make everything up to her in the most romantic way possible. And this time he was going to keep all of the promises he had made to her in his heart and in his wedding vows.

The next day Clay was called out of a meeting by an urgent transatlantic call. It was Marcus, telling him that Big Benny had had a mild stroke and was hospitalized. Marcus thought rightly that Clay should be the one to tell Bennie, and he immediately agreed. Telling Marcus that he and Bennie would be in Detroit as soon as possible, he left Martin to handle the rest of the meeting and started making arrangements to get Bennie and himself to Detroit. He tried vainly to figure out what time it was in L.A., and where Bennie might be at that moment. Deciding that she was probably at the airport for her return flight, he took out his cellular phone and punched in the speed-dial for Bennie's phone.

The phone rang several times, and Clay was about to hang up when an unfamiliar voice answered. "Hello? To whom am I speaking?" asked the voice.

Clay's brow wrinkled. "This is Clayton Deveraux. Who are you and why are you answering my wife's telephone?" he asked gruffly.

There was a silence on the other end of the phone. "Mr. Deveraux, this the Queen of Angels hospital in Los Angeles. I am sorry to have to inform you, but your wife was in a car accident this evening."

The next hours were the most hellish that Clay could ever remember. Even when his father had died and Clay had to identify the body and accompany it back to Atlanta, the feeling had not been anything like what he was going through now. He knew only that Bennie was in intensive care. The doctor could not give him the full range of her injuries, because there had been several people involved in the accident and the triage process was making it difficult to complete evaluations of each patient. All Clay could do was get from Tokyo to L.A. as fast as possible. It was a sheer act of luck that Martin was with him—had he been alone there was no telling what he would have done to relieve the desperate anxiety.

It was Martin who pulled strings to get them on the next nonstop to L.A., Martin who telephoned Bennie's family and Lillian, and Martin who kept Clay from going over the edge. When they finally arrived at the hospital the next day, Andrew was there—Detroit was a lot closer to L.A. than Tokyo.

"Clay, Benita is doing as well as can be expected. She has some facial fractures, and her right lung is punctured. She has a broken arm and collarbone and she has lost a lot of blood." He paused for Clay to take in that information before he delivered the final blow. Putting his hand on Clay's shoulder, he added sadly, "The baby didn't make it, Clay. The shock to her body was too much. There wasn't any trauma in the pelvic region, and she will be able to have more children. But . . ." His voice trailed off for a moment before he continued. "She is in deep shock, Clay. She's in a coma. They have not been able to revive her since the accident, and that is their main concern right now."

Clay's unshaven face grew more ashen with each word from Andrew's mouth. By the time Andrew finished speaking, tears were rolling down Clay's face, but he could not trust himself to speak. Finally he asked to see Bennie. Andrew hesitated. "Dammit, where is my wife? I have to see her now," Clay demanded. The panic that had grown in him since the initial phone call was about to erupt into hysteria.

Andrew spoke soothingly, saying that he would take Clay to Benita right away. "But I want you to prepare yourself, Clay; she looks pretty rough."

Nothing could have prepared Clay for the sight of Bennie with half her face bandaged and the other half bruised. Her eyes were closed, but even in slumber she did not look like she was resting; she looked to be in terrible pain. There was a breathing tube in her nose, and an IV was dripping slowly into her arm. A blood-pressure monitor was registering her heartbeat, and some other machine appeared to be attached to her scalp. Clay almost fell over at the sight of his beautiful, broken wife, but he managed to find the chair next to her bed and take one of her cold, pale hands in his.

"Peaches. Oh, God, baby, what have I done to you?" he whispered before he broke down in great, racking sobs.

From far away, Bennie observed the scene with great interest. The handsome man was crying as though his heart would break, while the poor woman in the bed seemed to be completely unaware of what was happening. It seemed very, very sad, but sad like a movie, not like anything real.

It was warm and fragrant where she was, where ever that was. She could hear a humming noise, like soft music. She could make out a golden, lovely glow that was coming closer and closer. It—whatever the glow was—seemed to be coming for her. Or maybe she was going toward it; she wasn't positive. She didn't seem to be walking, that was for sure. Maybe she was floating—whatever it was, it was an indescribably nice sensation, like swimming in a warm, fragrant ocean.

"Hello, Fish-face." Bennie smiled. Gilbert used to call her Fish-face. Fish-face, Bird-face, Monkey-face, and whatever else he could come up with. The glow seemed to dissipate a little. It was Gilbert, walking toward her with his same sweet smile. She reached out a hand to touch him but he stopped. "Not yet, Benita. It's not time for you yet," he said softly.

"Why are you here then?" she asked plaintively. "I miss you. I want to go with you."

Gilbert looked very sad and peaceful at the same time. "I had to come for this," he said quietly. Bennie noticed a blanket-wrapped bundle that Gilbert was carrying. The blanket moved softly and a glow seeped out of its folds. Bennie suddenly felt cold and empty and afraid. Gilbert knew exactly what she was feeling, the way he always did.

"Don't be afraid, Fish-face. He needs you. He loves you. Take care of each other and love each other. I love you Benita. I always will."

The glow started to fade and the warmth and fragrance slowly disappeared, leaving her alone and lost, except for the feel of her hand in Clay's.

Ten

Clay's heart nearly leaped out of his chest when he felt the unmistakable pressure of Bennie's hand in his. He gently squeezed her hand again, and she responded again. "Baby? Peaches, can you hear me?" he said urgently. Bennie's hand moved gently in Clay's and she clung to its familiar contour. "Benita, I have to get the doctor, baby. I'll be right back," Clay said, moving away. Bennie's face puckered and she clung tighter to his hand, as if begging him not to leave her. Clay panicked momentarily—he had to get a doctor or a nurse, but he couldn't leave her.

Luckily, a nurse came in while making her fifteen-minute rounds, as was the habit in the intensive-care unit. Her face brightened when she realized that poor Mrs. Deveraux was showing signs of life. She hastily called the doctor and pried Bennie's hand away from Clay so that the doctor could examine the patient. "It's all right, Mrs. Deveraux; he'll be right back," she said soothingly. "He hasn't left your side in two days, Mrs. Deveraux; he'll be back as soon as the doctor looks at you." Once the examination began, Frances, the night nurse, urged Clay to stretch his legs and get something to eat. "I'm worried about you, Mr. D. You can't help her if you keel over, now, can you?"

Clay barely heard her words, or the concern in her voice. His thoughts were totally with his wife. Clay ignored the advice to rest—he did what he had been doing every time he was forced to leave Bennie, and paced up and down the corridor. Bennie had hovered near the brink of consciousness for two appalling days, and she was finally showing signs of reviving. Clay had never felt as helpless in his life. The person whom he loved more than anyone else in the world had come close to dying, and it was his fault. No one else had come to him with that accusation, but it was true nonetheless.

If he had not cajoled Bennie into coming to L.A., none of this would have happened. She would have been safe at home in Atlanta, happily preparing for the birth of their child. *Our baby.* Fresh pain racked Clay as he thought again that while he had come close to losing his wife, they had truly lost their baby. How was he going to face her? How in the name of God was he going to help her get over the pain that was threatening to kill him now?

Clay paused in his endless walking and leaned against the cool tile of the hospital corridor. He felt a hand on his arm and looked down to see Renee's face awash in concern for him. "Clay, you have to go the hotel and get a shower and some sleep. You have to. You're not in this alone, Clay. You have me and Andrew and Martin and . . . and everybody in Detroit and Atlanta, too. We're all here for you and Bennie. But honey, wearing yourself out is not going to help anyone. You have to get some rest," Renee pleaded.

Martin joined the two of them, carrying a paper cup of coffee, which he handed to Clay. "Renee, take him to the hotel. Sit on him if you have to, but keep him there for four hours at least. I'll stay with Benita until you come back," he said in a voice that indicated no bargaining.

Clay was too exhausted to argue anymore. Almost placidly he went with Renee, after insisting that Martin call him immediately if there was any change. Clay docilely followed Renee out to her rental car in the parking lot. He did not speak until they had almost reached the hotel where she, Andrew, and Martin had a suite. He finally turned to Renee and said bleakly, "How am I going to tell her about the baby, Renee? What words am I going to use?"

* * *

Bennie felt nothing but pain. For a while she had been holding Clay's hand, but he wasn't there now. Someone was in the room with her—a man, she thought. It must be the doctor. But there was relative silence except for the incessant beeping of the infernal machines that were apparently helping her to stay alive. Someone was speaking to her in a soft voice, but Bennie could not understand what he or she was saying. Her chest felt like a slab of stone lay across it; she could barely breathe. And she couldn't swallow; something was keeping her mouth from opening. It was hot in the room, and she couldn't breathe.

She tried to move, to sit up, to get air, and she couldn't. Bennie was alarmed at first; then panic set in. *Why can't I move? Why can't I breathe? Can't they see I can't breathe?* Through her haze she heard a voice saying, "Breathe through your nose, Benita. There is plenty of air, and you can get it if you breathe through your nose." Strong arms raised her up a little, and she vaguely heard the whirring sound of her bed being raised. When she was arranged in an upright position, she really could breathe.

She lay there, savoring the sweet air. She opened her eye gratefully to see the person who had helped her. *Martin.* His eye patch and his height gave her his identity immediately. *Martin knows; he understands.* Bennie tried to look around the room. She saw no one but her brother-in-law. Martin saw her searching look and assured her that Clay was with the doctor. "He'll be here in just a minute, Benita." Bennie closed her eyes, knowing that Clay was nearby. Only one hand seemed to be working and she reached out to Martin. He held her hand tightly, as if his life force could flow into her from their contact.

Bennie felt the pain ebbing away and started drifting with it. There was something she had to tell Martin, so that he could help Clay. It was a secret that Gilbert had told her, but she couldn't remember what it was. *You have to help Clay, Martin.* Bennie wanted desperately to say the words, but her mouth would not open. She fell asleep with tears running down the side of her face.

Mercifully, Bennie slept for several hours. When she awoke, she was still in the almost upright position that was most comfortable for her. She was still in terrible pain, but she was beginning to understand that the pain was in different parts of her body. She tried opening the eye that was not bandaged. Slowly she raised the lid; it blinked a few times and she was able to focus. Sitting beside her bed with his head in his hands was Clay. He looked so sad, so tired. Bennie reached for him with the one hand that wanted to cooperate. The movement roused Clay, and he saw that Bennie was looking at him.

He immediately took her hand and brought his chair as close to her as possible. He kissed her hand repeatedly while she clung to his strength. "Benita. Oh, Benita, I'm so glad you're awake, baby. You're going to be fine, baby. Just fine." Bennie pulled her hand away to indicate her other arm. "It's in traction for a while, Benita; it's broken," Clay said carefully. Bennie pointed at her mouth and patted her jaw to show that it wouldn't work. Clay gave her face the barest touch with his long finger. "Your jaw is wired, Benita. You have a facial fracture along that side," he said gently. Bennie stared at Clay for a long moment. She took his hand and laid it on her abdomen, never taking her gaze away from him.

Clay's eyes filled with tears and before he could answer, Bennie knew. She remembered what it was that Gilbert had shown her in those hazy moments. Bennie let go of Clay's hand and covered her face with her free arm. Despite the wires clamping her fractured face in place, she sobbed like a child. Clay had as much of her in his arms as he could manage, trying his best to calm her down. "Benita, I'm sorry, I'm sorry. Please forgive me, Benita; I'll make it up to you somehow. Please forgive me," Clay said brokenly. Bennie could not hear a word of what Clay was saying; she could not feel his arms or see his tears. All she felt was emptiness and pain.

* * *

The worst part of the entire ordeal was what he could not share with anyone. Over and over the scene played through his mind like an endless loop of video that could never be erased. Soon after his arrival at the hospital, while Bennie was undergoing the surgery to repair her punctured lung, a nurse had approached Clay and asked him to sign a form to dispose of the abruption. Clay's lack of knowledge of the term had shown on his face, and the nurse had reddened while she gave him the simple, horrifying explanation.

"An abruption is . . . a medical term for your wife's, um, mis . . ." the woman stammered, obviously uncomfortable with the message she had to deliver. Clay's knees had buckled as he realized that this woman was talking about their baby, the baby that he and Bennie had made and that had so tragically died. The nurse was trying to get him to sign some kind of release form to destroy his child's remains. Tremors overtook his body as the full import of the words sank in. *Our baby. Our child.* And the hospital was going to . . . *what?* "No," was all Clay could say. The nurse looked at him in alarm—he was paler than death, and sweat had broken across his forehead. She wasn't even sure that he was listening to her. "No," he said again. "You are not going to . . . to . . ." He couldn't finish the thought.

The nurse thought he was going to pass out, which he probably would have. Helping him to a chair in the deserted waiting area, she ran for her supervisor. The supervisor was a middle-aged African-American woman who saw right away that Clay was on the verge of a total breakdown. Very quietly and gently, Mrs. Bady explained that when the baby was less than twenty-one weeks old, the remains were discreetly disposed of, unless the family wished otherwise. And between twenty-two and twenty-five weeks, the policy was approximately the same. Clay had shuddered at her clinical assessment, although she had spoken kindly. Bennie had been twenty-six weeks pregnant.

"Every family deals with their grief differently, Mr.

Deveraux. If you would like to have some kind of service for your baby, it would be perfectly appropriate. I will be happy to assist you and your wife. . . ."

Clay shook his head. "My wife is in surgery right now, and will be in intensive care right afterward. I don't want this to wait, and I don't want to further distress her with the details," he said simply.

Mrs. Bady nodded her head. "All right then, Mr. Deveraux, let me call a friend of mine who is a funeral director and we will make the arrangements."

The arrangements. The words had a hollow ring to them. Clay would never forget the pathetic Styrofoam container that held the body of their child. The fact that the funeral director provided a small, white casket to inter the remains with the hospital-issued receptacle safely inside was no comfort. Clay stared at the tiny casket that contained so many of the dreams that he and Bennie had shared, and wept silently. With tears running down his face, he removed the gold bracelet that Bennie had presented to him and laid it in the casket. He was alone in the funeral parlor—he had not told anyone what he was doing because he could not bear any discussions on the proper course of action. He did not want to hear arguments for and against a service, whether it should be done in Atlanta or California or Timbuktu; he just wanted to know that his baby—their baby—was put to rest. Whether he would ever rest again was another story.

Somehow they made it through the subsequent days. Bennie's condition continued to improve, although she had a setback when it was revealed that Big Benny had suffered a stroke. Benny actually recovered faster than his daughter and had to be forcibly detained from making the trip to California to see about her. Around that time that Bennie's family had to return to their home bases to make further arrangements. Andrew left first, having assured himself that his sister was getting the best care possible. Before leaving, he talked seriously to Clay about Bennie's continuing care.

"She's going to need a stay in extended care, to make sure that she is getting the physical therapy and monitoring that she requires," he cautioned. "Then, if a nurse is not available, she will need to go into a rehabilitation facility until she can travel and take care of herself."

Clay shook his head. "I can get Benita whatever care she needs, however she needs it. What I need to know is when she will be able to travel. I want to get her home as soon as possible," he said decisively.

Andrew looked at Clay and shrugged eloquently. "That is pretty much going to be up to Benita. She is young and she was in superb condition when this happened. Her recovery should be fairly rapid, all things considered. Her mental state is critical, however. What I am afraid of, more than anything, is depression. She has had an awful lot to deal with over the past few days—it is essential that we take into consideration her mental state as well as her physical one."

Clay could not disagree with Andrew in his capacity as a physician or as his wife's brother. Clay was more alarmed than he could articulate about Bennie's general lassitude. Her injuries seemed to be healing, but she was withdrawing from Clay and from everyone else. Clay was feeling more and more helpless and liking it less and less. Running his hands through his hair, he turned to Andrew with his anxiety plain to see. "Andrew, what am I supposed to do? How can I help her? I keep telling myself that once I get her back to Atlanta everything will be fine, but it won't, will it? It's only going to get worse, isn't it?"

Clay was about to start pacing again when Andrew grabbed his shoulder. "Clay, listen to me. What Benita has gone through no one should have to suffer. Especially not my sister, because we all love her and want the best for her. I can't tell you what is going to happen right now. All I can tell you is not to expect miracles. It is going to take time for Bennie to heal physically, mentally, and emotionally. I'm a damned doctor and I can't tell you what's going to occur next. All I can give you are some guidelines. And I know that's not what you want to hear," he finished, anticipating Clay's next remark. "We all want the same thing, Clay, and that's for Benita to be well and strong and to help her through this as much as possible. And there is no perfect formula to do that. We have to follow Benita's lead, here. We have to do what is going to be best for her, after all."

The two men were sitting in the waiting area of the ICU area, waiting for Bennie's bed to be moved into progressive care, a downgrade from the ICU. This move meant that she was recovering to an extent that she did not require constant monitoring. Renee and Martin joined the two men. Renee was also going back to Detroit temporarily, to make arrangements to return to California to stay as long as Bennie needed her. There was no way she was leaving her friend alone during this time. And Aunt Ruth had stopped her globe-trotting to come to her niece. With her years of nursing experience, she was just the person to take over in the wake of the tragedy.

Martin listened to the discussion without comment for a while and then spoke. "You may not like what I'm going to say, but I think the best thing you can do is to leave Benita alone for a while," he said frankly. He looked at his brother's expression of disbelief calmly. "I know it seems like the totally wrong thing to do, Clay, but I was where Bennie is not too long ago," he said, recalling his own accident and its aftermath. "There were so many times when I needed to be able to be quiet, without looking better or feeling better or being cheerful for the relatives. I just need to be alone for a while to blank everything out. I'm not suggesting that we let Benita take it as far as I did," he said self-deprecatingly, "but she could probably use some privacy right now. This is a lot for her to get used to," he pointed out.

Clay lowered his head into his hands and tried to still the pounding in his temples that was almost constant now.

There didn't seem to be a logical or right course of action for him to take. This was not like the boardroom, where he laid out his objectives and devised a plan for accomplishing them. This was real life, and his real wife was down the hall suffering the worst pain of her life, pain that he had inadvertently caused. No one was saying it, no one was blaming him, but he blamed himself. Even when Donnie had come from Detroit to see his beloved sister with his own eyes, he had looked at Clay with compassion and not censure. For some reason, the behavior of her family made him feel even worse.

He had to put his own feelings aside, though, and deal with what was best for his wife. The depression that Andrew had spoken of was quite real; Bennie was more and more listless every day. The fact that her jawbone was still wired was no help. Even though it was an impediment to speech, she still should have been able to say a few words—but she didn't even try. Day after day, Clay would sit by her bedside and talk to her, holding her hand and trying to be reassuring. Sometimes it was as though he was not even in the room, Bennie would be so still and unresponsive.

Her doctors tried to be reassuring, but their efforts were without merit. Dr. Dantes, a small Filipino woman with a sincere and engaging manner, laid it on the table for Clay. "Mr. Deveraux, your wife has suffered a great trauma to her body, as well as to her mind and her spirit. It is never easy to lose a loved one, but to have a miscarriage in this fashion is exceptionally traumatic. You get up in the morning and you are pregnant, and when you wake again, you are not, with no warning and no chance to prepare yourself. This is trauma enough for the psyche. And to awake in dreadful pain, unable to speak, unable to have full movement, this compounds the suffering." Clay could barely stand to hear what Dr. Dantes was saying, but he knew that she was explaining Bennie's condition as clearly as it was possible to explain.

"Your wife, Benita, is suffering as a soldier would who

has seen terrible things in war. It is like a form of Post-Traumatic Stress Disorder, very severe. It may be weeks or months before she is strong enough emotionally to pick up the pieces of your life together. I do not like to say it so bluntly, but this is what you must be prepared to accept," she said in a grave tone of voice.

Clay looked at the small woman across the oak table in the triage room where they were cloistered. Martin, Renee, and Donnie were all present, as Clay saw no reason to keep them out. They would have been told any developments as soon as he left the room anyway, so he had no reason to bar them from the conference. Clay finally spoke. "Dr. Dantes, are you saying that I shouldn't take Benita back to Atlanta? Is she going to have to stay in the hospital indefinitely?" His voice was close to breaking as he asked the dreaded question.

Dr. Dantes answered quickly, "No, I do not think the hospital is the place where she will regain her strength and stability. There are many facilities where she can get the care and counseling that she will require. There is a very fine facility in Atlanta, as a matter of fact. I will tell you, though, that the ultimate decision will have to be your wife's. By that I mean that she will have the most work to do in her own recovery. There will be highly trained people helping her every step of the way, but the lion's share of the work will be hers."

Dr. Dantes left the room after answering more questions for Clay and Donnie. Renee and Martin had been mostly silent during the discussion. Renee broke her silence to say that it was immaterial where Bennie recuperated; she was there for the duration. Donnie mentioned that there were some facilities in the Detroit area as well, but that it would be unthinkable for Bennie to be away from Clay for any length of time. Furthermore, it was impractical for Clay to be away from the Deveraux Group for an extended period.

Clay's head went up at the mention of The Deveraux Group—for the first time in twenty years he had literally forgotten that there was such a place as the business he had built into a media monolith. He immediately said, "The company is not my priority right now. Benita is my only priority. My brothers can take care of the company for the time being."

Martin finally spoke. "I don't have a problem with that, Clay. But before we get too entrenched in making plans for Benita, I suggest we find out what would be best for her by asking her. She is injured; she's not simple. You need to talk to her and find out what she wants."

Clay did not say it, but that was the very conversation he wanted to avoid. Benita had every right to never want to see him again, and he did not want to risk hearing her say the words that would destroy him.

"Benita, you're still having the dreams." The statement, coming in John's soft, measured voice, was no less frightening to Bennie. The dreams that Bennie had been having since the accident were no better, even though she was practically herself again, at least physically. There was no danger that Clay would have to nurse her or treat her like an invalid. The scars had done a remarkable job of healing, thanks to the repeated use of the surgical gel packs and emollient lotions assiduously applied. But still a fear lingered in Bennie. She turned her big eyes to John, afraid to answer him and afraid not to.

"John, it's been over four months since the accident. And yes, I am still having those dreams. In fact"—she hesitated—"they're getting worse," she whispered. Bennie lowered her head and looked at her hands.

John leaned toward her in a gesture of support and concern. "Try to tell me about it, Benita. How are they getting worse?"

Bennie sighed and sat up straight, still not meeting John's eyes. "Benita, I have a cottage that is on the beach, about twenty-five miles north of here. There is room for you, your Aunt Ruth, and Renee, and there is a very good physical therapist who will be willing to make daily home visits.

"It's not too isolated; there is a big mall within a few miles. And there is a lap pool right in the backyard. The previous owner was an Olympic swimmer who swam daily," he added. as if that information were vital. He leaned closer to Bennie and spoke quietly and persuasively. "The thing is, Benita, I think you can get better there. I think you need to be away from anything that looks like an institution, from people in uniforms and from anything that reminds you of a hospital. I think it's time that we tried something new to get you back on your feet."

Bennie actually looked at John then, for the first time. He took advantage of that moment and smiled. "We can have you out of here and settled in about two days, Benita. And then we can get you well." For the first time since she regained consciousness in the queen of Angels intensive-care unit, Bennie smiled. It was a weak and shaky smile, but it was unmistakable. And then she spoke. "Okay." It was all she said, but it was a beginning.

From that point on the change in Bennie was almost miraculous. She began to speak again, she participated in her therapy instead of lying passively and submitting to it, and she began the process of healing. But the dreams would not go away. Every night, almost, it was the same dream, although as she told John, it was somehow getting worse, more intense. She tried again to explain it to John.

"It's like before, when I was floating along and I hear this music and see this glowing light. And then I hear Gilbert's voice, and he talks to me and tells me that it's not my time. And I ask him why he is here, if he hasn't come to take me with him. He shows me a bundle in a blanket and says, 'I came for this.' This sort of golden light comes from the blanket, and Gilbert looks very sad and sweet and tells me that everything will be fine. And he . . . goes away, I guess." Bennie's brow furrowed in concentration as she tried to recall the exact nuances of the dream.

"Well, then I started having the dream more and more,

but this time I am trying to follow Gilbert. I don't care what he says; I have to be with him now, and I want what he has. It's mine, and I have to have it back; I *have* to. Because if I don't get it, something terrible is going to happen—not to me, necessarily, but to Clay. I think it's Clay who I am trying to protect, so I have to get it back from Gilbert. And he just runs from me." The pain was evident in Bennie's voice, and her eyes reflected the confusion of trying to sort through the dream.

"Now when I have the dream it's even worse. Because now I know that if I don't catch Gilbert something terrible is going to happen to Clay. I am running and running, and I can just see Gilbert in front of me through this dense, gray fog; it's almost black. I'm calling and calling him, and he won't answer me; he won't turn around. My feet are bare and there are sharp stones on the ground, and it is cold, terribly cold, and whatever I am wearing is not enough because I'm freezing and, and . . . then finally I catch him!" Bennie turned troubled eyes on John and repeated her last words.

"I finally caught up with him in the dream, John. And he turns around and it isn't Gilbert at all; it's Clay. And there is no bundle; there is nothing, just a piece of cloth. He looks right through me and lets go of the cloth and it floats away and disappears . . . and I wake up in tears," she finished with a small sob.

John reached for her hand and held it while she composed herself. "What does it mean, John? Why do I keep having the dream?"

John rubbed his thumb across her knuckles. There was a lot that he could do as a therapist, but he could not take a patient down a path that she was not ready to tread. And he knew that right now there was a terror that Bennie had yet to face, but the day was fast approaching when it would be inevitable.

John could feel Bennie's pain and fear as plainly as if she had said the words. He admired this beautiful, brave woman more than he could say—probably more than was ethical in a doctor-patient relationship. He had seen her in the beginning broken and in despair, and to see her now, strong, purposeful, and determined, was truly rewarding. But he did not delude himself that Benita Deveraux was completely healed. There were still some issues bubbling under the surface, like lava about to erupt through the thin crust of a volcano's surface. What they were and when they would surface was anyone's guess, but they had to come out if the healing was to come full circle.

John glanced at his watch and suggested that they end it for today. Bennie reminded him that he was to join her for dinner the next night. "My sister-in-law, Clay's sister, Angelique, is on her way out here. She'll be here in the morning. I think you'll like her," Bennie said cheerfully. "She's kind of a case study all on her own."

John smiled. "I'm looking forward to it. Try to take it easy until then—don't push yourself too hard, okay?" John flushed suddenly—he had been about to give Bennie a quick kiss on the cheek before he realized what he was doing. *What in the hell am I doing here?* he thought. *This is crazy,* muy loco.

Bennie watched John get into his car, and then walked back into the cottage and closed the door behind her. She was tired of working on the dream, but she knew that she must to get her life back. She looked down at her hand without her engagement and wedding rings. When she was brought into the emergency room, they had to remove her jewelry at once due to her injury. Bennie knew that Clay had the rings, but she could not bring herself to ask for them back. She didn't want the rings; she wanted what they symbolized—her husband, her family with him, and her piece of eternity. For a long time she did not think she would regain all that they had lost, but now she was determined. She had fought for Clay before and she was going to fight again. She was almost ready. Dream or no dream, she was getting ready.

Renee's departure had signaled the beginning of her readiness to resume her normal life. At Bennie's insistence,

Renee had returned to Detroit, albeit reluctantly. Renee had spent nearly all of Bennie's recuperation time with her, except for odd weekends when Donnie and the others had come out, and another weekend when Vera, Lillian, and Uncle Bump had come. Bennie had urged Renee to get back to Detroit. Renee had a most capable manager running Urban Oasis in her absence, but the spa still needed her professional touch. Moreover, it was not only her regular customers who were getting agitated by her absence—poor Andrew was beside himself. Their on-again, off-again relationship was definitely on; this time it seemed to be for the duration.

Renee was anxious to get home, but she could not help feeling that there was something more to the John Flores situation than met the eye. To her mind, he was taking more than a professional interest in Bennie. She had caught him looking at Bennie in a way that none of her other doctors had. She had gently pointed this out to Bennie, only to be met with laughter.

"Renee, please! John has nothing but a professional interest in me! He brought me to his cottage, yes, but if he hadn't I might be in a loony bin by now, and you know it! Besides," she added in a softer voice, "he reminds me of Adam, for some reason." And there was a marked similarity between the two men; although John was of African-American and Puerto Rican ancestry, he and Bennie's younger brother shared some similar traits. They were both well over six feet tall, they both had golden caramel skin and thick black eyebrows, both affected mustaches, and both wore their hair in long ponytails. John's hair was straighter in texture than Adam's, but they both looked like dashing, avant-garde intellectuals, which they both were.

Renee had to admit that there was a comforting familiarity about the man, due mostly to the fact that he hid from hair scissors, as did Adam. And she had to further admit that Bennie had made a miraculous recovery and could not have done so without John. But she also felt that it was time for Bennie to go home to her husband, which she gently tried to point out. "Bennie, you can't stay out here much longer," she began.

Bennie agreed immediately. "No, and I don't intend to. I just wanted to spare Clay the worst of my recovery. Ne-ne, you have no idea what it is like to care for a sick spouse. It was so humiliating for Gilbert when I had to bathe him and dress him and when he would throw up—it was horrible. For him, not for me—I would have done anything for him. But I know how much it hurts to see a loved one in pain, and I couldn't do that to Clay; I just couldn't." Bennie's eyes glazed over as she remembered her days of endless agony with Gilbert, as well as her own paralyzing pain right after the accident.

"But I'm better now. I want to be home soon—very soon. I just think I need to be here alone for a few days, to tidy up a few details with John," she stated. It was mostly true, after all.

And as Bennie pointed out, it wasn't as though she would be alone. "Every time I turn around there is someone else dropping in on me. My family calls me every night, and I talk to Clay at least once a day." Bennie did not look particularly happy as she related this last part—she and Clay did speak briefly every day, but it was awkward. He had stopped asking when she was coming home, and she had stopped making excuses. It was as though they were balanced on a high wire, which they were, in a manner of speaking.

Bennie missed Clay more than she thought humanly possible. Even before the thick veil of depression began to lift, she felt his absence so keenly that she could not eat or speak at times. At the same time, her insistence that she not burden him and her own sense of guilt over the tragedy made it paramount that she be whole and well when she went back to him. She had never complained about taking care of Gilbert, even when he was incontinent or threw up in bed or was delirious from medication. But she would have died a thousand times over before letting Clay see her in any of those conditions. And after the bandages came off her face and body, she was sure she had made the right decision.

The redness and newness of the scars would fade in time, especially the relatively small one down the side of her face. There were a few on her temple, but that was what bangs were for, she reasoned. It would not be so easy to hide the rib-to-rib incision that was a result of the partial lobectomy to repair her punctured lung. That was an angry, raised welt of crimson that would take time to fade. There was a special surgical-gel tape that she used day and night to speed up the process, and it was helping, but she still felt like Frankenstein's other experiment when she looked at herself in the mirror. She was too thin, for one thing. And the huge elastic pressure bandages that she had to sleep in for her arm and chest were not exactly sexy. But she would be out of them soon. She just prayed that Clay's feelings would still be the same. Losing the baby had been hard enough—losing Clay would surely kill her.

Everyone in the Deveraux Group trod lightly around Clay these days. Every since his return to Atlanta he was a changed man. It wasn't that he stormed around and threw fits of rage; it would have been a relief if he had. Clay was quiet, withdrawn, and somber, revealing a persona no one had ever witnessed before. He threw himself into work with a vengeance, working from dawn until nightfall on most days. He was the first person in the office and the last one to leave it. It was speculated that he slept there, but no one had witnessed him doing so. In truth, he might as well have slept there, for the little sleep that he got.

He made it a point to get home as late as possible at night. He could not bear the emptiness of the huge house without Benita's loving presence. She had changed the house in the short time she lived there, just as she had changed Clay during their time together. The house, under Bennie's ministrations, no longer had an empty, cold feeling. The sight of Benita's furniture mixed in with his gave him a sense of longing for her that was unbearable. The sight of her pillows and throws and enchanting objets d'art made his heart ache for the sight of her. The smell of her perfume and the sight of her clothes in their suite were too much—Clay had taken to sleeping in one of the guest rooms on the lower floor because he could not stand his bed without Benita in it.

Aretha was his only consolation. The big black cat had become totally attached to Clay. She would wait for him every night and follow him around until he picked her up. Where he sat, she sat; where he lay, she lay. She seemed to sense when Bennie was on the telephone and would lie across Clay's chest purring like mad. Aretha did not approve of Bennie's absence any more than Clay did. She sometimes looked at him in a manner that suggested that if he were any kind of man he would go and fetch her immediately. Clay ignored that look, although he felt the cat's disdain quite keenly. In truth, there were times when he was within a heartbeat of flying to California and abducting Bennie by force if he had to. But something stopped him every time.

Clay had never been able to rid himself of the idea that he was responsible for Bennie's accident. He never stopped regretting the position he had put her in. If he had only let her alone to pursue her writing and not insisted that she be a part, however small, of the Deveraux Group, none of this would have happened. Not a day went by that Clay did not calculate how close Bennie would be to delivering their baby if he had not convinced her to take that ill-fated trip. Bennie never accused him; her brothers, his brothers, his mother, all the sisters-in-law, everyone was on his side, yet he felt like the lowest form of life.

With the uncanny instinct of a bird of prey, Big Benny was able to feast on Clay's guilt. Andrew had confessed to Clay that he had called in a few favors to get Big Benny's doctors to refuse to let him travel, although in truth there was nothing to prevent him from so doing. It was the only way that Andrew could keep Big Benny away from Bennie's side—Andrew knew instinctively that his presence would cause more harm than good. He was not blind to the complexities of their father's relationship with Bennie, and he was also attuned to the way that Benny related to Clay. No purpose would be served by having Benny in his daughter's face while she was trying to recuperate. But that did not stop Benny from using the telephone. If he wasn't phoning Bennie to console her and quiz her on her state of health, he was calling Clay to remind him that he had predicted disaster if the wedding took place. The first time he had called, Clay had been shocked and hurt, but he was too wrapped up in guilt to formulate a defense. He just let Benny harangue him.

"So you were going to protect my daughter and my grandchildren, were you? You selfish bastard, you did nothing but put her in harm's way. You destroyed my grandchild and you ruined my daughter's life, you sorry Creole trash, and you're going to pay the rest of your life. She's never coming back to you; I'm going to see to it, you sorry dog." Benny's anger grew with every word.

Clay was afraid the old man would work himself into another stroke, something for which Bennie would never forgive him. So he took it as long as he could—he was thankful when Benny ran out of steam and cut the connection. Thanks to caller ID, Clay did not answer when he saw the Cochran Detroit number, but that did not stop Benny from leaving a number of hateful messages on the answering machine, messages that Clay erased immediately.

Clay could only hope that Benita would come back to him when the pain of seeing him lessened. He truly did not know how much more he could take of being away from her. He had all but stopped looking at calendars—the accident was in February and it was now the middle of June. The only things that brought him any comfort were the little letters that Bennie sent him every week, along with their brief daily call. Even those was beginning to cause more pain than they eased. Bennie sounded guarded and awkward on the telephone. He wasn't used to the polite conversation they made—even when they were first dating they had warm, rich, funny talks that made him hot and eager for her. He wanted that back. He wanted his wife back; their life back; but he did not know if he would ever have it, and he was beginning to be afraid to try. He had already hurt her enough.

Night after night he would put on the sweet, sexy CD that Bennie had made for his birthday, and listen to her miraculous voice singing just for him. Sometimes, although it caused him more pain than it eased, he would look at the magical pictures he had taken that morning and remember. Sometimes the memories, accompanied by her soft voice on the CD player, would lull him into a fitful sleep. Most times, though, they would haunt him to another pale gray dawn. He would remember the slight, insubstantial weight of that small container he carried from Queen of Angels hospital. He would remember his wife's broken body and shattered spirit, and he would remember that he was the unwitting cause of it all. And sometimes the tears would come.

Eleven

Angelique was the only member of the Deveraux family who had conflicting feelings about Bennie. She was past the stage where she despised the woman; Bennie was just too damned nice to really hate. But she did manage to stir things up in Atlanta. For one thing, there was that business with her mother and Bump Williams. For God's sake, they were running around like they were teenagers! With no shame whatsoever, they were traveling together and acting like young kids in the first flush of love. It was downright embarrassing at times. Although it was really quite sweet, too. Angelique could not lay this one at Bennie's feet, but it did start up in Detroit, due to the fact that Bump and Lillian had run into each other at Bennie's party.

Then there was this new feeling of family that had started since she came around. Every time Angelique turned around there was some kind of cookout or picnic or trip to St. Simons, and everybody was there—the whole family, including some relative or another of Bennie's who never all seemed to stay in Detroit. Not that it wasn't fun; it actually was. And Bennie had never seemed to lord it over anybody that she was a good cook and hostess. And she never seemed to know that the things that they were doing weren't totally normal for the Deveraux family. Like when Martin moved back to Atlanta.

That one took everybody by surprise. It was as though he had decided that it was time for him to become a member of the human race again. It was true that he was still reclusive, to an extent. He did not frequent the clubs and parties the way he once had, but he was no longer living on the houseboat in the keys; he was back home. And that Bennie had somehow influenced this was something Angelique did not doubt in the least. It was hard to dislike Bennie, but Angelique was not altogether sure that the woman was not a witch of some kind. She certainly had Clay by the short hairs.

Angelique could not understand what had happened to her brother since Bennie's accident. Every since he came back to Atlanta without her, he was a wreck. It just about killed Angelique to see him in the state he was in, but there did not seem to be anything that she or anyone else could do about it. Angelique actually felt sorry for Bennie—hell, no one deserved what had happened to her—but she failed to see how hiding out in California would make anything better. And her absence was destroying Clay. After spending a particularly grueling afternoon with Clay, whom she was trying to cheer up, Angelique came to a conclusion: if nobody else had balls enough to talk some sense into that woman, she did. By the next day, she was on a plane.

Bennie had been surprised to hear from Angelique, but pleased. Any connection to Clay was better than none, and she knew that Angelique saw her brother frequently, or she had since the accident. Bennie hoped that she would be able to get something more out of Angelique than the polite, distant phone conversations she had been having with her husband.

Angelique arrived at the cottage with shopping bags. No matter where she was in the world, Angelique managed to find a place or two to shop. She seemed to know the great malls of the world the way certain art connoisseurs knew the collections of the great museums. Despite her jaunty demeanor, Angelique had been disturbed by Bennie's appearance.

It had not occurred to Angelique that there would be such marked changes in her sister-in-law. Bennie had never been voluptuous, but the woman was a stick! And she had a huge bandage plastered across her face that made her look like the Phantom of the Opera. Bennie assured her that it was temporary, and had even taken it off to show Angelique that it was just to accelerate the healing process, but Angelique was appalled nonetheless. And it wasn't just that Bennie had scars from her ordeal; it was her whole demeanor. For some reason Angelique thought that Bennie was lounging around on the beach every morning and shopping every afternoon before dancing till dawn or something.

All she seemed to do was work out. She would get up in the morning at some god-awful hour and do tai chi exercises to limber up. Then she would work out with that big blond physical therapist of hers for what seemed like hours. Then, instead of taking a nap like a normal person, she would write a letter to Clay in the afternoon and send e-mail to her brothers and other friends. And all she wanted to do was talk about Clay. How was he, was he working too hard, was he eating right? The eagerness in her face for information about her husband was pathetic—Angelique couldn't decide who was the worse off, Bennie or Clay. It was obvious that her original plan to give Bennie a kick in the pants was not appropriate, but she was damned if she knew what was.

The next night, Angelique was taken aback as John Flores approached the house. "You didn't tell me your brother was in town," Angelique said as she stared at John's approaching figure.

Bennie smiled. "That is John Flores, my therapist. He does kind of favor Adam, doesn't he? I think it's the hair," she added. Bennie introduced the two of them and went to open the wine that John had so thoughtfully provided, along with a bouquet of flowers. Angelique immediately went on red alert when she saw the way John looked at Bennie. She had no illusions that Bennie was interested in John—

there was obviously no one in the world for Bennie but Clay. This John, however, would bear watching, in Angelique's opinion. She went out of her way to be relaxed, open, and charming, which was a side of her that few got to see.

Angelique was, in fact, the life of the party. She soon had them laughing at tales of the antics of her three nieces, tales of her childhood, and anything else that was light and amusing. While everyone was in such good spirits, Angelique grabbed her trusty 35mm camera and snapped a few shots. When they all decided to have a walk on the beach to walk off Bennie's excellent dinner of seafood Vera Cruz, green salad, and risotto, Angelique took the camera along to capture the sunset. She was altogether a different person from the spoiled little wretch who had given Bennie such a hard time a few months before.

Bennie was actually quite dismayed to see her leave. In the few days that Angelique had been visiting, she felt like a major milestone had occurred in their relationship. Even though Angelique had insisted on being mysterious about her visit—to the extent of asking Bennie to not mention it to Clay—Bennie was glad she had come out to see her. For the very first time she thought there was hope for the two of them to have a sisterly relationship. She was careful not to mouth that to Angelique, however—she was willing to take it slowly. There was no point in spooking her with a lot of mushy talk. She couldn't resist giving her a big hug before she left, though. And surprisingly, Angelique did not stiffen up—she gladly accepted the embrace.

Altogether, Bennie had nothing but hope for their future—she and Angelique had made up for a lot of lost time in the few days that she had visited. And it made Bennie hope that soon, very soon, she would have the same kind of reunion with her beloved husband. She couldn't wait. Missing Clay the way she did was draining all the life out of her.

* * *

A week later, Clay had just returned to Atlanta after a trip to New York. He was tired and listless as always, and felt disheveled from the plane ride. He was slowly going through the mail that had accumulated at home, hoping to find something from Bennie. He was surprised when he came upon a heavy mailer, the kind designed to hold photographs. He turned it over in his hand—curiously there was no return address. He opened the envelope and out fell several photographs of Benita with a strange man. A violent pain shot through Clay—what the hell was this?

That she was completely comfortable and happy with this man was evident by the happy smile on her face, a smile that should have been only for Clay. Clay dropped the pictures on the floor, and as he bent to pick them up, his trembling fingers found a typewritten note: *This is what your wife is doing when she is supposed to be "recovering." She looks pretty well recovered, wouldn't you agree?*

Blind fury gripped Clay. What kind of perversion was this? Who was the man, and what was he to Benita? All this time he had waited patiently for her to return to him, and she was apparently having the time of her life with some stranger. It was quite obvious that the man was more than a friend; Clay recognized the look of longing in the man's eyes. *Well, to hell with that!* Clay's head felt like it was about to explode. He raced out of the huge, empty house and drove like a madman to the airport. He was going to get some answers tonight—his days of playing the lovesick chump were over.

Bennie was on the verge of hysteria. She could feel her heart pounding like a jackhammer, and her breaths were short pants. She kept telling herself to be calm and to breathe deeply, but she couldn't, not since she had opened the hateful package she had received a few hours before. The manila envelope had contained a picture of Clay and some simpering woman at a charity event held in Atlanta.

Clay looked to be having the time of his life. He looked utterly carefree and contented with the little slut on his arm. There was no return address, of course, and the postmark said only *Atlanta*, which told her nothing.

Bennie was trying to think rationally, but she couldn't. Was this what the dreams had meant? Was Clay leaving her? Had she waited too late to go home and try to salvage their marriage? Bennie stared at the phone for long moments—she wanted to call someone, but whom? John seemed a logical choice, but for some reason she couldn't bear to tell him what she had discovered. For that matter, what was it that she had discovered? Some cowardly bastard had sent her an incriminating picture, that was all. Bennie looked at the picture again and collapsed onto the sofa in the living room of the cottage.

Maybe it wasn't "all;" maybe there was a reason for the distance she heard in Clay's voice night after night. Maybe it was too late. Bennie drew an anguished breath as tears began to rack her body. It wasn't fair; it wasn't right, not after all this time and all her work. Despair, anger, and confusion swirled around her until she felt she would scream, but mercifully, she fell into a disturbed sleep.

There he is, there he is . . . I can get him. If I just push a little harder, run a little faster . . . Oh, God, it's so cold, so cold. Gilbert, wait for me! You have to stop! Gilberrt! Gilberrt!

The smoke grew thicker and obscured more of her vision. There was no sound whatsoever except the pounding of blood in her veins, the dull thumping sound that threatened to overcome her. Her feet were bleeding and sore, but she ran on and on.

I've got him . . . I have his shirt; he has to stop running now!

The man turned around slowly and in the dim light she could make out his features. It wasn't Gilbert; it was Clay.

*Her momentary joy turned to pain as she saw the hatred
on his face.*

Why, Clay? Why?

The pounding in her ears got louder and louder, and her
head felt as if it were about to burst when she realized that
the pounding was real—there was someone at the door of
the cottage. Bennie's eyes flew open, and she was awake
and disoriented in the dim twilight of the room. She turned
on a soft light by the sofa before opening the door. Before
she could ask who it was, the door flew open and there,
with a face of absolute fury, stood Clay. Bennie's mouth
fell open, and every possible emotion flitted across her
face. There was joy, shock, anger, happiness, surprise, and,
for Bennie, recognition. She took one look at her husband
and knew that wherever that picture came from, it was an
old picture.

The Clay who stood before her was as skinny as a rail,
for one thing, and for another his hair was longer, so long,
in fact, that he had it in a ponytail. There was also a generous amount of gray in it that had never been there before.
He looked worn and haggard and absolutely miserable, she
surmised in a few seconds. Not that it would have mattered
anyway. Before she could stop herself or question the wisdom of what she was doing, she had her arms around Clay.
She could not speak; she was so profoundly moved by his
presence. She buried her head on his shoulder and would
have stayed there forever if Clay had not intervened.

This was not the reception that Clay had imagined, although it was close to the one he had dreamed about. How
could Bennie just step into his arms like that if there were
something evil afoot out here in California? And why was
he so willing to let her? His eyes raked over her hungrily—
she was thin and drawn, but she was still his beautiful
Benita. But he wasn't about to sink back into their familiar
passion until he got some answers. "Benita, what the hell
is this?" he demanded, putting the pictures in her hands.

"These came in the mail today, and I need to know just what the hell has been going on out here while you are supposed to be recuperating," he ground out. He knew he sounded like a total bastard, but he could not help it; he knew that if his veneer slipped an inch, he would be lost, and this time he could not afford to lose.

Bennie walked over to the light to see the pictures more closely, and in the process turned on another lamp to better see Clay. She knew, even before examining them, what they were—the pictures that Angelique had taken while she was visiting. Turning to him, she said, "I'm afraid you have had a fast one played on you," she said. "This man is my therapist, John Flores. And these pictures were taken by your sister when she visited me last week," she informed him.

Clay sat down in the nearest chair, feeling like ten kinds of fool. Before he could say anything, though, Bennie spoke. "Well, I personally think we owe her a new Porsche or something. Her methods may have been unorthodox, as usual, but they worked. Here we are in the same room, at least," she said gamely. "I'm going to get you something for that headache," she added. Clay just nodded. Bennie had known from the very first day when he was in pain, so there was no point in pretending otherwise.

Bennie returned with a headache powder and a glass of cola, her usual remedy. She poured the powder on his tongue without having to coax him, and handed him the glass to wash it down. As he drank it, she drank him in with her eyes. "Benita, I feel like such a idiot," Clay began.

Bennie put her hand over his mouth to forestall any more of that. She took his hand and led him into the bedroom to lie down. Kneeling, she took off his shoes and socks, then helped him out of his shirt and slacks. She covered him with an afghan and lay down beside him. "We'll talk later, sweetheart. Right now you need to get some rest," she crooned as she held him to her heart.

It was a sign of how exhausted he was that Clay actually fell asleep. Bennie's arms around him soothed him into the first restful sleep that he had since the day of Bennie's accident. Bennie was much too keyed up to sleep. She could not stop looking at Clay and touching him. He looked terrible. He was much too thin, and it was obvious that he had not been sleeping well or eating properly. And he was in a terrible state of nerves over the picture incident, not that she was one to talk. She decided not to mention the little package that she received; it would serve no purpose whatsoever. He awoke with a start, and called Bennie's name frantically. "I'm here, sweetheart, I'm right here," she answered, kissing his face tenderly. He felt hot and feverish to her. "Let me get you something to drink," she said, trying to pull away from him. Clay wouldn't have it, though. In the end, she turned back the covers, took off her clothes, and they held each other all night, like children in a fairy tale. Which was perfectly fine with Bennie. From the moment he walked in the door looking like the very wrath of God, Bennie knew there was nothing that could take her out of his arms again.

The next morning Clay lay very still, afraid to open his eyes. He was afraid that last night had been just another in the long series of dreams that had plagued him for the last four months. He knew that when he opened his eyes it would be just another morning when he awoke without Benita in his arms. But something was different today—he felt a hand moving gently across his chest and felt soft lips on his face. And he heard Benita's voice speaking to him.

"Good morning, sweetheart. Wake up and take a shower so that you can eat this really fattening breakfast that I'm making you. Hurry up." Bennie's smiling face was really looking down at him, and those really were her hands touching him. Clay could finally breathe again. He looked at Bennie for long, precious moments before speaking. "Good morning, Peaches," was all he said, but it was more than enough.

This was not what he had expected in the way of a

reunion, although he had not, for so many weeks, permitted himself to think about getting back with Bennie at all. Yet there they were, sitting in the cozy, sunlit kitchen, eating the breakfast that she had prepared for him. They did not speak much, but each word was steeped in context. Clay could not stop looking at Bennie, drinking in her sweetness, and taking in every slight change. Her hair was different— she had thick bangs that feathered toward her cheeks. Clay knew without being told that she was covering up a scar, and the knowledge twisted in him like a knife. He was trying to find a way to address the issue when Bennie spoke.

"Clay," she said carefully, "this is not going to work." Clay almost dropped the cup of coffee he was raising to his lips—surely she wasn't saying that it was over! Not now. But Bennie was looking at Clay's hair, which flowed down to his shoulders. Leaning forward, she flicked a long, damp strand. "Cochise, this has got to go. What were you thinking about, letting it get this long?" Clay's hands started trembling with relief, and Bennie saw how her words had affected him. In an instant she was on her knees next to his chair with her arms around his waist.

"Oh, baby, I'm sorry! I'm not trying to be flip; it's just that I want everything to be the way it was, and I don't know what to say—I just don't," she cried. "Oh, Clay, it's been so long, and I missed you so much, and I'm so sorry for everything I put you through. I'm so sorry!" She wept. Clay was astounded, but he pulled Bennie up into his arms and held her as tightly as he could. "Stop, baby, stop crying," he begged. "Benita, please don't ever cry again, baby."

Clinging to each other, they walked into the living room and sat down on the sofa. When Bennie's cries had slowed down to soft hiccups, Clay began to speak. "Benita, I am the one who needs your forgiveness. What I put you through was wrong, it was selfish, it was thoughtless, and I almost lost you. I need to hear that you forgive me,

Peaches. I need to know that we have a chance of putting everything right."

Bennie looked at Clay as if he were speaking another language. "Clay, what are you talking about? Nothing that happened was your fault. You are not responsible for a drunk driver on the 405 crashing into the limousine. If I had had the balls to tell you that I didn't want to go on the stupid trip, none of this would have happened. If I had told you that I just wanted to be a fat, happy homemaker for a while, you wouldn't have asked me to go. And, and . . ." Her voice trailed off as fresh tears began to cascade.

Clay was astounded by what he was hearing. Yet he could not resist the lure of Bennie's arms another minute. He pulled her into his lap and held her as close as he could while they both murmured all the things that they had needed to say for so long. All he could think was how sad it was that they had wasted so much time thinking they knew what the other was feeling, when in reality they were clueless. But they were at least in the same room now, and where there was life, there was hope. "We're going to get through this, Peaches. We're going to be fine," he vowed as he inhaled the sweet scent of her hair. They looked at each other for a long moment, before Clay lowered his head to hers and kissed her the way they both remembered—a hot, sweet explosion of love and promise.

When they finally pulled away from each other, it was only to walk into the bedroom and complete their journey of rediscovery. Bennie's hands began unfastening Clay's shirt, and his did the same for her. Bennie panicked momentarily, remembering that her body was not quite the same. She tried to stop Clay from removing her shirt, but he was too quick and too gentle. The look of tenderness in his eyes let her know that for him, nothing would ever change. They were standing in front of each other with everything exposed, including their never-ending passion for each other.

Clay's heart cried as Bennie's hands instinctively crossed

her rib cage to protect her scars from his sight. Laying her gently across the bed, Clay first stroked her face gently and kissed her on the temple that bore the small scars. He kissed her softly, then deeply, with passion and love, across every inch of her body. When he came to the line that intersected her ribs he paused only to stroke it gently and look deeply into her eyes before continuing. Gently, deliberately, lovingly, they became one again and again.

John Flores had known for some time that his feelings toward Benita Deveraux were veering dangerously away from doctor-patient into something that could cause a lot of problems. He tried vainly to think of her as just another case, but it was impossible. Her sweetness, her intelligence, and her charm had won him over completely. He had thought of her as being extremely fragile, because she certainly was when she came into his care. But watching her reclaim herself, watching her confidence return along with her strength, was one of the most gratifying experiences of John's career.

He kept telling himself that it was just that—the knowledge that he had helped a wonderful woman recover after a tragedy—that made Benita so special to him. He found it more and more difficult to convince himself of that as the days passed, however. He had been out of town for a few days, which had caused him to miss a few sessions with her. Now that he was back in town, he found himself eagerly anticipating his visit with her. He was so deep in thought that he missed the fact that there was a strange car parked near the cottage. Hearing Benita's laughter, he went around to the back to see what the cause of her happiness was. He did not have to wonder as he observed her laughing and feeding pieces of ripe fruit to a smiling man who could only be her husband.

They were so involved in their sensual play that John had to clear his throat several times before Bennie looked up. A radiant smile lit her face, and she rose to greet him.

"John, I'm so glad you're back! This is my husband, Clay Deveraux," she said as she looked at Clay with her heart in her eyes. "Clay, this is John Flores, the man I have been telling you about. This is my special miracle worker," she said fondly. Clay rose to shake the other man's hand, expressing his pleasure at meeting John. Before John had time to feel awkward or uncomfortable, Bennie made him join them for breakfast, pouring him coffee and going back into the cottage for extra rolls and napkins.

John tried—successfully, he hoped—to look nonchalant and happy about Clay's arrival. "So how long have you been in town, Clay?" was the best he could manage. It had been five days since Clay's tempestuous arrival in Mission Del Vista, the village where John's cottage was located. It had been five days of utter bliss, as far as Clay and Bennie were concerned. The haggard, drawn look that they both had worn had been replaced by the rosy glow of contentment. Clay still needed to regain the weight he had lost, as did Bennie, but they both looked alive and vibrant for the first time since the accident. Bennie's incandescent glow was not lost on John, although he tried to ignore it. She was returning from the kitchen when she heard him ask about Clay's arrival.

"It's been five days, John," she answered. She set down the tray that she had carried out of the kitchen and went to Clay's side. She smiled up at him adoringly and touched his face. "Five amazing days," she repeated. "And John, I have so much to tell you that I don't know where to begin." Clay kissed Bennie's cheek before reluctantly stepping out of her embrace.

"I know you have a lot to discuss, so I'm going to get out of your hair for a while," he said easily. Bennie was about to protest, but Clay insisted on giving her the privacy she needed to talk with John. "I'll go get a paper or something. I'll be back soon." Nodding to John, he kissed Bennie again before going to the car, which was parked in front of the cottage. Bennie watched him leave with a smile playing around her lips. John finally spoke.

"I take it that you have had a happy reunion," was all he said. Bennie did not hear the slight note of resignation in his voice. She looked like a supplicant looking at an icon of her patron saint. Her eyes were completely serene and love-filled as she agreed with him. "John, it's been absolutely unbelievable," she said softly. "I had been anticipating and dreading the moment we would see each other for weeks and weeks, and when it happened it was . . ." Her voice trailed off as she tried to find the right words. "It was not what I expected, but much better than I hoped, if that makes sense." John nodded resolutely.

Bennie went on to explain how Clay's appearance had come about. John drew in his breath and shook his head. "Angelique was taking a huge chance with that maneuver—she had no way of knowing how the two of you would react. It could have led to a total disaster for all concerned," he said frankly.

Bennie had to agree, but reminded him of what she had told him about Angelique. "She's a totally unique person—she leads with her heart. Whatever comes up, comes out, and not always for the best. She doesn't think things through, I must admit. Remind me to tell you about a little shower she had for me in Atlanta," Bennie added. She went on to tell John as honestly as she could her feelings about Clay's appearance in California.

"I am thrilled—beyond thrilled, John. I am so happy I could burst. I want to go home now, tonight, and just pick up our lives where we left off, just start over again like these past months never happened," she confided. "But I know we can't do that, not really. Clay for some reason feels terribly guilty about what happened. I feel guilty for what happened. I blame myself, he blames himself, and there's things that we should have talked about, but didn't, and I think that's a part of it, too." Bennie sighed and idly rearranged items on the al fresco dining table.

"John, I want to go home with my husband. And he wants me to come home. But I don't want us falling into any of the little traps that people fall into after a tragedy occurs. And I don't want us going through life thinking that we know what the other person wants and we aren't able to talk it out. But I don't want to turn our marriage into some kind of New Age encounter group, either," she said firmly. As was her habit when she was deep in thought, Bennie began to pace the sunny patio. John took this opportunity to address the issues she had brought up.

"Well, what does Clay say about this? Have you discussed this with him?" Bennie nodded. "We talked about it for quite a while, and he agrees with me on this. Especially after I told him about the dreams." Bennie looked almost apologetic. "I had to—I had one the other night. And John, it has changed again."

Two nights earlier, Bennie had been deeply asleep in Clay's arms when the dream took over her subconscious. She was once again chasing Gilbert out of a sense of dread for the well-being of Clay. Or that was the way it was in the beginning. Soon it became obvious that Gilbert was chasing her, and instead of being in thick, black fog, she was surrounded by gray. The stones were no longer sharp and jagged, but mildly uncomfortable, which allowed her to run faster. And just when she thought she was safe, the man grabbed her from behind. Turning her around in his grasp, she once again saw that it was Clay, not Gilbert. And this time he had a look of peace on his face, but there was no other explanation for the chase.

Bennie had awakened with a start, but without the feeling of panic and despair that normally accompanied the dream. She attributed it to being in Clay's arms, where nothing could ever harm her, and partially to the fact that the dream had altered itself to the point where it was no longer as menacing. "But I have to say, John, I still want it over with. I would give a lot to know exactly what the dream means so I can get it behind me," she admitted.

John looked at Bennie for a long moment before making her an offer. This could be the most tortuous thing he had ever done, but he did not see how he could do otherwise. "Benita, how would you and Clay feel if I conducted a couple of sessions for the two of you? It would give you a chance to work through some of the kinks you were talking about before you go home. If you feel uncomfortable about it, I can recommend someone else, here or in Atlanta. But I think you are on the right track when you say that you want to enhance your communication levels with one another," he said.

Bennie was surprised and touched by his offer. "John, I trust you completely, and I will ask Clay if he would feel comfortable with the idea. I can't thank you enough for thinking of it," she said. John smiled to himself and accepted her effusive thanks as if it were nothing. Despite his doomed feelings for Benita, he wanted only the best for her and her husband. And if he could help them maintain their happiness, good for him.

The session with John was more comfortable than Clay would have anticipated. It was clear that John's interest lay in helping Clay and Bennie maximize their communication skills, and anything that would get Bennie back to Atlanta was something that Clay endorsed heartily. Besides, there were some things that he felt that Bennie had a right to know—things that he had not yet been able to tell her. John started off slowly and easily, asking them about their meeting and their courtship, which was easy for them to talk about. Bennie was particularly fond of the incident involving the pink dress when they were in Chicago. She laughed when John asked her where the dress was now.

"I think it's under glass in the Smithsonian, John. Clay is never letting me wear it again; yet I think he worships that dress," she said cheekily.

Clay's arm was draped around her and he did not deny her words. "She was . . . amazing," he agreed. "I went down for the count that night."

Bennie looked at him with surprise. "Clayton Deveraux, I remember it slightly differently. I had to propose to you, if you recall!" she exclaimed, laughing.

Clay looked at Bennie without trying to hide the love in his eyes. "Do you know when I bought your engagement ring? The day after I got back from Chicago, Peaches. So talk about what you know, okay?" Clay smiled, loving the stunned look on Bennie's face.

John cleared his throat and asked a perceptive question. "So, Clay, I take it that you were less than candid with Benita about your feelings?"

Clay had to agree. "Yes, I was. I did not want to admit that I was completely knocked out by a beautiful, smart, funny woman who took me home for lunch to get rid of my headache. I did not want to admit that I had fallen madly in love with a woman who was brave and open and honest with her feelings and who loves baseball and Chinese food. I never told Benita how I really felt; I let her do most of the talking and most of the reacting because it was safer that way," he admitted.

John paused to let that sink in. "Benita, did you ever feel that Clay was holding back from you? Did you ever want him to say more of how he felt toward you?" Bennie immediately denied any feelings of that sort. "Clay always acted as though he cared about me. I grew up around men, and I think that they just aren't as verbal as women. Women *tell* you how they feel, and men *show* you how they feel. And Clay always acted as though he cared a great deal about me. He was sweet, generous, kind, affectionate, and he respected me. Sometimes a little too much, if you ask me. But I always felt like he cared about me," she finished.

Clay shook his head as Bennie was making this recitation. Bennie still had not heard from his lips how much he loved her, how passionately he adored her. Well, he would remedy that situation this very night. *Care* was far too neutral a word for what he felt for Bennie. John noticed Clay's expression, and guessed that it stemmed from a need to express things that were not appropriate for the ears of a counselor. He tried to build on that without venturing onto extremely personal ground.

He had watched the two of them carefully, and saw

through their body language that they were a couple who shared deep feelings and deep desires and were willing to work for their happiness. In telling John stories of how they met and how they courted, they were happy and animated, laughing and smiling and finishing each other's sentences. They looked at each other the entire time and were obviously crazy for one another. They touched often and listened to one another, but they had real concerns about their future. John tried to summarize what he was sensing from Bennie and Clay.

"You met during the course of business, you had an instant attraction to one another, and you built a passionate relationship on that attraction. But there may be areas that you did not discuss fully before getting married, and the reality of the situation may be not as you perceived it. Or, due to the tragedy that befell you, you fear that the reality you face is one that you are not prepared to deal with effectively.

"In other words, you have a lot at stake and you want to make sure you have it right this time," he paraphrased himself.

Bennie nodded somberly. "John, both of us feel such guilt about what happened. I know that we can't put it away as though it never happened, but we have to find a way to deal with it, don't we? And what I would like more than anything is for Clay to understand that I don't hold him in any way responsible," she said, looking directly into Clay's eyes.

Before Clay could speak and direct the same comment to Bennie, John intervened. "I think we have to make it plain that neither one of you is responsible. When tragedy happens, it is logical to look for someone to fix blame on. I find it interesting that you each blame yourselves. Clay, Bennie could have fallen down a flight of stairs, or been in a car accident in Atlanta, or eaten tainted food, and the outcome would have been the same. As much as we want to protect our loved ones from harm, we can't hover around them like a protective shield twenty-four hours a day."

Before John could go on, Clay broke in. "But I could have done a better job of listening to Bennie and understanding what she wanted. I was no better than her brothers and her father, constantly hanging on her and getting her to do this and do that until she had no life of her own. I was supposed to love her and cherish her, and I wasn't any more taking care of her than the man in the moon. I was only thinking about myself and what was best for me," he finished bitterly. "I wasn't taking care of her the way I should."

Bennie was plainly distressed at Clay's words. "Clay, honey, I'm not a plant or a child—you don't have to take care of me! I'm a very strong woman, in case you haven't noticed. I'm as tough as old boots! I need you to love me, yes, to care about me and support me, but I don't need to be tended to—you can't possibly feel guilty over how you have behaved toward me in this marriage."

Clay held Bennie's hand tightly as he tried to explain the relationship he had had with his father, and how disillusioned he had been when he had discovered his father's sordid affair. It was the central issue in his life, which explained why he had such an ironclad need for control, and why he had fought giving in to his passion for Bennie for so long.

Bennie quickly put her arm on Clay's arm. "Clay, you don't have to explain—I know everything about your father," she said softly.

Clay was thunderstruck. "How in the world . . . ?" he began.

Bennie arched an eyebrow with a hint of weariness. "My father, who else? He paid one of his stooges to dig up dirt on you, and that's what he came up with. I told him to take it and shove it, and that if he tried something like that again, I would disown him." Hastily she added, "I'm sorry I never mentioned it, but I thought you would tell me when you were ready, and I didn't want you to know what a crackpot Daddy can be when he gets started. Please forgive me," she added.

"Forgive you? I continue to be amazed by you, Peaches," he said softly. Momentarily forgetting that John was in the room, Clay pulled Bennie closer to him on the sofa and kissed her. John interrupted with a cough and a hearty, "Well, I think we can wrap this up for today."

He left, asking the couple to continue to think about ways that they could be more candid in expressing their positive and negative feelings on the future. "And Benita, I think we have a pretty good handle on Clay's sense of responsibility to you. Next time we'll talk about those same feelings that you have toward him."

Nothing in Bennie's face revealed how she felt about that statement as she waved good-bye to John from the doorway.

Despite its auspicious beginning, the evening session had taken a toll on Bennie. Instead of feeling reassured and heartened by John's words, she felt off center. There was a lot of merit in what John said—she and Clay had plunged headlong into marriage without a lot of discussion. There was a lot of passion, certainly, and a lot of love, but what else was there? When all was said and done, did she and Clay have enough of what mattered to make a successful marriage? Doubt and uncertainty rushed over her, leaving her shaken to her very foundations. All this time she had just assumed that as soon as she was well and able to return to Clay, things would go back to the way they had been before. Now, after just one counseling session, she was confused and frightened.

Clay, as always, sensed that something was on her mind. He had followed her out to the kitchen, where she was washing the glasses they had used earlier. Everything about her posture screamed tension. He walked up behind her and wrapped his long arms around her rigidly held body. Resting his head on hers, he breathed deeply and felt her relax into him. "Benita, don't worry," he said softly. "We are going to work everything out, and we will be back at home and happy before you know it."

Bennie, unmindful of her soapy hands, turned around to face him. She put her arms around his waist and just stood there, drinking in his comfort. "Clay, I love you. I want us to be together forever, and I want it to be right," she said. "I don't want to end up divorced or in some horrible marriage because we couldn't figure out how to talk to each other. If you stopped loving me or we didn't want to be with each other anymore, I don't know what I'd do," she confessed tearfully. Clay just held her tighter.

"Peaches, where do you get these ideas? We may not have had a very conventional courtship, but that doesn't mean that all the elements aren't in place for us to have a good marriage. We already have a good marriage, if you ask me. And you and I are the only two who count in this; remember that. As long as we're committed to each other, everything else will fall into place, especially since we're working on it." He looked down at Bennie and lifted her face to his. "Do you trust me, baby?"

Bennie gave him a radiant smile. "What all my heart," she answered.

Clay touched his lips to hers. "That's all that matters, then," he said.

However, as the old saying went, wishing did not make it so. That night, despite the fact that Clay was holding her as she slept, Bennie's dream came, and this time it was more horrifying than ever. The vague sense of peace that had pervaded it since Clay's arrival in California was gone, replaced by the now-familiar dread. This time she seemed to be chased by Gilbert and running after Clay, and the eerie silence was replaced by the sound of sobbing, whether it was Bennie's or someone else's, she wasn't sure. But the crying got louder and louder and sounded more like the wailing of an infant. She was so astounded by the noise that she had stopped to listen, and when she did, Clay suddenly turned on her and grasped her by her shoulder, shaking her. His expression was stern and unforgiving as he shook her over and over without saying a word. Terrified, Bennie began to scream.

Clay nearly jumped out of his skin when he heard the heart-wrenching sounds coming from his wife. He had gotten up to get a glass of water, and had returned to the bedroom doorway in time to hear Bennie cry out. In an instant he was across the room, holding Bennie and rubbing her back. "Wake up, baby; you're having a bad dream. Come on, Peaches; wake up, baby." His soothing words finally penetrated through her panic, and Bennie began to calm down. Her breathing was still irregular and she was still choking back sobs as Clay continued to stroke her and speak in a soft, reassuring voice. "Benita, can you tell me about it? What is in this dream that frightens you so?"

Bennie drew one last hiccuping breath and sighed. She took a swallow of the water Clay offered her, and licked the moisture away from her lips before looking up to meet Clay's steady gaze. To Clay, she looked adorable, like a beautiful child with her tousled hair and tearstained face. Finally she put the glass of water on the stand next to the bed and started talking. She told Clay about the experience of seeing Gilbert in the hospital, and about the subsequent dreams. She related all the imagery that she could recall, and told him how frightened she was in the dreams, not for herself, but for him. She concluded by explaining how the dreams had changed since his arrival, and about this dream in particular and how terrifying it was. Clay did not move a muscle during her entire recitation. When she finished, she looked at him almost shyly. "Now you know the truth. Your wife is nuts," she muttered.

Clay did not speak for a moment. Bennie was propped up on a pile of pillows, and Clay was seated on the side of the bed facing her. He moved so that he was lying next to her and pulled her into the shelter of his arms. Finally he spoke. "Peaches, I think I understand those dreams. I think you haven't been able to figure them out because you're missing some information. And I think that once you get it, you will be able to put those dreams behind you." Bennie looked up at Clay as if to ask what he was talking about. But before she could prod him any further, he gave her the answers she had been seeking.

The next day, Clay and Bennie were standing in the courtyard of the Queen of Angels retreat, a small religious post that was part of the order after which the hospital was named. They were about to enter the tiny memorial gardens that were a part of the retreat grounds. This was where their baby had been interred during the terrible time when Bennie was in the coma. When Bennie told Clay about the dreams she had been having, he knew instinctively that they were in part due to her sense of incompleteness with regard to their baby. Whereas he had had a chance to grieve and find a kind of closure to her miscarriage, Bennie had not really had the opportunity. It was as Dr. Dantes had said—she was pregnant and then she wasn't. And when she had regained consciousness there was the pain and immobility to deal with, and she was still not able to express her grief properly. She didn't even know about the memorial service—no one did, other than Clay.

The night before he had slowly explained to her what he had done and why. The knowledge that Clay had taken care of everything so lovingly had brought new tears from Bennie. There were tears for the life that had ended as well as for Clay, who had been alone during the terrible time. Bennie was struck afresh by the strength of her love for Clay. What she had done to deserve someone as loving and sensitive as her husband she had no idea, but she was profoundly grateful, and told him so. Clay had just held her closer and told her that he was the one who was grateful and would be for the rest of his life.

The next morning, Bennie had asked Clay to bring her

to Queen of Angels so that they could say good-bye to their baby together.

Bennie was pale and had huge circles under her eyes from her sleepless night. She had not trusted herself to go back to sleep—she was afraid that the dream would return, even though what Clay had told her made it seem less ominous. Clay was somber as he led Bennie to the tiny brass plate that marked the spot where their infant lay. *Baby Deveraux* and the date, with Bennie and Clay's names, was all that was engraved on the simple plate, but the poignancy was unmistakable. Bennie leaned on Clay and quietly cried. Turning in to his shoulder, she felt his tears join hers as they prayed together. Finally they were able to leave. Bennie did not let go of Clay's hand once on the entire drive back to the cottage.

"So Bennie, tell me something that you dislike about Clay," invited John. The three of them—Clay, Bennie, and John—were in the living room of the cottage. After a nice dinner served on the patio, they had repaired to the living room for another session. This time, though, Bennie was much more relaxed. All the anxiety from the previous session had left her after the agonizing night and emotion-charged visit to the cemetery. Whatever lay ahead of them, Bennie had no doubt that they could face it together.

John was also able to discern a transition. Bennie had told him what had occurred after their first session, and he agreed that they had made some major progress. He could see for himself the happiness that radiated from Bennie, along with a new sense of calm. He could not help but regret in some small way that she was not free; he was angry with himself for feeling so much for her, but the human heart did not understand propriety. Building on their last session, when it was obvious that they adored each other, John decided to play devil's advocate to encourage them to continue to communicate honestly. He repeated his question to Bennie about what she disliked about Clay.

"I love Clay the way he is," she answered. "If Clay didn't have his faults and peculiarities, he wouldn't be the person whom I fell in love with," she pointed out. Clay looked smug until she added, "That doesn't make him perfect, however. Clay likes to be Daddy Rabbit," she said, laughing at his look of affront. "There is nothing that escapes his attention, nothing that he does not like to tweak," she pointed out, referencing his work habits. "Clay is the HMFIC, and you'd better not forget it." Clay pretended to throw a sofa cushion at her, while she laughed.

"But John," she said fairly, "Clay runs a multibillion-dollar international corporation. He's supposed to do what he does. So I wouldn't try to change that; I just acknowledge it. Like the fact that he's possessive. If another man looks at me, Clay gets this laser-beam glare going—he doesn't say anything; he doesn't have to. But I have seen him scare the pants off a few fellows," she finished.

John looked at Clay and back at Bennie. "How does that make you feel, Benita?" he asked. Bennie gave him a Mona Lisa smile before answering.

"I suppose I should feel any number of ways about it, but I don't. I knew that about Clay before I married him. He knows I would never look at another man, and I know that he would never make a scene or accuse me of anything. So I have to be truthful and say it doesn't affect me negatively in any way. I mean, it's not like that towel thing of his," she added.

Clay immediately asked, "What towel thing?"

Bennie looked at him with great affection and asked, "How do wet towels get to be dry towels, Clay?" At his look of complete bafflement, Bennie raised her hands in triumph. "That's exactly what I mean! He has no idea how this happens. He leaves the wet ones all over the place and waits for the miracle of the towels every day."

After she finished laughing, Clay had the grace to look slightly embarrassed, although he leaned over and said, "You're going to pay for that, Peaches," in his sexy voice.

Then John turned the tables, asking what Clay disliked about Bennie.

Clay looked at Bennie with his heart in his eyes for a long moment before answering. "Benita is absolutely perfect in every way. There is absolutely nothing about her that I would change in any way."

Bennie frowned and said, "That's not fair—I was honest about you."

Clay did not look at Bennie; he looked at John. "I'm being totally honest. Bennie makes me feel extremely humble because she is truly perfect. She is intelligent, talented, warm, friendly, open, caring, generous, giving, loving—she does everything right all the time. Sometimes I wonder what she ever saw in me," he admitted.

Bennie's cheeks were red with embarrassment by now. "I am not *perfect;* by no means am I perfect," she protested. "You make me sound like some kind of automaton, some kind of android. I am a real, flawed human being like everybody else," she said hotly.

Clay could see that she was really upset and he tried to make amends. But how did one apologize for seeing only the best in the person one loved? Clay looked to John for help.

"Benita, what I hear Clay saying is that he admires you tremendously for the person you are. From what I understand, you are a very giving, compassionate person who has always gone out of her way for others, particularly for your family. And there is no question that you are a talented, accomplished woman. But it seems as though this description makes you uncomfortable. Why is that?" His gentle probing seemed to strike a chord in Bennie. She had reduced her hair to a tangled mass while he was speaking; now she withdrew her hands from hair and stood up. As always when she was agitated, she started pacing around the room.

"I wasn't always Little Miss Perfect," she said. "I was a goofy little kid, always in trouble. Andrew and I were the worst children on the block. We got in so much trouble

the neighbors offered to pay our way to boarding school."
She related a few of the escapades she and Andrew had
initiated, which were indeed hair-raising.

Clay and John listened intently as she talked. Bennie
seemed barely aware of their presence. John continued to
probe, to get her to keep talking.

"What changed, Benita? When did you become a model
child?" he asked quietly.

Bennie's answer was simple and terrible. "When my
mother died. It was my fault she died," Bennie said softly.

As a mother of six, Lillian Cochran did not work outside
the home. And it was a good thing, as she was constantly
shuttling the children from one event to another and running over to the school to deliver forgotten lunches, homework, and equipment. One sunny morning, Bennie had
forgotten her science project and called her mother from
the school. After Bennie's fervent pleas and promises to
never forget anything again, Lillian agreed to bring it to
her. She was not thrilled with the turn of events, however.
Before she hung up the phone she had fussed at Bennie,
"Andrea Benita Cochran, you're going to be the death of
me yet!" Those were the last words her mother ever spoke
to her. On the way to the school her car was hit broadside
by a truck and she was killed instantly. And the then-ten-
year-old Bennie had always felt that she was responsible
for her mother's death.

"If I hadn't been so careless, I wouldn't have had to
call her. And if I hadn't called her, that truck wouldn't have
hit her. And my father would have had his wife and my
brothers would have had their mother. It was all my fault,"
Bennie murmured. By this time Clay was at her side with
his arms around her.

"Benita, baby, it wasn't your fault. It wasn't your fault.
You can't blame yourself for that, baby," he said over and
over.

John was struck by the sadness in Benita's face as Clay
led her back to the sofa. He could only imagine what she
had gone through as a child. In a way, it was a textbook

case. Children were particularly susceptible to thinking that they were responsible for bad things happening, things like the death of a loved one, or a divorce. And they developed coping behaviors to help them deal with the guilt. This revelation explained a lot of things about Bennie's personality and her sacrifices for her family. Choosing his words carefully, John began to speak.

"Benita, I'm terribly sorry that you did not have someone that you could confide this in when it happened. They could have helped you understand that you were not responsible. They could have also prevented you from assuming the role of model child. You were so anxious to make up to everyone for the loss you wrongly thought you caused that you became all things to all members of your family. You were the straight-A student, the surrogate mother, the loyal friend, and the adoring sister. You became your father's trusted associate, and you were never allowed to be a child, to be a daughter. Benita, you have been so afraid of letting someone else down that you haven't been taking care of someone very close to you."

Bennie looked guiltily at Clay, who held both her hands in his as they sat next to each other on the sofa. John saw the look and sighed softly. "No, Benita. It's *you* whom you haven't taken care of. I think Clay would agree that you take care of him very well indeed. It is you who needs the tender loving care, you and the little ten-year-old girl who misses her mother very much and is in terrible pain for something that she did not do."

At John's soft words, a deep, choked breath came from Bennie, and her chest started heaving with great, racking sobs. Clay rocked her gently and spoke soothingly to her, although it was apparent that she could not hear him. Clay finally stood up and led her to the bedroom, where he laid her down on the bed. When her tears subsided, she drew a few shaky breaths and fell asleep on Clay's shoulder.

Clay rejoined John in the living room. He looked at John, whose handsome face was full of concern for Bennie. "I never said this, John, but thank you for helping my wife.

Your friendship means a lot to both of us. I think that Bennie's life will be a lot easier now that she has that off her heart."

John waved away Clay's thanks, but he was pleased nonetheless. "Benita is the one that did the hard work," he pointed out. "And it's not over. But she has made tremendous progress, and she's such a fighter that she is not going to let anything get between her and the happiness she wants to share with you. You are a lucky man, Clay. The two of you are lucky to have each other." Clay could not have agreed more.

A little while later, Clay joined Bennie in bed. John had left, and Clay had done what little straightening needed to be done in the kitchen. As soon as Clay wrapped his arms around Bennie, she awakened at least enough to speak to Clay. Drowsily but firmly, she said, "Clay, let's go home. I want to go home with you as soon as possible."

Clay kissed his sleepy wife and smiled. "That's fine with me, Benita. The sooner the better."

Bennie was awake enough to return the kiss. "Thank you, sweetheart. I love you very much," she said, before falling into a deep and dreamless sleep.

Twelve

In a very few days, Bennie and Clay were on their way back to Atlanta. Bennie wasted no time in making the necessary preparations for their return home. She assembled all of the clothes she had accumulated during her time in California and had them laundered or cleaned in order to give them away to charity. As she pointed out to Clay, she had more than enough clothes at home. What she did not say was that these clothes would only remind her of a painful time in her life. It was with no regret that she got rid of the casual workout clothes and sundresses that made up her California attire.

The next thing she did was to have final appointments with all of her doctors and arrange for the transfer of her records to her Atlanta physician. She also made generous donations to the hospital that had taken such good care of her, as well as the Sheltering Arms extended-care unit and the Queen of Angels retreat. It was with a profound sense of gratitude that she wrote out the checks. She had so much to be thankful for, a fact of which she was reminded when she discovered that Clay had also made a donation to each organization some months before. Clay liked to think that Bennie was some kind of saint, but he was as generous and caring as she—he just didn't seem to realize it.

She wanted to give something personal to the people who had helped her through her recuperation. She bought very thoughtful gifts for her physical therapist, Sam Janderwski, and for Mrs. Ayala, the housekeeper who came once a week whether Bennie needed her or not. Mrs. Ayala just liked checking on Bennie, especially after Aunt Ruth and Renee went back home. And finally, she bought a gift for John Flores, who had given her back her life, as far as she was concerned. It was one thing to have her physical body mended, but quite another to have the peace of mind that John had helped her find. And the fact that he had helped bring her even closer to Clay was the most priceless and treasured gift that Bennie could think of. She pondered over what to get him for a long time. An engraved fountain pen seemed too impersonal, and jewelry seemed a bit much. But whatever it was, Bennie wanted it to be something that he would have always, to remind him of her.

It was Clay who suggested a piece of artwork. Bennie's eyes shone when Clay brought it up. "Clay that's perfect! There is a very nice gallery not too far from here—let's go pick out something right now!" she exclaimed. They found the gallery and Bennie was able to find exactly what she was looking for—a small sculpture by an African-American artist that expressed all of her feelings. It was the figure of a woman whose face was tilted upward, as if she were facing the sun. Although her eyes were closed, the thrusting posture of the figure indicated that the subject was rejoicing. Her arms were held away from her sides and she looked as though she were about to leap in ecstasy. Everything about the statue suggested freedom, joy, and release. Bennie looked at the figure for a long time, examining it from all angles. Looking at Clay, she confided, "This is how I feel, Clay. This is what you and John have done for me. I am free of so many things, thanks to you."

Clay was so touched by her words that he could barely reply. Bennie still had no idea how much she meant to him, and how privileged he felt to have her as his wife. He knew, though, that if he told her one more time that she was remarkable, she would brain him, so he held his tongue.

John was equally tongue-tied when Bennie presented him with the statue. He actually reddened along his cheekbones when she told him how much he meant to her. "Benita, I don't know what to say," he began.

Bennie hushed him by assuring him that he did not have to say a word. "Just promise me that you will stay in touch. I don't ever want to lose you as a friend," she said. John gave her his solemn promise. As she hugged him tightly, he could not help feeling a last regret that circumstances could have been different for the two of them. There was something inexplicable that continued to draw him to her, although he knew it was totally hopeless. Still, when she looked at him with that amazing smile, with that warmth and sweetness that was hers alone, it felt as though a soft hand were squeezing his heart.

John insisted on driving them to the airport. Clay returned his rental car to a dropoff point in the village, and John drove them to LAX, even accompanying them to their gate. It was a complete surprise for them to encounter Bump Williams, this time without his entourage. Uncle Bump was in L.A. for a day to take a meeting, and would be returning to his home in New York the next day. He was thrilled to see Bennie and Clay, especially since Bennie was so obviously recovered. Oddly, he did a double and then a triple take when meeting John Flores. Bennie picked up on it immediately.

"He kind of favors Adam, doesn't he, Uncle Bump? I think it's the height and the hair," she said, smiling at John.

Bump quickly agreed. "Oh, definitely, that's it for sure," he said distractedly. "Well, I'll be in Atlanta this weekend, so I will be sure to see you children then. That is, if my best girl lets me out of her sight," he bragged, referring to Lillian Deveraux. "You know I'm irresistible," he added, raising his eyebrows comically. Bennie and Clay were still laughing when they got on the plane.

First-class accommodations were not a luxury for Clay—with his long legs they were a necessity. Which was fine by Bennie; she liked the extra legroom herself. She also liked the fact that she could sleep on Clay's shoulder for most of the flight. She was happier than she had been in months. Although she would never put the pain of losing her baby completely behind her, she had so much to be grateful for, and so much more happiness ahead, that she knew she was blessed. She told this to Clay, and was touched to see his eyes grow moist. He kissed the hand that he was holding, and she returned the favor by kissing his.

"Clay, I missed you so much. I don't ever want to be away from you again. Never."

Clay kissed her softly on the lips. "Then Peaches, you never will be. I promise."

Bennie was in a state of bliss. Her homecoming had been wonderful—it was sweet, private, and showed her once again how much Clay adored her. He had called ahead to Mrs. Harrison, their housekeeper, to make sure that the refrigerator was stocked with Bennie's favorite foods, and that there were fresh flowers in the bedroom, the living room, and the dining room. He also arranged to have Mrs. Harrison pick poor Aretha up from the kennel, where she had languished while he was out of town. Aretha had disposed of her normal catlike aloofness and was all over Bennie, purring her joy.

"Oh, Clay, I am so happy to be home again." Bennie sighed. "I may not ever leave this house again," she said dreamily. They were in the gigantic tub in their bathroom, enjoying a bubble bath together.

Clay wasn't saying much of anything—he was leaning back against Bennie and luxuriating in the feel of her wet, warm body against his back. "Whatever you say, Peaches," he murmured.

They had been back in Atlanta for a week. During that time she had been visited by all of Clay's family, including the irrepressible Angelique. Bennie had looked at Angelique with a mixture of love and exasperation before hugging her hard. Then she looked her in the eye. "Angel, I don't know what I'm going to do with you. What you did was quite crazy, you know. It could have very easily back-fired and hurt all three of us. Not to mention poor John, the innocent bystander."

Angelique snorted. Bennie was totally clueless about that man, but she would still bet her last pair of Ferragamos that the man had designs on her brother's wife. She was not going to be the one to point that out, however. All she said in her own defense was, "Well, it worked, didn't it? You two would still be miles apart mooning over each other if I hadn't made a move."

Bennie opened her mouth to say something and then shrugged. What was done, was done. And in this case, at least, the end had justified the means. She was back home where she belonged, and she was fiercely glad that Angelique had cared enough to interfere.

Her family was also elated to know that she was back home—at least, her brothers were. Renee was also thrilled, although she seemed a bit distracted when Bennie had talked to her. Whatever was on her mind was paramount, although Renee promised her that a full explanation would be forthcoming soon. The only person who wasn't jumping for joy was Big Benny. He, in fact, had seemed rather sub-dued, and if Bennie had not known better, she would have thought he was disappointed that she was no longer in re-habilitation.

"Daddy, did you hear me? I said I'm home! I'm back in Atlanta with Clay and I am a hundred percent better. I am better than that, actually. The doctors say that they have never seen anyone recover as fast as I did, considering my injuries. Isn't that good news, Daddy?" Bennie was waiting to hear some effusive response from her father, but she was disappointed. He was cordially glad to hear her good news, but he was strangely distant.

"Well, dear, that's just wonderful. Just wonderful. I hope that you'll be coming this way soon—I'm able to travel now, but it would be nice to see you up here. I know your brothers feel the same," her father said evasively. And that was about all she could get out of him.

Luckily, Martha was much more excited about her news. After Big Benny relinquished the phone, the two women chatted quite volubly about Bennie's homecoming and the possibility of travel in the near future.

Altogether, Bennie had nothing but warm, happy feelings about being home. She had missed everything—her husband, her home, and her family and friends. She was having lunch one day with Vera Jackson and was talking about that very thing. "Well, Vera, you're married; you know what I mean. You know how it is when you have that special closeness with your husband—it's like you become an integral part of each other," Bennie said, not noticing the shadow that passed over the other woman's face. Bennie prattled on happily, unaware of Vera's tension.

"You know," she confided, "I was thinking the other day that you must have an exceptionally strong marriage to handle all the traveling that your husband does." Looking up from her crab salad, Bennie looked directly at Vera and was dismayed at what she saw. Vera's eyes were full of tears, and she was plainly very unhappy. Bennie dropped her fork and reached for Vera's hand. How could she have been so tactless as to go rattling on about something she obviously knew nothing about? Clearly something was very wrong with Vera's marriage, but Bennie had not realized it until that minute.

Vera tried to smile bravely but failed. All she could say was, "Bennie, you and Clay are very, very blessed. Don't ever forget that or take each other for granted."

Bennie was chagrined at the thought that she had inadvertently hurt her friend, but she took the words to heart. After what she and Clay had been though, every day seemed like a precious jewel. And she had every intention of keeping it that way. So apparently did Clay, judging from his behavior.

Clay's dramatic reappearance had occurred in the first week of June. Their subsequent reunion and return to Atlanta had brought them to the first week of July, when Bennie's birthday fell. Bennie had not even remembered the date, but Clay had. He had made the occasion sublimely special, with flowers, champagne, and a lovely dinner that he had prepared with his own hands. Bennie's was absolutely enchanted with the little grotto he had arranged on the patio; there were candles everywhere, as well as soft music playing to enhance the mood. And as always, Clay had come up with the most amazing gifts.

There was another Judith Leiber bag for her growing collection, this one heart-shaped. There was every item ever made in her favorite fragrance, from bath oil to perfume. Bennie's eyes widened when she saw the sumptuous array; she could never get enough perfume. But the pièce de résistance was the magnificent ring that he slipped on her right hand. Clay had brought her wedding set to California with him, and she had not taken the rings off for any reason since he put them back on her left hand. As far as she was concerned, she did not need another piece of jewelry in life, she was so satisfied. This ring changed her mind about that, though. It was an emerald-cut green tourmaline that had to weigh at least six carats, judging by its size. It was bracketed on either side with trillion peridots that balanced the deep green of the main stone with their pale green light. It was set in a heavy yellow gold setting that was delicate and dramatic at the same time.

Bennie had sighed with happiness upon looking at the ring. "Clay, it's beautiful. Everything is beautiful. But sweetheart, it's too much. I don't need for you to buy me things like this—I just need for you to love me, that's all," she said with love and sincerity.

Clay looked lovingly at Bennie. He pulled her out of her chair and held her close to him for a long moment before speaking. "Benita, it still amazes me that you are so special, so unique and wonderful, and yet you are the humblest person I have ever met. Your love is the most precious thing in the world to me, Peaches. Before I was lucky enough to meet you, I had no idea that life could be as wonderful as it is. I want to spend the rest of my life making you as happy as you make me. I want it all, Benita—all the love, the joy, the pain, the laughter, the sorrow; whatever life brings us, I want to share with you. And all the babies, Benita, as many as you'll have with me. I want us to have a big family, Peaches, big enough to hold all the love I feel for you. I love you, Andrea Benita Deveraux, and I always will," he finished in his deep voice before kissing Bennie with all the love he had just expressed.

Bennie cried with happiness. She felt as though she had cried more in the last six months than she had in her entire life, and she couldn't help telling Clay that. Trying to wipe away the tears of joy, she laughingly told Clay that she was in danger of being mildewed. "Clay, honestly, I had no idea that there was so much water in my body! I can't imagine how many of your shirts I have soaked," she added.

Clay kissed away all of her tears, vowing that she would shed only tears of joy from now on. "From now on, Peaches, everything I do is for you, for us. I am dedicating my entire life to you from this moment on," he said softly.

Bennie's eyes filled with tears again as she took in what he was saying to her. There was nothing, she thought, that she would not do for the man who was holding her in his arms.

Bennie finally found out what Renee had been keeping from her. Bennie had tried vainly to call Andrew on their shared birthday and was unable to reach him. After a few days, though, Andrew had checked in with her and had the most startling news—he and Renee had been away for a few days together. *Well, that explains why I haven't been able to catch up with Miss Thing,* Bennie mused. And there was more news—Renee was having a big party that would not be complete without Clay's and Bennie's presence.

It sounded just the thing to Bennie—she had been looking forward to going home to Detroit to see all of her family, and this would be the perfect opportunity. So it was

with great anticipation that Bennie began to make preparations to take their trip. She was packing their bags in the
master bedroom when the telephone rang. It was Clay, making his daily midmorning call. After a brief, flirtatious conversation, they hung up the phone. Bennie looked at the
number of messages on the answering machine. She smiled
and shook her head. Clay's belief in the answering machine
fairy had not abated—the man would let messages pile up
forever. Bennie sighed and started erasing messages. She
was distracted by Aretha hopping into the suitcase, only to
have an old message broadcast from the unit. Recognizing
her father's voice at once, Bennie was shocked, then horrified and deeply ashamed as she realized what he was
saying to Clay. *Oh, my God, how could he? How could he
do this to Clay?*

Bennie paced the room nervously and frantically combed
her hands through her hair. Clay had never mentioned a
word of this treatment to Bennie—*treatment* being the op-
erative word. She had no doubt that this was not an isolated
incident; when roused, her father's wrath could go unchecked like a wildfire. This was so uncalled for, so unfair!
It was the last thing that she wanted to deal with at this
point in her life. Things were back to normal between her
and Clay, and she wanted to keep them that way. The last
thing she wanted was to have to choose between her father
and her husband.

And it wasn't as though she could let it go, the way she
had so many other conflicts between her and Big Benny.
This was the deal breaker, as far as Bennie was concerned.
She was so upset that she was getting physically ill. The
room tilted to the left and Bennie tilted to the right. She
was gripped by a sickening nausea so quickly that she did
not have time to do anything but react.

After she came out of the bathroom she picked up her
electronic organizer from the bedside table and called her
doctor. There was something altogether too familiar about
what she had just experienced. Luckily, her doctor was able
to work her in that afternoon. Bennie immediately show-

ered and dressed—this was one appointment that she couldn't wait to keep.

If Clay was to be perfectly honest with himself, he had to admit that he had mixed feelings about the impending visit to Detroit. There was no telling what his father-in-law would pull during this visit. He already knew that Big Benny was capable of any number of low machinations and outbursts, and he wanted Bennie exposed to none of them. He had naturally not said a word to Bennie about her father's phone attacks; he had seen no point in distressing her further. Besides, he was a strong man with more than enough self-confidence to deal with Big Benny. He actually felt sorry for the man, although he could not figure out exactly why. All he knew for sure was that he loved Benita, and anything he had to do to keep her happy, he would, up to and including forcing himself to have a cordial relationship with her father.

Clay was nearly consumed with the trip to Detroit, so much so that when he arrived home the night before the trip, he was totally preoccupied. Not so much that he did not lose himself in Bennie's kiss, but so that he did not notice her animation.

Bennie was visibly excited and giddy, fairly bursting with joy. She saw right away that Clay was in another world, however, and decided to ease him into the evening. She led him upstairs and insisted that he get into the tub for a relaxing whirlpool bath. Clay gladly let her fuss over him; he really was tense.

After his bath, he dressed and joined Bennie on the patio, where she had set the table for an intimate dinner. He stood in the doorway and watched Bennie put the final touches on the table, in the form of elaborately folded linen napkins. She had placed a stand next to the table that held an ice bucket with a bottle of wine already surrounded by crushed ice. He loved looking at his wife when she was unaware of his scrutiny. She was so lovely that she continued to leave him breathless every time he beheld her. She was wearing a long, sheer caftan of some sort in a peachy color that made her bronze skin glow. Her glossy hair was loose and full around her shoulders, and she had it pulled back on one side. That she was perfectly content was obvious by the serenity on her face and the fact that she was singing. Clay could have watched her forever, but she looked up and saw him standing in the doorway.

Her face lit up, becoming even more radiant. She floated over to meet him halfway and led him over to the table. Kissing him sweetly, she bade him to sit down. There was a package on his plate, which he turned over and over before opening. Bennie sighed in exasperation. "Clayton Arlington Deveraux, that drives me crazy! Open it; open it this minute!" she ordered him. Clay enjoyed teasing Bennie, and this was no exception.

"Benita, you know I don't need gifts from you to make me happy. I just need you to love me forever," he said, smiling.

He was paraphrasing what Bennie had said on her birthday, something that she found totally endearing, enough so that she relented in her quest. "Oh, okay, I can return it, I guess. But I have a new bracelet and I got you one to match it, is all," she said sweetly.

Clay's eyes lit with curiosity and he gently grasped her wrist, where there was indeed a bracelet he had never seen before. It was yellow gold and made of flat, interlocking links, and in the middle of those links were block letters that spelled out *MOMMA.* Tears flooded Clay's eyes, and he looked at Bennie.

"Yours says *POPPA,* she confirmed. Clay rose unsteadily to his feet and pulled her up with him. He held her to his heart and cried unabashedly while he whispered his thanks over and over. "Peaches, baby. Thank you, Benita, thank you," he murmured.

Bennie tried not to cry, but she couldn't help it. "Clay,

I love you so much," she whispered. "I should be thanking you for this, for us, for everything."

It was much, much later before they remembered to eat.

Finally the day that Bennie had both dreaded and anticipated was here. They had arrived in Detroit late the night before—it was unthinkable to start dropping in on people at that hour. Bennie had not actually planned it that way, but she was pleased. It gave her a chance to get her bearings before meeting her father. Renee and Andrew had picked them up at the airport, and there was so much conviviality and joy that all thoughts of Benny's perfidy had been momentarily pushed from her mind. Renee looked wonderful, more radiant than Bennie had ever seen her, and that was saying a lot—they had known each other for a thousand years.

The next morning, Bennie had gotten dressed while Clay was still lounging around in the Outhouse, because she wanted to gossip with Renee and find out what was going on between Renee and Andrew once and for all. Renee was in the kitchen making coffee when Bennie cornered her.

"Okay, spill it. What is going on around here? For years you and Andrew have been sniping at each other, and then you're all kissy-face, then you can't stand each other, and now you're traveling together. Inquiring minds want to know, sister-friend, what is up?" Bennie demanded playfully.

Renee gave her a really irritating Cheshire cat grin and acknowledged that she and Andrew had had a tempestuous past. "But things do change, Bennie. You missed quite a bit while you were in the hospital and while you were recuperating in California," Renee said mysteriously.

Bennie pondered that statement. "Yes, but you were with me a lot of the time that I was in California, Renee. So what was it I missed?" Bennie was not quite getting it. Renee took pity on her best friend.

"Let's just say that tragedy has a way of letting people know what is important and what isn't," Renee said. She was forestalled from making further comment by the arrival of Andrew in the kitchen. It was apparent that he had spent the night—he was wearing a beautiful bathrobe that Bennie would not have credited to her brother's wardrobe.

Finally the penny dropped. Bennie's eyes got huge and her mouth dropped open. "Are you two . . . do you mean . . . are you *engaged?*"

Renee just wrapped her arms around Andrew and giggled. Life as Bennie knew it was over. Renee was giggling in the arms of a man, in full view of another human being. The ever cool, calm, and collected Renee had been transformed in front of her very eyes. "Well, there's obviously a long story in here somewhere," mused Bennie.

Andrew looked over Renee's head to smile lazily at Bennie. "If you only knew, Benita. If you only knew." He sighed before kissing Renee.

Bennie decided that two was company and made a hasty escape back to the Outhouse, where Clay was just finished dressing. "Let's go out for breakfast," suggested Bennie. "Boy, have I got a lot to tell you!" She and Clay breakfasted at a small café and decided to make a few social calls before getting ready for Renee's party. They went by the radio station to visit with Donnie, then stopped by Adam's loft apartment before heading out to see Alan and Andre. Those visits took the longest, because Bennie had been away from her niece and nephews for so long. They were so beside themselves with joy at seeing their beloved Bunnie they didn't even notice the presents she had brought them. Lillian was especially glad to see Clay, with whom she associated her "grandma" Lillian.

After bestowing many sticky kisses on Bunnie, she attached herself to Clay like a limpet, demanding to know where her grandma Lillian was. "She's in Atlanta right now, but you'll have to come visit her soon," Clay said.

That was fine with Lillian. "Okay, I'll come with you now," she offered.

Bennie started laughing. "That's what you get for flirting," she informed her husband. "We may have an extra passenger on the way back," she warned him. "Lillian is known for her tenacity. The word *no* means 'try harder' to her."

Clay could not possibly have cared less. He was never going to sweat the small things in life again, nor the big ones. He had a second chance at the kind of happiness that most people were not lucky enough to have once in a lifetime, and nothing was going to ruin it for him again.

Renee had elected to have a casual buffet in the backyard of the Indian Village house that she and Bennie had shared. Of course, *casual* for Renee meant quietly chic and tasteful. To her mind, *casual* did not mean *slovenly*, so the buffet was catered and the attire was festively summery. The men did not wear sports coats, but there were no jeans or shorts in attendance except on the children. The women were wearing summer dresses in a variety of fabrics and hues, so the whole effect was like an extremely upscale tea party.

Bennie drew a deep breath as she saw her father enter with Martha on his arm. Clay felt, rather than heard, her sharp intake of breath, due largely to the fact that his arm was firmly around her waist. "Are you all right, Peaches?"

Bennie smiled up at her handsome man. "I'm fine, honey. I just haven't seen Daddy for such a long time that it feels a little strange, is all."

And it was a partial truth; she had not seen her father in months, and she anxiously scanned him for changes. He did not look a day older, and there was no sign that he had suffered any kind of stroke: no tremors, no limping, no halting of his speech. Benny Cochran looked very well, indeed. She went to greet him and was surprised by the hug she received, given his absentminded conversation the last time they had spoken. Benny was obviously happy to see her; his eyes grew moist and he could not let go of her. Martha could barely get a kiss and a greeting in before Big Benny was monopolizing his daughter. He seemed to hesitate when Clay approached the group, but after Clay's easy handshake and greeting, he was back to being his usual ebullient self.

As the evening went on, it was that fact more than anything that made Bennie take her father into the house for a talk. She could not get over how cavalierly he had treated Clay in the garden. It was as though he realized that Clay had not said anything to Bennie about his horrible behavior, so he thought he was in the clear. More than once Bennie had looked at Clay during the evening and felt, rather than saw, his acceptance of the situation. *There is nothing he would not suffer to make me happy,* she realized. That knowledge, coupled with the smug look on her father's face, led her to the action she had decided to take. When they were in the living room of the house she had lived in for so many years, she invited him to have a seat. He looked surprised that she did not join him, but she shook her head.

"This is not going to take long, Daddy. I know what you did to Clay. I know all about those filthy, hateful phone calls you made to him while I was in California," she said quietly and evenly. The panic and pallor that descended on her father's face did not sway her in the least. "No, Daddy, Clay did not tell me about them. I found out by accident while I was erasing messages from the answering machine." Benny's head dropped, as if to say that he knew the jig was up. But Bennie was not finished.

"Daddy, you have no idea how it affected me. I was so ashamed! I was actually embarrassed that you were my father. You, the man I adored and looked up to all my life, had done something so hateful and so unforgivable to the man I love. How could you? Do you have any idea—*any* idea—what Clay went through after my accident? Do you have any clue what it did to him to lose our baby? Do you? You didn't even stop to think about him—or me—did you, Daddy? It was all about you. Your show pony had gotten injured and you were afraid it couldn't race again," she accused.

Benny looked up then to defend himself. "Benita, daughter, you know that's not true. You know how much I love you. . . ." His voice trailed off as Bennie raised her hand.

"Daddy, I don't want to hear it. I know you think that you love me, and I suppose in your own way you do. But that does not excuse what you did. You know, until I heard that message on the answering machine I could have forgiven you anything. I *have* forgiven you everything in the past." Bennie did sit down then, so that she could look into her father's eyes at his level.

"While John was helping me in therapy, I made a discovery. I have always blamed myself for Mommy's death. I always thought I was responsible because she was leaving the house to bring me something at school. John said that if I had told someone when I was ten, when it happened, that I would not have had to carry the burden of all that guilt. He said that a caring adult would have made me understand that it was not my fault, and would have helped me get through the guilt." Bennie's eyes filled with tears, but she dashed them away roughly with the heel of her hand. Crying was not going to make it easier to say.

"There was one thing he didn't know. I couldn't tell him the truth that I *did* tell someone what I thought I had done. I told *you,* Daddy, and you have used that knowledge to keep me under your thumb. You preyed on that guilt and kept me as your little puppet for most of my life. But you know what? I forgave you for that. When I was in California, John and Clay helped rid me of that burden, and I swear to God, Daddy, I forgave you. But this I cannot forgive.

"I told you before, when you had that detective digging up dirt on Clay and his family, that if you even thought anything ugly about Clay you would never see me again. And I meant that, Daddy. Clay is more than my husband; he is my dearest friend, my strongest support, the keeper of my heart, and the father of my child. And since you have forced me to choose between the two of you, I choose

Clay. He is my life now, and you cannot be a part of it, not now. Right now I have to take care of my husband and have a healthy baby. When I am ready to deal with you again, if I am ever ready to do that, I will contact you. Until then, you must stay away from me and stay out of my life. I hope I make myself clear on this, Daddy. Anything you do to Clay, you do to me. And you went too far." Bennie rose on unsteady feet and left the room without looking back.

Benny sat alone in the gathering darkness and tears coursed down his face. Martha had warned him over and over what would happen if he did not let go of Bennie. Every word that his daughter had said was true; he knew it. But to hear her say it in her calm, measured voice—it would have been better if she had been screaming at him. The finality of her words, coupled with the startling news he had gotten from Bump Williams a few weeks earlier, was just too much. He abandoned himself to his grief for a few minutes before stiffening his back in resolve.

He would get Bennie back, no question. There was no problem that they could not overcome, given time. And this other thing, the thing that Bump had laid at his doorstep . . . well, he would just have to see about that. In the meantime, he was down, but not out. Nobody had ever gotten the best of Big Benny Cochran, and nobody ever would. Before leaving the living room, Benny rose painfully from the sofa and went over to the rosewood desk in the corner. Picking up the telephone, he punched in an indispensable number. Gruffly he said, "It's me. I need you to do a check on someone. John Flores, in Los Angeles. Dr. John Flores, that's right."

Bennie was surprised and appalled to find Clay in the dining room. He had come in search of Bennie and heard every word of the exchange. He clasped her upper arms with his big hands and looked deeply into her eyes. "Benita. Benita, are you all right? I'm sorry; I did not mean to eavesdrop, but by the time I realized what you were saying I couldn't leave without making sure you were okay. Are you?" he asked anxiously.

Bennie nodded her head. "Yes, Clay, I'm fine. I am not happy about what I just did, but I would do it again if he or anybody else tried to hurt you. I just won't have it, Clay. We have been through enough. I am not letting anything or anyone come between us ever again." Bennie put her arms around his waist and rested her head on his shoulder for a moment. She looked up at Clay with her heart in her eyes, and a look of utter trust and contentment.

"I meant every word I said, Clay. You are everything to me. You belong to me, and I belong to you. I love you and this baby more than anything, sweetheart. And I am afraid that I am prepared to go to some pretty primitive lengths to keep you both safe and happy. And I am not going to waste a minute of that time. So let's go and get this party over with so we can get on with our life, baby. Are you ready?"

Clay looked down at his wife, the woman who had taught him how to love, and who kept teaching him every day about tenderness and caring, and felt his heart swell with the love he felt for her. "You bet I am, Peaches. I'm always ready for you." They smiled beautiful smiles at each other and went back into the garden to share their joy with the people who loved them.

Epilogue

"Oh, Clay, you know if you talk to him he's just going to want to play," Bennie fussed, but it was obvious that her heart wasn't in it. They had gone through the same scenario for months now, and there was no stopping Clay. He had made good on his promise to help with the two A.M. feedings. He would awake as soon as Clayton Arlington Deveraux III did, and go and change him, a task that he had mastered quite handily. He would then bring their son to Bennie to nurse.

Their routine never varied. Clay would hand the baby to Bennie and then get into bed with them so that he could hold them both while little Clayton greedily drank his fill from his mother. Bennie loved these times. She loved lying drowsily in her husband's arms with their baby. She was completely content and fulfilled—or she was until the baby got old enough to be sociable. That was when he started viewing his early feedings as a cocktail party. He would hear his father's voice and start smiling, and smiles would lead to laughter, and then he would be awake and playing for an hour before going back to sleep.

Bennie despaired of them both. She leaned back on Clay's shoulder and puckered her lips for a kiss. "If you two want to hang out and be *boyz,* that's your business. Momma is going back to sleep. Daddy and Martha will be in rather early tomorrow, and I don't want to be yawning all over the place when they get here," she said with a huge yawn.

Clay relented and agreed to put little Clayton back in his crib before he got too rambunctious. "I am truly glad they are coming, Peaches. I'm glad you were able to forgive your father and let him be a part of your life again," he said sincerely. Bennie moved a little, so that she was sitting up more and could look at him while she was holding their precious son.

The baby was the image of Clay, with a full head of silky black hair that had given Bennie much heartburn during his gestation. He had the same perfect lips as his father and the beginnings of the same noble nose. What was particularly cute was the fact that his eyebrows were surprisingly dark for a three-month-old infant. Bennie joked that all he needed was a mustache and he and Clay could pass for twins. She gazed sleepily at her beautiful husband, who grew more handsome every day, as far as she was concerned.

"Clay, I have to tell you, darling, I am not mad at a soul in this world. Not a soul. And it's all because you love me so well that there isn't room for anything in my heart except love." She smiled and kissed him thoroughly, which still made his heart race and his pulse accelerate.

Clay returned her kiss with fervor, then scooped their sleeping son up and returned him to his crib in the sitting room/nursery. He slid into the massive bed, wrapped himself around Bennie with the agility born of practice, and confessed, "Everything I know about love I learned from you. I love you, Peaches. And since you want to get up early, I'd better let you sleep now." He turned off the bedside lamp and smiled as he heard Bennie's familiar, delightful throaty laugh that meant one thing only.

"You know what, Clay? I'm not that sleepy after all," she purred. And she proceeded to show him once again how special their love was, even in the early-morning hours.

Dear Readers:

I truly hope that you enjoyed getting to know Bennie and Clay and sharing their story as much as I enjoyed creating these characters and bringing them to life. In case you're wondering about Renee and Andrew, you'll find out all about this dynamic couple soon. Their story, UNTIL THE END OF TIME, will be released in March.

And yes, you will also find out more about the mysterious John Flores in future stories about the Cochran and Deveraux families. In the meantime, I'm very pleased to have a novella in the upcoming Valentine's Day anthology to be released in January. The very first Arabesque novel I ever read was LOVE LETTERS, a Valentine's Day collection from a few years ago. That was the book that set me on the path to writing romances, so I am especially thrilled to be in the 2003 edition.

Please write; I love to correspond. Please send a stamped, self-addressed envelope for a faster response. You can reach me at: P.O. Box 5176, Saginaw, Michigan 48603. I look forward to hearing from you. Until then be blessed, everyone.

Melanie
I Chronicles 4:10

ABOUT THE AUTHOR

Melanie Woods Schuster currently lives in Saginaw, Michigan, where she works in sales for the largest telecommunications company in the state. She attended Ohio University. Her occupations indicate her interests in life; Melanie has worked as a costume designer, a makeup artist, an admissions counselor at a private college, and has worked in marketing. She is also an artist, a calligrapher, and makes jewelry and designs clothing. Writing has always been her true passion, however, and she looks forward to creating more compelling stories of love and passion in the years to come.

DO YOU KNOW AN ARABESQUE MAN?

1st Arabesque Man HAROLD JACKSON
Featured on the cover of "Endless Love"
by Carmen Green / Published Sept 2000

2nd Arabesque Man EDMAN REID
Featured on the cover of "Love Lessons"
by Leslie Esdaile / Published Sept 2001

3rd Arabesque Man PAUL HANEY
Featured on the cover of "Holding Out For A Hero"
by Deirdre Savoy / Published Sept 2002

WILL YOUR "ARABESQUE" MAN BE NEXT?

One Grand Prize Winner Will Win:
- 2 Day Trip to New York City
- Professional NYC Photo Shoot
- Picture on the Cover of an Arabesque Romance Novel
- Prize Pack & Profile on Arabesque Website and Newsletter
- $250.00

You Win Too!
- The Nominator of the Grand Prize Winner receives a Prize Pack & profile on Arabesque Website
- $250.00

To Enter: Simply complete the following items to enter your "Arabesque Man": (1) Compose an Original essay that describes in 75 words or less why you think your nominee should win. (2) Include two recent photographs of him (head shot and one full length shot). Write the following information for both you and your nominee on the back of each photo: name, address, telephone number and the nominee's age, height, weight, and clothing sizes. (3) Include signature and date of nominee granting permission to nominator to enter photographs in contest. (4) Include a proof of purchase from an Arabesque romance novel—write the book title, author, ISBN number, and purchase location and price on a 3-1/2 x 5" card. (5) Entrants should keep a copy of all submissions. Submissions will not be returned and will be destroyed after the judging.

ARABESQUE regrets that no return or acknowledgement of receipt can be made because of the anticipated volume of responses. Arabesque is not responsible for late, lost, incomplete, inaccurate or misdirected entries. The Grand Prize Trip includes round trip air transportation from a major airport nearest the winner's home, 2-day (1 night) hotel accommodations and ground transportation between the airport, hotel and Arabesque offices in New York. The Grand Prize Winner will be required to sign and return an affidavit of eligibility and publicity and liability release in order to receive the prize. The Grand Prize Winner will receive no additional compensation for the use of his image on an Arabesque novel, website, or for any other promotional purpose. The entries will be judged by a panel of BET Arabesque personnel whose decisions regarding the winner and all other matters pertaining to the Contest are final and binding. By entering this Contest, entrants agree to comply with all rules and regulations.

SEND ENTRIES TO: The Arabesque Man Cover Model Contest, BET Books, One BET Plaza, 1235 W Street, NE, Washington, DC 20018. Open to legal residents of the U.S., 21 years of age or older. Illegible entries will be disqualified. Limit one entry per envelope. Odds of winning depend, in part, on the number of entries received. Void in Puerto Rico and where prohibited by law.

ARABESQUE
A PRODUCT OF
BET BOOKS